MAKING WAVES AT PENVENNAN COVE

LINN B. HALTON

An Aria Book

ALSO BY LINN B. HALTON

First published in the UK in 2021 by Head of Zeus Ltd
This paperback edition first published in 2022 by Head of Zeus Ltd,
part of Bloomsbury Publishing Plc

9 7 5 3 1 2 4 6 8

A CIP catalogue record for this book is available from the British Library.

ISBN (PB) 9781800246287
ISBN (E) 9781838938017

Head of Zeus
5–8 Hardwick Street
London EC1R 4RG
www.headofzeus.com

Printed and bound by CPI Group (UK) Ltd, Croydon, CR0 4YY

Dedicated to the unsung heroes of small communities everywhere. You know who you are, and you make the world a better place!

PART ONE
OCTOBER

ONE

WISHFUL THINKING

In hindsight, coming home to Penvennan Cove was the easy part. It's the entanglement with the past that is making my life increasingly difficult with each passing day. While Dad is my number-one supporter, in an ironic twist of fate he is fast becoming my number-one problem.

'That's a big frown you're wearing today, Kerra.' The voice of my neighbour, Drew Matthews, seems to come out of nowhere as I step out onto the pavement outside of Pascoe's Café and Bakery.

Clutching a waxed paper bag in my hand, I shrug my shoulders nonchalantly. 'It's one of those days, I'm afraid. And when I'm in need of comfort food, this is where I come for the best hevva cake.'

'I'm sorry to hear it, but thanks for the heads-up as it's something I haven't tried yet. If you can hang on while I pick up a pasty for lunch, I'll walk back with you.'

'Okay. Don't rush. It's bracing out, but I could do with a little fresh air to clear my head.'

As Drew makes his way inside Pascoe's, I cross the road

towards the low, stone wall on the far side of the council cark park. Gazing out over the beach, I see that it's a cold, murky, inhospitable morning and even the seagulls have been driven inland. The sea, too, is a dirty shade of grey, and on the horizon it's hard to tell where the water ends and the sky begins. It looks as grim as my mood. I scuff the pavement with the toe of my shoe. A fine layer of gritty sand is swirled around by the wind every time it gusts, creating curious, snake-like trails.

Stooping down, I perch on the uneven surface of the stone wall to look back at the picturesque cluster of buildings that is the heart of Penvennan Cove. The café and bakery has the prime position, situated on the large corner plot at the bottom of the long hill that leads up to the village. Out of sight, just beyond the bend, is what must qualify as one of the tiniest newsagent's shops in Cornwall. But it's been here for as long as I can remember, and Gryff still sells loose sweets. The old-fashioned screw-lid jars line the wall behind the counter and there's something for everyone.

I watch as Drew strides towards me, stuffing a bag into the pocket of his coat before buttoning it up to the top. This wind seems to get into every little nook and cranny, and it feels more like winter, than autumn.

'Do you fancy a walk along the beach before we make our way back? I think we've seen the worst of storm Alexa now, thank goodness.' Drew grins at me. 'The choice is yours.'

'Why not? I've been working online since five this morning and, like Alexa, I'm running out of steam.'

Jumping up I fall in alongside Drew. Tall, with dark brown curly hair, he's one of those people you can count on in an emergency, or a listening ear if you're in need of one. We hit it off from day one when I returned home in April and took up residence in Pedrevan Cottage, which is attached to Drew's beautifully named Tigry Cottage.

'Why the long face? I thought you and Ross were getting on well.'

The wind catches my hair and I use my free hand to scoop it away from my eyes. 'We are, in a low-key, *inconspicuous* manner,' I reply, labouring the word.

'Oh. My lips are sealed, you know that. But seriously, Kerra, anyone who is around the two of you for even a short period of time will twig what's really going on.'

'One's first love is always a special bond, isn't it? Coming home I knew that old memories might return to haunt me, but not my teenage crush. I simply wasn't prepared for the emotional pull I felt when I saw Ross Treloar for the first time after so many years.'

'And now you know that he feels the same way, isn't it time to put the past behind you both?'

I heave a huge sigh and it's carried away on the wind. If only it were as easy to shake off the hurts of the past. 'If it was just down to us, then it wouldn't be a problem. But it isn't and that's why we're avoiding being seen together. I know that Sy and Tegan won't let anything slip, but it's Dad I'm worried about.'

My two closest friends always have my back. Tegan runs *Clean and Shine*, the bulk of whose work is servicing holiday lets and offices, with a small domestic market. Sy followed me here from London. Little did I know that not only would they begin working together as a team, but also end up getting engaged.

'Eddie seems okay around Ross,' Drew replies, as we step over the wrack line, where kelp, shells and other debris are deposited at high tide.

Being an *emmet* and an incomer, someone who wasn't born here, Drew has no idea of the level of animosity between my dad, Eddie, and Ross's father, Jago.

'He is, but that's because he isn't aware that there's anything going on between Ross and me. Jago always considered his family to be a cut above everyone else. When they moved away from the village into their huge, manor house, he knew he was going up in the world. Jago has connections everywhere and a little power can go a long way.'

'I can't imagine Eddie getting pulled into that,' Drew comments, frowning.

'The enmity between our two fathers stems from a feud that began shortly after my parents bought Green Acre. Dad put in a planning application for a change of use for the land to set up the kennels. Jago was a local councillor at the time, and he was also on the planning committee. He's a man who likes to flex his muscles and put people in their place. Even though he no longer lived in the village, and given that no one else objected, he tried his best to veto it.'

'Why would he do that? It's not as if the kennels can be seen from the road into the village. It makes no sense if the locals didn't have a problem. And it has its own off-road parking.'

This is hard to explain as it doesn't really portray Dad in a flattering light.

'Ross and I... well, he was popular with the girls at school and Dad knew I liked him. Dad didn't make Ross welcome, because he felt I deserved better. But it wasn't Ross's fault. He didn't play games, and most of the rumours about him weren't true. While girls threw themselves at him, the boys were jealous of him, and Ross suffered through no real fault of his own. Dad believed what he heard and let that be known. And that's why Jago fought so hard to scupper my parents' plan to set up the business. It was personal.'

'And now you're caught in the middle, not wanting to hurt Eddie, but... well, let's face it, you and Ross spark off each other. I think you're fighting a losing battle, Kerra.'

Drew is right, but I came back to Penvennan to support my dad after the death of my mum, not to alienate or upset him.

'The irony is that Dad has always respected Ross's work ethic. Not least, for the way he's managed Treloar's Building Limited since his parents decided to move to Spain.'

'Well, that's a start,' Drew points out.

'Hmm. Not really. Ross's very public divorce simply confirmed Dad's view that Ross isn't reliable when it comes to relationships. And Ross is treading carefully, because if he upsets my dad then we have a real problem.'

'It's an uphill battle, then?'

I laugh, but it sounds as hollow as I feel. 'As you know, before she died I promised Mum that I'd come home, to put her mind at rest. I'm not sure who she felt was in most need of a little support – Dad or me – but her instincts were right, and I have no regrets. But Dad won't understand that Ross isn't ready to jump into a full-blown relationship, anyway, given what Ross has been through. And that suits me fine. I'm in no hurry myself so we're taking it a day at a time. Admittedly we are having a little fun in the process, but there are no guarantees and neither of us are taking anything for granted.'

'You mean that Eddie is old-fashioned, and he wouldn't approve of the two of you creeping around and having sleepovers?'

We burst out laughing at the same time.

'It's not funny,' I declare, robustly. 'I left here as a teenager and Dad missed the years in between. Now I'm back, he feels it's his job to protect his daughter from...' I cast around for the right words.

'From being seduced by the charms of her childhood sweetheart?'

'It's a little late for that now, but Dad doesn't want to see me get my heart broken. And Ross and I were only ever friends – Dad made sure of that.'

'Then go on being discreet, and gradually Eddie will come to see how happy you are and, hopefully, realise it's because of Ross.'

'You make it sound so simple, Drew. I feel like I'm living in a goldfish bowl at times after the anonymity of living in London. The pace of life is so fast there that people don't have time to worry about the small stuff and, often, they don't give a damn anyway. It's as if I'm doing something wrong, which is ridiculous at my age. I'm a grown woman and a free agent. And so is Ross.'

Drew tuts. 'Ah, but the rumour mill loves talking about him, Kerra, and you – *the returner*. In a small community like this one, not much goes unnoticed,' Drew continues. 'You'll need to be clever to keep something like this a secret.'

'I know. But it will be easier now that Ross is living up at Treylya, at least until it's sold. He's installed a cat flap for Ripley.'

Drew stops to pick up a stone, rooting around until he finds one flat enough to skim.

'That's a start. At least she won't be sitting on the doorstep at two in the morning, miaowing to get in when you're not there. I still haven't forgiven her.'

I watch him as he positions himself, his right arm across his body, his focus full-on. Pulling a sad face, he glances at me and then does a few practice pitches as he gets ready to throw.

'Don't make me feel guilty, Drew,' I groan. 'I can't help that your cat wouldn't come home to you after I looked after her for a while. She must be the noisiest Bengal in the world. Honestly, the conversations Ripley has with me are exhausting at times. Especially when it's in the early hours of the morning. At least she loves Ross.'

'That makes two of you, then.' He grins back at me, finally releasing the stone in his hand. It looks promising as he stands back and we both squint, watching as the rock glances off the water twice and then disappears.

'It's the waves,' he tells me, solemnly. 'It's too choppy.'

'They all say that,' I reply, amused.

I pick up a similar stone, then do one or two practice manoeuvres before launching it horizontally through the air.

'One, two, three... four! Yes!'

'Gloat, why don't you? But you lived here for eighteen years before you ran off to London and had plenty of time to practise. For a newbie like me, two isn't bad.'

'Hmm. You'll get better over time,' I reply, encouragingly. I don't like to tell him that I've never done less than three and when the water is calm, I can do five.

We stop to gaze up at the sky and the seagulls wheeling overhead, squawking away. Their raucous calls are eerie when the weather is so grim. I think about how cold the water is and it makes me shudder. My granddad Harry drowned when I was only ten years old; his small fishing boat smashed against the rocks at the bottom of the cliff. It was an awful way for his life to end, especially given that the sea was a big part of his life for so many years. He survived violent storms at sea when other men didn't make it back to dry land. Coming here I feel close to him, but it's always tinged with great sadness.

'I'm fed up trying to keep the hair out of my eyes and mouth. Shall we head back?'

Drew nods in agreement. 'Let's take the shortcut through the pub car park.'

We walk diagonally, heading towards the gate in the far right-hand corner where the beach meets the steep cliffs. It's almost lunchtime and there are at least a dozen cars parked up. The Lark and Lantern is owned and run by Sam Saunders and his daughter, Polly, an old school friend of mine.

'Do you think they'll survive another year?' I ask, glancing in Drew's direction.

He screws up his face. 'Sam stays positive, but Polly has her doubts.'

'I know. It's the heart of Penvennan Cove when the tourists are here and for the locals when they aren't. Imagine the winter months without anywhere for folk to congregate for a chat, a pint and some pub grub.'

As we walk within a couple of feet of the windows, I peer in and it looks so cosy at this time of the year. The log fire in the main bar is inviting, but I have work to do and so does Drew, who is a freelance architect. He's designed and project-managed the building of an extension to the rear of both of our semi-detached cottages, and I've come to know him well in a relatively short time.

'How is Bertie settling in, these days? Is Ripley still terrorising him?'

Drew was very gracious allowing me to keep Ripley, not that he had much say in it at the time. But I couldn't leave him without any company at all and when darling little Bertie's owner died and Dad was asked to find a new home for him, I knew he'd be good company for Drew and loyal.

'You know what Ripley's like. She might not want to live with me anymore, but she still regards him as an interloper. I usually keep an eye out if Bertie wants to have a run around the garden. If I see Ripley perched on the fence, I call Bertie in.'

It's hard not to smile. 'I have tried talking to her,' I inform him, feeling bad. 'I'm sure she'll get used to Bertie being around eventually, as he's so friendly.'

Bertie is a miniature Schnauzer and his previous owner trained him well. But he hates the rain and if he gets caught in a downpour he refuses to move and will stand there, with his legs locked rigid. I've caught sight of Drew on countless occasions recently, returning home carrying Bertie back from a walk. It's hilarious.

Halfway through our uphill climb, our pace slows a little as we pass the row of tiny fishermen's cottages that time has hardly changed. They've all been renovated over the years, but in keeping with their original character. It's one of the reasons why families flock here in the summer months. It's such a pretty little Cornish village, leading down to a picturesque cove with a sizeable beach, a welcoming pub serving great food and the best bakery for miles around. It's also a little off the beaten track and small enough not to be an option for anyone towing anything more than a two-man boat.

At the top of the hill, we stop for a moment to catch our breath.

'It's an amazing property, isn't it?' Drew turns to gaze up at the clifftops in the distance. Renweneth is several miles away by road, but as the crow flies it's just a trek through the forest of trees. Treylya stands proudly looking out from the tip of the headland.

'Yes. It's way too big for Ross, obviously. What was he thinking letting his wife talk him into building it? He told me that he'll probably end up losing money when he manages to find the right buyer.'

'Is that why he's moved back in? I suppose it isn't easy to arrange viewings when a property is rented out.'

I avoid Drew's gaze. 'Sort of.'

'Oh! Right. I see... hence the cat flap! It's not just because Ripley has this tendency to visit him because she enjoys a little romp up through the woods, then?'

'No. Ross didn't like me driving home alone in the early hours of the morning from The Forge and it was an hour round-trip for him to drop me back. It's a fifteen-minute walk from my cottage up to Treylya, so he can walk back with me to the end of the village and check I get home alright.'

'And while your car continues to be parked up outside Pedrevan Cottage, when Eddie looks out the corner bedroom window at Green Acre, all is right in his little world.'

We saunter along, past the Penvennan Convenience Store run by Mrs Moyle and her husband, Arthur, and I peer inside, catching her eye and returning her wave.

'I have a plan and, if I do say so myself, it's a particularly clever one to hopefully get Dad and Ross working together.'

As we cross the road, Drew and I stand for a few moments outside of Tigry Cottage. The wind is finally petering out and I shake my head to untangle my hair.

'Really? Ross and Eddie? You know what they say about the best laid plans and all that. Alternatively, you could just let Eddie come to his own conclusion in the fullness of time.'

Seriously? 'A decade wasn't enough time for Dad to

forgive Ross for a wrong that he never perpetrated in the first place. We simply hung around together with a bunch of school friends, that's all, so now it's time Dad got to know him a little better. I'm optimistic that I can get him to see Ross in a different light.'

Drew shakes his head, a forlorn expression on his face. 'You make it sound like a PR exercise. Hmm... good luck with that! And enjoy your hevva cake. I'm off to eat my slightly squashed pasty.'

'Enjoy. One day I will present you with a proper Cornish tin miner's pasty, like my grandma Rose used to make, with apple at one end.'

Drew is already at his front door, inserting the key. 'Now that's an offer I wouldn't refuse. You don't like cooking, though.'

'I know,' I call out, as I walk away from him. 'But I know a man who can. He's quite a chef, on the quiet.'

As I walk up the path to Pedrevan Cottage I can hear Drew chuckling away to himself. I'm feeling refreshed, if wind-blown, and ready to start work again.

TWO

TIME TO WORK AND TIME TO PLAY

Nothing brightens my day more than paying a visit to The Design Cave, albeit that it's for a meeting with my business partner, Sissy Warren. The unit opened a month ago and it's doing well.

'Morning, Sienna, how are you and the family?' I wave out as I step through the door. Sienna's husband, Logan, and I went to the same school. As I headed off to London, they were planning their wedding and now they have two young boys.

Sienna is standing on a stepladder behind the point of sale, arranging a display of scatter cushions.

'Oh, we're all good, thank you, Kerra. And you?' Sienna asks, looking down at me.

'Wonderful, thanks. How's your mum coping with the afternoon school run and looking after the boys?'

'Oh, she loves it. Oscar and Cadan say she's like the home-work police, though.' She laughs. 'But it's great, because by the time I get home at five it's all done, and we can enjoy a little quality time together. I'm encouraging them to play board games rather than going online – you know what kids are like.'

'I can imagine! I'm glad it's working out for you. Is Sissy out the back?'

'Yes. She's on her own; James is out on a delivery.'

'A big one, I hope?'

'It is, actually. One property and it's two trips to fit everything in.' She gives me a thumbs up and an enthusiastic grin.

Sienna was working part-time in a school as an admin assistant, which was perfect when the boys were small, but she was eager to find something a little more challenging. When I met Sissy, she was stuck in a tiny retail unit in the centre of Polreweek and had no online presence at all. Putting the two of them together was a win-win situation. It's a steep learning curve for them both, but Sienna is a well-motivated and capable assistant manager to Sissy. In return, Sissy is happy to be flexible about Sienna's working arrangements in the school holidays.

As I wander through the display area it all looks immaculate. You can literally furnish an entire room, complete with soft furnishings and knick-knacks, all in one shopping trip. Aside from the section where customers can pick the smaller items off the shelves, the larger displays are laid out in individual room settings.

Heading for the rest area, it reminds me that it's time to talk about creating an office. The kitchen is just one large room that was divided off from the shop floor. With a fridge, tea and coffee making facilities in one corner, and an oversized pine table there's a lot of unused space. But every penny of the investment I put in was spent on organising the sales floor and getting the website up and running so that we can sell online. It's time to plough some of the profit back in and the first priority is erecting an office for Sissy.

As I'm about to reach for the door handle there's a ping

and I retrieve my mobile from my bag with the intention of turning it off.

How do you fancy dining out tonight?

It's from Ross and it puts an instant smile on my face.

Sounds good. I assume it's not local? 😊

Would I take a risk like that? Meet you at the lay-by next to the vet's surgery at 7.30 p.m.

Perfect. 😉

I know for a fact that Dad and Mum's best friend, Nettie, are going out tonight to watch a play in the old cinema at Trehoweth. I bumped into them yesterday morning when they were doing the first dog walk of the day. It's about a half-an-hour drive away, so by the time Dad drops Nettie home afterwards, my car will be safely parked up outside the cottage and he won't be any the wiser.

After giving a gentle tap on the door and opening it, I poke my head around the side. 'Morning, Sissy.' She's sitting at the aged pine table, a furniture catalogue laid out in front of her.

'Come on in, Kerra. I'm almost done here. I'm working on a special one-off order for a new client. She wanted a couple of items we don't stock. Take a seat; I'll just gather everything up. The coffee is freshly brewed if you want to grab a cup.'

'I'm fine, thanks. You look well and your hair is amazing.'

After having had a make-over from my cousin Alice for the launch party last month, Sissy now has a mass of curly hair and it really suits her. She tosses her hair back and forth in quick succession as if she's in a shampoo ad, grinning back at me.

'I went with Alice's suggestion to have a perm and now I get up, shower, and let it dry naturally. It's perfect for someone who hardly ever stops to look in the mirror,' she confesses.

Sissy is like me, a natural entrepreneur: self-motivated, proactive and with that instinctive drive to succeed at whatever we do. Failure is simply not an option and if a plan begins to unravel, then it's back to the drawing board to find a solution. It's the fuel that keeps us going. I wake up each morning eager to get on with the day ahead and I can sympathise over the hair, because I rarely fuss with mine unless it's for a special occasion. But when it comes to customers, nothing is ever too much trouble for Sissy, and having been on the receiving end of that, I was so impressed I went from being a satisfied customer, to an investor. And what a way to begin setting up my new business portfolio.

Settling myself down at the table, I pull the laptop out of my bag.

'Before I outline the final changes I've made to the website and walk you through the updated version of the online store, are there any supply problems from the manufacturers?'

'No. They're keeping up with our orders. It makes so much sense getting them to deliver direct to the customer on the bigger items.'

'And how is James doing with the local deliveries from stock?'

'Oh, what a gem he is and so polite, too. When he's not out in the van, he's more than happy to lend a hand with whatever needs doing on the shop floor.'

'I'm delighted to hear you say that, Sissy. James and his

parents – you know Tom and Georgia? – have been my dad's closest neighbours since he was tiny.'

'He told me that his dad owns the car and boat repair yard, down by the beach.'

'Yes, The Salvager's Yard. Trade isn't what it used to be, but Tom manages to keep it ticking over. And how are things with you?'

Sissy's cheeks begin to colour up. 'Everything's fine,' she blusters. 'It's busy and that's how I like it.'

Hmm, that's a little out of character for Sissy. She's not one to get flustered easily and I hope she doesn't think I was being nosy. 'Right, if you're ready, let's begin.'

'Thank you for all the work that you've put in to get everything up and running, Kerra. Without your expertise I wouldn't have known where to begin to take the business to the next level and beyond. From here on it's down to me to prove to you that I have what it takes to grab this opportunity and run with it.'

The last thing I want is for Sissy to feel any undue pressure. 'Look, being *a silent partner* means I'm only silent unless you need my input. If you have any problems at all, I'm a phone call away. You started your business on a shoestring budget and turned it into something worth growing. Don't underestimate what you've achieved.'

She looks at me anxiously. 'It's overwhelming to think that you are putting your trust in me, and I won't let you down, Kerra.'

'It's what investors do, Sissy. I have organisational and IT skills, but I've never sold anything in my life. That's where you excel. You have a good eye when it comes to buying furniture and soft furnishings, and I was happy to buy from you. So, it seems, are an increasing number of the locals.'

'This is my dream, and I can't thank you enough, Kerra. Do you have another project already lined up?'

I tilt my head, smiling. 'Ideas don't always come to fruition, but when they do it's a marvellous feeling. I'm not sure where to turn my attention next, but something will crop up.'

There are times when I miss my life in London but selling The Happy Hive – a subscription website connecting people with a need, to people who have the requisite skills – has given me financial freedom. Money sitting in the bank doing nothing isn't helping anyone and it's not solely about making my considerable nest egg grow, it's about investing in people's hopes and dreams. People like Sissy. I think I've finally found my niche in life and at the age of thirty, I'm no longer feeling burnt out, but re-energised. Sissy is right. The question is, what's next?

* * *

Pulling into the lay-by, which snakes around the edge of a wide grassy area abutting the pavement, I decide it's far enough back from the road for the car not to stand out. I'm early, curious about where Ross is taking me. Hopefully, a romantic little pub a reasonable drive away so we can sit and relax. I put my hair up in a clip tonight and have even curled a couple of the strands that managed to escape. Checking my lipstick in the vanity mirror, I decide that I'll do, and I know he'll notice the effort I've made.

It isn't long until I spot the headlights of a car coming towards me and as it pulls in alongside, slowing to a halt, I grab my bag and jump out. It's chilly tonight but I'm warmly dressed in a grey woollen coat over a pale lilac jumper dress, black leggings and ankle-length boots. As Ross leans across to open the passenger door for me, he rewards me with his bewitching smile.

'You look nice.'

Before I strap on my seat belt, I lean across to give him a kiss. He wants to linger, running his fingers gently down the side of my cheek, but the engine is idling. 'Come on. There's plenty of time for that later,' I respond, grinning at him.

He grimaces. 'If you say so. But you look and smell lovely. Just the tonic I need after a troublesome Saturday.'

I settle back, indicating that I'm impatient to get going. Ross reluctantly engages first gear, and the car begins moving.

'Has your father been harassing you again?'

Ross shakes his head, straining to look past me and check it's clear to pull out onto the main road.

'No. He's gone quiet again, thank goodness. There's a problem with one of the jobs we're on. We began digging out the footings yesterday and this morning I received a call from the foreman. They've found something that might be of archaeological interest and that means everything is on hold until we can get it checked out. It just blows a hole in our schedule for next week.'

'Oh, Ross, I am sorry to hear that.'

'It happens. But there is good news, at least for you.' I watch his side profile and see his lips twitch as his annoyance gives way to a little smile.

'For me?'

'How do you fancy having three of my best guys invading your garden on Monday?'

I clap my hands to my face. 'You're not joking? I'm going to get my new office?'

'You are. It'll take them three days to assemble the kit

and I still need to sort out an electrician, but you should be all up and running barring any unexpected hitches, by Thursday.'

'It's already been delivered and is sitting in one of your units?' I ask, indignantly.

He grimaces. 'It's a small job, Kerra, and I knew if I told you it had arrived that you'd have expected it to be done immediately. What do you not understand about work schedules?' He laughs.

'Yes, but...' I pause.

'You're sleeping with the boss and you think that entitles you to special treatment?' he teases.

'No, that's not what I was thinking!' I reply, emphatically. 'What I was going to say was that I should be a valued customer, given that you recently completed my lovely new extension. I thought that might count for something.'

'You're not fooling me. Kerra Shaw likes everything done asap.'

'Are you implying that I don't have any patience?'

He pauses. 'Changing the subject ever so slightly, aren't you curious about where we're going?'

Ever the diplomat, it's hard to be cross with him when I know full well that Ross is a businessman and not even Dad would dispute the fact that he treats everyone fairly. Ross's principles are the rules by which he lives his life and it's one of the reasons why he's so well regarded, despite the interest people take in his personal life. It's impossible to be cross with him when I know he's in the right.

'Surprise me.'

'We've been invited to dinner at Treeve Perran Farm.'

'Ross! This is such a bad idea. How on earth did Yvonne and Gawen find out about us?'

He shifts uncomfortably in his seat. 'They don't know anything. I asked if I could bring a date.'

I'm floored. 'A date?'

'Okay, so once they see us together, they'll know what's going on anyway. They're old friends of mine, Kerra, and it's not as if you don't know the farm.'

I groan out loud. 'They arrived in Cornwall long after I'd left. I helped clean their holiday lets a few times shortly after I arrived back. That was only because I was repaying a favour by giving Tegan a hand when Clean and Shine was short-staffed. I probably waved to Yvonne and Gawen on my way in and out, two or three times at most.' It's difficult trying to keep myself from panicking. I remember visiting the farm shop as a child and I'm pretty sure my parents didn't stop buying from there after I left.

'I'm sorry. I didn't mean to upset you but who is going to know? It's the other side of Polreweek, and it's not exactly on our doorstep, is it? Gawen and Yvonne already suspect that I'm seeing a special someone, but they're discreet people who are on my side. This kind invitation is their way of letting me know they can keep a secret if I'm... we... are prepared to share it with them.'

I can't help feeling a little disconcerted that Ross is springing this on me without talking it through first.

'We agreed to keep a low profile in everything we do, Ross,' I point out.

'I know and this doesn't change that. It's not like we're having a meal together in The Lark and Lantern in full view of the entire village, is it?'

'No,' I mutter, begrudgingly.' He has a point, but then so do I. 'But now you've moved back to Treylya, you're in the heart of the village again. I think it was a big mistake doing that, Ross, I really do. You escaped for a reason and that was to have a little privacy.' He's as intent as I am on not becoming the focus of local gossip again. But everyone knows Ross and his family, because of their business and social connections, which extend way beyond sleepy little Penvennan.

'I'm back for two reasons and one is because of you, Kerra. Besides, it's too late now as Tegan and Sy are happy renting The Forge. Until I sell Treylya, I have nowhere else to go.'

I love The Forge, as it's where we spent our first night together, but he's right and it is too late to reverse his decision. 'Which is why it's important that we're careful.'

'Please trust me that it will be okay,' he implores, and my resolve weakens. 'Won't it be nice to act like a normal couple for a few hours, without having to watch what we say, or do?'

The truth is that I'm not sure I'm ready for this. It's a big step for us both and a leap of faith for me with two people who are essentially strangers.

'Look, I'll level with you, Kerra. If, and I hope it doesn't happen, word gets out about us before we're ready, I'd hate it to come as a surprise to Gawen and Yvonne. They had my back and were there for me throughout the entire unpleasant-ness of the divorce. I owe them big time because they kept me on an even keel. To me they're family.'

It pulls on my heartstrings to hear Ross admit that. He's always had a difficult relationship with his parents, but his very public and messy divorce sent them scurrying away to live in Spain. The scandalous behaviour of Ross's ex-wife, Bailey, sparked a level of gossip unheard of in our little community apparently and, unfortunately, news spread far and wide because he's a Treloar.

'I didn't realise quite how close you were to them, Ross. I'm sorry I overreacted.'

'No, it was wrong of me to spring it on you like this. Would you rather turn back, and eat at my place instead? I can call and make an excuse.'

'That's not necessary. I'd love to get to know them better.'

Ross has been so understanding about the situation with my dad, so it would be wrong of me not to go along with his request. But I am nervous, as even in my wildest dreams as a young girl, I never saw myself as being the woman in Ross's life. Me, the IT nerd who was always on the edge of the little group of village kids. I longed to blend in and shine as brightly as the other girls trying to attract his attention. Even now, with everything that has happened in the few months that I've been back, that little seed of doubt is still buried deep inside of me. I'm not glamorous, like his ex. And I'm not a social climber, but then neither is he.

THREE
A WARM WELCOME

'This is a lovely surprise,' Yvonne exclaims, as she welcomes us through the door. 'It's Kerra Shaw, isn't it? Your mum used to visit the farm shop once a month. I was so sorry to hear of your loss. She was a lovely woman. I haven't seen Eddie in a long while.'

Everyone knows everyone and nothing goes unnoticed.

'He's been busy relaunching the kennels,' I explain.

'Ah, of course. Anyway, come in out of the cold.' Yvonne looks directly at Ross, seemingly delighted by this unexpected revelation. He follows me inside, stopping briefly to kiss Yvonne on the cheek before she shuts the door behind us.

As we slip off our coats and hang them on the well-worn pegs, a cute little Labrador puppy suddenly comes bounding towards me, jumping up and nearly knocking me over.

'Gawen, come and get Poppy, will you, please? I'm so sorry, Kerra. She's still settling in and she's so excitable whenever anyone new comes to visit.'

'It's fine. Hello, Poppy, aren't you gorgeous?' I kneel down on the flagstone floor, to rub her back. She's full of life and such a beauty, with her cream coat and her biscuit-coloured ears.

Gawen appears and we're all huddled into the narrow entrance hall.

'Come on, girl,' he says, patting his leg to attract Poppy's attention.

'Gawen, this is Eddie's daughter, Kerra.'

He thrusts out his hand and we shake, as Poppy sits patiently between us wondering what's going on.

'Good to finally meet you, Kerra. You were here with Tegan a couple of times in the summer, I remember, sorting out the holiday lets. We never got a chance to chat. Come on, let's head into the dining room and warm you up. The fire is blazing. Farmhouses are such draughty places.'

Gazing up at the oak beams overhead, I'm envious. 'That may be, but it's utterly charming.'

'Hmm,' he replies, sounding a tad jaded. 'Old plumbing, cold floors and windows through which the wind howls when it's coming from the east. But it has its redeeming features.' He laughs.

As he ushers us inside, the atmosphere is relaxed, and Ross is like a different man. He banters with Gawen as we walk into the dining room and the two men head over to a rustic dresser to sort out the drinks. Yvonne invites me to take a seat and says she'll be back shortly. I was about to ask if there is anything I can do to help, but she's gone before I get a chance.

'Kerra, what can I get you?' Gawen enquires.

'A small glass of red wine, please.'

'Small? Isn't Ross driving?'

Oh dear. 'I'm a lightweight,' I reply, breezily. When I glance at Ross his eyebrows are raised as he stares back at me, indicating that I should relax and not be so guarded.

The door begins to swing back, and I hurry across to hold it open so that Yvonne can enter. She's carrying a large tray and gives me a grateful smile.

'Kerra's car is parked up by the vet's surgery on the edge of the village,' Ross continues. 'So, we're both watching what we drink tonight.'

'Ah, that's a shame!' Yvonne joins in. 'If we'd known that, you could have stayed overnight.'

I focus on helping Yvonne pass the plates around, my stomach rumbling. 'I was brought up on roasted Cornish game hen and have fond memories of Grandma serving up this same dish when my grandparents lived in Pedrevan Cottage. This is wonderful, thank you, Yvonne.'

I intend to sit back and enjoy this home-cooked meal. I'll let Ross explain why we're creeping around as if we're having a clandestine affair, fearful of being found out. Neither of us is in a relationship, but secrecy is the price to pay for wanting a peaceful life, at least for now.

'Is it okay to ask how long you two... I mean, when did you discover...' Yvonne tails off, not wanting to say the wrong thing.

Ross coughs, clearing his throat before taking a quick sip from his glass. As he places it back down on the table, he looks across at me sheepishly. 'It began when I was about fourteen years of age, Yvonne. Gaining Kerra's attention wasn't easy – I knew nothing at all about writing computer code, or how to speed up a PC. Whenever I did manage to engage her in conversation, I always ended up tripping over my own words and feeling like a total fool. I lived in the hope of one day being able to impress her. But out of a sense of self-preservation I kept that thought to myself at the time,' he says, laughing at himself. 'And when she left for London, I was devastated – she didn't even say goodbye.'

He's right, I never did get a chance to wish him luck before I left. It's illuminating sitting here listening to Ross talking about us and seeing things from his perspective. And it quickly becomes apparent how strong the bond is between these three people, that he's comfortable speaking from the heart.

'Well, once Treylya is off your hands I'm sure it will feel like a fresh start, Ross. How are you coping, being back in the village?' Gawen voices the big question, one I haven't had the heart to ask.

Turning to look at Ross, I watch as he loads up his fork before pausing to answer. The frown on his face is touching.

'I have good and bad days. Fortunately. I have a little company at times,' he answers, raising his eyebrows. 'And I don't just mean Kerra, her cat Ripley pays me visits, too. I think both of them sense that Treylya is the last place I want to be, but maybe life is teaching me a lesson.'

'An expensive one, at that,' Gawen points out and Ross shakes his head, sadly.

'I'll be lucky to get my entire investment back, I know that, but it represents everything I've worked for, so far. Every penny of my savings are tied up in it, when it could give me flexibility for the future. The pity is that it could take a while to find the right buyer. There's a cut-off price below which I'm not prepared to go just for the sake of a quick sale. It was a big mistake not building something more traditional and I knew that at the time, but it was a calculated risk, even if I was pushed into it.'

I catch Yvonne giving Gawen a fixed stare across the table as she decides it's time to change the subject.

'I hear that Pedrevan Cottage has been undergoing some

major work since you returned, Kerra. Are you all settled now?'

'Yes. My neighbour, Drew, was the architect and project manager. Treloar's did a wonderful job of extending both our properties. It feels like home and yet the old memories are still there.'

'How lovely. The best of both worlds. Do you miss London?' she enquires, genuinely interested.

'Not really. Although I do miss the anonymity at times,' I confess, trying hard not to sound jaded.

'I can't begin to imagine what it's like to return to a place where everyone is watching your every move with interest. Not many who leave end up coming back for good. The odd visit isn't quite the same as trying to slip back in unobtrusively, when everyone wants to know your business, is it?'

'Oh, come on, Yvonne,' Gawen remarks, taking offence. 'That's a bit unfair.'

She stops what she's doing to give him a semi-apologetic look.

'Well, maybe not *everyone*,' she grants, 'but it's often the people with the loudest voices who seem happy to repeat whatever they hear, whether it's based on fact, or pure speculation.'

What ensues is a hilarious retelling of some of the classic examples Yvonne can remember hearing, and it becomes even more amusing when Ross joins in.

'Do you remember when you disappeared for a whole month, Yvonne? Word was that you'd run off with your lover,' Ross informs her, putting his head back and laughing. 'Like you'd ever leave Gawen.'

Yvonne shakes her head in disbelief. 'Can't a woman even

take a trip home to visit her parents without someone making something of it?'

'That's rich!' Gawen, looks appalled. 'Good job word never reached my ear; I'd have had something to say about it, you mark my words.'

'It's just the way it is,' I offer. 'No one means any offence, but other people's lives always seem so much more interesting, don't they?'

Yvonne purses her lips. 'Personally, I think some people have too much time on their hands and not enough to do. They should try running a farm. Most days I'm too tired to care what everyone is tattling about.'

'You had a bit of a time of it with your ex-tenant I hear, Kerra? Nasty business that. He was dealing in stolen cars, I hear?' Gawen sympathises.

'Yes, it was a bit of a shock, I will admit. He was vetted by the letting agency and always paid on time.'

'See,' Gawen points out to Yvonne. 'If it weren't for people keeping an eye out, that gang of crooks would probably still be in business. They'll get their just desserts in court.'

'They most certainly will,' Ross endorses.

'Okay, that's one of the few examples when twitching the curtains to watch what your neighbour is doing, might actually pay off.' Yvonne laughs. She stands to begin clearing the plates and I join her.

As we make our way out into the hallway and into the kitchen, she says over her shoulder: 'Only emmets like me, or people like you who have spread their wings, can understand. In a curious way the likes of you and me will always be classed as different. It's not a bad thing, because people are naturally curious. Gawen knows that I mean no offence, I'm simply stating the truth.'

She edges open the kitchen door with her foot and we both step through.

'You have no idea how good it is to talk to someone who can see both sides, Yvonne.'

'Well, I was born in Bath, but my family ended up on a farm in southern Ireland. It was a culture shock for me when, at the age of ten, we moved from an elegant Georgian house within walking distance of the world-famous Roman Baths, museums and a shopper's paradise, to being surrounded by nothing but fields.'

'My goodness, it can't have been easy leaving your friends behind at that tender age.'

'My grandfather had a heart attack and died a few days later. My parents had no choice but to go and rescue the farm. My grandmother was distraught and within a year she'd given up on living. It wasn't the same without the love of her life by her side.'

As I help Yvonne to load the dishwasher, I can see the sadness that still lingers in her heart reflected on her face.

'Losing a soul mate is heart-breaking,' I acknowledge, sadly.

We both stop what we're doing to exchange an empathetic glance.

'It made me realise that when you know you've found the one, it doesn't matter what other people think. Every single day you have together is precious and you shouldn't let anyone rob you of that. I've never seen Ross as happy as he is right now, despite the problems. You'll get through it and come out stronger at the other end.'

I'm guessing Yvonne's parents weren't exactly overjoyed when she met Gawen and moved to Cornwall.

'Can I ask you something in strictest confidence?'

Yvonne looks at me, cagily. 'If it's something I'm able to answer, then go ahead.'

'Is Ross really over his ex-wife, Bailey? From what Tegan told me, she was beautiful, well-educated and from a wealthy family. *A proper catch*, as people around here term it.'

'I think I'm the only one who can answer that.' Ross's voice looms up from the doorway, rendering both myself and Yvonne speechless as we turn to face him.

'You ran away, Kerra. I didn't think you'd ever come back, well, not for good. And when you did visit, you never sought me out. Not once. I was mesmerised by Bailey, but now I know that I was never *in love* with her, I just didn't know any better.' He turns to look at Yvonne, who stares back at him sadly. 'You sensed that from the start, Yvonne, didn't you?'

'Personally, I didn't take to her. She thought a farm was an unhygienic place to live and she made that abundantly clear. You'd have thought I walked around with pieces of hay hanging out of my hair. Pushing my personal feelings aside, I think it was such an awful experience that it has helped to make you realise what really matters in life, Ross.'

Ross begins to laugh, turning to face me. 'That day I got out of the van and saw you standing in the doorway of Pedrevan, I knew what was going to happen. And so did you, Kerra.'

It's an awkward moment as we stare at each other, knowing that Yvonne is looking on. She clutches her hands to her chest, touched by Ross's admission. 'It's time we convinced Eddie that Ross is the one, Kerra, don't you think?' Her voice wavers and I can see how moved she is as Ross wraps his arm around my waist.

'I think I might have a plan to get him on our side,' I muse, feeling pleased with myself. 'I'd be interested to know what your thoughts are on it, though.'

'Can't wait to hear the details!' Gawen's voice makes us all turn around to look at him. 'You'd best kick it off soon, though, as it's impossible to keep a secret round here for too long.'

'This calls for strong coffee and a slice of autumn cake from Gawen's grandmother's Women's Institute cookery book,' Yvonne declares. 'I do love a good plan. You can make the coffee, Gawen, and we'll have it in the sitting room,' she says, crossing the kitchen to retrieve a cake tin from the walk-in larder.

Ross pulls me even closer, nestling me against his chest. 'I told you,' he whispers softly into my ear. 'We're among friends and everything is going to be fine, I know it.'

* * *

'Morning, Nettie,' I call out, hurrying to catch up with her. She's an old friend of my mum's and has recently started work at the kennels to give Dad a hand. I've been anxiously keeping an eye out for her first dog-walking session of the morning and on Sundays, unless it's raining, Dad stays behind to do what he calls his weekly deep clean.

'It's unusual to see you out and about so early at the weekend, Kerra,' Nettie replies, as one of the dogs begins jumping around tangling the leads.

'I thought I'd get some fresh air before I order the furniture for my new office. Here, let me take two of those leads from you. Who is this overactive little guy?'

'He's new. His name is Buddy, and he's not used to walking alongside other dogs. We only have him for a week and this is his second day, so he's still adjusting to it. If you wouldn't mind taking him for a moment, while I untangle this little mess, then I'll be fine.'

I bend, grasping Buddy's lead near his collar and pulling it through so Nettie can sort out the others.

'I'm heading up to the woods too. We can walk together. Why don't I take his lead? He'll probably settle down once he's on his own. It's Rufus he's in competition with.' I smile, knowingly.

Rufus is the most gorgeous red setter, and he comes to the kennels to give his owners a rest. Mr Thomas has an arthritic knee, which means he can't always walk him, and Mrs Thomas struggles at times to keep up with Rufus's boundless energy.

'Well, if you're sure, that would be much appreciated.'

It doesn't take long to untangle the leads and with Rufus in one hand, and the two smaller dogs in the other, Nettie is all sorted.

'Right. We're going to be fine together, aren't we, Buddy?' I kneel down next to him, smoothing his back to calm his excitement before we set off. He waggles his little tail vigorously, basking in the attention. He's a jolly little chap, with a totally white coat and muzzle, his head and ears a rich cinnamon colour. 'You're just soooo cute, aren't you?'

'How's it going at The Design Cave?' Nettie enquires, as we set off.

'It looks really promising. And James has settled in well, although I suspect my dad is missing him.'

Nettie nods her head. 'He is, Kerra. It was so convenient having James on the doorstep to help with the walks and he'd turn his hand to anything, but it's nice to know he's in full-time employment now.'

'He told me that he's going to save every penny he can for a deposit, as he'd like to rent a place of his own.'

The look we exchange is maudlin. 'What chance do the youngsters have to buy or even rent, with house prices as they are these days?' Nettie says the words that were on the tip of my tongue.

'I know. It's crazy.' On the one hand holiday rental properties bring in the tourists to boost the economy, but on the other it makes it almost impossible for the next generation to live independently. 'How's Dad?'

'Eddie's good. He's agreed that he needs to look for a replacement for James. I don't know if he mentioned it to you, but I packed in my part-time job at the vet's. In the interim I'm working a few extra hours each day at the kennels, but I've just started writing a new play and it is a bit of a struggle to fit everything in. Eddie knows I won't let him down, though,' she replies, her voice softening. It was a pleasant surprise to discover Nettie has a passion for writing. What started as a hobby seems to be taking over her life now and she's in her element.

When Mum set up the kennels, Nettie was a nurse in the vet's surgery, a stone's throw away. She'd help Mum out with the early morning and late afternoon walks. Often, she'd spend long periods here at the weekends and she was a part of our family. Dad was working with Uncle Alistair in the family business, Shaw & Sons Joinery, at the time and rarely walked a dog. When Mum became ill, he gave up his job to look after her and keep the kennels going. When Mum passed, things began to go downhill and when I returned to Penvennan to honour the promise I made to her, Dad realised something had to change. Ironically, I did very little to help him other than to upgrade his website, sort out the mess he'd made of the online booking system and produce new advertising materials.

'Is Dad's heart really in running the kennels, Nettie?'

We step off the pavement and begin the climb up through the woods. Swinging open the gate, I wait for her to go through, and let Rufus off his lead. He needs to bound around and knows these woods as well as we do. Poor Buddy begins whimpering and straining on his lead, so I let it out and he heads straight to a large oak tree to sniff around.

Nettie and I walk slowly, the track still a little muddy from the recent heavy rainfall.

'Honestly?'

I nod.

'He wouldn't know how to let go of it even if he wanted to, Kerra. Meryn was a remarkable woman and the love of his life. He's surrounded by memories wherever he turns.'

'I think I already knew the answer, but I value your opinion. He's not unhappy, is he?'

'No. He gets lonely sometimes, that's all,' she confides as our charges urge us forward. Rufus comes bounding back, setting off Buddy who can't understand why he isn't free. I slacken his lead a little more, hoping he doesn't wind himself around one of the trees and tie me up in knots.

'It's been better for him since you've been back.'

'Ah, I do hope so, Kerra. He pushed everyone away for a while and I can understand that. Seeing me around was the last thing he wanted, as it just reminded him of your mum. I do thank you for bringing us back together. I miss her just as much.' I can tell from the sadness in Nettie's voice that the loss of a dear friend is equally hard to bear. She was a part of Mum's daily life and vice versa.

'Uncle Alistair still misses working with Dad. I know they

argue all the time, but family is family.' Several years after they married, Granddad Harry could see that Grandma Rose was homesick and longed to return to Cornwall. He uprooted them from Kinross, determined that he'd build a legacy. And he did; there's a big market for Shaw's hand-crafted kitchens and bathroom cabinetry. Adding & *Sons* to the business name was his proudest moment. 'Do you think Dad misses working in the family business?'

We stand, watching the dogs as they ferret around, snuffling at piles of autumnal leaves and dying vegetation.

'I'm not sure. He's not exactly a man who shares his thoughts, is he?'

'I know. But he's angry with Uncle Alistair and they haven't spoken for a while again. This time I think it's because after Uncle Alistair begged him to go back under any terms at all, Dad didn't want to admit he's tempted. But you know what Dad can be like when he doesn't see eye to eye with someone, and this is all about the way Uncle Alistair treats Alice.'

Nettie frowns. 'That's always been a bit of a puzzle to me, Kerra. Eddie dotes on her and is quick to forgive Alice, no matter what problems her gossiping has caused in the past.'

'I wish it were as simple as that, but it's more about the fact that Auntie Marge hoped Alice would take over from her and run the office side of the business.'

'Alice? Really?' Nettie immediately realises how disparaging that sounds. 'Oh, I'm not implying that Alice isn't up to... what I meant to say is that Alice's skills lie elsewhere,' she corrects herself.

'My thoughts entirely. Sadly, Uncle Alistair can't see that, and it makes Dad fume how dismissive he is about Alice's career, expecting that at some point she'll see sense, as he puts it. As far as Dad is concerned Alice can do no wrong, even though that isn't always the case. But when something upsets Dad it's virtually impossible to talk it through with him, because he simply goes off the deep end.'

'Now it's all beginning to make sense, Kerra. Two wrongs don't make a right, although I doubt Eddie would appreciate me pointing that out to him.'

She's being polite and I think what she wanted to say is "anyone pointing that out to him". And she's right to warn me off because Dad would simply dig in his heels even more.

'Having a stubborn streak can cloud one's judgement; it takes one to know one, as they say,' I concede.

'The irony of the situation is that what Eddie is doing with regards to your situation with Ross, is much the same as Alistair thinking Ian isn't right for Alice.' Nettie sighs, but she's hit the nail on the head. Dad is slow to forgive even when he's proven wrong, because it's hard for him to swallow his pride and say sorry. When his emotions are in turmoil his coping mechanism is to push people away until he's ready to face the facts. I think it's time to change the subject as this is getting a tad depressing.

'Old habits die hard,' I reply, shrugging my shoulders. 'On a happier note, Ross says the rehearsals are going well for the Christmas pantomime.'

That puts a huge smile on Nettie's face. Penvennan Amateur Dramatics club is dear to her heart and this year they're performing one of her plays *Santa and the Ice Palace*.

'It's a bit of a nightmare for Ross. There are quite a few scenery changes and I know some of them are a bit of a challenge.'

'Well, children have big imaginations and that's what a pantomime is all about. He says it's wonderful, but I know he is struggling a little to get everything built. He's such a perfectionist and safety is a real concern for him.'

Nettie screws up her face. 'Yes, I'm afraid my imagination knows no bounds, too, and I never gave thought to how we were going to represent some of the scenes on stage. From Santa's sleigh to the castle and the ice palace.' She laughs. 'It's a tall order.'

'Well, I've offered to give him a hand with the painting, so I'll be there every Thursday evening when he needs help.'

'Oh, how lovely! That's most kind of you, Kerra. All newcomers are welcome. Sy has been amazing, too.'

'I can't believe he's playing Santa Claus. That costume is going to require an awful lot of padding,' I retort.

We exchange a mirthful look. Sy is tall and very slim, but he's always had a theatrical air about him. Initially, he brushed off my suggestion that he join the local group, but at last he came around to the idea and it's something he is really throwing himself into. Tegan says he's in his element.

It's a nice walk and the trail takes us in a loop. We pause in the clearing to gaze out across the bay and with a pale blue sky, the water looks cold but so pretty, as the watery sun's rays dance over the surface. It's like someone has put a filter over the lens through which we are looking, and everything appears to be bathed in a liquid silvery sheen.

'It's breath-taking, isn't it?' I ponder.

'There's nowhere else I'd rather be,' Nettie replies, as she reluctantly drags herself away to call Rufus back and put on his lead.

It's been a great walk and I hope I've sown a seed that will flourish. Ross is in need of help to build the set for the upcoming pantomime and he has already turned to me, so I hope that Nettie starts to connect the dots. Dad is, after all, a professional carpenter and she just might succeed in dragging him out of his armchair to lend a hand. Yvonne and Gawen would be proud of me. I think I've done a great job of subtly dropping a big hint. It's time to head back and I can start thinking about storage solutions for my garden office.

FOUR

IT'S NOT WHAT YOU KNOW, BUT WHO YOU KNOW

'Hi, Polly, it's Kerra.'

'Oh, hello, Kerra. Goodness, what's that noise?'

'Sorry, I'll shut the window. There's a Hiab crane outside the front of the cottage. It's delivering the timber for my new home office.'

'An exciting couple of days for you, then!'

'Yes, I can't wait. That's the reason I'm calling you. I wondered if you have an hour spare so I can pick your brains about storage solutions?'

Even though Polly works full-time helping her father Sam run the pub, she studied interior design when she was in college. It's her passion, but her loyalty has always been to her dad, who brought her up single-handedly. Even though that meant putting her own dream on hold to keep his dream alive.

'Why don't you join me for brunch? I usually grab something at elevenish before the lunchtime rush begins. Dad will be downstairs in the bar and we can have the kitchen table to ourselves.'

'Perfect, if you're sure you don't mind.'

'Suits me, fine. I'll enjoy the company.'

'Great, see you in a bit then. And thanks, Polly, I appreciate it.'

There's a sharp rap on the door and I know that knock so well. Rushing through to open it, I feign surprise.

'Oh, Ross. Good morning.' I swing the door open wide, inviting him to step inside. 'The off-loading seems to be going smoothly,' I add raising my voice a little and sounding business-like.

The moment the door is shut he turns to grin at me. The problem with an open-plan ground floor is that his guys are walking back and forth with the bundles of timber and we're in plain sight.

'It's feels like ages since I've been here. I'd forgotten what an amazing job my team did on this,' he boasts, shamelessly. 'Are you alright?'

I lead him on through and he takes a seat at the dining table.

'I am. Yesterday I managed to churn through a list of annoying little items that were outstanding, and it was good to clear my desk ready for the move later this week. Coffee?'

'I'd love one, but I can't stop for long so it's a *no*, I'm afraid,' he replies, placing his clipboard down in front of him. 'We'd better look like we're going through the paperwork.'

Ripley appears, lured by the sound of Ross's voice.

'Here's my girl,' he calls out as soon as he spots her. She pads across to him, arching her back as he lets her sniff his hand first. Then she puts her head down so he can ruffle her ears. 'You haven't paid me a visit for a few days, Ripley. I thought you loved those chicken treats?' Ross declares, sounding miffed.

'She prefers the salmon ones, now,' I inform him. He looks at me, throwing his hands in the air accusatorily and I raise my eyebrows. 'Mrs Moyle has them in stock, but she's been keeping them under the counter for me.'

'That's unfair. And I can't exactly ask her for them, can I?' He stares back at me, shaking his head. 'It's not right, is it, Ripley?' He asks and she miaows back at him in agreement.

Ripley is ignoring me, as she does whenever Ross is around. I take the seat next to him and half-turn so that my back is to the garden. It's hard not to lean forward and kiss Ross on the mouth, but we're being watched with interest by Ripley and the guys traversing the path outside. What I'd give for a little privacy right now.

'You've forgiven me for Saturday night's little surprise, then?'

'Considering I had a great time, I guess you can consider yourself off the hook.' I beam at him.

He smiles back at me, for the briefest of moments a more serious look taking over. 'It made me feel a little sad when I walked in and overheard you asking Yvonne about Bailey.'

I can feel my cheeks begin to glow. 'I'm sorry about that. It just slipped out.'

'No, it's fine. I thought I'd said enough to reassure you, but I'm not one to dwell on the past and I've closed the door on that period of my life. That doesn't mean to say that you don't have questions, though. You only have to ask.'

As my eyes search his, I can see his only concern is for me – he has nothing at all to hide.

'Your answer swept away any lingering doubts I had, Ross. It's just that... well, your life with Bailey was so different. Lots of social functions, a glamorous wife, that stunning house and mixing with influential people. By comparison, my life is low-key, cosy and family-orientated.'

Ross narrows his eyes. 'Well, that might be the case, but life with you will never be boring, Kerra. Your head is constantly full of exciting ideas and you shine without even knowing it. To me you are perfect, exactly as you are.'

My heart is pounding as his words take my breath away and I compose myself before replying.

'Gawen and Yvonne were very understanding and kind. Oh, and I managed to catch Nettie yesterday morning.'

Ross looks pleased. 'Well done you. And were you able to slip in the fact that I need a little help building scenery for the play and make it sound credible?'

'I did. I'm fully aware that less is more, and Dad is no one's fool. If it had come from me it would have been too obvious, but as there is a great deal of truth in what I said, I'm sure it set Nettie thinking. I pointed out that Dad is a craftsman.'

Ross looks content. 'The sleigh is almost done, and if I do say so myself, it's a pretty realistic version for the stage. But the castle is taking forever to make it really stand out and turn it into 3D. And as for the Dark Queen's Winter Palace, well, Nettie keeps referring me to the film *Frozen*. Goodness knows what that will involve to make it look credible!' Ross sounds like he's griping, but he loves a challenge. It's something he gets involved with because he enjoys it and if it's a way to build bridges with Dad, then where's the harm in it?

'Is there any chance of catching up with you one evening this week?' he asks, a hopeful expression on his face. How can I resist?

'How about Friday? Nettie mentioned in passing that Dad's going to hers for dinner. I thought that was rather nice. They're getting on so well.'

'Find out what time they're leaving, and I'll pop down and pick you up. It'll be too dark for you to walk up through the woods.'

I sigh. He's right. And everything is a risk. 'What if Mrs Moyle or Arthur are looking out and spot us?'

'I'll give you a five-minute warning and you can begin walking towards the vet's surgery. I'll pick you up from the lay-by. Is that okay?'

'Perfect.'

'Right, I really must go, or the guys will begin taking the rise out of me. I'll call you late this evening, but you are serious about Friday night, aren't you?' His voice drops and I can sense his uncertainty. It's a big ask for me to stay overnight and we both know it. It's tough living like this, but it would be a lot tougher for those around us if our personal business was common knowledge. I can hear it now... 'She's only after him for his money' and 'What does Ross see in her?' I don't need to rely upon a man because I didn't come back a failure, I walked away a successful businesswoman but it's not common knowledge. And what I learnt is that money in the bank means nothing, it's what's in your heart that matters.

'It won't be like this forever,' I promise, as Ross follows me to the front door. 'And yes, I'm serious about Friday night.'

Do I really want to stay overnight in the house that he once shared with Bailey? The answer is *no*, but that's not his fault and we don't have a choice. It's not as if he can sleep here. Once the garden office is built, Ross will no longer have a legitimate reason to knock on my door.

He groans as I let him out. Our faces pass within mere inches of each other and it's hard to keep that distance between us.

'I love you, Kerra Shaw. You've turned not just my life, but my entire world upside down. And it's scary but I love it and I love you.'

Aww... to hear him talk like that takes my breath away. My eyes sparkle as I gaze at him before opening the door. As he steps across the threshold, I raise my voice a little as I speak.

'Well, I'm pleased to hear that you are confident everything will be completed by close of play on Wednesday,' I state, matter-of-factly, trying not to laugh.

'Treloar's Building Limited aim to please and nothing is too much trouble for a valued customer,' he calls out over his shoulder. I doubt anyone can hear us as they're making way too much noise, but Ross is walking away from me sporting a huge smile on his face.

All I can say is, roll on Friday!

* * *

Will is back as the foreman in charge, but he explains that he's splitting his time between two jobs, as mine was a last-minute change to the schedule.

'Don't worry about your new lawn, Kerra,' he reassures me before I leave to meet up with Polly. 'We've going to lay down some temporary boards. It'll flatten the grass a bit, but it won't churn it up. Ross has left specific instructions that we leave everything in the same condition we found it.'

'Thank you, Will. I'm glad you're in charge. Is it really possible to assemble all of this timber in just three days?'

He gives me a knowing smile. 'These kits fly up and our guys know what they're doing. The electrician will be here on Wednesday afternoon and he'll need access to the cottage.'

'Oh, that's not a problem. I'll be around all day. Right, I'm just heading out, but you have my number if anything crops up. I'll leave you to it, then.'

The sound of a nail gun assaults my ears before I've even reached the side of the cottage and I hurry off in the direction of the cove. I can't believe how organised Ross's guys are and I can hear Will's voice as he gives them their orders. No wonder Ross is so busy, and he seems happier these days. It makes a huge difference when his father isn't trying to interfere with the day-to-day running of the business.

I'm a little early, so I pop in to see Mrs Moyle first, but she's serving someone. I give her a quick wave but as I turn to go, she calls me back.

'Hang on there a moment, Kerra. I'm almost finished here.'

I loiter aimlessly, wondering what this is going to be about, but the open conversation suddenly turns into a whispering session and after she waves her customer off, Mrs Moyle disappears. I wait patiently by the counter until she returns, full of apologies.

'Sorry about that, Kerra. A little problem has come up for Arthur to sort out.'

'Nothing serious, I hope?'

'Your dad might be getting a call, shortly, that's all. Just a neighbour who has just been whisked into hospital, I hear, after breaking her ankle. Her dog is being looked after by another neighbour who will pop in, but the poor little chap will need a temporary home for a while.'

Everything is word of mouth because that's the way it's always been amongst the older folk around here. I don't know how they'd cope if it wasn't for Mrs Moyle's husband, Arthur. This is the central hub of the village and it's more than just a shop, it's an essential service. If anything is wrong and Mrs

Moyle hears about it, she's straight upstairs to see Arthur. He knows who to contact and does so in a very discreet way.

'Anyway, that'll all get sorted. On another matter entirely, I know it's none of my business, but there's something I thought I'd mention in passing. Your cousin, Alice, is seeing a chap and she's keeping it on the quiet.'

Good for Alice, realising it's best to keep a low profile. 'It's probably early days, then,' I reply, thinking the least I say on this subject the better.

'No. That's not the reason I'm bringing it up. He's getting the rough end of the stick just now, to take the heat away from someone else and it's all wrong. There's trouble brewing in my opinion but that's all I'm prepared to say, and you can do with that as you wish.' Goodness, when Mrs Moyle is this pointed in her remarks then it's time to take note.

'Well, um, thank you for the heads-up. I'll... uh... keep an eye out for her.'

'Make sure you do, Kerra. I hope you don't mind me saying something, but although Alice might unwittingly make trouble for herself at times, on another level she's not a worldly girl – if you know what I mean.'

'No problem at all. Thank you. And, before I forget, can you save me one of your apple pies for Friday afternoon, please? I thought I'd spoil myself over the weekend.'

'Of course, I will. Now don't forget what I said, will you? Are you off somewhere nice?'

Mrs Moyle doesn't gossip for the sake of it, and she won't put up with baseless rumours. But she says what she thinks. I'm guessing she has her suspicions about my situation and I'm wondering if she approves.

'I'm having brunch with Polly. My new garden office is being erected as we speak.'

'Arthur shouted out earlier on that there was a lorry outside the front of the cottage. And I spotted Ross just now when I was redoing the window display. He keeps himself out of trouble these days, doesn't he?' I don't know quite what to make of that remark.

'I believe so,' I reply, cautiously.

'Well, I'm glad of it. He's a nice man and he hasn't always been treated fairly around here. I'd best not keep you, Kerra, Polly will be waiting.'

Mrs Moyle isn't one to stand around talking once she's said her piece. But she has oodles of patience when it comes to her elderly customers who call in daily for a pint of milk or a loaf of bread, and a chat.

As I step outside and stride out along the street, I don't know what Mrs Moyle thinks I can do about Alice's situation. Our paths don't cross that often as she lives with Uncle Alistair and Auntie Marge. It's a good ten-minute drive from here and if she visits the village it's only to pop in and see Dad. Alice and I have had our issues over the years. She has an unfortunate knack for saying the wrong thing, at the wrong time. As a peace offering, I reached out to her and she was kind enough to use her skills to do a hair and make-up session for Sissy, Sienna and me for the launch party. We made our peace, but laying the past to rest is one thing, being friends when our paths rarely cross is another. Alice hasn't maintained any form of contact and who she's seeing is hardly any of my business, so there isn't really anything I can do.

'You're in a hurry,' Dad's voice booms out behind me and I turn to see him striding to catch up with me.

'Oh, hi, Dad. I'm off to catch up with Polly before she starts her lunchtime shift.'

'I thought you'd be watching them builders. I saw Ross

was here earlier on. Watch yourself there, m'dear. A woman on her own needs to be wary.'

Inwardly I groan.

'Will's there for a bit and I'll only be gone an hour. I'll be glad to get my new office up and running so I can reclaim my guest bedroom,' I reply breezily, ignoring his warning.

'I'll walk with you. I'm on me way to see if Gryff still has a copy of last week's local paper.'

As he steps forward to plant a kiss on my cheek, I put an arm around his shoulder, giving him an affectionate pat on the back. 'Ah, you're a man on a mission this morning.'

'I am, that, my lovely. There's lots to do and I thought I'd look in the ads section to see if anyone local is advertising for a bit of work.'

He's walking quite briskly and it's good to see. When I first returned home, he was a shadow of his former self and now he has a spring in his step again. I like to think that Nettie is the reason for that.

'Ah, yes, to replace James.'

'I do miss that lad, but I'm happy for him and it worked out well for Sissy. Are the rumours true that you're looking for another investment already?'

I turn to look at Dad, quizzically. 'What rumours?'

'So, it is just gossip, then. I did wonder as you hadn't mentioned anything. No worries, I know me daughter has got her head screwed on right and doesn't rush into things.'

Do I quiz Dad about what exactly he's heard, or do I ignore it? It's pure speculation anyway, as although I have a couple of ideas I'm mulling over, I haven't approached anyone yet. Besides, my next project is likely to be a non-profit-making one, but first I need to do a little more research.

As we turn the corner and begin the downhill walk to

Penvennan Cove, there is a light breeze coming off the water, carrying with it that distinctive salty tang.

'Do you remember when I was small, and you'd take me over to Draketown to watch the fishing boats return?'

'I do. And you'd wrinkle up that nose of yours and the fishermen would laugh at you. And your granddad, Harry, would be there offloading the catch from his trawler *The Wild Rose*. Fond memories, my lovely.'

Named after my Grandma Rosenwyn, it was an impressive vessel, and they were often out at sea for several days at a time. She could never rest easy until he was back on dry land and it was like that until the day he died. I think that she always felt the sea would be the death of him, and she was right.

'Grandma told me once that none of her family went to her wedding. I always thought that was rather sad.' As I stare straight ahead, I consider that on a day like this the water looks beautiful, a true blessing from nature. But staring off into the distance at the rocky outcrops almost covered by waves makes me shudder. After selling *The Wild Rose,* Granddad often took his small two-man boat out to do some handline fishing. On the day he died, he got caught in a squall that drove him onto the rocks. It smashed the hull to bits before anyone could reach him and just like that he was gone.

'It was a different time, Kerra. Let the past go, my lovely. I can tell by the look on your face what you're thinking about right now. Your grandparents were happy, and money never meant much to Rose. Her family didn't understand that she had to follow her heart.'

'And Granddad's untimely death ended up breaking it,' I reflect, sadly.

We walk past the row of fishermen's cottages, their rustic,

whitewashed stonework façades an iconic tourist photo opportunity. Originally, they were all two rooms up and two down, with a coal house on the back and a toilet at the end of the garden. Most have been extended now, of course, and only two of them are still owned by ex-fishermen.

'Did you know one of these is coming up for sale?'

'No. Which one?'

'The second one in from the left. It's been a holiday let for more than ten years, now. It's a pity, as the owners always holidayed here. Do you remember the Bartletts? Nice little family, with two daughters, but they're in their late teens now and seldom get down here.'

'I never knew them. They must have bought it after I'd left.'

'Right, I'm heading inside for a chat with Gryff. If he hasn't got a paper, he might have an ad pinned up on his noticeboard. You never know. Tell Polly I'll see her later.' Dad grins at me. I'm guessing that means he'll be sloping off for a pint and a chat in the bar, at lunchtime.

'Okay. I hope you find someone very soon, Dad. If you ever need a hand, you can always call on me.'

Dad gives me one of his looks. 'I know you have better things to do with your time, Kerra, but remember that there's more to life than just work. Maybe you should think about getting out a bit more and socialising. You're stuck in every evening and I thought you'd miss getting out and about after your time in London.'

Oh, Dad! If only you knew. 'I've been really busy online, and you know what I'm like. I'm happiest when I have a challenge to focus on and when I'm good and ready, I'll take some time off. Besides, when the nights draw in who wants to venture out?'

He makes a grumbling sound. 'Well, don't turn into a hermit, that's all I'm saying.'

I lean in to give him a kiss on the cheek and his eyes sparkle. 'I'm hoping that Sy and Tegan will set a date for their wedding before too long. Just giving you a heads-up, as you'll no doubt want to take someone along with you.'

'Dad! Stop it! I'm off, I'll see you later.'

I dig my hands into my pockets, knowing that Dad's vision for my future is different to mine. He means well, but just because I'm back doesn't mean I don't have ambitions still to chase, or that I'm looking for a quieter life.

As I approach the pub, I up the pace. The front door is locked still, so I go around to the back. The rear door is ajar, and Sam is standing outside, hands on hips as he surveys the patio area, deep in thought.

'Oh, hi, Kerra.'

'Hi, Sam. Did Polly mention I was popping in?'

'Yes, she did. She's upstairs, I'm sure you can remember your way.'

'Problems?' I enquire, noting his frown.

'Always. Never-ending. Just thinking about Polly's idea for brightening this up a bit in the spring. That girl of mine is full of ideas and I wish I had pockets full of money to turn them into reality.'

Goodness, Sam does sound down.

'Well, the recent upgrades inside have made an enormous difference. It's so fresh and welcoming now. I'm here to pick Polly's brains myself.'

'I'm right lucky, I know that. It's just that time of the year when trade falls off a bit weekdays, and it's always a worry. We're still here, though, aren't we?' he jokes, but he isn't fooling me.

'And I hope you'll be here for a long time to come, Sam.'
'Me too, Kerra. Me too.'

FIVE

FAVOURS

'Bang on time,' Polly informs me with a beaming smile. 'I hope you like doorstop bacon sandwiches. The bread is fresh out of the oven courtesy of Pascoe's bakery.'

'As I walked up the stairs, I hoped that delicious smell was coming from here and not the restaurant kitchen below us.' I laugh, slipping off my coat.

'I've just made a coffee for myself. I'll grab you one if you'd like to carry your plate over and get settled. Ross's crew turned up then?'

'They did. Bright and early. The kit arrived in two separate loads, but everything is now on site and I'm so excited. Not that I intend inviting anyone to stay in the foreseeable future, but I can't wait to make the spare bedroom look nice again.'

'And you'll be staring out across the garden when you're working in future. What a bonus!'

Polly walks over to join me, plonking herself down into her seat and then getting straight back up to grab a bottle of tomato sauce. 'You'd think with all my waitressing experience I'd remember the ketchup,' she muses, handing it to me.

She glances at the clock. 'We have fifty minutes until I need to head downstairs. Shall we look at a few things online while we're eating?'

'Suits me,' I reply, before taking the first delicious bite of my sandwich. 'Mmm, this is seriously good bacon.'

'We get our meat from Treeve Perran Farm.'

'Oh, isn't Leath's Farm closer?'

'Yes, but they've dramatically downsized their farming operations over the years. The farm shop only sells organic ice cream now and it's a big attraction in the summer for the tourists as they have a kiddies' playground. They serve milkshakes, too, but it's seasonal and they shut the shop in the off-peak periods. Their main business is supplying ice cream to restaurants and pubs like us, all around the south-west.'

'They were huge at one time,' I reply, putting my hand up in front of my mouth as I chew. A bacon sandwich doesn't last long when you've been up since 6 a.m. and have only had two cups of coffee.

'There are a lot of hoops to jump through to gain that organic label these days, and the cost of certification isn't cheap. They get their milk from Treeve Perran and the only animals they rear are to support themselves.'

'What a shame.'

'It is, and it isn't,' Polly replies. 'It's less hassle and they make a reasonable living.'

'Mum never got on with the wife – I can't remember her name. That's why she wouldn't shop there. They did veggies, too, if I remember correctly.'

'Old Mrs Warren was a bit sharp, at times. You do know

that she was Sissy's grandmother, of course? Her son and daughter-in-law ran it for a while and the old lady kept the herb and the vegetable garden going. Now I think the Jenners keep it for their private use only.'

'I didn't make the connection with Sissy,' I confess, as I push my plate away and make room for Polly's laptop. She turns it on, and I wait impatiently for the screen to light up.

'The family sold it seven, maybe eight, years ago. The new people, the Jenners, are lovely. They moved here from Kent and they've turned the business around. They were the ones who started running a car boot sale in one of the fields.'

'So much has changed, hasn't it? And that hit the spot, thank you so much, Polly.'

'I Imm,' she says, popping the last of her sandwich into her mouth. 'I can think better on a full stomach. Now, do you prefer open shelves, or cupboards?'

'I want everything hidden away,' I reply, resolutely. 'No clutter. No distractions. I'm thinking of a zen-like environment – just me, my PC and nature.'

'Ooh, I like the sound of that, and I have just the modular units to solve your problem,' she informs me. 'You will need *a man who can* to install them for you, though.'

'That's not a problem.'

As she opens the web page I can see it's like storage heaven. If I can smuggle Ross into my house without anyone being any the wiser, he'd get this sorted in less than a day. It's hard not to heave a sigh, though, as I accept that I might have to go with the safer option and employ a stranger to do it for me.

'I'm so grateful to you, Polly, and if there's ever anything I can do in return, just let me know. I really mean that.'

* * *

'Wow. I have a floor,' I comment, shocked at how quickly it went down. It looks much bigger than I'd anticipated. Ross got his team to lay the concrete base and run the electrical wiring when they were building the extension, back in the summer. Having grown used to seeing the ugly, dull grey slab at the far end of the garden, it gives me a real buzz to see it obliterated.

'These kits are pretty quick to assemble.' One of the men stops what he's doing to come over and chat. It's just the three of them and Will is probably long gone. 'The sections are modular, so the shell will be finished by lunchtime tomorrow with a bit of luck.'

'Including the bi-fold doors?'

'Sure. After that it's a case of putting the exterior finish on the roof, fitting the insulation inside and then we'll start affixing the wallboard inside. Wednesday we'll lay the laminate flooring.'

'I think that deserves a mug of tea all round, don't you?'

He gives me a wink. 'You're an angel. One black, two white and no sugar, ta very much.'

I head up to the cottage, thinking that as soon as I've taken the drinks out to the guys, I really should get on with some real work. After popping on the kettle I dig out a packet of biscuits and lay up the tray when my phone kicks into life.

'Hi, Sy, how are you?'

'Good thanks, Kerra. We're literally just coming up to the turn-off to the village and wondered if we could pop in? Say if it's inconvenient – it's not urgent.'

'Oh, yes, of course. The kettle is on. I'll leave the side gate open, as I'm just popping out into the garden. See you shortly.'

As I carry the tray down to the guys one of them looks up to see me coming and his eyes light up.

'I'll tell e wot,' he says, sincerely, 'that'll go down a treat. Thanks, missus.'

'It's Kerra,' I reply. 'Tomorrow I'll make sure to pick up some saffron buns from Mrs Moyle.'

He digs one of the others with his elbow. 'Worth comin' back for tomorrow, then.'

We all start laughing and I turn, retracing my steps just as Sy and Tegan walk around the side of the house.

'Hi,' I call out. 'This is a nice surprise. Is this a day off?'

'I wish,' Tegan complains, coming to give me a welcome hug. 'It's been ages, hasn't it? We just signed up another six rental properties, not far from The Design Cave. All with the same owner, which is rather convenient.'

We head inside and Sy stoops to kiss my cheek. He was my right hand man for five years at The Happy Hive and I do miss working with him five days a week, as we always had a laugh.

'I'm coming along to the rehearsals on Thursday night, so I'll get to see you twice in one week!' I declare and he gives me a smirk.

'Really? What're you up to?' Sy knows me so well, but I feign a look of innocence.

'Nothing! I volunteered to help paint some of the scenery.'

As I sort out the drinks, the two of them wander around. 'I forgot just how lovely this place is now,' Tegan enthuses.

'And how are you finding life at The Forge?'

She stops, turning to look at Sy and they smile at each other. 'Wonderful. It was so the right thing to do, Kerra, and it's kind of Ross to let us rent it at a discounted rate. Business is good but we're ploughing every penny back in and will be for a while.'

There's a loud miaow as Ripley decides to join us.

'I wondered where she was. Hi, girl!' Tegan calls out.

Ripley is in no hurry to join us and instead decides to sit and have a bit of a wash, first.

'Has she gained some weight since I last saw her?' Sy asks.

'No. It's her winter coat and it'll probably get a bit thicker yet. It looks much darker, too, doesn't it?'

'It does. The golden tips have gone.'

'Yes. She's a darker cinnamon bun now, but once the summer comes around again her coat will begin to sparkle. Do you want to go through to the sofas, or sit at the table?'

'Let's sit here so we can look out at the garden,' Sy says, as he pulls out one of the rustic hand-painted chairs.

'It's very relaxing – this country cosy feel,' he continues. 'You and Ross have somewhat similar tastes. I do love the open plan and the light, but it's the furniture that stops it feeling stark, if you know what I mean.'

'Sy's been on at me to add a few touches to the cottage,' Tegan explains as she sits down next to him.

'Ah, yes. It needed a woman's touch.' I laugh. 'A few cushions here and there, and some roman blinds to dress the windows. I do love the white, wooden-slatted blinds for privacy, but with that flagstone floor it's a bit echoey, isn't it?'

'That's exactly what Sy has been saying. I'll ask Ross if he minds; it won't cost us very much but will make it more homely.'

It's touching to hear her say that. Tegan had a tough time following the death of her husband Pete, just over two and a half years ago. When Sy moved in with her, I feared they were moving forward too quickly, partly because the home she shared with Pete is so full of memories. Although she's not ready to sell it yet, renting it out is the perfect solution and The Forge is just the right size for them.

'Okay. I'm a confessed minimalist to the nth degree, but I know when I'm beaten,' Tegan admits, putting her hands up in surrender.

Judging by the way Tegan is gazing at Sy, she'd do anything to make him happy and it's wonderful to see my best friends from two quite different worlds, so happy together. I never, ever, thought Sy could be lured away from the bright lights and excitement of London, but boy, was I wrong about that! And Dad's right – I don't think it'll be too long before they begin planning the wedding.

'That's quite a home office you're having built there, Kerra,' Tegan remarks, as we turn to watch the guys beavering away.

'I know. Now that it's being built, it looks a lot bigger than I thought it was going to be and it will all be done in three days.'

'And you're finding plenty to keep you occupied?' Sy enquires, casually, but there's something on his mind and I can see that reflected on his face.

'Yes. Now that The Design Cave is up and running, I'm looking for my next investment opportunity, but I'm in no hurry.'

'Locally?' he asks, his eyes narrowing.

'It depends. Why?'

'I've had a call from my ex-boss, the guy who took over just before I walked out. I knew he had an uphill battle, but the slide has continued. The Happy Hive isn't quite so happy right now, from all accounts.'

I sip my coffee. Sy isn't thinking about going back and leaving Tegan to cope all on her own, is he?

'That's a shame, Sy, but you and I suspected as much. Too many changes in quick succession and a hike in the charges levied. What did they expect?'

'Well, not the reaction they got, that's for sure. Over a third of the members have cancelled their subscriptions.'

There's always churn, as we called it, people leaving and new subscribers joining, but that's a mass protest. 'Hopefully, it will teach them a lesson. I bet they were spamming people with ads based on their profiles, too,' I reply, sadly. It's my brainchild we're talking about and they're destroying it. 'So much for their company ethos of giving back to the community. If they're making a loss there won't be anything to give back.'

'I'm not telling you this to upset you, Kerra, please don't think that. Javier has reached out to me and I've agreed to take part in a video conference call.' Sy can tell that it makes me cross, but that was my old life and there is nothing I can do about it.

'To what end?' I ask, confused.

'He's been told to offer me a consultancy to help steer The Happy Hive back to profitability.'

Tegan is looking extremely uncomfortable about this conversation.

'Is that what you want? Surely, you have enough on your hands already. Clean and Shine is expanding and isn't it risky to pull yourself away from it, even for a short while?'

Sy looks at Tegan, but she turns her head to stare out the window, feigning an interest in watching the guys drilling and hammering.

'It will give me something to do in the evenings and it

won't take that long. Besides, the money will come in useful, Kerra, and although it's not an ideal situation, it's not easy to turn down an offer like this.'

'Why do I feel there's a *but* coming?'

'Javier has asked me to talk you into taking part in the meeting.'

'Why?' I'm stunned.

'Because he feels you may well have your own thoughts about how to get things back on track.' Sy is measuring the effect of every word he utters.

I shake my head, sadly. 'And you know that I won't say no, because of the guilt factor.'

Sy rubs his hand down along his jaw, a clear sign that this isn't an easy ask for him. 'Listen, Kerra. You created that business from nothing and when you left it was something of which you were extremely proud. You didn't walk away because of the money on the table; you'd taken it as far as you could, and these tech giants said what they thought you wanted to hear. Well, they messed up and now Javier has been tasked with finding a solution to get their plan back on track and take it to the next level. He's willing to pay for your time, and he understands that if you do agree to take part in the call, there are no strings attached and you can choose not to voice your opinions.'

'But you're hoping that I will?'

'Javier has asked me to look over the figures and consider the changes they've made to the website as a starting point. The meeting is to kick around some ideas, based on my findings.'

'And how do you feel about this development, Tegan?' I ask, pointedly.

She turns her head in my direction, a serious look on her face. 'As Sy said, we need the money, Kerra.'

It's more than that, though. Sy left The Happy Hive because he saw what was happening. He warned his boss on numerous occasions that the subscribers weren't happy and told him the numbers would begin dropping quite dramatically. Sy was right and the fact they've approached him for help now substantiates his actions. I have never known him to lose his temper under any circumstances and for him to have walked out demonstrates just how bad it was at the time. It wasn't solely the high level of customer complaints, but the staff were feeling totally demoralised under the new ownership.

'Okay. One meeting and no obligation on my part, understood?'

Sy gives a little smile. 'Understood. Tegan and I are so close to getting the new structure in place for our cleaning business and this little job could make all the difference.'

I'm so proud of what they've achieved, and they've proven to me that I was wrong in thinking they'd jumped into their engagement too quickly. When you find the one, deep down inside you know and there are no doubts. But making it work long-term isn't always easy and it's how you get through the ups and downs of life, that makes the bond stronger. Or else it starts to fracture and gradually things fall apart, and I've seen that happen so many times.

'The plan is going well, it seems?' I enquire, and Tegan immediately perks up again.

'It is! Sy's idea of Clean and Shine being the middleman means we're gradually changing over from being employers, to contracting self-employed staff with their own vehicles. No more having to do runs in the minibuses to ferry people around and drop off materials. It's a genius idea.'

I glance across at Sy and he does look satisfied with himself. 'We negotiate the contracts with property owners, saving our contractors the hassle of the paperwork and getting new leads. We look at each contractor as a small business and do our best to get them enough properties within a given area to make it profitable for them. They buy their own materials, and we don't have transport costs or payroll to worry about. It's just a simple case of money in, deduct our fee and a monthly bank transfer out.'

I'm impressed. Tegan was barely breaking even and working herself into the ground. 'That's such a simple solution, Sy.'

'We encourage our contractors to cover for each other in an emergency. The majority are women with young children, and they work around school pick-up times, which isn't a problem. If a child is sick, they can phone around to get someone to cover for them on a reciprocal basis. We do that by circulating a monthly newsletter to keep everyone in touch,' Tegan explains. 'And twice a year, we're hoping to get them all together for a night out.'

'I think it's the perfect solution. It's a lot less pressure on you, Tegan. Changeover day on Saturdays used to be awful, didn't it? All that dashing around between holiday properties you and I did, covering for people who phoned in sick and that day one of the minibuses broke down was a total nightmare. It was one problem after another. We had some laughs though, didn't we?'

She nods in agreement. 'Remember when you locked yourself out of that bungalow and got stuck climbing back in through the bathroom window?'

I burst out laughing and Sy raises his eyebrows.

'You what?'

'I had to stand on the dustbin as it was a narrow window and only the top half opened. One of the neighbours spotted my legs flailing around and phoned Tegan.'

'Kerra simply needed a good shove, and afterwards she was back at it wearing her bright yellow, rubber gloves,' Tegan replies, straight-faced.

'No wonder you were both so pleased to see me when I turned up,' Sy declares, looking at us as if we're crazy. 'That's no way to run a business.'

'Sometimes a good belly laugh is just the tonic for raising the spirits. I still giggle whenever I think back on that day,' I reply.

'A lot has happened since then,' Tegan points out. 'It scares me to realise how close I was to going under both financially and physically. If you hadn't come home for good, Kerra, I dread to think where I might be now. I certainly wouldn't have Sy by my side.'

He reaches across to grasp her hand in his and it's touching to see the look they exchange.

'It's time we headed off to process today's paperwork. Thanks, Kerra, for being so... understanding.' Sy looks at me in earnest.

'Let's hope I can add something meaningful to the conversation, but I can't promise to come up with a miraculous solution. The ill feeling they've caused might mean the damage is irreversible.'

He shrugs his shoulders, and I can see that he's thinking the exact same thing.

'Anyway, thanks for the drink and the chat. I'll see you on Thursday evening then, with a paintbrush in your hand.'

'You will, that!'

As they jump up to pull on their jackets I look out at the workmen and am amazed to see that my office already has a back wall and half of one side. That deserves another round of tea, I think. The one thing I've learnt having all this work done is that builders are cheerful guys, and it doesn't take much to keep them happy.

SIX
TREADING WARILY

Ross leads me into a windowless storage room and when he turns on the light I'm surprised to see that the shelves along one wall are crammed full of tins of paint.

'Anything left over from a job ends up in here,' he says, grinning at me. 'There's a reason why they asked me to make the scenery. It saves us wasting offcuts of wood, too, and you never know when something is going to come in handy.'

'Is it always as busy as it is tonight?' I ask him, as he grabs me a paintbrush and scrutinises the labels on the tins.

'It varies. Tonight, it's the first run-through for the entire cast, so we'll keep out of their way. We'll be in the back room painting. Here you go, one brush and one large tin of red paint.'

I take them from him, and he goes to turn, then spins around on the balls of his feet, coming closer. He looks over the top of my head to check no one is in the narrow passageway and then bends to kiss my lips, lingering for a few seconds and reluctant to pull away.

'Stop. Stop!' I whisper, stepping back. 'Anyone could catch us. It's not worth the risk.'

'It was to me,' he replies, grinning before turning around and grabbing an armful of items. 'Would you mind carrying that dust sheet with your free hand?'

'Yes, sir. Right, lead the way.'

As the crow flies, Penvennan village hall is directly behind Lanryon Church, but it's only accessible from the main road at the top of the village. There's no way to walk between the two, as there's a dense forest of trees on the grounds of a big manor house that sits on top of the hill.

'Do you want to pop in and say hello to Nettie before we begin?' Ross calls over his shoulder.

'No. I won't interrupt them. I'm guessing she came on her own?'

'Yes, same as usual. It doesn't bode well for a visit from your dad. There are about a dozen of them in the hall rehearsing. I did see Sy in passing, though.'

We trudge into what is called the meeting room, our arms full. We place everything down on the floor and begin moving back the sectioned table and chairs.

'We'll need to clear the entire space,' Ross informs me. 'Then we'll spread out the dust sheet and carry the sleigh through.'

It doesn't take long to clear the floor space and I follow Ross into the main hall. Nettie and her assembled cast are sitting in a big circle, reading from scripts and Ross and I tiptoe as quietly as we can past them. He holds back the plush velvet curtain at the side of the stage, which is heavier than it looks. After stepping through we walk around to the back where various items of scenery they've used in the past are stacked against the rear wall.

'I'll pull out the sleigh; if you can grab the two flaps at the side so they don't clatter as we walk, that would be great.'

It is heavy, made of stout MDF, but we manage it between us, although it's an awkward thing to carry. The walkway is narrow and then when we get out into the hallway, inevitably the cast stop reading as we manhandle our load.

'I'll get the door.' Sy jumps up as Ross and I make our way across the room. So much for not disturbing them.

'Sorry, guys,' Ross says, apologetically. 'We promise not to interrupt you again.'

Sy is standing with the door wide open when Dad suddenly appears.

'Let me give a hand with that,' he calls out and comes over to grab one of the flaps on the side of the sleigh.

'Thanks, Dad, that's made it a bit easier.' I reward him with a warm smile, and I can see Nettie watching us intently as we shuffle out through the door.

'Thanks, Sy,' I call over my shoulder as the three of us negotiate the passageway.

'A couple of hooks on here wouldn't go amiss. It would anchor these bits of wood when you're moving it around,' Dad comments.

'I think you're right, Eddie. This isn't easy, is it?' Ross replies, graciously.

'Dad, if you can just steady this piece a moment, I'll get the door.'

I pin back the door to the meeting room with my foot and we ease the wooden structure through. Reaching over to hold the flap, I let my foot slide against the door to keep it from hitting Dad in the back.

'Are we laying this down?' he asks.

'Yes. I'll find a couple of bits of wood to raise it up afterwards, ready for painting. Easy does it. There. Good job. And thanks, Eddie.'

'How does it work then?' Dad asks, scratching his head.

Ross tilts it back up, so it's standing on its edge. The sleigh is just a shape and he turns his attention to the contraption on the back.

'This flap folds down flat and then these two pieces drop down and lock into place like this,' he demonstrates. 'Then that becomes a seat and it also stabilises the sleigh. Santa sits here, like this.' Ross demonstrates and both Dad and I look at him, impressed. It's pretty solid.

'It just needs painting red and where it rises up at the back that's where we'll staple on some sacking and pad it out to give the impression that the sacks are full of presents. Maybe add red bows at the top where the shapes narrow.'

'It doesn't have runners,' Dad points out.

'Not yet. I thought we'd get two coats of the red paint on and let it dry first. Then see what wood there is in the store cupboard and add that afterwards. Maybe paint them white, or black perhaps.'

'Do you want me to take a look and see if I can find anything suitable? You two can start painting.'

'If you don't mind, Eddie, that would be a big help. I doubt I'd get both coats on tonight if Kerra hadn't offered to give a hand. As the meeting room isn't being used tomorrow, we can leave it out overnight to dry. I'll pop back in the morning to put everything away. Someone should be around to help me carry it back into the hall.'

'I'm glad I called in, then. I was just checking Nettie had everything she needed,' Dad says as he turns, sounding glad to be of use.

As soon as the door closes behind him, I give Ross a beaming smile and a thumbs up.

'Dad's a dab hand with a paintbrush, too,' I half-whisper. 'With a bit of luck, you have yourself a work buddy.'

'It's funny that this is the first time he's ever popped in. Anyway, stop talking and start painting,' Ross says, rolling his eyes. 'This had better work, Kerra. I still have my doubts. Now, start at the top, ignore this bit as that's where you're going to get creative with the sacking once the first coat is touch-dry.'

As I cautiously dip my brush into the scarlet paint, I begin singing softly under my breath: 'Rudolph the red-nosed reindeer...'

Ross flashes me a look, his eyes sparkling. 'You love it when one of your plans come together, don't you?'

'*Yes I do, yes I do, yes I do,*' I sing, and he waggles his finger at me.

'All I can say is roll on tomorrow night,' he whispers, softly. 'It seems like—'

Ross is cut short when Dad reappears. 'There are a few bits here we can use to attach the runners, but I have just the thing in one my garages. I'll pop back and fetch it. Do you have any tools here?'

'In the boot of the car, Eddie. I'll fetch them in before you return.'

'And I'll put the kettle on,' I add.

It seems we have a bit of a team effort going on here, although I have a sneaking suspicion that Ross wouldn't feel quite so comfortable if I wasn't around. Maybe my presence will help with the bonding process, but Dad was humming cheerfully as he left the room and that's always a good sign.

* * *

When I return home, Ripley is lying on the bottom tread of the staircase, patiently waiting for me.

'You look like one tired girl,' I comment, as I walk past her to grab a tube of her salmon treats. She ambles into the kitchen area, not having made a sound, and I know she's cross with me for disappearing for the entire evening.

'Here you go, Ripley.' I bend to tip a small pile of the dried cubes onto the slate floor. Leaving her to eat them, I slip off my coat and go to hang it up on a hook in the hallway. When I return, she gives me a begrudging miaow and goes to sit in front of the folding glass doors.

'It's dark out there. Shall we put on the lights?'

Miaow, miaow, miaoooooow.

'I guess that's a yes.'

Walking over to the bank of switches, I turn them on one by one and join her to stare out. The garden really comes to life at night. From the inset lights on the large deck that is a seamless transition when the doors slide back, to the new garden office, with four uplighters making it look like a little house down at the very end. It's nice not to see the back fence anymore and somehow it feels more secure. Only the middle bit of the garden is cast in shadow. I turn the key in the lock, sliding the doors back three or four feet, to step out onto the wooden deck.

It's nice to stand here and draw in a few deep breaths, even though it's chilly.

'Are you going to join me?' I ask Ripley, when a voice looms up expectedly out of the darkness.

'Well, that's an invitation I can't refuse,' Drew replies. 'Are you making hot chocolate?'

I look down at Ripley, smiling and she turns tail and pads through to go upstairs in disgust. It's bedtime, and she expects me to join her.

'Why not? I'll let you in. Bring your coat and I'll show you my new office,' I call out.

Bertie starts barking, unaware that Ripley is no longer around. 'Hi, Bertie.'

'I'll just settle him down. Give me a couple of minutes to grab him one of his chews.'

I find myself wondering what it's like to have children. Animals are fairly easy to please, well bribe, but kids – that's another thing entirely. Will Sy and Tegan start a family once they're married? I wonder if Ross would like kids one day. As for me, I've never given it any thought. Is that a bad sign?

Closing the doors, I pop a pan of milk on low and go to fetch my coat and a bobble hat. Seconds later, Drew taps on the front door.

'Come on in.'

'I wasn't spying on you, honest. I literally opened the door to let Bertie out for a couple of minutes just as you turned on the garden lights.'

He follows me through to the kitchen and I grab a whisk, adding some cocoa powder and a dash of hazelnut syrup before I begin to froth up the milk.

'Here you go,' I hold out the tall mug to him. 'Do you want anything on the top?'

'No. I'm good.'

After pulling on my coat and hat, I pour the remainder of the mixture into my mug and we head outside.

'I don't have anywhere near enough lights in my garden,' Drew informs me, as he stares around him. 'It's looking fabulous, Kerra. Have you had a chance to set the office up, yet?'

'Sadly, no. I'm waiting for the storage cupboards to be delivered.'

The grass is a little spongy as we walk. The thick turf has taken well although most of the new shrubs will take a year or two to establish. Only a part of the old hedge dividing the two properties remains and the rest is new fencing.

To our left the tall laurel bushes form an impenetrable boundary with the garden of the large, detached house the other side. It's enough to soften the newness of the majority of the planting. I can still gaze out and in my mind's eye see the large mud pit that it was while the major building work was underway.

'They didn't make any mess putting this up, did they?' Drew remarks, sounding impressed.

'That's probably down to bribery, involving endless cups of tea, biscuits and buns.' I grapple in my pocket for the key and turn it effortlessly, pushing back one of the two, bi-fold glass doors. 'Come in.'

'My shoes might be a little damp,' Drew points out but I usher him inside, closing the door.

'Sorry about the basic seating arrangements.' I laugh.

It consists of two of the chairs from the garden set, the rest of which is now safely put away in the shed next to the barbecue.

'This is cosy, and warmer than I thought it was going to be.'

'It's eco-friendly and there's some sort of special reflective foil thing in the walls, floor and ceiling, in addition to the insulation, to keep the heat in. The electric radiator pumps it out and I think if I warm it up first thing in the morning, I probably only need to keep it on for an hour, or two, and it will last all day.'

We position the chairs in front of the four glass panels and sit to enjoy our hot drink.

'Goodness me, it seems like forever since you moved in and we sat outside that first evening, on your old stone patio drinking hot chocolate and looking up at the stars.'

'I know. And so much has happened since. A lot of that is down to you. See how beautiful it is looking back on our cottages now. My grandparents wouldn't have believed the transformation.'

'No regrets, then?' Drew asks, peering at me in the half-light from the uplighters around the structure.

'None at all. This is my forever home.'

'And, at some point Ross will be joining you?'

I sigh and it's as much with tiredness as it is with the frustrations of our situation.

'Hopefully. We're working on that, but it's slow going and that's fine. Neither of us is in a tearing hurry. He has to sell Treylya first, of course. Oh, before I forget...' Instinctively I find myself lowering my voice, which is ridiculous as no one can hear us. 'I won't be here tomorrow night, well not until very early the following morning, probably around 6 a.m. Hopefully Ripley will come with me.'

'If I hear her outside howling, I'll give you a call. There's little point in me trying to entice her inside my place, because she'll only set Bertie off barking.'

'Aww... poor Bertie. I wish Ripley wasn't quite so territorial. I mean, she doesn't live with you anymore and yet she begrudges Bertie taking up residence. That little madam wants to have her cake and eat it.'

Drew sits back in his chair, warming both hands on his mug. 'Felicity said the same thing when I was telling her about

Ripley sitting on top of the fence and teasing Bertie the other day.'

'How is Felicity? She hasn't made it to Cornwall for a couple of weeks now.'

Felicity is Drew's girlfriend. Drew originally bought Tigry Cottage as an investment and a place they could come to spend their weekends and holidays. Then he was made redundant, and it made sense, financially, for him to move here permanently. Felicity is still adjusting to the reality that Drew's future is here, in Penvennan Cove.

'She's fine. Just family stuff, as usual. She's heartily sick of it. Everything her brother does affects the finance department, and he seems to enjoy creating problems. I fear that all this will ever be is her escape.'

'I sympathise but moving here permanently would be a huge upheaval for her. There's no chance she'll talk you into heading back to Gloucestershire?'

He looks at me, frowning. 'I sincerely hope not. I like the relaxed atmosphere and the walks along the beach and the headland are amazing. I know she loves it, too. But it's that transition isn't it? Cutting the ties and walking away from the only life you know and starting over afresh. She's coming down the weekend after next, and I can't wait.'

'I'm sure Bertie is going to be a big draw, too. Those two have really formed a bond, haven't they?'

'Yes. It's "Hi, Drew, where's my little Bertie?" when her face appears on the screen. Never mind about poor old me and how I'm coping.' He grimaces and I almost choke on a mouthful of velvety smooth hot chocolate.

'Did you know one of the fishermen's cottages is up for sale? There's no sign up, but I think it's the second one in from the left. Dad mentioned it the other day.'

'I hadn't heard. Why?'

'I might be interested, you know, as an investment.'

'Jump online. I'm sure it will be listed on one of the websites. Are you thinking of getting into holiday lets? At least you know a company who will keep it ship-shape.' Drew laughs.

'No. I would probably rent it out on a medium to long-term lease. Yes, I'll find out who the agent is and book a viewing.'

'Are you struggling to find something to occupy your time now that Sissy is all sorted out?'

'Not really. There's a little community project I'm considering, but it needs a bit of research first, and another thing has come up that I might get pulled into, albeit reluctantly. But I'm in no hurry.'

'So, uh... you're up at Treylya tomorrow night?' Drew gives me a cheeky grin.

'Maybe. My car will be parked outside of here, of course.'

'My lips are sealed and if Ripley lets you down, I'll get straight on the phone before she wakes everyone up.'

'Thanks, Drew. I know I can always count on you. That means a lot to me.'

'Still feeling like you don't fit in?' His voice is full of empathy.

'I never did, which is crazy as my family go way back. As hard as I try to melt into the background, I think I'll always be the odd one out for some reason.'

'Hmm. That's why you and Ross get on so well, Kerra. Interesting people are fun to be around, and other people often look on with envy because your life isn't mundane. That's why you left Penvennan in the first place. Don't let it put you off now that you're back. I seem to have slotted in, even though I'll always be *not from round 'ere,'* he says in the worst impression of a Cornish accent I've ever heard in my life. 'But I don't exactly lead an *interesting life,* do I?'

The difference is, this is where I was born and brought up; this is where my roots are and yet I still feel that I'm that square peg in a round hole. And I don't know why.

SEVEN

GROWING MY PORTFOLIO

'Hello, I'm Kerra Shaw.'

The smartly dressed man in front of me offers his hand and we shake cordially.

'Oliver Sinclair. It's lovely to meet you, Kerra.'

What a charming tone of voice and he has a smile to match it. I wait as he inserts the key into the door of Gwel Teg. It's the first time I've been inside one of the fishermen's cottages at Penvennan Cove.

'*Gwel Teg* translates into beautiful view,' Oliver informs me, talking over his shoulder as I step across the threshold.

'I know,' I reply. 'I was born and brought up in the village.'

'Oh, sorry! I wouldn't have guessed you were a local from your accent.' As we move through into the narrow hallway, I close the front door behind me. When I join him, he looks a little unsure of himself.

'Don't worry. I spent ten years in London and I've only recently returned.' I didn't mean to sound condescending just now, but the moment I mention London he visibly relaxes.

'Ah, I see. That's something we have in common, then.

Not the Cornish roots, but the company I work for have just bought out several independent estate agents in the area. I'm down here for a while to oversee the process of bringing them all under our corporate banner.'

'That's a huge change, then. And quite a task for you, I should imagine.'

'Yes, but I'm getting to see a beautiful part of the country I'd never visited before. Anyway, let's head into the dining area first and I'll dig out a brochure for you.'

I'm delighted to find that Gwel Teg has a small extension to the rear that doubles the size of the original room, turning it into a kitchen/diner. At the far end there's a door to a tiny patio area and next to it is the sink unit, above which is a large window.

'It's much lighter in here than I'd expected,' I comment, as I wander over to look outside. A sloping bank of mixed shrubbery and heathers behind the row of cottages rises gently and it's almost like looking out over a secret garden. Some twenty metres beyond it, the ground rises steeply, peppered with large outcrops of rock.

'Who owns the swathe of land adjacent to the small courtyard?'

'It belongs to Lanryon Church, who maintain it. It's a pretty outlook considering how tiny the gardens are for these traditional fishermen's cottages.' I glance at him and he smiles. 'Sorry, I guess you know more about this little terrace than I do.'

'I've never been inside one of them, though.'

'You said you're interested in this as an investment property?'

'Yes.'

'Right, well here's the brochure and you'll find my business card inside. I've also put in a list of comparable properties in the wider area indicating what level of rental you could expect. We can help you out on that, as we are also in the process of setting up a local arm of our property management company. We already have a list of potential clients looking to rent on a medium to long-term basis in and around this area.'

'You work quickly, Mr Sinclair.'

'Oh, please call me Oliver, Ms Shaw.'

That suits me. 'Just Kerra, will do, Oliver. Have you heard of a locally based company called *Clean and Shine?* They specialise in contract cleaning for landlords with portfolios of properties. They don't just cover holiday lets, but also one-off deep cleans between rental contracts, or when selling a property. I can thoroughly recommend them. Here, I'm sure I have a card, somewhere.' I dive into my handbag and luck has it that I have a few cards tucked in the little side pocket. I withdraw them and Oliver raises his eyebrows as he takes them from me.

'That's useful, thank you, Kerra. I'll get in touch with them as it might be worth including their details in the packs we give out to potential clients.'

'I know what it's like when you're new to an area. Albeit adjusting to life in London isn't quite the same as coming to Cornwall, where word of mouth is everything.'

'It's funny you should mention that, Kerra.' Oliver pauses, checking his watch and I realise we're chatting and not viewing.

'Sorry, I only need a quick look around because my mind is already made up.'

'Oh, I wasn't implying... There's no need to rush. In fact, I was going to ask if you had time to grab a coffee in the bakery afterwards? If you don't mind, I'd rather like to continue this line of conversation.'

I look at him in surprise. 'I'm no expert in the property field, I'm afraid.'

'But you're clearly a businesswoman and you have local knowledge. Maybe there are other contacts you wouldn't mind recommending to me, too?'

I'm no one's fool, and I know he has another question, one he doesn't want to pose until he knows me a little better.

'Right, show me around the rest of the property, Oliver, and then we can head to Pascoe's bakery for a coffee and a chat.'

* * *

'No Ripley?' Ross asks as I jump into the passenger seat.

'No. Drew is going to keep an eye out and if she makes a fuss he'll give me a call.'

'You told Drew that you're staying overnight?' Ross sounds shocked.

'It's fine – relax. He knows what's going on between us and, to be honest, if we're going to have sleepovers at Treylya then I need him keeping a look out at Pedrevan. And I've left piles of treats for Ripley to discover all over the place. If she's not content, then she'll make her way to Treylya. It's not like she's a stranger when it comes to appearing on your doorstep, is it? I'm just perplexed by the fact that she'll happily use your cat flap, but is reluctant to use mine.'

'Okay. I just thought we were going to keep this bit of our relationship a secret.'

'Drew guessed, a while ago.'

'What's in the box?' Ross's curiosity getting the better of him.

'One of Mrs Moyle's apple pies.'

'You know how to look after me, don't you?'

I smile at him, knowingly. I might not be creative in the kitchen, but I know a woman who is a baking guru.

'How did the sleigh look this morning?' I ask, eagerly.

'Pretty good, actually. Two coats are enough and the sacks at the back look the business when it's viewed from a distance. The padding just makes it more realistic. All it needs now is a little decorative detail to enhance the scarlet paint job and once Eddie's runners are fixed in place, I was thinking of gluing on some large balls of cotton wool, or something similar so it will appear that it's sitting on snow. What do you think?'

Ross turns right at the end of the road, and I duck down in my seat.

'What are you doing?' he asks, quizzically.

'I don't want anyone to spot me. On this stretch it's so well lit, I feel exposed. There won't be much traffic once we turn off into the lane heading up to Renweneth.'

Ross heaves a sigh. 'This is crazy, you do know that?'

'I agree but, hopefully, not for much longer. Dad was really perky last night and I'm glad he managed to complete his little task.'

'He did a good job, but then he's a carpenter whereas I'm just a bit of an all-rounder. Stuff I've picked up being in the building trade. I'm a manager, but when it comes to hands-on I'm a jack of all trades.'

'Which is perfect, because Dad will feel he's making a difference. He misses getting hands-on and he loves building things. I bet he turns up next week without you having to ask him, just you wait and see.'

Ross looks pleased, his eyes crinkling up at the sides.

'I hope so. But you'll be there too, won't you?'

'If you think it will help.' I know Dad isn't good at small

talk unless he really gets on with the person concerned. While he respects Ross, he doesn't regard him as a friend, just an acquaintance.

'How was your day?'

'Full of surprises,' I declare, contentedly. 'I had an offer accepted on one of the old fishermen's cottages at the cove.'

'What?' Ross momentarily takes his eyes off the road to glance at me.

'I'll be renting it out, of course.'

'You didn't say you were going to invest in property.' Ross seems surprised.

'It was on at a good price and it's a pretty little place. They don't come on the market very often and after having a look around I decided to go for it.'

'Hmm. Getting into holiday lets now, are you?'

'No. I'll be renting it to one of the locals, probably.'

'And that stacks up financially?'

I should have known that there's no fooling Ross.

'Okay, maybe I'd get more if I didn't opt to find a tenant, but I'm looking for an easy life.'

He laughs out loud. 'You... an easy life? Never in this world. I'll find out what you're up to in the fullness of time,' he replies, knowingly.

I pretend I don't know what he's talking about and instead stare out the window at the darkness, as we travel along the winding lane that leads up to the headland. There is the odd house set way back from the road, their wide gates lit up, but in between the landscape is eerily black. The trees tower over-head on both sides of the lane, some meeting in the middle and forming a natural arch. It's pretty in spring and summer but forbidding in autumn and winter. Up here the winds can be punishingly strong at times and dead branches often litter the road after a heavy storm. Tonight, the wind is beginning to whip up and I wonder why Ross chose to build the house of his... or Bailey's... dreams, on the top of a headland.

We drive up to the gates in front of Treylya, and Ross slows the car, pressing a remote control, and we wait while they slowly ease back. The drive up to the house is lit by solar lights and it does look enchanting. In the background, the house is lit up like a proverbial Christmas tree against the darkness.

It's only the second time I've been here. The first time was a few days after I arrived back in Penvennan. It was a Saturday, and Tegan was panicking because she was two staff down. We had four hours in which to get Ross's property and the holiday cottages over at Treeve Perran Farm, which is at least a half an hour drive in the opposite direction, ready for the incoming holidaymakers.

'You've gone very quiet.' Ross's voice breaks my reverie.

'I was just thinking what fun it was cleaning your house.'

He bursts out laughing. 'I know. Six bedrooms, six and a half bathrooms and high-gloss floor tiles everywhere you look. Imagine what it's like when Ripley visits me. I find her fur balls rolling across the floor like tumbleweed in a ghost town.'

Now it's my turn to laugh... at him.

'I guess I'm not one to lecture anyone on their investments,' he states. 'But I'm not downhearted. Somewhere out there is someone who wants a Los Angeles style home overlooking a cove in Cornwall. I'm sure of it.' As the car pulls to a halt at the head of the turning circle, he turns to smile at me, ruefully.

'It might take a while, although I know a man who might be able to help. How long has it been on the market now?' I question.

'Two and a half months,' he admits.

'How many viewings have you had?'

Ross shrugs his shoulders as he unclips his seat belt. 'None, yet. The estate agent has already broached the subject of a price drop, knowing full well they only have another fortnight before the contract is up. I said I'd think about it.'

We get out the car and I walk around to stand next to him as he reaches for my hand. We stare up at the glass façade. 'It has energy-efficient solar and recycling systems, which create as much energy as the house uses. I built it to have a net-zero carbon footprint and yet standing here, it looks out of place,' he acknowledges with a touch of irony in his tone.

'It's a real achievement, Ross, it really is, but does it feel like home to you?'

'No. It never did, and it never will. Come on, at least there's a nice casserole bubbling away in the oven and a good bottle of red wine, uncorked and waiting for us.'

He turns to kiss me briefly on the lips, then changes his mind and wraps me in his arms, instead. 'If I'd built this for you, my darling Kerra, it would have been something traditional, instead of a big, glass box.'

'Well, the views are amazing, that much I know, and someone will fall in love with it, Ross. You did an amazing job, truly you did.'

'You hate it,' Ross proclaims, pulling back and laughing at me. 'But it's not too shabby for our little clandestine nights together and I promise to do better in future.'

As he leads me inside, my thoughts turn to Bailey. I'll never feel relaxed here, but at least we're away from curious eyes and twitching curtains, so that's a reason to be grateful I suppose.

* * *

'Good morning, sleepyhead. I didn't miss anything, did I?' Ross asks, sweeping the hair away from my cheek with his hand.

'No phone calls and no Ripley. I guess she found the treats I left for her, and probably couldn't believe her luck!'

Yawning, I stretch out my arms and arch my back. I hate sleeping in a strange bed, but I slept like a log. Well, once we did, actually, get to sleep.

Ross scoots up the bed a little to lean against the head-board, plumping up his pillows and stuffing them behind him. 'It looks good but it's so darned uncomfortable,' he declares.

It is a stunning feature: a three-metre-square, hammered metal piece of art. Either side of the bed, suspended from the ceiling are six light tubes of varying lengths and the effect is dazzling at night.

He helps me to pull myself up next to him and sort out my pillows.

'My goodness, the view is incredible,' I declare, but it also sends me into a panic. 'Why did you let me sleep so late?'

'It's only six-thirty and I've literally just woken up. We'll grab a cup of coffee and I'll walk you down through the woods. If we meet anyone, we'll just pretend we were out walking our dogs and hang around as if we're passing the time of day.'

I turn to gaze at him sternly, but my resolve disappears as our eyes meet. I love that boyish little smirk that creeps over his face unbidden when he's happy. His eyes sparkle and how I wish we could take our time, watch the sun come up properly and sit here staring out to sea. With nothing to obstruct our view it feels as if we're floating, not set back on a headland high above the beach. All that exists is a vast wall of blue striations of colour from the darkest at the top as it graduates down until the sky meets the sea on the horizon. A glow as the sun makes its appearance sends long shards of light reflecting out over the water like tendrils reaching out towards us.

'I got something right, then,' Ross murmurs, leaning his head against mine.

'It's all lovely, but it's not homely. I... uh, sat and had a cup of coffee with an estate agent yesterday. It might be worth you having a chat with him. His company have bought out some of the independent estate agents in the area and the bonus is that their head office is in London.'

'Hmm. Don't they all use the same websites though, to advertise the properties?' Ross doesn't sound at all interested.

'That's true. But houses like this don't come up very often and that view is what will clinch the deal. It's a secluded location and a perfect getaway for someone with deep pockets. The sort of people who don't actively look because they have people who keep an eye out on their behalf when something unusual comes up.'

'This guy obviously charmed you, and you think he might have some wealthy contacts?'

'Oliver Sinclair will impress you and what do you have to lose? Zero viewings to date doesn't really bode well, so maybe the marketing is wrong.'

'Why did you have coffee with him?'

'He showed me around Gwel Teg. He's interested in working with some local businesses as they rebrand the various offices and get them networking. I suggested Clean and Shine, obviously, Treloar's and a few other contacts I felt might be useful. He's also keen to ensure the changeover goes smoothly and they retain that local connection, while providing a wider range of services.'

'Clever chap, realising a big name above the door doesn't always guarantee success. If you rate him, then text me his number and I'll give him a call. I'm not promising anything, even if he has impressed you.'

'Are you jealous, Ross Treloar?'

I run my hand down his cheek, grazing my fingers lightly against his stubbly chin.

'Are you sure you have to go?' he groans. 'Couldn't we amble down later and hope no one notices you aren't around?'

'No. Ripley will only behave herself up to a point and this is pushing it. I'll jump in the shower and head off immediately afterwards.'

'Well, I'm walking down to the edge of the village with you. I'll be quick, I promise.'

After vaulting out of bed, we head off in different directions. I use the master bathroom and when I'm finished, I make my way downstairs to retrieve my coat and shoes.

The space is a little overpowering and yet it reminds me of my loft-style apartment in London. It's ultra-modern and I didn't have many personal items around me. It was mostly for show. I was always about the work and it was a place to sleep and entertain on a third date if the guy was mildly interesting. Consequently, the times I entertained there were few and far between.

When Ross rushes downstairs apologetically, I'm ready and waiting.

'Sorry, I didn't hurry as I assumed that you'd take longer than me. You should have shouted up.' He disappears into the downstairs closet and two minutes later we're trudging across the gravelled drive towards the woods.

'I think I'm going to sell the apartment in London,' I confide in him.

'Because you're buying the cottage, or because you know that you're not going back?'

Is there a grain of truth to that? The man who rents it has already expressed an interest if I decide to sell, but was it my safety net if things didn't turn out well here, once Dad was back on his feet?

'I'm never going back, Ross. You can count on that. My life is here now, in Penvennan Cove.'

'Then I must do my best to convince Eddie that I'd make a good son-in-law. We can't move forward until the way has been smoothed, can we?'

As we take the winding track that leads us down through the mass of trees, the smell of the sea on the breeze is tantalising. I keep straining to catch glimpses of it as we weave in and out, stepping off the path where it's a little churned up and still muddy from the recent storms. Ross draws to a halt, putting a finger up against his lips and pointing to someone in the distance. A man with three dogs, two of which are on leads.

'That's Dad,' I whisper. 'Go back. I'll cut across and say I'm looking for Ripley. Go on, go! Speak later.'

He disappears and by the time Dad spots me at least I'm nowhere near the path leading up to the private access to Treylya.

'Morning, Kerra. What are you doing out and about this early?'

'Just checking if Ripley's around. She hasn't appeared for her breakfast yet.'

'Well, she was sat on your front wall just now.'

Oh no. 'Was she wailing?'

'No. Quiet as a lamb and enjoying watching the sun come up.'

Rufus comes bounding up and I give him a smooth. 'You're full of energy this morning, Rufus. Don't go overdoing it, Dad. Is this your first walk of the day?'

'Yes. Thought I'd get one in before Nettie arrives to help. I have seven boarders over the weekend and it made sense to do the easiest three first.'

'At least it's a pleasant morning and quite mild today. I'd best head back if Ripley is waiting for her breakfast.'

'It is a grand time of the day, isn't it?' Dad replies, wistfully. 'It's impossible to tire of that view.' Is he thinking of Mum? I wonder.

I lean in to kiss his cheek. 'It certainly is the best, Dad.' And now I know that I'm never going back to London, no matter what happens. It will always be on my doorstep whenever I need to blow away the Cornish cobwebs.

EIGHT
LAUGHTER AND SURPRISES

'What's the plan for this evening then, Ross?' Dad's wearing his overalls and he also brought a toolbox along with him tonight to the church hall.

'I loaded up the van with a whole stack of wood and various offcuts, if you don't mind carrying some of it inside, Eddie.'

'Do you want me to give you a hand with that?' I ask but Ross shakes his head, a mischievous smile on his face.

'No, I have a special job for you. Come with me.' He leads me into the storeroom, and I'm surprised to see Santa's sleigh is leaning up against the wall.

'Oh, it's ready and waiting.'

'Sy gave me a hand carrying it through. There's a pot of gold paint somewhere amongst the tins and smaller brushes in one of the boxes. I suggest you go online and look at a few pictures before you begin embellishing it.'

'Yes, sir!'

Ross edges closer, leaning into me. 'I thought if Eddie and

I are working alone together it might spark a little conversation. What do you think?'

'I think it's a great idea,' I whisper back to him.

We're both conscious that the cast are still wandering around and, reluctantly, Ross turns away as Dad is waiting for him. I know that he was hoping to steal a quick kiss, but I'm happy, even though I've been relegated to what is little more than a big cupboard. Grabbing the phone out of my pocket I tap in *sleighs* and begin scrolling through the photos until I find one that looks handmade. The decoration is simple and I think I can make it work.

It doesn't take long to gather together the bits and pieces I need and I use a pencil to draw some large, fancy curls in the two lower corners. It takes a while to paint them as the lines need to curve gracefully, but also be wide enough to really stand out from a distance. The side of the sleigh is quite high, so that it's not obvious it only has one side to it and when I stand back, I realise it needs something else. I decide to add a line of golden holly leaves to follow the sweeping curve along the top edge.

When I pop my head around the door of the meeting room, Ross and Dad are leant over a large piece of wood suspended on two wooden stools. Dad is pressing down to keep it steady, as Ross is cutting out a shape with an electric jigsaw. Due to the noise they don't notice me, so I back out and head for the kitchen. There must be a piece of cardboard somewhere that I can use as a template to speed up the process.

'Oh, hi, Nettie. How's it going in there tonight?'

She turns around, surprised to see me. 'I didn't know you were here, Kerra. Still working on the sleigh?'

'I am,' I reply, grinning. 'I'm desperate for a piece of thin cardboard.' My eyes alight on the large box of biscuits she's emptying out onto a platter. 'If you're going to empty the entire box, could I have it?'

Nettie smiles. 'Of course! I figure they deserve a treat for putting up with me. It's the first time I've been in the director's chair as well as having written the script, and my first ever pantomime. But they're all doing such a wonderful job, and they're a jolly bunch of people.'

It's funny, but I would never have guessed that Nettie was a writer. It's lovely to see someone realising their dream. After a lengthy career working with animals, I had hoped that... well, she'd partner with Dad in running the *Home from Home* kennels. Now I can see that it will probably only ever be a part-time thing for her, and Dad really does need to find himself another helping hand.

'And writing is keeping you busy?' I enquire, as Nettie takes out the last of the biscuits.

'Here you go, Kerra.' Nettie hands me the box. 'Very busy and it's such fun. It's not making me much money, it's true, but everyone has to start somewhere.'

'Thank you. Well, judging by the laughter I heard just now when I walked past the door to hall, they're all enjoying themselves.'

Nettie grins at me. 'Santa has just delivered the presents to the Dark Queen's Winter Palace and it's a trap. She's freezes him in a solid block of ice because she intends to spoil Christmas for everyone,' Nettie informs me, rather dramatically.

'Oh my! I hope you have a good guy in the wings waiting to come to Santa's rescue.'

'I do. But I haven't mentioned this part of the plot to Ross just yet. How on earth he's going to conjure up a special effect for that, I have no idea.'

We both laugh, good-naturedly, as I head back to my cupboard.

* * *

There's a tap on the door and when it swings open Dad and Ross are standing there.

'Are we allowed in to have a look?' Dad asks, tentatively. 'We wondered if it wasn't going well, given that the door was shut.'

'I just needed to concentrate. What do you think?' I stand back as they step inside, so they can see my handiwork.

The rail at the front that extends across to help stabilise the seat, is now painted gold, as is the rail at the back. The holly leaves are all done, and I'm pleased with the effect.

'Crikey, you did that fast,' Dad remarks, giving me a wink and Ross looks impressed.

'All that's missing now is a little snow, but rather than stick anything onto the sleigh, I wondered if it would be better to slide a board underneath, paint it white and create a few little mounds using polystyrene, or even something I could just paint white?'

Ross looks at Dad, who nods his head. 'We can sort something out, can't we, Eddie?'

'Sure can. Great job, Kerra.'

'How's it been going in there?' The look they exchange is non-committal.

'An ice palace isn't the easiest of things to conjure up, but we've made a start,' Ross confirms, jovially.

'Can't imagine what else Nettie has up her sleeve for us,'

Dad adds, 'but it's going to test our skills, that's for sure. She's not a lady I'd want to disappoint and she's not easy to talk around when she has a firm picture in her head of what she wants.'

Goodness, they're both going to be staggered when they hear about the frozen Santa.

'I'm sure you're up to it,' I reassure them.

'She'll certainly let us know if she isn't happy,' Dad confirms, as Nettie suddenly appears behind him.

'Who isn't happy? I love what Kerra's done with the sleigh. It's perfect. You're doing a great job, guys – I knew you could do it!'

Well, it seems that all is going to plan. I have nothing at all to worry about but, as the saying goes, patience is a virtue.

* * *

'Hey, Bertie. How are you little fella? Is Ripley behaving herself these days?' He does his usual cute little thing of sitting in front of me, one paw half-raised and his head tilted to the side. Miniature Schnauzers are so adorable and it's upsetting that Ripley won't make peace, even if they can't be friends.

Felicity steps forward and we hug. 'You're looking well,' I remark. 'And I'm glad it was possible to get away. Drew has been pining for you.' I shoot Drew a pointed look and he rolls his eyes.

'That's not true, but I know a little fella who has... isn't that right, Bertie?' Drew isn't fooling anyone, and Felicity walks over to throw her arms around him, planting a kiss on his cheek.

'I know they both miss me, and I do intend to get down here more regularly in future. Things are starting to change for me at work and I hope it will be for the better.' Felicity's comments are unusually guarded, and I can tell from her expression that something has happened. Drew seems oblivious as he starts pulling out items from the freezer and then scrutinises the instructions. Felicity and I leave him to it, walking over to the glass doors to look out onto the garden.

'I was telling Drew that he doesn't have enough lighting. Look how pretty the soft glow is from your place, Kerra. It's a long way down to the bottom of the garden and I know the last ten metres this side is all veggies and herbs, but it's a bit spooky looking out onto a big black void.'

'Do you want to pop around to mine and I'll show you the new garden office?'

We look across at Drew.

'Oh, don't mind me. I'll dog-sit and get on with heating up the food.' He tries his best to sound put out, but we grab our coats, still chatting as we make our way to the front door.

'Ripley is still being a minx, then?' Felicity asks, as she pulls the door shut behind us.

'Bertie is beginning to fight back. He no longer runs away to hide if Ripley jumps up onto the fence and hisses at him. He won't get too close, but he'll stand and bark at her incessantly until she jumps down.'

'So I hear. It's driving Drew mad, at times. He says he's constantly up and down, and it breaks his concentration. I suggested he either installs a dog flap in the shed so Bertie has somewhere he can run and hide or consider buying him a little dog kennel. He'd bark when he wanted to go back inside but Drew can't hang around for long spells waiting for him to make up his mind when he's trying to work.'

'What a great idea. I do feel so guilty about it, at times.'

I unlock the side gate and after Felicity steps through I immediate fasten it again.

'Still reliving the nightmares of your unwanted visitors?'

Catching up with her, I nod my head. 'I don't know what I'd have done without Ripley here. I moan a lot about how vocal she is but, in all honesty, if anyone steps inside the garden or approaches the front door, she senses it and she'll wake me up every time.'

'I'm glad how it worked out. Bertie needed a home, and Drew was in need of a little company. Cats choose their owners, whereas owners choose their dogs, or that's what I believe, anyway.'

Walking down the path towards the far end of the garden, Felicity seems enchanted.

'My goodness, that's some garden office. I was expecting a kit to look a little basic, like a posh shed, but this is very stylish indeed.'

With the low-level lighting all around the base, it high-lights the hedges on both sides and the only shadows at the end of the garden are in the far corner, by the barbecue.

'Treloar's did an amazing job. Come and have a look inside.'

I rummage around in my pocket for the keys and when I push back the bi-fold doors, Felicity is eager to step inside. 'Now this is a home office that I could work in. Heck, I could live in here!' she exclaims.

'Ross will be here tomorrow and I'm going to give him a hand putting up the storage cupboards that will line the back wall.'

Felicity turns to face me. 'Ross? Not one of his men? I thought it was still a secret about the two of you?'

'It is, but he'll come in his four-by-four and I've told Dad that he's offered to do it in his own time as a favour. I'm helping Ross painting some of the scenery for the pantomime.'

Felicity looks surprised. 'Well, things are moving forward. I'm glad for you, Kerra. And this is amazing.'

She falls silent and I'm conscious that Drew will wonder where we are. I turn to lead her back out into the garden when she touches my arm.

'There's something... Can I ask your opinion on a personal matter? But it's in strictest confidence. It has to be just between the two of us, because I need to get my head around it before I say anything to Drew.'

'I knew there was something on your mind – that's why I suggested we come outside. You know that you can trust me, Felicity. It's not bad news about the family business, is it?'

She pauses and I can see this isn't easy for her. 'Drew and I agreed a plan and, of course, it never goes quite as smoothly as you hope it will. I'm trying to extricate myself before I drop the bombshell. But there's a complication and it's not one either of us expected.'

I wait patiently for her to continue. She comes to stand next to me as we both stare out at the moon, high above the roofline of the cottages.

'I'm pregnant,' she states, sounding as if she can't quite believe it.

It takes a few seconds for her words to sink in. 'When did you find out?'

'I suspected last month and then thought it was maybe stress delaying things. But I did a test the day before yesterday and it confirmed my suspicions. I'm not ready to tell Drew yet, because the timing is all wrong. It wasn't even on our agenda. I'm not saying it wouldn't have been at some point, but if I walk away from the family business, I'll have no income at all.

Moving to Penvennan will mean either looking for a job or becoming self-employed. And you know the risks that entails. Drew's work is getting busier, but he still has gaps in between projects and... well, I need to come up with an action plan before I tell him.'

Relief floods through me. Felicity is the type of woman who – like me – needs to plan ahead, and I turn to give her a comforting hug.

'Listen, once you get your head around what needs to happen and when, Drew will be delighted, I promise you.'

'Thanks, Kerra. I thought as much, but it's nice to hear you mirroring my own thoughts. Drew is stressing over his work, as his current job finishes shortly and it looks like a major project he tendered for is going to be delayed. I'll have to think carefully about the timing of handing in my notice and starting to look at my options. By the time I figure that out, I hope Drew will have received the go-ahead on his next job and he'll be more relaxed.'

I'm torn between offering my opinion, which is that if she tells him now, I have no doubt they could work through it together, but I accept that Felicity knows him even better than I do.

'I'm always here for you, Felicity, if you want to talk anything through. You notice that Drew still hasn't done anything to the bedrooms? He's waiting until you move in.'

'I know and it worries me a little.'

'Why?'

'Do you think he still doubts I can walk away from my old life? He says it's because he wants me to feel it's our house and not simply his, and we'll decorate them together.'

'He's living in limbo, Felicity, and that's the truth of it. He was excited about building the extension because you were involved in choosing the final finishes. Then things went awry, and he thought he'd lost you and that your first loyalty would always be to your family. But until you're here permanently, he's afraid to take anything for granted. In the meantime, he buries himself in his work and nothing else matters while he's waiting.'

Felicity takes a deep breath, a half-sob catching in her throat.

'I intend to come down the weekend after next and I'll tell him then. It's all a little overwhelming, but just being able to share it with someone is a huge relief. Somehow or other, I'll sort this out. I don't want to be giving Drew happy news, only for him to start worrying about our immediate future. One person who will be ecstatic when I hand in my notice will be my brother. Having bailed him out of the last disastrous decision he made, he's going to have to learn to wise up, because I intend moving here sooner, rather than later.'

The positivity in her voice is heart-warming. As I lock up and we make our way back to Tigry Cottage, I know it's going to be a happy home for them. And I can't wait to see the look on Drew's face once he knows he's going to be a father. But Felicity is right, if she doesn't want him to go into panic mode, she'll need to have a clear plan of action ready to lay out before him.

Wow! That's something I didn't see coming, but it does put a huge grin on my face.

NINE

A PERFECT SATURDAY CHILLING
AT HOME

'Was that Felicity's voice I heard out in the garden talking to Bertie, just now?' Ross asks as we start shifting the boxes around to make a start.

'Yes. She arrived yesterday afternoon.'

'How late am I allowed to stay?'

'Why?'

'I wondered if we could all get together this evening and I'll order takeaway.' I know Ross is simply keen for us to enjoy some sort of normality as a couple, but with Felicity being on edge, I don't think company is what she needs right now.

'I think that would look a bit like two couples getting together to socialise, don't you? You can get away with staying late, as this little lot is going to take us a while to assemble. It's an excuse, anyway.'

Ross's face falls. 'I don't get to have any fun in return for my hard labour?'

'Cheeky. You have the pleasure of keeping me happy.'

He throws me one of his roguish smiles and my heart

melts. *I love you, Ross Treloar, and I can't wait for the day when the pretence is over,* I tell myself.

'Right, time to flex your muscles. We need the four heaviest boxes over here and we'll unpack them first, as they're the carcasses,' he instructs me.

I'm just the builder's mate, today. Ross assigns me little tasks like sorting out brackets and putting screws and fittings into little piles. I push, I pull, I stand around waiting to hand him the next piece and shut my ears when he catches his finger, or drops something.

For lunch I make a picnic and we sit on the two garden chairs eating off trays, the doors pulled shut as although it's a bright day it's cold, but it's toasty inside.

When I'm with Ross everything seems different. The way I think, the things I do. I slip into couples' mode as if it's the most natural thing in the world. And yet, I still can't quite believe it. Even at Treylya, it's not the same and that troubles me, because after today I doubt that we'll be able to conjure up any excuses for Ross to spend time here.

'You've suddenly gone quiet,' Ross interrupts my thoughts. I turn to gaze at him and he looks so relaxed and happy, it's good to see.

'I've never known you to take a Saturday off work, before.'

He chuckles. 'You call this a Saturday off? It feels like work to me.'

'You know what I mean.'

'I think it's time I backed off a little. My foremen are all good guys, and they know what they're doing.'

This is a big deal, because Ross feels the need to constantly be on call. 'If there's a problem they'd phone you, Ross. I know you like to keep up to date with every job, but trust helps people to grow. Treloar's have a solid reputation, and you should be proud of that. The business isn't going to suffer if you don't always do the rounds on a Saturday when the men are working overtime, is it?'

He shrugs his shoulders, too busy eating to reply.

'Sy asked me to sit in on a video call with the man in charge of The Happy Hive, yesterday.'

Ross looks up, surprised. He pops the last of one of Mrs Moyle's feta cheese and olive scones into his mouth. I love watching him eat. He devours everything as if he hasn't eaten for ages.

'I thought that was all behind you now. And why is Sy involved?'

'He was approached because the changes aren't going down well with the subscribers. They want Sy to work as a consultant to analyse what's going wrong and he asked me to take part in case I could come up with any ideas.'

'Sy has a full-time job, I'm surprised he has time to get involved.'

'Sy and Tegan need the money, I'm afraid. Clean and Shine was on the brink of going under and change requires funding. That's why I agreed to take part in the meeting, but I won't be getting pulled into it.'

'I'm glad to hear it. If they've messed up, that's their problem. You're building a new empire.'

I laugh. 'No, I'm not. I'm just spreading my investments, that's all. It's called managing the risk.'

He gives me a shifty look.

'What?'

'I spoke to Oliver Sinclair, yesterday. I've um... decided to renew my contract with Truscott and Sons for another three months.'

'You weren't impressed with Oliver?'

Ross looks a tad uncomfortable. 'He knows his stuff, but I like to support family businesses where possible. It's no reflection on Oliver, and I did tell Kenneth Truscott that if they don't manage to find a buyer within that timescale, then it will be a case of giving another agency a chance. They did offer me a half-a-per-cent reduction in their fee.'

I know that was a goodwill gesture and the incentive wasn't a factor in Ross's decision. I, too, believe in supporting local companies – of course I do. But it's clear they aren't targeting the right market, which means they haven't established links with agents further afield. Businesses need to change with the times, creating new opportunities by thinking outside the box, or risk going under. And that's not good for the community or the families of the employees those businesses support.

'The company Oliver represents want to integrate their brand into the community, in a meaningful way. We had an interesting chat about the differences in how business is conducted in large towns, as opposed to tiny villages. And they intend to give back, not simply provide employment to local people. But the choice is yours, and I'm sure Truscott's will do their best.'

'I wondered whether you might be cross with me, for sticking with them,' Ross, replies, meekly.

'We're both businesspeople, Ross, and they've been around a long time. Anyway, on a similar topic, the ball is now rolling with regard to selling my apartment in London, but I haven't mentioned it to Dad. You know how he panics.'

'I think you've more than proved you know what you're doing, Kerra. You'll no doubt earn a tidy profit once it's sold.'

Ross wipes his mouth on the paper napkin, placing his tray on the floor and sitting back with a bottle of beer in his hand.

It's a snapshot I'll keep in my head forever. Even the sun has come out to shine down on us and this all feels so right.

'Yes, prices have jumped up since I took a mortgage out on it. I'm excited about what's to come and why have equity tied up in something that links back to my past and not my future?'

Ross holds up his bottle and we chink. I know he's used to grander things, but that doesn't seem to bother him.

'I think it's time we carried these trays back up to the cottage and then made a start again, don't you?'

'Great idea. I'm surprised Ripley hasn't joined us, but she'll be waking up soon and expecting her dinner.'

As we walk across the lawn, I can hear Bertie the other side of the hedge. It sounds like Felicity is throwing a ball for him. As soon as we step through the glass doors Ripley rushes downstairs and begins miaowing, in quick succession.

'What is it, girl?'

Ding dong. Ding dong.

I glance at Ross. 'Let's put the trays in the sink and why don't you pop upstairs for a minute? It's probably only someone selling something, but just in case, eh?'

He nods. Whoever is outside is getting impatient. *Ding dong. Ding dong.*

'Coming,' I call out, waiting until Ross is out of sight. When I swing the door open my cousin Alice is standing there, wiping her eyes with a tissue.

'What's wrong?' I gasp, ushering her inside.

Ripley has already run back upstairs, as the minute Alice is inside, she begins sobbing noisily.

'Dad has thrown me out,' she wails.

I'm dumfounded. Uncle Alistair must have had a really good reason, because I can't imagine Auntie Marge not stepping in and trying to smooth things out between them.

'Slip off your coat and take a seat.'

She does as I bid, pulling a fresh tissue from her pocket and blowing her nose.

'It's because I won't stop seeing Ian. Dad says the Adamses are trouble and it's not what he wants for me. When I said that it was none of his business, he told me that he didn't want *us* under his roof any longer.'

'You and Ian have been living together?'

Alice is clearly distraught. 'Yes. Ian lost his job and had nowhere else to go. Mum talked Dad into it, but it's been a horrendous four weeks and when I popped home for lunch, Dad and I got into an argument. I don't know what to do, Kerra. It's all so... unfair. Ian isn't a bad person. I know his brother has an awful reputation, but Ian has calmed down a lot now he's older and yet people won't give him a break.'

I feel for Alice. Ian's older brother, Fraser, always mixed with the wrong crowd when he was at school. There were some rumours about his little gang shoplifting, but Ian simply tagged along, being four years younger and not wanting to be left out. What makes it worse is that their father is known for his dodgy dealings, but as far as I know he always manages to get away with a caution whenever the police pay him a visit. Fraser's posse were a lot younger than my peer group and I don't really know what happened to any of them after I left Penvennan.

Alice begins crying again, but this time it's nowhere near as loud.

'Slip your coat back on and I'll grab mine. Let's head over to see Dad.'

'You think Uncle Eddie will let us stay with him for a while?'

'I don't know, Alice, all we can do is ask. Since James went to work for Sissy, Dad still hasn't found anyone to replace James at the kennels and that counts for something if Ian is desperate.'

I don't add that Dad has always had time for Alice, and if that in tandem with a helping hand isn't a tempting offer, then they're sunk. There is no way I'd live under the same roof with her, let alone someone I hardly know. We both know that wouldn't work.

'Ripley, I'm just popping out. Good girl,' I call out. Alice looks at me quizzically, but I simply nudge her in the direction of the front door.

* * *

'You've done well!' Carrying a mug of coffee in each hand and a paper bag very gingerly under my arm, I step inside the garden office.

Ross immediately turns around. 'I wondered where my helper went. And that coffee is most welcome.'

'And I have two of Mrs Moyle's saffron buns. Sorry about that; family drama.'

'Is Alice alright?'

'Dad's going to let her and Ian Adams stay there while they sort something out. Ian recently lost his job.'

'Well, at least she chose the right brother, I wouldn't trust the other one to hold a piece of wood, let alone my toolbox from what I've heard,' Ross replies, sharply.

'It's a temporary arrangement for a week, in return for Ian helping out, and then Dad will review the situation. I couldn't have her here, Ross. I know that sounds awful, but we've only recently called a truce and I'm not used to living with anyone.'

Ross stops what he's doing and stares at me. 'That makes

two of us. It's a compromise even when you're happy to have someone in your home, but if you don't really get on it would be a living hell. Did I overhear right, that they'd been staying with Alistair and Marge? That can't have been easy, and it will have left a bad feeling all round if they've fallen out.'

I put the mugs down next to the chairs, closing the doors behind me. Opening the paper bag, I offer it to Ross. He immediately reaches out to grab a bun.

'It's looking good, isn't it? I can start putting the doors on next, so you've returned at just the right time. It'll take two of us as they're rather heavy.'

The floor-to-ceiling cabinets are now securely screwed to the walls. With a range of shelving inside, it's all the storage space I could ever want.

'I can't wait to unpack the last of the boxes,' I declare, happily. There's a loud series of miaows and I slide back the glass doors so Ripley can come in.

'Sorry, Ripley. I don't have any treats for you in here. We'll remedy that soon, I promise.'

She sniffs around and when we sit down to enjoy our coffee, she jumps up onto Ross's lap.

My cat, my man, my office. Heaven.

'You might as well stay for dinner this evening. Dad will be much too busy sorting out his guests to worry about what's going on over here. Alice is taking the afternoon off work to collect a few things from the house and break the news to Ian. He managed to get a day's work helping a mate move some furniture to a house on the other side of Truro. What do you fancy to eat?'

Ross looks happy, stroking Ripley's back with one hand as she purrs contentedly and sipping from the mug of coffee in his other hand.

'Surprise me.'

'Chinese it is, then.'

Ross looks at me, shaking his head, disapprovingly.

'I'll cook. I'm sure there's something in your fridge I can throw together. Do you have eggs, potatoes, maybe an onion and some frozen peas?'

'Probably. It doesn't sound very interesting, though.'

'I'll make you the best Spanish omelette you've ever tasted. Seriously, even though I usually throw in a red pepper, it'll still taste wonderful.'

Perfect. And by the time he's standing in front of the cooker while I'm gazing at him adoringly, my office will be ready to move into. Lucky, lucky me!

* * *

'It's hard to imagine a time when we won't need to creep around,' Ross murmurs into my ear. I roll over into him, pulling the duvet up over my arms as the temperature has dropped.

'If only every day could be like this. Well, you know what I mean. And thank you for doing such a wonderful job of assembling those cupboards.'

'I like to make my woman happy,' Ross quips. 'And how was dinner?'

'Lovely. I'd certainly let you cook that for me again,' I answer laughing, and he joins in.

'Do you mind if I have a quick shower before I go? I don't suppose you fancy coming back with me? We could take Ripley with us and no one would be the wiser.'

'That's not fair and you know it. We're pushing the boundaries as it is and what if Alice turns up on my doorstep later this evening, in need of a listening ear?'

Ross groans as he wraps his arms around me and neither of us want to make a move. But it's gone seven and if he stays any later it will look like a date. I'm sure Mrs Moyle and Arthur have craned their necks a few times today, to see if Ross's vehicle is still parked up in the lay-by opposite the cottage. Not that either one of them gossip, but my business is just that and privacy is very important to me.

'I know, it's time. I'll be out of here in ten minutes, I promise. Just sixty seconds more, that's all I ask.'

Ripley comes running upstairs, jumping straight on the bed and lying across our feet.

'See, even Ripley doesn't want me to go,' Ross moans.

'I don't either, but your time is up.'

Reluctantly we break apart and it's a mad dash before that final kiss goodbye. Ripley is most upset as I try to straighten the bed.

Just as Ross is walking out the door, toolbox in hand, Uncle Alistair approaches and he doesn't look happy.

'Oh, hello, Ross,' he calls out. 'Problems?'

'No. I've been putting up some cupboards in Kerra's office.'

I turn to face Ross. 'Thank you so much for stepping in at the last moment as a favour. Email me your invoice and I'll pay it immediately. I'm sorry that the units were such a nightmare to put up.'

'It's no problem at all and I'll send it across on Monday. Have a great evening, Kerra, Alistair.'

As Ross steps out, Uncle Alistair steps inside and Ross disappears into the darkness.

'I only wanted a quick word about Alice. I hear that Eddie

has taken them in. She's making a big mistake and the only way to make her stop and think is not to make it too easy for them.'

Oh no. I really do not want to be party to this at all.

'Come and sit down. At least you know Alice is safe with Dad around. Better that, than some friend puts them up and you don't know where she's staying.'

'I'm glad you understand.' He lets out an exasperated sigh as he sinks down onto the sofa. 'You can talk Auntie Marge round, then, because she's not speaking to me and I don't know what to do for the best.'

Oh well, I guess that asking for a perfect Saturday was reaching for the moon. I'd better go and get my coat and follow him back home. That'll get the village talking, as Tremont is even smaller than Penvennan.

TEN

THE STORM CLOUDS COME ROLLING IN

'Morning!' Stepping out my front door to see Alice and Ian walking past with a dog lead in each of their hands, I'm amazed. Dad didn't hang around long before making them work for their keep. 'Those clouds look threatening.'

'Yes. Eddie suggested we make it a quick one. He was up early to start the deep clean and Nettie is on the way over. Ian, do you remember my cousin, Kerra Shaw?'

Ian frees up one hand to hold it out and we shake. He towers over me, but the last time I saw him he didn't even come up to my chin.

'It's been years, but nice to see you back again, Kerra. Is it for good?' His reaction seems genuine and obviously Alice hasn't been talking about me, which means she really is changing her ways. Poor Alice, she has a reputation for being a gossipmonger, but it's usually a case of careless chatter.

'Yes. I'm really settled in now at Pedrevan.'

I pat Rufus's head, trying to stop him from jumping around, as Alice tries to rein him in a little.

'Your grandma would be happy to know you're back. It

ain't going to be a day for a walk along the beach, that's for sure,' Ian replies, amiably.

I nod in agreement. 'This little one is Willow, isn't it?' I ask, surprised to see Sissy's sweet little Westland Terrier. She's such a patient little dog and is sitting quietly next to Alice.

'I think Eddie said she's only in for the day,' Ian informs me. I glance at Alice and she looks happy. After the state she was in yesterday, this is good news indeed. And Ian is no longer the boisterous youth I remember, so why is Uncle Alistair so concerned for Alice? I wonder.

'We'd best get off before that rain sets in, Alice. I'll do the second walk on my own. Anyway, it's good to see you, Kerra.' They both give me a parting smile as I swing open the gate and shut it behind me, before crossing the road.

I fall behind a little as the dogs are hurrying them along, eager to explore in the woods but Alice is struggling a little. They stop for a moment and Ian takes Rufus's lead from her. Alice is much happier with just Willow and it's reassuring to see Ian looking out for her.

Stepping inside the convenience store, I grab a basket and begin browsing as Mrs Moyle is serving someone. There isn't much I need, but I grab some more cat food and a tub of hot chocolate. When I hear the door shut, I head straight for the till.

'Good morning, Mrs Moyle, how are you today?'

'I'm well, thank you, Kerra. And you after all the excitement?'

I can see from her face she's aware of Dad's new boarders and not just the dogs.

'Wonderful now that my office is ready. I was... um... wondering if you and Arthur could spare me an hour sometime to talk through a little idea I have.'

She looks at me, curiously. 'What sort of idea?'

The door opens and two people step through.

'Why don't you pop in at four-thirty as I'm closing up, and we can go upstairs and have a cup of tea together?'

'That would be perfect, thank you.'

I place the items into my carrier bag and pay, eager to leave Mrs Moyle to chat to the two old ladies who have obviously come in for a natter. 'See you later, then.'

* * *

Sunday lunchtimes at The Lark and Lantern are always busy. The locals outnumber the tourists at this time of the year and it's a gathering place. After dropping my shopping back at the cottage, I take a brisk walk down to the cove. It's not a day for hanging around, as the wind is whipping up and when that rain starts to fall it's going to pour, but I need a quick word with Polly.

Tapping on the back door of the pub I step inside, calling out. 'Anyone around?'

Polly appears at the top of the passageway. 'Hi, Kerra. Come on through. I'm just emptying the glass washer.'

I follow her through into the bar. Luckily, she's on her own although there's a lot of banging and clattering coming from the kitchen, so I need to be quick.

'I know you're busy, but if an opportunity came up to get involved with a little interior design work on the side, would it be of interest to you?'

'That's a temptation I wouldn't be able to resist, but I can't see anyone wanting to employ *me*. It's all well and good having a certificate, but I don't have an awful lot of hands-on experience, do I?'

'You have enough to put on a CV. The thing is, do you have the time?' I ask, getting straight to the point.

'I have mornings and a couple of hours in the afternoons during the week.'

'This might be something that could work for you. I'll email you with the background details of a conversation I had and a phone number. The guy's name is Oliver Sinclair.'

Polly beams back at me. 'Wonderful! Thanks so much for thinking of me, Kerra. I'm desperate for any chance I can get to demonstrate what I can do. But... uh, let's keep this just between us for now, eh?'

'Understood. I'll call him first thing in the morning to let him know you'll be contacting him direct. Let me know how you get on.'

Walking back up the hill to the village, I stop for a moment in front of Gwel Teg. I've always adored this wonderful little row of cottages and I'd love to be able to rent it out to someone local.

As I'm daydreaming and fighting a battle to keep wisps of hair escaping from my hood, I turn around to gaze out at the tumultuous waves. When the sea is this angry, it's ugly and it strikes fear into my heart for anyone out at sea.

'It's got a great view,' Drew calls out and I turn around to see him and Felicity, hurrying towards me hand in hand.

'Hasn't it just?' I retort.

'Tempted?'

'Done and dusted.' The grin I give him is one of pure satisfaction. 'But I'm keeping it quiet.'

The two of them glance at each other smiling and Drew lifts his hand to put a finger up against his lips, teasingly.

'We're having lunch at the pub later. Do you fancy joining us?' Felicity asks, but I shake my head.

'Thanks for the offer, but I'm just popping in to check on someone. Enjoy, though.' It's more that Felicity might change her mind and over a leisurely lunch decide to open up to Drew. She can't do that if I'm there.

We head off in opposite directions and when I reach the top of the hill, instead of turning left I find myself turning right and taking the path up through the woods. The rain begins to fall, and I speed up, but it's tough on my calf muscles and by the time I reach the private gate at the top, I'm hot and bothered. Strands of hair are sticking to my face and although my coat is waterproofed, my jeans are soaking. I pull out my phone to call Ross.

'Hello. What are you up to?' He sounds chilled and I can hear music playing in the background.

'I'm standing at the rear gate. Can you let me in?'

There's an almost instant click and the phone goes dead. As I step through and the gate slowly shuts behind me, Ross flings open his front door and comes racing out with a large umbrella. He hasn't even stopped to put on a coat.

'You must be mad! You're soaking wet,' he shouts as the howling wind on the clifftop threatens to blot out his words.

He throws his arm around my shoulders and lowers the umbrella to try to shield us, but the rain is coming at all angles and it's a struggle. As soon as we're inside I stand there dripping and he rushes off to get a towel as I ease off my coat.

'It was a spur-of-the-moment thing,' I explain as he hurries back to me.

'Here, wipe your face and dry the wet bits of hair. There's a dressing gown in the cupboard of the downstairs cloakroom. You'd better pop your jeans into the tumble dryer. The utility room is the door next to the cloakroom. Coffee?'

'Please. It would have made more sense to have phoned for

a chat, wouldn't it?' I reply as I scoop as many sodden clumps of hair as I can up into the towel. 'I just thought that no one is going to be out in this, so it seemed like the perfect opportunity to pop up for an hour, or two.'

Truthfully, I wasn't even thinking straight. He could have had company, for all I know but he's smiling from ear to ear.

'I'd rather have a visit than a call, believe me. Especially as I was wondering what happened after I left last night. Anyway, go peel off those jeans and get yourself sorted. We'll soon warm you up.'

Polly would love it here and whoever chose the furniture knew what they were doing. Everything is pristine and shiny. I even end up using the towel to wipe around the splashes I make after washing my hands in the stylish silver glass oval bowl that sits on top of the white granite worktop in the cloakroom. As a family home, you'd need to employ someone to come in daily and clean up behind everyone.

When I join Ross, he's sitting on the long, white leather designer couch that looks out across the bay. The wall of glass is floor-to-ceiling and an extended canopy and side wings shield the front elevation from crosswinds. Treylya sits at a point on the headland where it returns and the cliff slopes down to meet the woods. You can see in two different directions at the same time. Depending on the weather, sometimes if you look out you can spot the turbulence in the water where the currents from east to west meet, as they come around the bay.

He stands, handing me a mug. 'I never tire of this view. On days like today it's a reminder of how harsh the elements can be.'

The heat from the coffee is welcoming, but it doesn't take

long for my chilly fingers to start feeling it and I hold the mug by the handle as we stand gazing out.

'I always think about the fishermen,' I confess, and Ross gives me a look of empathy.

'And your granddad.'

I nod, biting my lip. 'It wasn't like him to take a risk and it still makes me shudder when I'm at the beach and looking at those rocks. Have you ever looked up at Lanryon from the cove? It looks like a face, and the arched wooden doors look like a big gaping mouth. With the tombstones in front of it, it spooks me every time.'

'That's because many of the graves are those of fishermen. But I've never noticed a face. I'll look next time I'm walking on the beach. You don't think it's just because it holds bad memories for you, of his funeral?'

'Maybe,' I sigh. 'But it reminds me of those gargoyles some churches have to catch the rain running off the roof. Why would they use faces as ugly as demons? Why not angels and cherubs? I'll never set foot in there, ever again.'

'Can I ask you a delicate question?' Ross asks, his voice softening. 'Is that the real reason why you left Penvennan?'

'It was a part of it, I can't deny that. Granddad and I were so close. My fondest memories are of him taking me out fishing in his little boat after he sold the trawler. It's only now I can look back and think about those times without feeling as if my heart is being ripped apart.'

'And that's why Pedrevan means so much to you.' His frown furrows his brow and I wonder what he's thinking.

'Right,' he says, cheerfully as he smiles at me. 'Drink up and let's see what we can find for lunch. If I'd realised I'd be entertaining, I'd have cooked something special.'

'You don't have to fuss for me.'

'But you can stay for a bit? You're not rushing off?'

'I'm popping in to see Mrs Moyle and Arthur at four-thirty but I'm in no hurry to head back in the rain.'

'Well, I'm not letting you walk back in this, so either you stay until it goes off, or I'll drive you back and who cares who sees us.'

Turning away from the view, I know that I could never live here, even to please Ross. While the cove will always be a place that is dear to my heart, Pedrevan Cottage is where my mother was born and it's where I feel closest to Mum, Grandma, and Granddad. Grandma left it to me in her will and I rented it out because I couldn't bear to part with it. Green Acre might have been my home, but I spent more time over at the cottage. Dad worked long days alongside Uncle Alistair, and Mum worked tirelessly at the kennels. My grand-parents enjoyed spoiling me and I loved spending time with them.

Ross calls out, 'It's time to switch off that brain of yours. Help me find something and then I want to know what happened with Alistair. He looked almost as distraught as Alice sounded.'

* * *

'You know who caught this sea bass?' Ross pushes his empty plate away from him as I finish the last of the sautéed potatoes.

'Well, I know it wasn't you.' I laugh. Ross doesn't have the patience for fishing whether by boat, or with a rod.

'Tom.'

'James's dad?'

'Yes. He often turns up with a few fish for the freezer.'

'I didn't know you knew him that well.'

'Oh, I put a bit of work his way. As well as repairing cars and boats he makes bespoke garden gates and he's done a few one-off jobs for me.'

'He was hoping James would follow in his footsteps, but his heart isn't in it. Besides, I don't think trade is brisk enough to support them both and I'm sure Tom and Georgia are pleased that James is doing well with Sissy.'

'It's troubling when a business is in decline,' Ross agrees. 'The buildings are nothing more than a cluster of rusty old sheds that are rotting away, and Tom's biggest problem is that he's a hoarder. All those bits of old cars he keeps locked up that he'll never use. Most of his work nowadays are jobs like mine, or small boat repairs. People go to the main garages to get their cars serviced and Tom simply doesn't have the latest diagnostic equipment.'

'James is at an age where he wants to spread his wings and see what he's capable of doing. I wondered if he'd be interested in renting Gwel Teg. Once the survey and the searches have been done, it should only take a couple of weeks until the contract is ready to sign. I'm buying it fully furnished and the owners, Mr and Mrs Bartlett, want it off their hands as quickly as possible.'

'That sounds ominous,' Ross replies, concern etched all over his face.

'Oh, the reason is legit. One of their daughters has just started at university and they've recently bought a property for her to share with some friends, apparently.'

Ross shakes his head. 'That's a risky business.' He laughs. 'It'll end up being a party house.'

'They're young and that's the time to have some fun. But what do you think of my idea about offering it to James?'

'He's a nice lad and he's been really good to Eddie. But can James afford it?'

'I know how much he earns, and I can make it affordable. He told me he'd like to move out and I think he'd be a good tenant. James will look after the place and it's only a stone's throw away from his family.'

Ross purses his lips. 'You feel you owe him. He might see through that.'

'Well, I do. If he hadn't helped Dad through those early weeks after Mum died, I dread to think what would have happened. The truth is that James probably could have found himself a full-time job much sooner. But he has a good heart and he put his own ambitions on hold to help.'

'It's a nice thought, Kerra, and if James goes for it, then I know it will make you happy.'

That's all the endorsement I needed.

'And this thing with Alice is sorted?'

'Alice and Ian are staying with Dad, at least for the next week. Ian seems happy to help at the kennels, which is a relief, as it takes the pressure off Nettie. She's so busy on the writing front and Ian seems happy enough walking the dogs. It means Nettie doesn't have to rush over each morning and each evening.'

Ross raises his eyebrows in surprise. 'I am a little shocked Eddie took them both in, I will say. He's a bit of a stickler for everything being done properly, isn't he? I bet it troubles his conscience having both of them under the same roof.'

'I know. It was a bit of shock to me, too, I will admit, although they have separate rooms. But Dad has always had a soft spot for Alice, as he feels Uncle Alistair is too hard on her at times. You know what trouble Alice has caused in the past, but she's more circumspect now. Auntie Marge talked Uncle

Alistair into letting Ian live with them after he lost his job. That turned out to be a big mistake.'

'Trouble always followed the Adams brothers around when they were in their teens and the father isn't much help, by all accounts. He's not the nicest of men. But I can honestly say that I thought that was all in the past. I don't know either Ian, or his elder brother Fraser, personally. What do you think will happen?'

'I honestly don't know. I went to see Auntie Marge and she's now talking to Uncle Alistair again. It's clear he won't have Ian in the house, but he is prepared to take Alice back.' I make a face, indicating that's unlikely to happen.

'So, Alice is digging in her heels, is she?'

'She is and it's time for Uncle Alistair to realise that Alice is more than capable of making her own decisions and taking responsibility for any mistakes along the way. As long as Ian doesn't let Dad down, it's really no problem having them there, as Dad rattles around in that big house all on his own. James has left a hole and Dad's eager to fill it with someone reliable. Having not seen Ian for the best part of ten years, I can't begin to gauge whether Uncle Alistair is being unreasonable, or not. Still, it isn't my problem, but Dad won't put up with anyone who treats Alice badly. I intend to stay out of it, if possible. Last night wasn't pleasant, but at least Auntie Marge let Uncle Alistair back in the house.'

Ross rolls his eyes. 'It was that bad?'

'Auntie Marge is a lovely lady and she's the glue that keeps everything together. Uncle Alistair didn't realise that until last night. It came as quite a shock to him, I can tell you. I couldn't get out of there quickly enough.'

'Have you spoken to your dad this morning?'

'No. I thought I'd hang back. He knows where I am if he

wants to talk, and the last thing I want is for Dad to think I'm on Uncle Alistair's side. You know how family arguments can blow up just like that. The Shaws are a passionate and stubborn family, and they don't back down easily once someone raises their hackles.'

'And the Pascoe side of your family, being Cornish, are inclined to be more accommodating?' Ross asks the question, but his expression is one of amusement. 'I can speak with authority that the Treloars aren't easily talked out of something when they put their minds to it, either. I thought that was a part of our heritage.'

I burst out laughing. '*Cain telly*, as my granddad would have said.' I love all the old Cornish sayings, and that was one of my favourites. As a young child I was constantly asking questions and Granddad would look at me, quite seriously, and simply say he couldn't tell me. I always thought it was because it was some sort of secret. Then I started school and found that kids tell you everything, including the things you don't want to know.

'Come on, let's tidy this away and sit and watch a film together.'

Just hanging around like this makes me glad Ross is living on my doorstep now and not a half-an-hour drive away. But the truth is that I preferred The Forge. It wasn't spacious and full of expensive stuff like Treylya, but it was very him. It wasn't cluttered, but his library of books was amazing and the big log fire in the sitting room is so romantic. He must miss it. Instead, we're going to sit in the spacious cinema room and watch a film on an enormous screen. It'll be nice, but it won't be cosy.

My thoughts begin to stray. Is it too much to dream of a time when Ross and I are together permanently? When after a hard day's work, we can relax in each other's arms and shut the door on the world without a care? Of all people, I should know better, I suppose. Nothing worth having ever comes easily and if it does, it rarely lasts the course. And I'm in for the long haul.

I mustn't forget to keep one eye on the clock. Even if the rain doesn't ease off, I can't be late leaving, as Mrs Moyle will instruct Arthur to have that kettle boiled at four-thirty on the dot.

ELEVEN
NEVER A DULL MOMENT

'Well, it's rather nice to have a visitor, isn't it, Daphne?' Arthur watches as Mrs Moyle pours the tea, using a tea strainer because she doesn't believe in using teabags. She even has a knitted tea cosy to keep the pot warm. It's so reminiscent of Grandma, although instead of cups and saucers the Moyles are happy to use mugs, I see.

It's the first time I've ever been invited up to their flat above the shop and it's larger than I thought it might be. Arthur, of course, sits in his chair in front of the window, his walking sticks hooked over the arm.

'How are you doing, Arthur?' I enquire, politely.

'I had a rough night, but I've been worse. Old age don't come alone do it?'

Arthur has had his back condition for as long as I can remember. He's still only in his early sixties and it must be so frustrating for him. He's active mentally, albeit he's house-bound and I can't even recall seeing him and Mrs Moyle out together when I was growing up.

'He's not a complainer, my Arthur,' Mrs Moyle says, proudly.

Arthur shifts his position, letting out an involuntary groan. I can't even begin to imagine what it must be like having to watch the world go by and not being able to join in. But he is a lifeline to so many people and an unsung hero of the community.

I often wondered what the street looks like from up here and he doesn't even need to lean too far forward to get a good view of the front of Pedrevan and Tigry cottages. They're situated on the opposite side of the road, just a little further down. As the shop is on the same side as Dad's property, Arthur can't see the house at Green Acre, or the kennels beyond. But the general coming and going of passing cars and pedestrians on their way to the cove must be a comfort to him. The stairs are quite steep, I noticed, and will be almost impossible for him to negotiate, I should imagine. It's a wonder they've never thought of installing a chair lift; at least then he could get one of those motorised scooters. I find myself wondering whether he's ever seen the cove, as Mrs Moyle once told Mum that Arthur hurt his back a few months before they moved to Penvennan. That's at least twenty-five years ago, as I started school shortly after they took over the shop.

'No point moanin' is there? 'Ow are things with you, Kerra? I watched all the builders in and out with interest. I bet it looks amazin' in there now.'

'It does, Arthur. And Treloar's erected my new office in the garden last week, so now I'm all sorted.'

'Must be satisfyin' and I'm glad you didn't sell up. Are you gettin' on alright with Drew? Daphne says he's a nice enough chap.'

I give Mrs Moyle a smile. 'Yes, Drew is a wonderful neighbour.'

'That Ripley has a mind of 'er own, don't she? Makes me laugh at times, she does.'

'And I must thank you for looking out for me when those awful men were around.'

Arthur looks at me, sternly. 'They was trouble, no doubt about it. 'Ave you 'eard the latest? Daphne will tell you. I'm supposing that your Alice knows all about it.'

I turn in my seat to look at Mrs Moyle.

'Now, Arthur, you know I hear a lot, but only say a little. But, I suppose word is getting around and Kerra ought to know. Ian Adam's brother, Fraser, was arrested but he's out on bail. It's connected to what was going on under our noses with the stolen cars. He was involved in the theft from Sissy's first shop in the arcade in Polreweek, too.' A burglary that nearly put her out of business earlier this year.

I'm stunned. 'I had no idea. Oh, my goodness, now I understand.'

Mrs Moyle and Arthur both nod their heads at me. 'When we saw Alice appear and then her and Ian out walking the dogs this morning, we guessed what had happened. Your uncle won't stand for it.'

'But Ian wasn't involved, was he?'

Mrs Moyle sucks in a deep breath, letting it out slowly. 'The trouble is, Kerra, those boys got themselves into scrapes when they were younger, and you know what people are like. Ian's a nice young man and I've always found him to be very polite. Fraser, I was never keen on as he always had a chip on his shoulder. But the father has had his brushes with the law and people tend to steer clear of the Adams lot. I hope Eddie is doing the right thing encouraging Alice. To be honest, I thought that was what you wanted to talk about, given what happened yesterday evening.'

Naturally, Arthur would have seen Alice turn up at Pedrevan and no doubt watched me take her across to Dad's place. And then Ross leaving a little later, just as Uncle Alistair arrived.

'Well, I am grateful to you for letting me know.'

'I thought maybe Alice would have told you,' Mrs Moyle replies, frowning.

'When I saw her yesterday, she was upset and not very talkative. If you hear anything further, I'd be grateful if you could let me know so I can keep an eye out for her. But I wanted to talk about another matter, entirely.'

I stop to sip my tea. It's so strong my mum would have approved but for me it's a taste I haven't acquired. Both Arthur and Mrs Moyle stare at me with interest.

'Penvennan Convenience Store is the hub of our little community and I know you both do a lot of good work looking out for our less able residents.'

Mrs Moyle looks directly at Arthur. 'I only have to shout up if a customer says someone isn't well and Arthur is on the phone. We don't let anyone go short, or manage on their own, if they need a bit of company. Arthur has his little black book, don't you, my love?'

Arthur colours up, nodding his head. 'I do that, Daphne. My mobile phone is always next to my chair. Some days I'm rarely off it.'

'What if there was an easier way of checking on people?' I pose the question.

'Can't think how,' Arthur replies, his bushy eyebrows knitting together forming a unibrow.

'What if we had a Penvennan community website? Somewhere people could log on to chat as a group, or post messages if they need anything, or have a problem? They could access it from their phone, or the computer if they have one. I'd be happy to pop round to show anyone who wasn't sure how to access it. You'd be in charge of it, Arthur, and if you have any problems once the system is up and running, you can give me a call and I'll fix it.'

Arthur puts down his mug and as he sits back in his chair, I can see I have gained his interest. 'So rather than relyin' on people poppin' into the shop or givin' me a call, I'd be able to check on folk, like?'

Mrs Moyle's eyes light up. 'And Arthur would be in charge?'

'Yes. He'd be what is called the administrator. So, if someone abuses the system, or uses bad language, let's say, Arthur could remove them. It could be as small, or as large, a group of people as you wanted. You'd simply send them an invite via email and I'd show you how to do that, and they accept. Once they have access, they can post messages, ask for help, or generally have a chat if they are in need of a little online company.'

'Like one of the social media apps, then?' Arthur jumps in.

'Yes, but smaller and you control who is a part of the group, Arthur. No one would be bombarded with spam messages from people they don't know.'

'How about those who have family, or friends, in other villages?' he asks, as he mulls it over.

'Then they message you and you send an invite to that friend, or relative. You can organise different threads. One for those requiring urgent help, another for a daily chat and maybe even set up topics like gardening, for instance. But, as I said, it would be entirely up to you.'

'It's a clever idea of Kerra's, Arthur. It would save a lot of phone calls, wouldn't it?'

'Hmm, it would that. There's a few of 'em now who are housebound and not all of 'em like havin' strangers in to give a helpin' hand. But if the neighbours they rely on to pop to the shop are on holiday, it's always a jugglin' act getting cover in the summer months. And you know how to set all that up?'

As I watch them interacting, I reflect that they're such a well-matched couple. It's depressing to think that there's nothing that can be done to help Arthur, but Mrs Moyle says he gave up on doctors years ago. She says that he's in pain much of the time and he's often up in the early hours, with little else to do but watch TV or keep a lookout for anything unusual. They both turn to look at me and I realise I was lost in my thoughts for a moment, there.

'IT is my field, Arthur. It's an easy enough thing to do. I've been meaning to mention it for a while.'

'I think it's an amazin' idea. It'd save you a bit of time, Daphne, wouldn't it? She's up and down stairs a dozen times a day with messages for me to sort out.'

My little idea seems to have gone down well.

'How long will it take to get it sorted?'

'Only a few days, although I do have a couple of things to attend to before next weekend. But I won't hang around, I promise.'

'I think it's a wonderful opportunity,' Mrs Moyle declares, happily and Arthur looks delighted.

'That's worthy of another cup of tea, Daphne,' he declares as they look at each other like I've just given them a present.

'I'm good, thanks,' I say, taking a few more mouthfuls and wishing I could drown it in milk. But I'm glad I finally approached them, and it will make me feel that I'm giving something back.

'I always said she was a clever one, Daphne, didn't I?'

'You did, my love, you certainly did.'

* * *

'Hello, Oliver, it's Kerra Shaw.'

'Oh, hi, Kerra. I was about to ring you. I hear the survey is back for Gwel Teg. I spoke to your solicitor first thing this morning and he said you've already signed the contract. I gave Mr and Mrs Bartlett the heads-up to expect a call imminently from their solicitor, to agree a date for a simultaneous exchange and completion.'

'It seems we're both on the ball this morning. I've been pushing from this end, too,' I reply, enthusiastically. 'I'm phoning about that contact I mentioned, Polly Saunders? I passed your number to her and she's going to ring you some-time today for a chat.'

'The timing is great. After sending out an email to customers whose properties are languishing on the market, I've already had two clients express an interest in speculating a little cash to maximise their return. I will look forward to having that conversation.'

'I hope you can work something out, Oliver. And fingers crossed that before the day is over, I'll have a date for Gwel Teg,' I say, unable to hide my excitement.

'I'm sure you'll have those keys in your hand very soon, Kerra. And thank you for the introduction.'

As I press end call, I notice the time and quickly text Dad.

Morning. I wondered if you had five minutes free to pop over and check out my lovely new office. 😊

Next on my to-do list is to ring Sissy. 'How're you doing this morning?'

'Good, thanks, Kerra. And you?'

'Absolutely fine. I just thought I'd let you know that I won't be around much this week as I'll be setting up my new office and then head down working. If you need anything urgently, call me, as I'll only be picking up my emails at the tail end of the day.'

'Will do, although everything is running well. Saturday was the busiest one so far and James has a full delivery schedule right through until the end of Wednesday.'

'That's great news. I hope you managed to put your feet up yesterday.' I throw that in quite casually.

'Um, actually, I uh... was away for the day, but it was just the tonic I needed.'

'I'm glad to hear it.' Well, judging by the lift in her voice, nothing has gone wrong so I can relax. I knew there had to be a reason Willow was in the kennels for the day. Nettie is Sissy's neighbour, and she looks after Willow when she's working at home. Unfortunately, now she's spending more time helping Dad out, that's an issue for Sissy.

'Right, Dad has just texted me and he's on his way over, so I'll leave you to it. Have a great day, Sissy.'

'Thanks, Kerra, and you!'

Well, she sounds happy this morning and when I open the door to Dad, he has a big smile on his face, too.

'Morning, my lovely. I didn't want to poke my nose in last week when it was all in turmoil. I figured you had enough people traipsing through your garden, but I've been dying to come over and have a look.'

'I've just made a start carrying the boxes down from upstairs. Anyway, let me show you.'

As we step out onto the decking area, Ripley rushes out behind us and takes a running leap up onto the fence. Poor Bertie immediately begins barking as, no doubt, she made him jump and she wasn't alone, there. 'Ripley, leave Bertie alone. Come on, come inside and have some treats.'

I hand Dad the key and pop back to distract Ripley, who is now hissing at Bertie, who starts to howl. Drew calls out, 'Don't worry, Kerra. He's been out for a while, so I'll encourage him to go indoors now.'

'Sorry, Drew. I'll be back and forth with some boxes for a while, but after that hopefully Ripley will sit with me while I'm working. I'll put her nest next to the radiator – that always does the trick.'

'No worries. If you need a hand, just let me know.'

'Thanks. See you later, maybe this evening for a natter if you have time,' I add, as Ripley winds herself around my left ankle. 'Come on then, girl.' I bend to smooth her and that cute little face stares back at me innocently. 'You'd better start being kinder to Bertie, Rippers. It's not nice upsetting him all the time and I might have to think of a way around our little problem.'

Ripley thinks she's a guard dog and is very protective of me, but in Bertie's case he's not an intruder.

Before I can catch up with Dad, he pops back into the cottage.

'I'll give you a hand with those boxes. Ripley is being a bit of a madam, isn't she,' he reflects. She devours her treats as if she hasn't been creating an unnecessary fuss.

'I don't know what to do about it,' I reply, anxiously.

'Why not have a word with Nettie? She's had quite a bit of experience of Bengals from her years working at the vet's.'

'Thanks, Dad, I will. Treloar's did a great job, didn't they?'

'They sure did. And it was good of Ross to sort out those units on Saturday. But don't feel beholden to him. He's made a fair few quid out of the work you've put his way. I'd have come over to give a hand, but it was one of those days when it was either my phone interrupting me, or the online booking service firing questions from potential new customers. Anyway, enough about me. Once your stuff is moved in you won't know yourself. You have a lot going on and more to come, knowing you.' He grins at me. *Oh, Dad, you don't know the half of it, but all in good time.*

'Before we start, I have to ask. How is Alice doing?'

'She got off to work alright. I feel sorry for Ian. Alistair is dead against the two of them being together. But he's not the wayward lad he once was; they all grow up. I believe that everyone deserves a chance to prove themselves. If he messes up, of course, he'll be gone in a blink of the eye.'

Inwardly I sigh. Ross, too, deserves a chance to prove himself and it's crushing that Dad can be so blinkered at times.

'I was horrified to hear that Ian's brother was involved in the stolen car scam.'

Dad's face falls. 'I didn't know. He must be out on bail, then, as I passed him in the car on the way to the wholesaler's on Saturday. That'll be what set Alistair off. It makes more sense now. That's probably why Ian lost his job. No wonder Alice isn't saying much. Still, I'll see how it all works out and Ian's certainly keen to help, although I can only pay him hourly, as I did James.'

'Where was Ian working before?'

'He was a painter and decorator for Newson's. Course, you can't have someone working in people's homes if there are rumours going around.'

'Surely they can't go firing people unless they've been accused of something?' I reply, adamantly.

'They told him they'd had some complaints about his work and he was upset about it. It's a small firm and they can't afford to lose customers, Kerra, even if it's the result of rumours going around. Ian doesn't seem to bear a grudge and I wondered if the job didn't suit him. But now I understand what was behind it. It's a sorry business. Let's get on and shift those boxes. I've left him hosing down the paths, so he'll be good for a while.'

If Dad had any concerns whatsoever, he wouldn't leave the house unattended when Ian's there on his own, because he's no one's fool. I wonder if Mrs Moyle is concerned *for* Ian, not *about* him?

TWELVE
LIFE'S UPS AND DOWNS

'Thanks for coming round, Kerra.' Sy opens the door, welcoming me with a big smile. 'I know I said I wouldn't drag you into the rescue plan for The Happy Hive, but I've come up with a few options and I need a second pair of eyes to check I haven't missed a trick anywhere.'

Tegan hurries in from the kitchen, a tea towel in her hands. 'Hi, Kerra. It's lovely to have you here at last. What do you think of the blinds?'

Standing in the sitting room of The Forge, I see that the log fire is crackling away, and it reminds me of the illicit evenings I spent here with Ross, when I first returned home. A feeling of sadness, of wanting to turn back the clock, washes over me. We had our privacy here, but I can see how happy Tegan and Sy are. It's a fresh start for them with no reminders for Tegan of Pete, everywhere she looks – only in her heart.

'What a difference it makes. And the soft furnishings you've added really make it homely.'

'It's not a bachelor pad anymore, is it?'

I gaze around, noting the floor-to-ceiling bookshelves

either side of the fireplace still stuffed with Ross's treasured collection. But already, with the small touches, Tegan has made it hers and Sy's.

'No. Have you done anything to the kitchen?' I ask, sounding upbeat and pushing away my own memories. It was here my life changed forever. From remembering the teenage crush I had on Ross, to discovering that the feelings we were never able to share at the time, were still there.

'Come on through and see for yourself. I brought my collection of vintage Cornish ware. I didn't want to risk leaving it at the house as the couple renting it have a dog. But I think it makes the kitchen, now.'

As I follow her through, I see that it does. The huge dresser I so admired, on which Ross had a few interesting pieces of china, has now been transformed. It's a collection fit for an old farmhouse and who doesn't love the traditional blue and creamy-white striped pottery.

The table has a cloth over it now as they did in Grandma's day and the white blind at the window has rows of blue and white striped fish in the exact same colour as the pottery.

'How clever. I love that blind. It's such fun, Tegan, and I'm so envious of your pottery. I remember it so well from my childhood. I bet there's some stored up in the loft at Pedrevan. If I come across any pieces, I'll put them to one side for you.'

'Ah, thank you, Kerra. Please take a seat. The food is almost ready. We can have a leisurely meal before the two of you sit in front of the computer, can't we?' She appeals to Sy.

'Of course! It's the least Kerra deserves for coming to my aid. And, besides, you want a word with her, don't you?'

The look they exchange is one of collusion.

'What are you two plotting?' I ask, as I take a seat.

'We'll discuss that a bit later.' She laughs.

Tegan has made a real effort to make the table look lovely. She collects crystal glasses, too, and the tall wine goblets have been polished until they gleam. Sy begins lighting a line of white candles in pretty glass pots and in between Tegan has threaded some tendrils of fresh ivy.

As I watch them both working together, pulling dishes out of the oven and plating up the food, I have never seen either of them as happy as they are right now. I was upset when Ross sprung it on me that he was moving back to Treylya. This was where we experienced many firsts, including spending our first night together. Now I understand that he wasn't moving back because he was hankering after his old life; it was a sacrifice. Here he could escape prying eyes, but at Treylya he's closer to me.

* * *

'They can't have it both ways, Sy. You're trying to achieve the impossible. There is a limit beyond which members feel they are being spammed with too much advertising and I think they're being greedy.'

Sy looks dejected. 'We're in agreement there. But it's not what they want to hear. So how do I get around it?'

'Honestly? I know this isn't what you're going to expect me to say, but on the free service I'd offer the choice of paying a small monthly premium to opt out of all advertising. Both online and email notifications of offers from their partners. The free community scheme never was intended to make money. That came from the subscription part of the website. People aren't fools and there's a limit to how much pop-up, sidebar, and email spam they will contend with, even for free. I wouldn't use the website now as it stands.'

It's the truth and I can see that Sy agrees with me but was hoping I'd come up with another option he hadn't considered.

'You've been thorough in your appraisal, Sy, but the truth is that free can't mean alienating people by flooding them with unwanted information, even if they're cleverly building individual user profiles to make it as relevant as possible. I'm of the opinion that in general people are turned off by click-bait advertising and find it annoying. Well, certainly the type of people who signed up for the community-based, free exchange of services side of the website. If they don't want to provide that to their customers, then why don't they close that part down?'

'And let someone else pick it up and run with it?' Sy recognises that the big tech companies run everything and having sold out to one of them, they've now proven it's all a means to a predictable end. It's all about the profit and if they think they can squeeze a pound out of something, they won't give up. Where's the pride in customer satisfaction?

'I see it all differently now, Sy. Big business and community are poles apart and maybe the two never can meet in the middle for a common purpose, even as a token gesture. They were clever, saying the things I wanted to hear that would allow me to let go. It was a valuable, if galling lesson.'

'Which is?'

'Big business isn't trustworthy. If you're putting your heart into something, then it's the small set-ups that make a difference. Real people, not the fat-cat CEOs and shareholders who don't give a damn, as long as they receive their dividends.'

Sy looks at me, surprised at my reaction.

'My baby is long gone, Sy. But I have no regrets. The subscription side of The Happy Hive would still be in profit if they hadn't hiked up the prices overnight to a level that was unjustifiable. It was a big mistake, and they need to rethink what they've done. Give them a couple of options, ignore my suggestion if you're not comfortable presenting it and walk away with a cheque in your hand. Then get back to what you love doing, and that's working alongside Tegan to build your future together.'

It isn't until the end of the evening, as I ease on my coat and am about to take my leave, that Tegan pipes up.

'We're going to tie the knot, Kerra. It will be a registry office wedding with no fuss, but we do need two witnesses. We'd love it if you and Ross would do the honours for us. Once we fix a date, we thought we'd invite you both over to ask you properly, but I'm so excited that I just had to share it with you now.'

It's wonderful news and Tegan is glowing.

'Of course, and congratulations, guys!' I reply, feeling overwhelmed as we do a group hug.

I'm tearful and I can't hide it. My two best friends. Even in my wildest imaginings when I brought them together this wasn't the outcome I was expecting. I thought Sy would simply help to get Tegan's business back on track and then he'd head home to London.

'It would appear that I'm joining the green welly brigade for good,' Sy comments. 'And now Tegan wants to get a dog. I mean, you know what I'm like with animals, Kerra,' he moans.

'A dog? How lovely,' I reply and Tegan and I start laughing. Sy is one city lover who intends to fight the transition every step of the way, but deep down inside he knows it's a losing battle. The heart always wins, even when the head hasn't quite caught up.

* * *

'Kerra, sorry it's late but it's been a hectic day.'

'Aren't you working tonight, Polly?'

'Yes. I'm on a break and I've popped outside just to fill you in on what happened today.' She sounds excited. 'I was so nervous making that call, but Oliver just jumped straight in and outlined what he felt his clients were looking for. You would have been so proud of me, Kerra. I took a deep breath and said I was sure I could deliver to a pre-agreed timescale and budget. He's going to take me to see one of his clients tomorrow morning, to talk through my ideas.'

She's almost breathless when she finishes speaking and I imagine her standing in the car park, in the cold, and not even noticing the chill in the air.

'That's an amazing result, Polly. I'm delighted for you.'

'My head is reeling, and it's so hard not to let on to Dad, but it would only unsettle him. I can fit this in around working at the pub as it's not like we're talking about a whole flood of work. Oliver says it's a service they offer in London, but it's on a different scale here. He'd been into the pub for a drink one evening last week and was impressed when I told him that I'd hand-painted all the furniture and organised a small team to do the decorating. I'll take my portfolio with me tomorrow, to show his client. I have photographs of every little job I've done so far. I know the pub is the biggest project I've tackled to date, but it wasn't the easiest of jobs.'

'It's enough to showcase your talent, though, Polly. I'll be thinking of you tomorrow. If you're passing and you have time to pop in for coffee after your meeting, please do. I'm excited for you.'

'All I can say is thank you so much. It would be nice to do something for *me*, for a change. I don't begrudge working for Dad, but every day is the same and I feel like I'm stagnating.

At least if I have a little project on the go it'll keep my brain occupied.' She laughs.

'Creativity is a blessing, but it can also be frustrating if you have to stifle it.'

'I knew you'd understand. Right, best get back to pulling pints, then. Night, Kerra, and hopefully see you tomorrow if I'm back well before opening at lunchtime.'

As I'm about to put the phone down on the bed next to me, it kicks into life again and this time it's Ross.

'Ah, you're off the phone, at last,' he says, and the next thing I hear is a huge yawn. 'I was worried I'd fall asleep before I could say goodnight.'

'Polly rang; she wasn't on long. You sound shattered.'

'It was a productive, albeit it a hard day, and then shortly after I arrived home my father rang. We disagree more than we agree, these days, and every conversation is a slog. He's lost touch with what's happening, and he accused me of not keeping him up to date with what's going on.' The frustration in his voice is tangible.

'That's unreasonable, Ross – we both know that. Is he still talking about setting up a second office?'

'I don't even listen now when he goes off in that direction. I've explained why it's not a good idea and I just switch off. Whatever I say, he counters but the nitpicking is grating on the nerves. Year on year our profit continues to grow because I keep a good handle on the number of guys we employ and the number of jobs we take on. He doesn't appreciate there's a tipping point and if you get it wrong things start to fall apart.'

'Ah, I wish I was there to just wrap my arms around you. I hate to hear you sounding dejected when you work so hard.'

'Just ignore me, I'll get over it. How was your day?'

'Good. My guest bedroom is now devoid of all office paraphernalia and it's just the internet to sort out now. Hopefully, that will happen tomorrow afternoon. I had dinner with Tegan and Sy, at The Forge earlier on. They've really settled in; it looks cosy and they're so happy to be there.'

'I'm glad. Tegan's house is nice but there are too many memories there. That invitation was a bit out of the blue, wasn't it?'

'Yes. Sy wanted me to look over the report he's produced on The Happy Hive. Well, the not so happy hive now. It's the same old problem that's rife today. Too many ads, spiralling subscription charges for a service where people can't see any real benefit in return. Hopefully, he's charging them an exorbitant hourly rate for the work he's doing, so it's not all bad.'

'And you don't sound upset. I wondered if you might be.'

'Not now. I don't believe in looking back. It was in excellent shape when I handed it over, so any damage is of their own making. Besides, my future is about to kick off and there are so many options, it's exciting.' There's another huge yawn down the line. 'Now put down the phone and get some sleep. Tomorrow is another day and hopefully your father won't ring again for a while.'

'I miss you. Wish you were here.'

Ripley is lying across both my feet and she lets out the loudest miaow as if she's saying goodnight, too.

'Did you hear Ripley?'

He laughs. 'I suspect anyone walking past the cottage would have heard her, too. Goodnight, Ripley. Look after my lady for me. Sleep well, Kerra. Love you.'

Aww. As the line disconnects that warm little bubble that was hovering around me instantly disappears.

'You miss him, too, don't you, girl? One day he'll be here with us and we'll forget about all the dark, lonely nights.' I reach out to smooth her back and she begins to purr. I don't know what I'd do without her to keep me company. She might wake me up in the small hours because she hates using the cat flap if I'm around, but it's a small price to pay.

'Let's get some sleep. It's been quite a day.'

THIRTEEN
IT'S ALL GO!

The irony is that this morning I'm working from my kitchen table as our local telecoms engineer, Sienna's husband Logan, won't be here until after lunch to connect up the hardwiring. I spend a little time on the phone talking to Arthur, getting a feel for what features he thinks would be most useful for the community link-up.

'You make it sound like it's my system, Kerra,' he remarks, cautiously. 'I'm no brain when it comes to IT stuff.'

'But you are good at being the point of contact, Arthur. In essence you're already running a network, and your phone is the communication system. All we are doing is replacing that with something much easier for everyone to access, for you to control, and to help you receive information in a timely fashion. But it will also be nice to incorporate some fun elements.'

'Puttin' it like that, Kerra, it makes sense. I'm pretty quick at pickin' things up, if I do say so myself. If I think of anythin' else, I'll email you. Off the top of me head, exchangin' recipes is one idea for a... what you do call it?' It's great to hear

Arthur's enthusiasm as I did wonder whether he'd find it a little daunting.

'A message board. There will be a link on the website that will take members straight to it and anyone can post there. I'll call in towards the end of the week and show you how it's shaping up, but I'll ring first to check when it's convenient for you.'

'Oh, don't bother about that. Just pop in whenever you're ready. It's not like I'm going anywhere, is it?' He laughs, good-naturedly.

When I settle back down to work, it's all about making the website visually attractive as I already have the bare bones in place. I want it to look professional as well as being easy to navigate. If I get a chance a bit later, I'll pop out and take a few photos in and around the village to brighten up some of the pages. I want everyone to feel that this belongs to them, even though Arthur's in control.

It's like the old days for me when I first set up The Happy Hive, before the idea exploded beyond all recognition. But the basic principle is similar, just on a much smaller scale. It's nice to be able to do something useful and if there are any problems Arthur knows I'm always around to sort them out.

Suddenly there's a loud *bonk* sound overhead and I see that Ripley has just jumped off the bed and is now racing downstairs. *Ding dong.*

Checking my watch, I hope it's Polly and when I swing open the door, she's standing there pink-cheeked and smiling. And looking incredibly smart, wearing a trouser suit and with a briefcase in her hand.

'I did it. I have my first job for one of Oliver's clients!' she discloses, happily.

'Well done, you. Come on in.'

Ripley suddenly rushes out through the open door, almost toppling me as I try to avoid standing on her. 'Ripley, slow down,' I call after her, but she ignores me. At least she doesn't head for the gate, but instead disappears under the big hedge to the side of the cottage.

'Take a seat. Do you have time for coffee?'

'No, sadly. I can't stay long. I just wanted you to know that Oliver was pleased and any future contacts he passes on to me I'll be handling myself.'

'That is good news. Take a seat – just push those papers to one side. And you're happy with the terms Oliver laid out to you?' Polly isn't totally new to business as she's in charge of the admin for The Lark and Lantern, but it's best to check.

'Yes. I'm happy with the cut the company is taking. The only problem I have is that I don't have a company name, or a logo. I'm going to set up a new email address and I'll need that for the sign-off and for invoicing et cetera. It won't take long to register and get the tax side of things in place, then I'll sort out a system for keeping records. I want to keep it simple to begin with, though, and see how it develops.'

'That's very sensible. There's no point in taking something on if it isn't possible to make a decent profit. If you like, I can design a logo for you if you come up with the name. I dabble with graphics all the time when I'm working with websites and it's easy enough to do.'

'Oh, Kerra. I wasn't hinting, really I wasn't.' Polly looks embarrassed.

'Seriously, it's a quick job for me. So, what are you going to call your new business?'

'Hmm... I was thinking of *Designed to Sell*?'

'Perfect! I'll come up with some suggestions. What colour scheme would you like?'

Polly stares at me blankly. 'What do you think will work?'

'Let me have a play around and then I'll put together a couple of options for you to look at. I'll send those across this evening.'

'Oh... but you look busy. Don't drop everything for me.'

'I love playing around with things like this; it's fun. Besides, I'm only twiddling around with this little project I'm working on, while I wait for Logan Williams to install my internet connection in the office. Working off the table isn't ergonomically correct, and I'll suffer for it if I sit in the same position for too long. It's easier to do bits and pieces, rather than get stuck into something too intense.'

'It's very kind of you, Kerra. This first job is exciting, but it will be a bit of a test, I will admit. I want all my dealings with Oliver to be as professional as possible, given the opportunity this presents.'

'What's the first project?'

'It's a two-bed, mid-terrace not far from the Polreweek town centre. The owner inherited the property recently when his uncle died. It's shabby inside, but the building is sound. It needs redecorating right through, which means finding someone to work with me. We agreed a reasonable budget to furnish it out afterwards, as it's going to be a holiday let. The location is good, being central, and it should be a nice little investment.'

'Who did you use when you did the work in the pub?'

'One of Ross's guys and two friends from college. We all rolled up our sleeves and did night shifts. Dad wouldn't shut the pub, obviously, so it meant clearing up after every stint and leaving it tidy for the next day. At least with this property there are no restrictions.'

'If you're looking for someone local, how about Ian

Adams? He worked for Newson's as a painter/decorator. Alice and Ian are staying with Dad for a while. It might not be long, but I have a feeling it will be a couple of weeks at least.'

Polly grins at me. 'I had heard on the grapevine. It can't help things between Eddie and your Uncle Alistair,' Polly replies, grimly.

'I know. And I had high hopes at one point that Dad would find someone to run the kennels for him, so he could get back to doing what he loves and that's working with wood.'

'Do you mean Nettie?'

It's nice to have someone to talk to about this, and Polly knows Nettie well.

'Yes. At first, I thought she disappeared after Mum died because she and Dad had fallen out, but Nettie says he pushed everyone away for a while, and that included her. When she offered to help Dad, I thought it was because she's interested in getting more involved now she's given up her part-time job at the vet's. But, sadly, that's not the case.'

'It's wonderful when a hobby turns into a career and that seems likely for Nettie if she gives it her all. I know how good it feels when things begin to take off. You have to go for it, or risk looking back and wondering *what if?* But I do feel sorry for your dad. He wants to keep your mum's dream alive.'

'I know. Ian seems to enjoy walking the dogs, but he can't survive on a couple of hours' work each day. And if the house you're working on is empty...' I pause, thinking of a delicate way of putting this without sounding like I think there's a question mark hanging over his head. 'Then Ian wouldn't feel uncomfortable about being there on his own if you're at the pub.'

Her eyes light up. 'That could be the perfect solution, at least for this first job. Anyway, I'd better get going. I slipped out without Dad seeing me but getting back in isn't going to be quite so easy. I'm going to leave my jacket and briefcase in the boot of the car and throw on a thick jumper to put him off the scent. If I can prove it's possible for me to take jobs on the side and keep Dad happy, then he won't get upset.'

As we walk towards the door, I give Polly an empathetic glance. 'Your free time is just that, Polly. And what you do with it, is entirely up to you. But if you need any help you can always call on me in an emergency – you know that.' She gives me an affirming nod of her head. 'And I'm a dab hand at sanding and painting furniture,' I add.

'Oh, I'm so excited and now I have to calm myself down and get a grip. Pub lunches don't serve themselves and if I don't wipe this self-satisfied little grin off my face the customers will wonder what's going on.'

* * *

'Hi, Logan. Coffee and cake?'

He rolls his eyes. 'If you insist... that's why I like coming back here.' He grins at me.

'Wow, that's a nice-looking office you have there,' he comments, as he walks towards the wall of glass doors. 'Treloar's do the business, alright. A kit, wasn't it? I overheard someone talking about it when I was standing in line at Pascoe's bakery the other day.'

'Yes. So, who was talking about me, then?' I rattle around with the mugs and spoons, feigning interest, but I am somewhat curious.

'Oh, they weren't talking about you, but Ross. It was old Zacky Carter. You know what he's like. Thinks he's the official village news. Ross is back at Treylya, then.'

It's hard not to sigh, thinking about how quickly word gets around.

'He is, until it's sold. Or so I hear,' I reply, laughing. The last thing I want is for Logan to suspect something is going on between me and Ross, as he'd tell Sienna, who might mention it to Sissy and even James.

Sometimes people aren't gossiping; they regard information as news. Zacky is retired and as he's on his own, for him there's a social aspect to being in the know. He also props up the bar down at The Lark and Lantern most evenings and that means word spreads quickly.

Zacky gets many a free pint put in front of him, because sometimes people have something to gain from the snippets he shares. I'm not saying that's always a bad thing if someone is looking for a job, for instance, and keeping their ear to the ground. But on occasion it can get personal. Disputes between individuals in the village and the surrounding area can go back generations. Personally, I'd be worried about bad karma, but when you've also been on the receiving end, it's only natural that it will give you a slightly different perspective.

As I slice up one of Mrs Moyle's fruit cakes and invite Logan to dive in, he does so without hesitation.

'Can we walk and talk as I eat? As I've already installed the Cat 5 ethernet cables, it's only a matter of fixing the outlet to the wall and drilling a hole to connect it. I can only really book an hour slot and my last job for the day is a new install, so time is tight I'm afraid.'

'Of course. I'll bring the coffees.'

We set off down the garden as Logan looks around, impressed.

'Last time I was here it was still a tiny little cottage and now look at it. Everyone is talking about what you and Drew have been up to, Kerra. It's the most excitement Penvennan village has seen since the big bust-up when your dad and mum applied for change of use to set up the kennels.'

I groan out loud. 'Don't remind me.'

'I am surprised you went with Treloar's to do your building work. They're the best, obviously, but given how your dad and Ross's dad never saw eye to eye, I thought you'd put your foot down.'

This is awkward. 'Well, Drew had everything all set up to push ahead with his extension. If I hadn't fallen in line with the plan it could have delayed it by six months.'

'Oh, right. That makes sense. And Ross is his own man, which is a quality I respect. Things looked up for that business once Jago and Harriet retired to Spain. The danger with constantly telling everyone you're better than them is that there comes a point when they step back and see it for what it is – repaying favours.'

I'm shocked to hear Logan say that. Is that the real reason why Ross's parents left and not the scandal surrounding Bailey and Ross's divorce? I wasn't living here at the time, but from what he's told me it was humiliating. Bailey was a woman with expensive tastes, and she ran up a lot of debt on his credit cards. If that wasn't bad enough, she had an affair with a local guy before leaving Ross.

I hold out the tray and Logan grabs the key to unlock the doors. 'This is very smart. My kids would love this – it would be their ultimate dream playhouse.'

'How long will it take to get everything up and running?' I ask, eager to get on with designing Polly's new logo.

Logan finishes off his cake and looks around for the point at which the electric cable enters the building. 'I'll need to take off this cover, as the cable is no doubt looped up and waiting for me to connect it. If I put the new face plate for the hard-wired cable alongside, you'll be up and running in no time.'

Ross's electrician situated it next to the desk and I've no plans to move things around. 'Sounds good to me. I'm glad you talked me into having it hard-wired, as opposed to a Wi-Fi connection.'

'In my opinion, even with a good booster, it's too far away from the cottage. You need something that transfers data at high speeds and also has the greatest bandwidth. With this Cat 5 ethernet cable and the package you have, you won't get any problems. And if you do, just give me a call, even if it's outside of normal working hours. You sorted out Sienna by recommending her to Sissy, and we're both grateful. My wife is full of ideas and she won't let Sissy down.'

'I know, Logan. And together with James, the three of them make a great team.'

'You don't hang around, Kerra, do you? It's refreshing, but for some people it's bewildering.'

That's an odd thing for Logan to say.

'If you hear anything you think I should be aware of, Logan, would you let me know?'

'Most of it goes over my head, Kerra, but as you've asked, I'll keep my ears open. Some folk don't feel easy around change, and that's the problem. But if things stand still, they eventually grind to a halt. When I think of what my job was like when I started my training and now it's hard to keep up with all the updates and upgrades. That's life now as we know it and if you can't keep up then you lag behind and everything seems bewildering.'

I decide to leave Logan to it as he's limited for time and I walk back with my mug in one hand and the tray in the other. There's a lesson to be learnt from Logan. If I worry about every little thing, then my life will become unbearable. If I let it go over my head, most things are a short-lived distraction and something else soon pops up to divert people's attention. For now, at least, Ross and I have a secret that isn't common knowledge and there's no reason to believe that will change. But I will be keeping an eye on old Zacky Carter. As Granddad would have said of idle gossip: 'T'aint right, t'aint fair, t'aint proper,' and he was spot on.

FOURTEEN

THEY SAY EVERYTHING HAPPENS FOR A REASON...

I work on Polly's new logo late into the night. Even Ripley gives up on me and pads quietly up to bed, having already accepted that when I'm focused on something, nothing can distract me.

This morning, looking at the two options with fresh eyes, I like both of them but for different reasons. The first one is a white feather on a turquoise background and the words *Designed to Sell* in a graceful, handwritten font hover above it. It's very Polly, is all I can say. The second one is a single block of lime green, with the company name etched into it in white. Along the bottom is a row of leaves to soften the effect and it stands out even when I reduce it to a small icon. It's time to get Polly's reaction.

Hi, Polly

I've attached two mock-ups. The colours can easily be changed if either of these ideas grab you.

Interestingly, when I did a search about white feathers, in a dream it represents a new start. I thought that might be a good omen. The vibrant green works well on the other one but let me know what you think.

Kerra x

I'm clock-watching and I think it's time I made a move. Dad and Ian will be walking the dogs now and if I nip over to the kennels I'm hoping that Nettie will be there, probably waiting to make the breakfast for them all.

Even with my thick padded coat, this morning's chill makes me shiver as I hurry across the road. Sure enough, Nettie is sweeping out one of the kennels.

'Morning, Nettie. The temperature certainly dropped last night. How are you doing?'

'Good, thanks, Kerra. Your dad and Ian have only just headed off for the first walk of the day. I thought I'd encourage them to *bond*.' She leans in, lowering her voice. 'Alice is getting ready for work and I thought I'd give her a little space.'

'And how is it going?' I ask, keeping my voice low.

Nettie comes closer. 'I feel sorry for the two of them, I will be honest. But it's not my place to express an opinion, of course. Eddie is protective of Alice, but you know that. Alistair has always been hard on the girl for some reason I can't fathom. As for Ian, I don't know him well. He's been as good as gold so far. And he has no problem getting up early.'

'Let's hope Dad takes to him, then, as Uncle Alistair isn't going to welcome Alice back if they're still together. Anyway, the reason I've popped in to see you is that I wondered if you had any tips on working with animals who have a problem socialising.'

'Socialising? Do you mean Ripley terrorising poor little Bertie?' Nettie has no problem speaking out when the occasion warrants it.

'Precisely. Poor Drew – it's getting ridiculous. If he lets Bertie out, he's fine until Ripley appears. And now Bertie has started howling, as he hates being hissed at. Drew is constantly being pulled away from his work and I must try to do something about it.'

Nettie leans on the end of the broom, shaking her head. 'It's a clash of personalities, Kerra. If you like, I'll do some research and come up with a suggestion, or two. There are no guarantees in a situation like this even if you get in a professional as a last resort. Bertie and Ripley don't live in the same house, for one, so their contact is fleeting. The other negative is that Bengals are best trained when they are young, and Ripley was the centre of attention for her first few years. She regards both Drew's home, and yours, as her territory.'

'Do you think it's worth a shot, or should I simply extend the height of the fence so she can't jump up and threaten Bertie?'

Nettie mulls it over. 'I think that's like accepting defeat before you've even had a go at solving the problem. They're both such delightful characters and it's a real shame that Ripley won't give Bertie a chance. I'll pop round one evening to have a chat with you and Drew. I'm sure I can come up with a few ideas to start you off.'

'That would be amazing, Nettie. Having literally stolen Ripley from Drew, I feel awful that poor Bertie is now driving Drew mad. And it's not Bertie's fault, at all; it's Ripley taunting him.'

'Animals sense stress in their owners, so stay calm and I'll give you a call very soon.'

'Thank you so much. I'd best get back.' I lower my voice. 'I'm avoiding Alice. I want to stay neutral as at least then Uncle Alistair has someone he can talk to.'

Nettie nods her head in total agreement. 'I'm with you on that one. I'm staying out of it, too. Hopefully, things will quickly settle down and at least Eddie is grateful to have another pair of hands.'

I lean in to give Nettie a hug. She's so good for Dad and he values her opinion. 'I'll leave it until you get in touch before I speak to Drew. I don't want to get his hopes up just yet.'

As I hurry back to the cottage my phone pings and it's a text from Sissy.

Are you up? I'm at the unit and the internet is down. In a bit of a panic.

I immediately dial her number.

'Hi, Sissy. Was it working when you first arrived?'

'Yes, but it's been timing out a fair bit recently. To the point where I can't even process an order now.'

That's not good. 'I'll jump in the car and come take a look. See you soon and get the kettle on. It's freezing this morning.'

'Will do. And I have biscuits.'

I head inside to grab a long coil of ethernet cable and in less than fifteen minutes I'm tapping on the front door of The Design Cave. It's just after 8 a.m. and I can see by the look on Sissy's face as she walks towards me that she's stressed.

'Thanks for coming. I've switched the router off and on several times, and just when it seems to be working again everything freezes. It's driving me crazy. I have a whole stack of orders to process and at this rate they'll never get done!' I've never seen Sissy so exasperated.

'The point of sale has its own internet connection, doesn't it?'

'Yes. It's hard-wired and that's not been affected at all, thankfully.'

I waggle the cable in front of her. 'I'm hoping that this will do the trick, then. You make the coffee, while I take a quick look. If I can't spot anything obvious, we'll run this lead straight from the modem. If we can at least get you up and running, we can put in a call to get Logan out as soon as possible.'

'It's been gradually getting worse over the last week, or so, but nothing like it is this morning,' she acknowledges.

While Sissy makes the coffee, I slip off my coat and sit down in front of her computer. After switching it off, waiting several minutes and then turning it back on everything loads up reasonably quickly. However, the minute I click to open the invoicing software, that ominous little circle dominates the screen. It won't let me save, or exit. I end up doing a forced quit. It's the same when I try to open a document, so it's not just a glitch in one of the programmes.

'Do you think it's the PC?' Sissy enquires, carrying two mugs over and sitting down next to me.

'I don't think so, as it fired up okay. Let's plug in the ethernet cable. Where's the router?'

Glancing around, Sissy takes the other end from my hand and walks over to one of the kitchen base units, opening the door. She stoops to plug it in. 'It just goes in the back, does it?' she calls over her shoulder.

'Yes. Why is it in the cupboard?'

'The guy who installed it said it was better in there in case it got knocked over.'

I guess he had a point. The room is large and aside from

the tiny kitchen area in the corner, there's nowhere to put it where it would be protected and that was bad planning on our part.

'I doubt Logan would have condoned that, but I'll give him a call. We need to get the line checked out as a starting point, but it might be a case of replacing the modem. We really must divide this room up, Sissy, as you can't go on managing like this. You need a bespoke office away from distractions and where you won't get interrupted.'

I give her a thumbs up as we're back online and start typing in the details from the first order on the pile.

'Well, that did the trick for now. Shall I get Ross to call in and give us a price for dividing the room into two?'

Sissy hesitates. 'I can manage for a while longer, Kerra. It's not a pressing issue.'

'Hmm... but it makes sense to get it sorted sooner rather than later, Sissy. That cable is a health and safety issue, so let's push the table back against the wall and tape the wire to run around the side of the kitchen unit. Just make sure no one tries to jam the door shut on it or it might sever the wire.'

'I don't like to think of spending more money right now,' she replies, hesitantly.

'If we're going to call in Logan anyway, it's the perfect time to get him to relocate the modem. It's up to you, but I'd suggest putting it in the far corner for now. I'll ask Ross to call in to price up the job, too. Just decide where you want the partition wall and he'll take it from there. This table will be too big for the smaller rest room area, but it's much too nice to use in this setting.'

She grins at me. 'I'll strip it down properly and wax it. Someone with a big farmhouse kitchen will jump at it. I suppose I'd better look for a bit of office equipment and a small table, then.'

'You might want to move the printer in here, too, once it's all done.'

Sissy is beginning to warm to the idea. 'The orders keep rolling in, don't they?' she acknowledges, as if she's reassuring herself that she's no longer managing on a shoestring budget. 'Oh... um... while you're here... Polly called in yesterday afternoon and was looking around. We got chatting and I think she's going to place an order. She didn't say it was for the pub, but I'm assuming it is. I know you two are great friends and she wouldn't ask, but do you want me to offer her a discount?'

Ah, how thoughtful. 'It's entirely up to you, Sissy, but that would be most kind. Polly has been so supportive since I've been back and that's the sign of a true friend.'

I can see that Sissy is pleased by my response, but it really is entirely up to her. 'Well, I'm glad I mentioned it. She puts up with a lot, does Polly. It can't have been easy not having a mother around and pub life isn't the best. When you live above the business there's no getting away from it, is there?'

Obviously, Polly didn't divulge why she was browsing, but Sissy isn't the sort to poke her nose into someone else's business, anyway.

'I saw some beautiful roman blinds the other day. One of them was in blue and white, which reminded me of the old Cornish ware.'

'That would be Tegan, then,' Sissy informs me, with some satisfaction and I chuckle to myself.

'Funnily enough when I visited The Forge I did wonder where she bought them, but I didn't like to ask. I should have known. Quality counts and you only source the best, Sissy.'

* * *

'I know you're busy, but I've just exchanged on Gwel Teg and we complete on Monday. I'm so excited and I just had to tell you!'

'That's great news, Kerra. Is this advance warning that you'll be needing some work done on it?' Ross replies, teasingly.

'It's quite tidy but I'll probably do a little updating before I rent it out. I know it's silly, but having inherited Pedrevan, being able to buy one of the old fishermen's cottages is a big deal for me.'

'But it's not the first property you've bought,' he points out.

'I know, but that's an apartment and it's not here, in Penvennan. When I was a child I'd wistfully imagine growing up and living in one of them. Ironically, it doesn't look down over the cove, but it looks across at the bay and the headland.'

'And when you're having some fun getting it ready you can stand in the front bedroom and wave up at Treylya,' he retorts.

'Stop laughing at me. I forget to mention that my London tenant, Mr Hornby-Smythe, has made an offer for the apartment. We're just agreeing a price for the furniture. It's the end of one era and the beginning of a new one.'

'Hmm... is that a tinge of regret I hear in your voice?' Ross enquires, tentatively.

'No. The profit I make will more than cover the cost of buying Gwel Teg, so I'm happy.'

'That's a handsome profit and it's nice when a childhood dream comes true, even if you aren't going to live there. I'm happy that you're happy. It means you really are putting down roots again.'

Ross is obviously on site, because he's now puffing a little as he walks, and I hear someone in the background calling to him. 'I must go, but I can't wait to see you tomorrow night.' There's a slight pause and muffled words. 'Speak later.' He disconnects abruptly and that momentary happiness begins to fade.

If only it wasn't just an evening of painting at the village hall he was looking forward to, but it's better than nothing; even though Dad will be around and we'll have to be on our best behaviour.

After sliding my laptop into the computer bag and zipping it up, I pull on my coat. It's time to give Arthur a sneak preview of the new website and having added a photo I took from the top of the hill leading down to the cove as a header, I'm pleased with it.

My phone pings and it's a text from Polly.

I LOVE the feather... it's perfect as it is. Virtual hug from me!
😊

Delighted you like it. I'll send over a hi-res version a bit later as I'm on my way out. If you need help with anything else, just shout! x

Miaow, miaow, miaoooooow. Ripley appears at the foot of the stairs as I sling the computer bag over my shoulder and go to give her a head rub.

'You've got fresh food and biscuits. When I get back I'll find you some treats and very soon Nettie is going to come and see you, Ripley. Won't that be nice,' I inform her as she stares up at me, unblinking. 'It's about time you made friends with Bertie.'

She makes no attempt to follow me out the door when I leave, and I suspect she'll have a quick bite of food and then head straight back to bed.

I hear Rufus's unmistakable bark as he spots me from the other side of the road. 'Hi, Ian,' I call out, as he stops to adjust the lead.

When the road is clear I hurry across to make a fuss of Rufus as he bounds about, excitedly. 'Is this an extra walk to get rid of some of that energy?'

'Yes. He's only back for the day as his owner has a hospital appointment. We're off to the cove for a change,' Ian replies, quite casually.

'I'm heading for the shop, but now I'm sorely tempted to join you. Rufus has long been a favourite of mine, but don't tell Dad as he says that all his charges should be treated the same way.'

Ian looks uncomfortable. 'Oh, well, I... we... probably won't be gone long. Eddie wants me to fix the gate as one of the hinges is loose.'

Hmm, how coincidental, as at this time of the day Polly is still off duty as the pub will have stopped serving lunch. I wonder if she has approached him about working with her and their paths will cross so they can walk and talk as they stroll along the beach. It's hard to suppress a wicked little grin.

'Oh, you'll have a go at anything, then?' I remark as Rufus continues to strain on his lead, and we fall in alongside each other.

'Can't afford not to, Kerra, is the truth of the matter.'

'Well, have fun down at the cove.' I stop as we draw level with the shop doorway and reach over to give Rufus's ear a ruffle. He's so engaging, but a real handful.

'We will and enjoy the rest of your day, Kerra.'

Ian's parting smile is one of relief and I feel bad that I unwittingly said the wrong thing, but I am envious as Rufus is such fun to take for a walk.

We part and as I'm about to reach out to push the door open, it unexpectedly flies back. I stand aside to let two men step out. One of them is Zacky Carter. They're deep in conversation, but he tilts his head in my direction, in acknowledgement. The last thing I need is to stand around chatting, as although Zacky is entertaining to talk to, I've always given him a wide berth. Mum always made time for him after his wife died and he's been on his own ever since, but he's a gatherer of information and I'm wary of him.

Heading inside, Mrs Moyle looks up and gives me a huge smile. 'Well, you were just being asked after and whether all the work on the cottage is done now. I said I had no idea, and they should ask you, but I see neither of them stopped for a chat.'

I grimace. 'And that suits me fine. But, yes, all the work is now completed, and I'm delighted with it, so please feel free to pass that on. I'd happily recommend Treloar's to anyone thinking of having work done.'

'You look it. What can I do for you, Kerra? Ripley's salmon treats are out of stock again and I'll get Arthur to let you know when they're back in.'

'It's Arthur I've come to see, actually. I want to show him the new website.'

'Oh, how exciting! He did say you'd be popping over sometime. Go on up. I heard his footsteps overhead a minute a go, so I suspect he's just made himself a cup of tea.'

'See you in a bit.' I make my way around the counter and out into the corridor linking to the back stairs, which lead up to the flat. I'm sure the creaking treads are enough to alert

Arthur of my presence, but when I stop at the doorway to the sitting room his chair is empty, and his sticks are hanging on the back. I turned around, slightly confused, to see Arthur standing in front of me with a mug in his hand and his jaw hanging.

'Um... well... right. Best come in and sit down, Kerra.'

I'm frozen to the spot and Arthur's expression is grim as he passes me. I hurry in through the doorway and busy myself slipping off the computer bag and my coat, but it's obvious Arthur has no problem whatsoever walking between the kitchen and this room while carrying a scalding-hot drink.

'Would... uh... you like one?' he asks, as he takes his seat and when his eyes meet mine, it's obvious he's embarrassed. No, it's more than that, he's mortified.

'I'm fine thank you, Arthur.' I'm trying to pretend nothing unusual has happened, but I'm a little bewildered to say the least.

'Would you mind shuttin' the door before you take a seat, Kerra? I expect you're wondering what's going on.'

I do as he requests and wander back to sit in the chair alongside him. 'Look, Arthur, I'm sorry if I surprised you,' I apologise. I don't quite know what else to say. 'You don't have to explain anything to me.'

He bows his head for a moment, his hands firmly clasped around the mug balanced on his knee. 'I don't always need the sticks, you see. Today happens to be a good one.'

I was shocked because Mrs Moyle herself told me that Arthur is unable to walk anywhere without aid, but it's really none of my business.

'And that's a blessing, Arthur,' I reply, reassuringly, before changing the subject. 'I've come to show you a preview of the Penvennan Community Link-Up. If I run through the various tabs, pages and links with you, I can make a list of things you'd liked amended and anything that you'd like added.' I'm waffling on a bit, but I can see he's relieved.

'I will just go and make myself a mug of tea if you don't mind. I won't be a moment.'

Making a quick exit, I don't know who is in greater need of a moment to pull themselves together, me or Arthur. He reacted as if I'd caught him doing something wrong and I don't know what to make of that. I'm going to make the tea and walk back in as if nothing out of the ordinary has happened. The thing I can't get out of my head is that this could be signalling an improvement in his condition. I would have expected that to have been the first thing Mrs Moyle said as I stepped through the door. He lives on painkillers, she told me once, and he's often awake during the small hours of the morning because of the amount of pain he's in. She dotes on Arthur and it's odd – very odd indeed.

When I walk back into the sitting room, we are both composed and as soon as I turn on the laptop the edginess between us begins to subside. Arthur has a few ideas of his own, and I make a list, adding a few things that I feel need tweaking. When we're done, I stand to put on my coat.

'Life sometimes doesn't pan out quite the way we hope it will, Kerra.' Arthur speaks slowly, as if he's considering every word. 'I believe in makin' the best of what we're given and that, ultimately, we pay the price for the mistakes we make. I'm payin' a price for somethin' I did a long time ago and since then my life is about keepin' my lovely wife happy and helpin' others.'

I look at him, frowning because I have no idea what he's trying to tell me. 'I do feel for you, Arthur. Life hasn't been easy for you, but a lot of people are grateful that you're there to support them.'

'Well, we all have secrets we want to keep from pryin' eyes and you know that only too well. If there's anyone I'd trust it would be you, Kerra. You see, Mrs Moyle is one of life's eternal optimists. On a day like today she'd get herself all excited, thinkin' a miracle has happened. But by tonight I'll be in total agony as usual and it would crush her. It's not fair to give her false hope, plus she'd be on at me to go back to see the consultant and there's no point. So, if we could keep this between us, I'd be very grateful to you for understandin' my situation. It ain't easy, I'm afraid.'

It's obvious that his wife is the centre of his world and that's wonderful. 'Oh, Arthur, of course I understand. My lips are sealed. And, um, if you have any more ideas for the link-up just give me a call.'

I walk away feeling dejected on Arthur's behalf. I wonder if there are times he wonders if the pain is gone for good and he's gutted when it returns. It's clear he's aware of what's going on between me and Ross and he was appealing to me because he feels I'll understand. I can't help wondering whether there is a glimmer of hope that he'll become more mobile, but perhaps he doesn't want to share that information until he can be sure he won't relapse. I can understand that and, as he said, we all have secrets.

FIFTEEN
PUDDLES EVERYWHERE I TURN

'Goodness, you're soaked!' Ross exclaims as I walk into the storeroom at the village hall. 'What on earth happened to you? Here, let me take that box.'

He leans in to kiss the tip of my nose, as everything else is dripping wet.

'I was crossing the car park and a lorry came in to turn around. You know the hole in the middle where the tarmac has subsided? Well, he caught it with his back wheel and the water was like a wave; unfortunately, I caught it full-on.'

Yanking off my sodden, knitted bobble hat I discard it onto the floor and then ease off my soggy coat. Ross puts down the box and grabs one of the clean rags we use for wiping the brushes. 'Here, you'd better mop your face. That water was a little muddy. I'll hang these over the radiator in the kitchen.'

Fortunately, my jeans aren't too bad. It's only the back of my left calf where the slick of water ran down off my coat that is sticking to me. I pop into the toilets to slip them off and put on my bib and brace coveralls.

Ross meets me in the passageway to grab my jeans and

says he'll find another radiator. I lean into him. 'Can you just check me out and make sure I'm presentable and you can't see through the fabric?'

'In all honesty, Kerra, although they're white the material is so covered in paint you're fine.' He turns to walk away. 'And that's not a criticism of your work,' he throws over his shoulder, trying his best to suppress a chuckle.

'I don't appreciate being laughed at,' I call out, tongue in cheek.

In the darkness, the lorry driver had no idea how close he was to me, or how deep that puddle is but I'm sure he'd have laughed his socks off if he'd seen the state I was in. I mean, who wouldn't?

'Right.' Ross reappears and follows me into the storeroom. 'Is this box of paint a donation?'

'Yes, from one of Mrs Moyle's customers. Some of them haven't even been opened.' As Ross checks out the colours, I can't take my eyes off him. That thick mass of dark, curly hair that flops down over one eye makes me want to reach out and touch him. I imagine running my hand down over the short hairs on the back on his head, where it's close-cropped. He's oblivious to the way women look at him and he always has been. Ross has a friendly smile, and a warm and welcoming manner. But there's a vulnerability hidden behind those mysterious, dark brown eyes of his and that, too, is a part of his charm. I've seen how deep it goes, but few can understand that. It's what I love about him – his modesty is genuine and not manipulative, and people sense that.

'Are you checking me out?' He turns his head, giving me a cheeky grin. As he does, only his left cheek lifts slightly, which emphasises the dimple in his chin. 'You might want to run a brush through your hair,' he remarks.

'Not fit for work, am I?' I retort. 'You'd better give me my task for tonight before I go and sort myself out. Oh, and before it skips my mind, can you call in on Sissy at The Design Cave to give her a quote? She needs that large room at the back divided up to separate off the kitchenette and create an office. Logan is going in next week to replace the modem and move the telephone point.'

'Will do. Now, how do you feel about painting the sky?'

'Blue with white clouds?'

'Yes. It's the backboard that will go behind the Dark Queen's Winter Palace. As we're not sure how much of it will show, I suggest you paint the entire thing blue first off and then add the clouds at the top once we know how tall the palace will be. There are two, five-litre tubs in the corner and if you need help decanting them, let me know as they're awkward to pour. Use the oblong paint kettle and there are a couple of hooks to hang it off one of the rungs on the stepladder. I suggest you start at the top and work down.'

I flash my eyes at him. 'I managed to paint the two bedrooms at the cottage,' I declare. Admittedly, with a little help from Tegan. 'I think I'll be just fine.'

'Okay. I've spread out the dust sheets and Sy helped me carry the backboard into the meeting room, so it's all ready and waiting.'

Although the door is ajar, Ross reaches out to put his hands around my waist and pull me closer. I close my eyes and sink into him. He smells of aftershave balm with a hint of sandalwood and amber. Our lips touch, but only briefly, as I can hear Dad's voice outside in the passageway. Reluctantly pulling away from each other, Ross whispers into my ear, 'It's killing me, us being apart.'

I jump back as Dad swings open the door and barges in, unaware of what we were doing mere moments before.

'You look a bit bedraggled there, Kerra.'

'A lorry just hit me full-on with a big puddle, Dad. Ross is too busy giving me my instructions to let me sort out my hair.'

'Well, it's not as if anyone's going to see you, is it? Are we going to tackle this palace, Ross, or the castle?' Dad queries. I guess I'm not going to get any sympathy here.

'As Kerra has kindly offered to paint the background for the palace, I think we'd better make a start on that first. How we're going to do it, I have no idea at all.'

Dad's face brightens. 'I've been thinking about it all week and I wondered if instead of one big set, we could create the two rooms needed and maybe have the outline of the exterior of the palace as a separate backdrop in front of the sky. It would make it easier to move the interiors around between scenes.'

Ross rubs his chin, in thinking mode. 'You might be onto something, there, Eddie. Right, Kerra, we'll leave you to it then. We'll be in the kitchen drawing up some plans if you need anything.'

Honestly, they're off to design an ice palace and I'm painting the sky. I know which job I'd rather do – it's a piece of cake.

* * *

You know that saying… *famous last words*? Well, just that.

'Help!' My voice wavers as I push open the door to the kitchen with my foot and both Ross and Dad look at me in total shock, before bursting out into raucous laughter.

As I reached across a little too far with the roller, I found myself having to grab on rather tightly to the ladder and it started to tip. Horrified, I quickly moved down a step or two, trying to steady it but one of the hooks on the paint kettle had disconnected, and suddenly the entire contents came raining down on me.

'We'd best mop up that dripping paint.' Dad jumps up out of his chair. He grabs a roll of kitchen towel and begins spreading it out around me as Ross rifles in the drawers next to the sink unit.

'Better be quick, Ross. This mess isn't going to be easy to mop up.'

The slick of thick paint is like a lava flow, as a couple of litres run down in ripples from my right side. Literally, from my shoulder to the fingertips of my right arm, it's a wonderful shade of sky blue. But it's so thick that big globules have dropped onto my leg and my trainers and as I turn my head a little in order to assess the damage, little splatters flick up off the ends of my hair.

'Don't panic,' Ross exclaims as he hurries over with a couple of black sacks in his hand. He spreads them out on the floor and I step forward. Dad is on his hands and knees using two wads of kitchen towel to scoop up the thickest blobs first.

'You're okay under all that paint, are you?' Ross checks suddenly concerned.

'I'm fine, just embarrassed that I overstretched and tipped the paint kettle over myself. There's a bit of a trail through the passageway and back across the meeting room floor, I'm afraid. I did call out, but no one heard me.'

If I was a little sorry for myself after the lorry incident, now I just want to call it a day and go home. Ross can see that I'm tearful.

'Eddie, I'm going to find a dust sheet to wrap around Kerra and then I'll drive her home.'

'Good idea, Ross. I'll sort things out here, don't you worry. You can pick your car up tomorrow, Kerra. If you want a lift just let me know. That was a bit of a shock, no doubt. Best stay and check she's okay afterwards, Ross, if you don't mind. A mug of hot, sweet tea might be a good idea too.'

* * *

'Is it still blue?' I ask anxiously as I tilt my head a little to avoid the cascade of water overhead from obliterating my vision. Ross is still massaging shampoo into the section of my hair that was coated in paint. I gaze down at our bare feet and the blue swirling water is at least now a quaint pastel colour.

'You have some on the side of your neck, but it looks like it's dried. Here.' Ross leans over to grab my shower mitt. 'Use this, but don't scrub too hard or you'll make the skin sore. If it doesn't shift easily try peeling it off with your fingers. That's what I'm having to do with the last bits in your hair.'

This is such a disaster. I love the thought of being in the shower with Ross, but not under these circumstances. My clothes and the dust sheet he wrapped me in are heaped in a pile on the bathroom floor and I don't think anything is salvageable. As he helped peel everything off, the paint had soaked through onto my underwear and, in places, onto my skin. At least now my body looks relatively paint-free even if the blue tinge has been replaced with a patchy shade of pink.

'I'm sorry,' I mutter, giving up on the mitt and running my fingers down the right-hand side of my neck. 'You're right, it's easier to peel it off.'

'It's specially formulated. It has latex in it and that's why you get good coverage. If I'd known you'd be wearing it, I would have picked up the ordinary stuff.' And then he begins laughing all over again.

'Just get it out of my hair!' I demand, feeling totally fed up as I continue to ease off tendrils of dry paint that are now beginning to gather around the shower drain.

'That's the best I can do, Kerra. Most of it is out and when your hair is dry, the rest will gradually brush out. It's only the very ends of it now. Aww... you look so dejected. What an awful day you've had.' He gathers me in his arms, and all I can think of is that this is nothing at all like our usual showers together.

Ross reaches out to turn off the water and, ever the gentleman, grabs the biggest towel off the rail to wrap around me.

'There. You sit on the stool with your feet on the bathmat and I'll tidy up.' It's rather fun watching him using a hand towel to dry himself before he jumps back into his clothes. They're scruffy ones he keeps for his evenings at the drama club, but there is quite a splattering of blue to join a myriad of other colours now.

I sit here like an obedient child. My skin is sore in places and I know there's still some paint on my neck, as it pulls a little when I turn my head to the side.

Ross is brilliant and it doesn't take him long to clean the shower and dispose of my ruined clothes.

'Hot, sweet, tea next!' He declares, waggling his finger at me.

'Can I have hot chocolate instead, please?'

'You can have anything you want. Do you need some help slipping into your pjs?' Ross raises his eyebrows, making me giggle.

'No. I think I can manage, thank you very much. But first I'm going to smother myself in moisturiser.'

He groans. 'While sending me off to make you a drink?'

I bat my eyelashes at him. 'I think we've had enough fun for one night, don't you?'

By the time I get back downstairs I'm feeling more comfortable and Ross is sitting at the table, Ripley curled up on his lap. She's purring so loudly as he smooths her back that it sounds like she has a bad chest. It reminds me of the time I had bronchitis but seeing them like this warms my heart.

'You'll feel much better once you've drunk this.' Ross nods his head in the direction of the mug he has set down next to him. 'Is your skin really sore?'

He's full of sympathy and no doubt feeling guilty for having laughed at me. Several times, actually.

'I'm just annoyed with myself. It was silly to overstretch. And you were getting on so well with Dad.' That's the annoying bit for me – pulling Ross away.

'It okay. He has some brilliant ideas and I'm happy for him to run with it. I think he likes having an assistant.' Ross sounds amused.

'You, an assistant?' I query, but he doesn't look at all bothered about it.

'Eddie is a craftsman and I respect that. His level of skill is passed down from one generation to another and it shows. Scenery isn't meant to be perfect close up, but it has to be fit for purpose as well as creating the overall effect. He's come up with the idea of using a turntable for the two rooms in the ice palace. I'm well impressed, as I'd been racking my brains over how to get around the problem of some quick scene changes.'

'I'm glad things are beginning to work out. And Dad

suggesting you bring me home, that was the last thing I expected.'

Ross gingerly reaches out for his mug, but Ripley isn't happy at being disturbed. She immediately jumps down, pushing out her front paws and lowering her head to stretch out her back.

I stoop down to smooth her head, but seconds later she runs off upstairs, no doubt blaming my arrival for the interruption.

'I hate to say it, but I think it's more about the fact that he was keen to finish getting his ideas down on paper. But I feel less awkward around Eddie now and that's a big step forward.'

'And how are things with your father? Is he coming around to your way of thinking?'

'He was so angry with me at one point today, that he forgot himself and ended up shouting down the phone. He came out with a few choice words, too. That's a warning sign, as he's as careful about not cursing as he is about not slipping back into dialect. He thinks both are beneath him,' Ross scoffs. 'But he's no gentleman, Kerra, when it comes to business. There are things he's done over the years that he wouldn't want raked up at his time of life. And he's aware that I'm probably the only person who knows most of what went on.'

I've never heard Ross talk like that before. Does he mean when Jago was a local councillor? I wonder. Jago was on several different committees at about the time his business really took off. That's when the Treloars moved from their lovely house on the outskirts of Penvennan, to a sprawling manor house up near Rosveth moor. That was a sad time for me because after that I rarely saw Ross outside of school. He was popular and I was one of the computer geeks; the two groups didn't mix that much. The days when we'd rush off the school bus to go home and change so we could all meet up down at the beach were suddenly over.

'You look sad,' Ross murmurs, as I sip my hot chocolate.

'Just thinking about the old days. They weren't all bad.'

He places his arm very gently around my shoulders. 'The only memories that make me smile are the times when you appeared. Even though you didn't always acknowledge me,' he complains.

'You couldn't always see me, and I wasn't going to fight off a horde of other girls, was I?'

'Something worth having is worth fighting for, Kerra. Remember that!'

'Oh, I'd fight for you now, believe me. That overly sensitive little thing is all grown up and these days I know exactly what I want.'

SIXTEEN
GETTING A GRIP ON THINGS

'Morning, Drew. I won't keep you, but I wanted to pop these in for Bertie. A little present from Ripley to say sorry she's been a nightmare again these past few days.'

I hand Drew a packet of dog chews and he gives me a hearty grin, standing back and inviting me inside.

'I'm just having a coffee before I start work. Why don't you join me. So, Ripley went shopping, did she?' he jests.

'I've decided to do something about it. Her behaviour is as disruptive for you, as it is for poor old Bertie. Nettie is going to pop in to talk about the subject in general and I wondered if you wanted to be a part of the conversation?'

He closes the door behind me, and I walk through to sit on one of the high stools around the central island. Everything gleams and it's all streamlined. Bertie comes bounding towards me and he's the only unruly thing in sight. I kneel to give him some attention. He tilts his head to one side, his cute little face a picture as he sits and puts up his paw. I give it a little shake and he wags his tail, happily.

'That's a great idea. I'm not available this weekend,

though, as Felicity is arriving later. Two visits in a month – things must be coming to a head,' he remarks over his shoulder.

Little does he know that he might be in for a bit a surprise that will turn their lives upside down. I wonder if she'll decide to hold on to her secret for a while longer, though. For any woman, learning that she's going to have a baby is a huge deal. But when two people's lives aren't just poles apart, but miles apart too, it's not a straightforward case of making the announcement.

Drew walks over carrying a mug and the chews.

'Perhaps they are, finally. Are you nervous about the future?' I enquire, gently.

He opens the packet and Bertie waits patiently, his whiskers flexing, and I swear he's smiling up at Drew. 'Here you go, Bertie,' he says as he offers the treat. Bertie rarely grabs anything, so very sedately takes it from Drew's hand and holds it in his mouth. Then he trots off to enjoy it from the comfort of his doggy bed.

'I've waited so long that there are times I still doubt it will happen, but I'm a patient man. I know Felicity loves me and that's all that matters.'

Drew is such a gentle man. The sort that my mum would have said doesn't have a bad bone in their body. Thinking of her makes me smile. The sense of loss never goes away but I'm finding myself looking back more often now with fondness and with fewer tears.

'Is everything alright with you? There's something blue stuck to your neck.'

'Oh, it's just a splash of paint. Things are beginning to move forward a little with Ross and Dad, but in the meantime I'm keeping busy. I get the keys for Gwel Teg on Monday.'

'That's great news! What's the plan for it?'

'A bit of general redecoration and replacing a few pieces of furniture that are a little tired, then renting it out. It's the first thing I've ever bought outright that actually means something to me,' I admit. 'I feel with Pedrevan that I'm just the caretaker and hopefully, one day, I'll pass it on to the next generation. Although as things stand, that looks like it could still be a long way off.' It's hard not to look and sound a little jaded.

'I can understand how you feel on both counts. If only we could speed up time, eh? But it's nice to think you own a little piece of property looking out over the cove that was your childhood haunt. I'm assuming you have a tenant in mind, because I can't see you renting it out to just anyone.'

There's a noise outside and Bertie's head sudden jerks up. He runs towards the glass doors. Ripley is now sitting on top of one of the fence posts, her back straight as if she's surveying her property.

'Come away, Bertie,' Drew calls to him, pulling out another chew, and he comes rushing back.

'James mentioned that now he has a full-time job he's saving up a deposit to see if he can find somewhere to rent. It's not easy, living at home after a certain age, is it? Once it's been tidied up, I thought I'd offer it to him at an affordable rent. It's young people like James we need to encourage to stay in Penvennan, as they're the future.'

Drew shakes his head at me, laughing. 'You never fail to surprise me, Kerra. If only everyone had a social conscience,' he replies.

'I have a business head, too. It's an investment,' I state, emphatically. I was going to mention the work I've been doing with Arthur, but now is not the time. Anyway, Drew is on edge and will be until Felicity turns up and he can relax once more. Which gives me an idea, one I can't believe I haven't thought of before.

* * *

As I sit at my desk and looking out over the garden, a sense of peace settles over me. Ripley is curled up in her new nest in the corner and I've placed a large, square wooden planter in front of her. She's totally hidden behind the five-foot-tall African fig, with its rounded leaves and flashy green foliage. It's also purported to clean the indoor air and help maintain the humidity levels. It wasn't cheap, but I love the jungle feel it gives, which softens what is a streamlined, uncluttered space.

At least a part of my life is shaping up nicely. If only I could get the rest under control then everything would be perfect. Talking of perfect – I pick up the phone and call Ross.

'I was just about to call you,' he says, the instant he picks up. 'Sorry I laughed at you so much last night. You were in such a sad state and I was trying really hard to control myself, but I failed miserably... several times.'

'It was funny, I just couldn't see it at the time,' I concede.

'You're not calling to tell me off, then?' He does sound genuinely apologetic.

'No. I'm calling to say that I love you and to thank you for looking after me last night. If you hadn't been there, I would have ended up sitting in the shower crying. It was one of those days that started well and went downhill.'

'Ah, my poor Kerra. No one deserves that less than you.'

'You sound very relaxed this morning.'

'I'm in the office and there are no ranting messages or

emails. I'm catching up on the paperwork and a bit later I'll be popping out to look at that job for Sissy. How about you?'

'I had coffee with Drew first thing this morning and he told me that Felicity is coming tonight and will be here for the whole weekend. She's travelling back early on Monday morning.'

'Goodness. She's really stepping up the visits. That's got to be a good sign.'

'I wondered how you felt about throwing a little lunch party on Sunday at Treylya? Too risky?'

'For Drew and Felicity?' Ross doesn't sound dismissive, which is a good sign.

'Yes, and I wondered if we could also invite Gawen and Yvonne. What do you think?'

'I like the sound of *we*. It will be the first time we've entertained as a couple. If you're willing to take the risk, so am I.'

'I'll extend the invitation, then. The only problem is that I can't really disappear for the whole day without attracting attention. If we say 1 p.m. for pre-dinner drinks, and I leave shortly before that, most people will be having lunch and I'll walk up through the woods. But that leaves you to do the cooking, I'm afraid. Is that awful of me?'

'It's not a problem; there are ways of getting around it,' he replies and it's obvious he doesn't intend to be the one slaving away in the kitchen.

'That's settled, then?' I ask, excited by the prospect.

'Why don't you invite Sy and Tegan, too? They're all in the know about us, so it's not as if we won't be able to talk openly.'

My stomach begins to flutter, nervously. 'I'd love to invite them. This is a big step for us, isn't it?'

'It is, Kerra, and I know we still have to be circumspect,

but what happens up here is out of sight. We should take advantage of that while we can as you never know, the perfect buyer could come along at any time.'

It's good to hear Ross sounding positive this morning, despite the flak he's had to put up with this week.

'I'll make those calls and then text you to confirm who is coming. Is there anything I can bring with me on Sunday?'

'Just yourself. Everything will be spotless, as Clean and Shine are in on Saturday. Can you sleep over on Sunday night?'

I'm tempted, so tempted. 'Let's wait and see what happens. Dad agreed to Alice and Ian staying for a week and that deadline is up at the weekend. Hopefully, they'll sort something out and I won't get dragged into it, but I can't be sure.'

'I understand, but it would be a real shame if you can't stay. After a nice meal and drinks with friends, it would be great to have some quality time together.' His tone is one of acceptance, but I can hear the longing in his voice.

'You never know, luck might be on our side!'

* * *

It's been a satisfying day but I'm desperate for a little fresh air, and afterwards I feel I deserve a leisurely evening in front of the TV. I'm too tired to cook and there are only so many evenings you can dive into the freezer and pull out the same old things.

Ripley is out and I haven't seen her for a couple of hours, which is unusual, but it often means that she's on mouse patrol. It's obvious now that the little critters know better than to come into my garden, so I suspect she wandered through under the massive laurel hedge into the garden of the detached house the other side. It's the weekend retreat of a couple who live in Berkshire, but even when they are here no one would know, and I've never bumped into them walking around the village. They keep the hedges well-trimmed, though, and the company they use always knock on my door and ask permission to trim this side, which suits me.

The sun has disappeared, and it's overcast as I lock up and head down to Pascoe's bakery before they shut. When I walk past Gwel Teg a smile instantly lights up my face and I'm tempted to stop and gaze at it, but I force myself to keep walking. It's mainly dog-walkers out and about, and a few families making their way up the hill towards me, as the rain clouds are now beginning to look threatening. It's too early for the mass exodus to the pub for the Friday night singalong. Hurrying into Pascoe's to get a pasty and a hevva cake, I figure it's marginally better than a pizza and a large bar of chocolate. Well, I can kid myself, but I'm in need of comfort food this evening.

Instead of walking straight back home, I pull up the hood on my coat and take a stroll along the beach. I love that swoosh of the water as it ebbs and flows, at times it even drowns out the eerie sound of the seagulls overhead. They fill my heart with a sense of dread and yet no one else seems bothered by them. I walk along to the far end and there are only three other people within sight now. Picking up speed I take the shortcut back through The Lark and Lantern's car park. I wave to Polly, who is standing outside with her phone pressed against her ear, holding her unzipped coat around her. The wind has whipped up and she's struggling. She doesn't wave back but hurries over to me as she pops the phone into her pocket to do up her coat.

'I'm glad I spotted you,' she calls out. 'I'll be quick. You'd best not hang around as those clouds look threatening.'

Polly comes up close, looking around furtively, but there's no one within earshot. 'I wanted to tell you that I've had a word with Ian, and we've sorted something out. He seems to think that he'll be staying on at your dad's for a while – is that right?'

I shrug my shoulders. 'You're more up to date than I am. If that's true, then I'm pleased for Alice and Ian, and it would be a relief to know that Dad has some temporary help. And Ian thinks he can handle it?'

'Ian said he'd be straight with Eddie and whatever spare time he has he'll crack on with the decorating. We're going to meet at the house tomorrow and agree a plan of action.'

'I bet you can't wait to start. When will you tell Sam?'

Polly looks at me, anxiously. 'When he quizzes me about where I'm going at some point. I'd rather avoid that conversation for now. Just until I can prove it's doable to juggle both. I guess I'll be doing lots of ad-hoc window-shopping trips to Polreweek.' She smiles, wanly. 'Is it wrong of me to keep this a secret?'

Who am I to comment on Polly's situation, when I'm an expert at keeping secrets?

'I'm the last person to ask for advice about that, Polly. No matter how honest and open we want to be, it's often complicated. All we can do is hope the decisions we make are the right ones, for the right reasons.'

'It's tough trying to protect the people we love, or at the very least, cause them less stress. Parents often find it hard to let go, don't they?' She sounds as sad as she looks.

'They mean well and it's wonderful to know that bond

continues, but like it or not we each steer our own lives. It's how we learn and grow.'

'I know – and I would hate to upset Dad if this doesn't work out. It would cause a great deal of anxiety and it could all be for nothing. Anyway, I now have a company logo thanks to you, and my very first quote has been emailed across to the client. I managed to go online and find a set of draft terms and conditions that don't need much altering to fit my situation. Aside from sorting an insurance policy, it's all good!'

Polly is a real entrepreneur and while she will always support Sam, she does need something of her own and an outlet for her creativity. I'm convinced that she'll be happier for it.

The wind is tugging at the bags in my hand, and I take my leave, walking as quickly as I can. After last night's escapades I have no intention whatsoever of letting the heavens rain down on me. Glancing up at the clouds, I screw up my face. 'Don't even think about it!' I declare, as the wind whips the words out of mouth and disperses them into the ether. It isn't until after I close the front door of Pedrevan behind me that the first drops begin to fall. I feel that in the battle of woman versus weather, I won – which makes me smile.

'Ripley,' I call out, expecting to see her appear but even after I've taken off my coat and walked into the kitchen there's no sign of her. Glancing out of the glass doors, I see that the rain is pounding and a sharp cracking sound is followed by a flash of lightning. It makes me jump and I hope she's not outside in this. I dump my phone and the two Pascoe's bags onto the worktop and go in search of her. She might be under the bed, sound asleep but before I can check the ping of an incoming message stops me in my tracks. It's from Ross.

I have a visitor. Ripley arrived about half an hour ago and she's curled up on the sofa. I was going to put her in the car and bring her back, but it's pouring down now. Not sure what to do!

She spent most of the day with me and has been out for a few hours mousing, I think. Perhaps she felt you needed some company. If the rain eases off she might wander back, but don't worry. She's her own woman. 😊

You lead by example! 😊 😊 😊

I chuckle to myself as I turn on the oven to heat up my pasty. If Ripley wants to stay at Treylya for a bit, then Ross must be feeling low. While Pedrevan is cosy, I should imagine that Treylya can be a lonely place at times for Ross, living there all by himself. I hope it sells soon, for his sake and mine.

SEVENTEEN
THE SHAPE OF THINGS TO COME

Sunday is usually a lazy start for me, but today is different. When I first arrived home, Dad and I were popping back and forth all the time, unobtrusively checking on each other. That all changed as it became obvious to me, and everyone else, how well Dad and Nettie are getting on.

While Nettie hasn't moved in, when she isn't at home working, she's at Green Acre. She helps Dad with the general chores, like cleaning the house and shopping, as well as doing what she can in the kennels. They spend their evenings together watching TV and she drives herself home late in the day.

It has taken me a while to get used to the change, but I know that Mum wouldn't want either of them to be lonely. It means that I no longer feel comfortable just letting myself in as I used to do. However, if I call beforehand, there's a note of surprise in Dad's voice as if he wonders why I'm giving him advance warning. But this morning I'm desperate to know what's going on over there before I head to Treylya. If there's trouble brewing, then now is the time to deal with it as I don't want anything to spoil this special lunch. To get six of our best friends around one table is a big deal and the last thing I want is Alice appearing on my doorstep again as I'm about to leave, preventing me from attending.

Ripley pads down the stairs and sits preening herself as I put on my coat and shoes.

'Do you think I should risk it, Ripley?' I ask her. She stares back at me and gives one, long *miaoooooow*. 'Is that a yes, or a no?'

She looks at me intently enough not to return to her preening.

'Just checking... what's cat speak for *no*?'

Miaow.

'Got it, Ripley, thanks! Wish me luck. When I get back you can have some treats.'

After talking to Polly, what I'm also hoping to find out is whether Ian has been straight with Dad. My instincts are telling me that he deserves a chance, and I don't think he'll mess Alice around. Boredom caused him to get him into a few scrapes when he was younger, but Dad thinks that also applies to Ross and look how wrong he was about that. Ross couldn't help being a magnet for the girls and I believe that Ian's reputation has suffered because of the rough crowd his brother mixed with. Unfortunately, Ian often tagged along, desperate not to be left out because he was the youngest of the group.

Today the sky is a pale blue, with fluffy little white clouds being moved on quickly by a light breeze, which is pleasant and refreshing. There is a steady stream of cars making their way to the cove and I'm sure they won't all be lucky enough to get a parking space. On a fine day like this, visitors from the wider area tend to come early. Sunday mornings are always busy anyway. Pascoe's do an all-day breakfast menu, and most people then go for a walk along the beach or take the path up to the headland. At this time of the year, at least three-quarters of the diners will be Cornish folk. Most end up in The Lark and Lantern at lunchtime and everyone knows you need to pre-book a table. Off-season prices for holiday lets mean that trade doesn't die off completely and Tegan's business confirms that, but the numbers are smaller.

'Seems like everyone is out and about today.' Zacky Carter's voice startles me as I wait for a gap in the traffic to cross the road. One of the cars is trying to reverse into a space in the lay-by opposite Pedrevan and it's about a foot too small for the car. They're blocking the entire road and Zacky comes to stand next to me, shaking his head sorrowfully.

'That int goin' to end well,' he states.

'Hi, Zacky. I fear you're right. The driver is getting a little flustered.'

A car further back begins honking their horn impatiently. I turn to face Zacky, good-naturedly. 'How are you?'

'Alive and hangin' in there. It's probably some sort of miracle, as I still smoke sixty a day despite what the doc says – and I like a pint, or two, as you know.'

Zacky is too old to change his ways.

'There's a skip in yer step these days, Kerra. Never thought I'd see yer back for good but it's nice for yer dad.'

'Ten years is a long time and life moves on.'

'It's true what folk are sayin' then? Yer plannin' on stayin'?'

'Why wouldn't I? Pedrevan is perfect now and I'm happy to be here.'

He lapses into silence as the car in front of us finally admits defeat. It takes the driver a couple of shunts to get out of the mess he's gotten himself into and now car horns are randomly tooting to hurry him along.

'Off to yer dad's?'

'Only popping in briefly. And you?'

'I've been in to have a chat with Arthur, poor fellow. Makes me count my blessings being able to get around like I do. I bet he'd love to get down to the pub for a pint.'

I'm not sure painkillers and alcohol mix, but I know what he means.

'Yes, it is a shame. If he could just get down those stairs, I'd happily drive him to The Lark and Lantern and bring him back.'

Zacky rubs his chin. 'That'd be a day to celebrate, fer sure. Talkin' about celebrations, people are sayin' it's about time Tegan and Sy tied the knot. Pete would be turnin' in his grave if he knew, or the fact that Sy ain't from around 'ere. It says summat when they have to hide themselves away like that, in Ross's old place.'

I stare at Zacky, unable to believe what I'm hearing. 'Well, I think it's high time people stopped poking their noses into other people's business, Zacky. I'm sure you agree, as no one wants to be labelled a troublemaker, do they?' I reply, pointedly.

The traffic begins to clear, and I say a hurried goodbye to Zacky, eager to get away from him before I start venting. Besides, I'm anxious to find out about Alice and Ian's fate, which is much more important.

* * *

'I'm so sorry I'm late,' I blurt out, as Ross swings open the door to Treylya. I can hear a great deal of chatter and laughter going on in the background. As I step inside, Ross pulls me into his arms. He gives me a quick kiss and helps me off with my coat.

'It's fine, don't worry. You've only missed the introductions. I knew that Felicity was meeting Gawen and Yvonne for the first time, but I had no idea Drew didn't know them either. Problems over at your dad's?'

'Not really, but it wasn't a quick in-and-out visit. Let's not keep everyone waiting.'

I run my hands over my hair to check for strays, as I've pulled it up and used a clip to fasten it. It's my version of a cheat's French plait. Ross is watching me intently.

'What's wrong?'

'Nothing. Everything is perfect and so are you.'

We stand for a moment just gazing at each other. Our first attempt at a social gathering and I'm the last one to arrive, but he grins back at me and his eyes are full of love.

'Come on. You look like you're in need of a drink.'

As we walk into the main room of the house, the views always make me stop and catch my breath. After last night's rain everything looks so fresh and bright today. The sea reflects the pale blue sky and the cotton wool clouds are mere wisps on the horizon.

'Finally,' Sy calls out, walking over to give me a hug. 'I was about to jump in the car and see what was holding you up.'

'Family drama,' I sigh. 'Sorry, everyone.'

I quickly move from person to person, dispensing hugs and feeling like the worst host ever.

'Relax,' Tegan says, as she brings up the rear. 'Ross has been sorting out the drinks while I took everyone on a tour of the house. Having cleaned every inch of it on numerous occasions I felt qualified enough to do it.'

We all laugh. 'Yes. I know the feeling.'

'Having cleaned this place once,' Ross joins in, 'Kerra said never again.'

'That's not fair,' I complain. 'I was helping Tegan and the people staying here left it in quite a mess. It's a huge job because everything is so shiny, and they were still in bed when we arrived.'

'Oh, I didn't know that was the case and I wouldn't have been happy either.' Ross has the good grace to look apologetic as he hands me a glass of red wine. Felicity, I notice, has something in a tall glass which I presume is a soft drink, but she's the only one. Drew isn't a noisy person at the best of times, but he's unusually quiet.

'I haven't shown everyone the cinema room yet,' Tegan informs Ross.

'Oh. Right. Come this way, then.' He seems very relaxed, considering that he's about to serve up a meal for eight people.

I hang back, bringing up the rear alongside Drew.

'Are you okay?' I whisper.

'Reeling, actually.' Oh dear, that wasn't quite the reaction I'd expected. We follow the others and, naturally, everyone is impressed by the huge screen.

'It really does feel like you're at the cinema,' Sy comments.

'We'd have to build an extension on the farmhouse to fit in something that big, but I want one!' Gawen declares as Yvonne shakes her head from side to side in opposition.

It seems the men are more impressed than the women.

'I wouldn't mind coming round to watch the football on that,' Drew joins in, starting to look a little livelier than he was a moment ago. Felicity walks over to stand next to him and grabs his free hand, giving it a squeeze.

A woman in a black dress and white apron appears in the doorway.

'Lunch is served if you would all like to come through.'

I look at Ross and he grins at me. 'You didn't think I was

going to risk cooking and mess up a fine Sunday lunch, did you?'

No wonder he looks so calm and collected. And hand-some. And kissable. I wander over to him. 'Are they doing the washing up, too?'

'Seriously, girlfriends are so demanding these days,' Ross replies as we saunter into the dining room and I hear a few chuckles coming from behind us. 'That's a no.'

It all looks lovely. There's a temporary serving table over against the wall, covered in a white linen cloth. The starters are on silver platters at one end. In the middle are six large, stainless steel heated serving dishes with lids and at the far end is a selection of desserts on two, tiered stands.

'Thank you, Meriel, and please give chef Louis my grateful thanks. I'll return everything in the morning.'

'It was our pleasure, Ross. I do hope you enjoy your meal.'

This is perfect and I can't believe Ross went to all this trouble to get someone to cook for us.

'How... where are they from?' I ask, as Ross invites everyone to help themselves.

'Pennington Hall Hotel. They usually only cater for large parties, but I called in a favour.'

'Well, this looks delightful,' Yvonne remarks, as she uses tongs to pick up some bite-size canapés. 'It's such a treat not to have to cook, isn't it?'

'For dinner last night I had a pasty and a slice of hevva cake from Pascoe's bakery,' I confess.

'It's traditional fare that reminds us of our childhood, although I'm not sure we work off the calories as we did in days gone by,' Ross replies. 'Our chef today is French, so I'm sure one of those hot plates will have something that was fresh off the trawler yesterday.'

It's a relaxed atmosphere and I sidle up to Felicity, who is engaged in conversation with Yvonne.

'We were just talking about the joys, or not, of living in a farmhouse,' she says, smiling.

'Your place is gorgeous, Yvonne,' I chime in.

'When the wind is in the right direction, but when it isn't the smoke blows back down the chimney and it whistles through those old glass windowpanes.'

'But don't you just love the charm and the character?' I reply, wistfully.

Ross has filled his plate and is about to take a seat at the oversized, walnut dining table. It's supported by two polished concrete pillars. 'Hear, hear. Charm and character win every time, says the man who built this eco-friendly glass box,' he interjects.

'Treylya is a perfect example of how to incorporate energy-saving features without compromising on design,' Drews speaks up. 'The location is unique and the way the glass outside reflects the sky, the sea, and the garden around the property gives it an organic feel in my humble opinion.'

'Spoken like a true architect,' Ross endorses, tipping his head at Drew in acknowledgement. 'Let's hope I can find someone willing to pay what it cost me to build it.'

'Did the schedule go to plan?' Felicity asks, as she takes a seat.

'No. It ran over time, over budget and over... everything.'

'But it is unique, and that view... well, I'd never get anything done if I lived here. It must be so dramatic when it's stormy and simply glorious in the height of summer.'

'I sound ungrateful, but to me it's just a millstone around my neck until it's sold. The bonus is that it's quiet up here and

I don't know why we haven't thought about having a little gathering like this before.' Ross looks directly at me.

'Because we're trying to be discreet and not make waves,' I spell out.

'Is that even possible in Penvennan?' Drew proclaims. 'From what I've seen nothing goes unnoticed, but sometimes it takes a while for the rumours to come to light.'

'And then there are the false rumours, of course,' Gawen adds.

'Wasn't I referred to as the *imaginary girlfriend*, for a while?' Felicity looks at Drew for confirmation.

'Not even that – it was just the *girlfriend* in a certain tone, implying I wasn't even capable of spinning a believable story to justify your existence.'

'I can vouch for that. And they'd lower their voices as if it was some sort of affliction,' I confirm, annoyed on his behalf. 'I wish someone would start a *positive* rumour about Ian Adams. As far as I can tell he's done nothing wrong, and he can't be blamed for what his brother has done.'

Tegan immediately joins in. 'I agree, Kerra. Even though he was a bit wild in his youth, he's a nice young man now. It is awful to think his brother might go to prison, though, for stealing cars.'

'That's the first I've heard of it. Does that mean Eddie's decided not to let Alice and Ian continue to stay at Green Acre?' Drew asks, frowning.

'He's extended their stay by two weeks. Ian has found himself a part-time job, but Dad wants to see how it pans out. Whether he thinks Ian will mess up and get sacked again, or that he will let him down helping at the kennels I don't know. Alice is simply delighted because they don't have any other options. Ian deserves a chance to prove himself, but Dad is keeping a very close watch on how things develop.'

Ross looks relieved. 'Your dad is very protective of Alice. For a moment there, I thought you were going to say Eddie has thrown them out.'

'I really hope it doesn't come to that. Uncle Alistair won't have them back and my conscience wouldn't let me turn them away.'

'They could come and stay here,' Ross offers, and I blink at him in rapid succession.

'Not when the house is on the market. With you here all alone it's easy to buff up the tiles, tidy a bed and clean a bathroom, but you'd have to get Tegan's crew in every time you have a viewing.'

'They're not exactly queuing up to take a look. It's just a thought if it comes to it.' I can see that Ross is serious, but I don't think it's a good idea.

'Are we finished with the starters?' I ask, jumping up to clear the plates. 'Am I allowed to load these in the dishwasher, or are they meant to be washed by hand?' I enquire and Ross stands.

'I'll clear these and they're going in the machine. If you can take the lids off the hot dishes, the dinner plates are in the plate-warmer at the back.' When Ross takes the dishes from my hand his eyes linger on me. I'm glad I made a special effort with my hair today. Wearing my favourite navy cable-knit jumper and slim-fit pale grey jeans, I feel comfortable entertaining and being regarded as the lady in Ross's life.

'Right, let's see what surprises we have in store for the main course.'

It's fun with everyone helping themselves and I can't wait

for the day that we can repeat this at Pedrevan, albeit lunch there will be a much simpler affair.

When we finally wave everyone off, I'm still none the wiser about what Drew does, or doesn't know with regard to what's going on with Felicity. I half expected them to make an announcement, but it wasn't forthcoming.

'There's something on your mind and somehow I don't think it's Alice.'

'Did you think Drew was unusually quiet?'

Ross is lying on the couch, his head buried back into the cushions. 'Not really. I think he finds Sundays a little tough whenever Felicity is here. Knowing that she'll be leaving early in the morning can't be easy. Is there any news about her upcoming plans?'

The only thing I do know for sure is a secret that isn't mine to share.

'Only that she is making plans, so things are moving forward.'

'Hmm. Well, that's been going on for a while now, hasn't it? What she needs is something to trigger that final push.'

From what she said, she's had that alright.

'You are staying, aren't you?' Ross checks, sounding hopeful.

'I shouldn't really, and you know it. I'll have to drop my car back to the village, first.'

'That's not a problem. I'll walk down through the woods and meet you at the end of the High Street. See if you can get Ripley to follow you. I like having her here.'

'Out of interest, did she wake you up around 3 a.m.?'

'No. She slept on the bed all night. Her snoring woke me up at one point, but I just pulled a pillow over my head and went back to sleep.'

Typical! 'Right. Let do this. I'll pop in and top up her food bowls just in case she's not around, but if she is, I'll carry a tube of her treats with me. She'll follow me anywhere for some dried salmon.'

'And what's the lure I should use to get you here more often?'

'Convince Dad how good you are for me.'

'Oh, I'm working on that one and I'd say it's going pretty well.'

Ross helps me on with my coat, wrapping his arms around me and homing in for a kiss. First one, then two, then three... he's reluctant to let me go.

'If you set off walking now, I'll be as quick as I can,' I promise, and he groans.

'Our life together is one long waiting game, isn't it?'

I beam at him. 'Some things are worth waiting for, now let me out!' I demand.

We have one last, lingering kiss before Ross swings open the door and as we pull apart and I turn to step over the threshold, there's a buzzing sound. Ross turns to press the pad on the gate's intercom.

'Hello?' He looks at me, puzzled. It's clear that he isn't expecting anyone.

'Ross, it's your father,' Jago's voice booms out and Ross looks at me, horrified. He hesitates as I stare at him, eyes wide, and I can see he's not sure what to do. He takes his finger off the pad.

'Jump in your car before I open the gate, Kerra. I can't refuse him entry but it's best that your paths don't cross. I'll let you know what's happening as soon as I can.' Ross pulls me close, and I can feel his anxiety. 'I love you, just hold on to that fact.' Then he encourages me out the door and I rush over to unlock my car and jump inside. As the gates swing open, I start up the engine. Pulling up the hood on my coat, I wait until the incoming vehicle moves past, before driving away as quickly as I can without kicking up the gravel.

My heart is pounding, and my stomach is churning. And I feel as if I'm abandoning Ross in his time of need. But my presence will be a red flag and I know that. I'm breathing so fast that if I don't slow it down, I'll begin to hyperventilate. *Be strong, Kerra*, I tell myself. *Ross is going to need you.*

But it's more complicated than that. Jago and my dad are enemies – there's no other word for it. There was even a point in the past when it almost came to blows between them. The image of Mum trying to restrain Dad, and a friend of Jago's yanking him away, remains etched on my memory. I had never before, or since, seen Dad as angry as he was that day. I was too young to understand why they were arguing at the time, but it was only the beginning and worse was to come. If Jago recognises me, then it's going to be like a red rag to a bull.

EIGHTEEN
THE NIGHTMARE BEGINS

I've been lying on the bed for hours, Ripley on my lap, and the phone next to me. She senses how distraught I'm feeling and has been unusually quiet, not even jumping off the bed to pad downstairs for something to eat. When Ross eventually texts me, I'm in my pjs and it's just after 1 a.m.

I need to talk to you, but I'm too wound up right now. He's here for a while and he's made it clear he won't be flying back until changes have been made. The first chance I get to talk properly, I'll give you a call. My options are limited, but I don't want to do anything until we've spoken. Miss you more than you can know. 🖤

Tears fill my eyes. Ross is a fighter and yet he already sounds defeated.

It was a tactic, turning up on your doorstep without warning. I'm here whenever you need me, you know that. Try to grab a little sleep, my darling. Love you. xx

Jago is an overbearing man and he's manipulative. He caught Ross unawares because that gives him the upper hand – he's obviously been planning this for a while. Ross is going to have to gather his wits together very quickly to withstand what I'm sure is going to be an onslaught of criticism. Ironically, what makes it seem so much worse is that we were having such a wonderful time, and just like that everything has changed. And who knows where it will lead, or how long it will last?

* * *

When dawn breaks, I'm already wide awake, having drifted in and out of an uneasy sleep for the last few hours. Unable to lie here any longer, I head downstairs and Ripley follows me as I go through the motions of our normal early morning routine.

By the time I'm showered and dressed, there's still no further messages from Ross and Ripley is driving me mad. She's refusing to use the cat flap, but obviously wants to go out. She sits by the glass doors wailing and I open them, but then she turns and runs off towards the front door. Then when I open it, she sniffs the air suspiciously as if sensing there's another cat on her territory. It's unlike her to be quite so contrary and she turns tail to run back upstairs. She's picking up on my frazzled nerves and, out of sheer guilt, I pour a pile of salmon treats into one of her dishes and carry it upstairs to her.

I find her hiding under the bed and she won't come out, so I slide the dish within easy reach and leave her to it. Today is the day I get the keys for Gwel Teg, but I can't even get excited about that now. Instead, I wander down to the garden office, as the only way to still my troubled thoughts is to throw myself into work mode.

When my phone rings a few hours' later, I snatch it up, but it's not Ross, it's Nettie.

'Hi, Kerra. I was wondering if it was okay to pop round and have a chat with you and Drew about Ripley and Bertie this evening?'

'Of course. Drew is up for it and I meant to let you know. What time?'

'Sevenish?'

'Sounds good. I'll make arrangements with him. Come to mine, given that Ripley is the instigator of the problem.'

She laughs and I let out the fakest of chuckles.

'Are you okay?' she enquires.

'Perfect. Just a little tired, that's all. Ripley is a bit unsettled. I think one of the other cats might have strayed into the garden and she won't go out this morning.'

'There's a fox around, so keep an eye out. We've seen it over here. Maybe that's it.'

'Thanks for the warning. See you tonight, then.'

I can hear Bertie in the garden with Drew, barking as he runs back and forth for the ball. It's easier to pop out and have a quick chat with him.

'Are you there, Drew?' I stand on the decking, listening.

'I am. I'm just trying to tire Bertie out a bit before I start work. He gets overexcited when Felicity is here and neither of us like it when she leaves. Her car didn't wake you, did it?'

'No, it wasn't that. I had a bit of a disturbed night. Oh, and there's a fox around, Nettie says. She just called to suggest we meet at Pedrevan at 7 p.m. to discuss the Ripley situation.'

I can hear Bertie snuffling around on the other side of the fence. He doesn't bark much, unless he's playing, or spooked.

'Is it alright if I call round for a bit before that for a chat? Felicity and I really enjoyed getting together for lunch yesterday and she really appreciated being a part of it. I wanted to have a chat about Felicity; I'm a little concerned about her right now.'

My thoughts are all over the place, but I hope that by then I'll be back in control.

'Yes, please do. Apart from heading out to the estate agent's, to collect the keys for Gwel Teg and popping in to take a quick look around, I'll be here.'

'Exciting times!' Drew replies, enthusiastically.

'Yes. As you say, exciting times. See you later, Drew. Bye, Bertie.'

As I amble back to my office, I can hear my phone ringing and even with a mad sprint I miss it. The call is from Ross and I immediately phone him back.

'How are you?' I burst out, sinking down into the chair.

'Lurching from one minute to the next. My father has been planning this trip for quite a while it seems. A car arrived about ten minutes ago to pick him up. He says he'll be gone all morning, thankfully. And I'm late starting work but I wanted to give you an update.'

'Do you know where he's going?'

'I suspect he's looking at office space, although I have no idea where that might be. He made it clear that he's here to get his plans for expansion moving but wasn't prepared to give me any details. I have no idea what's coming, so only time will tell.' Ross sounds despondent and that's not like him.

'Is there nothing at all you can do about it as the managing director?'

'Not without consulting someone experienced in business law.'

'You think it will come to that?'

'I sincerely hope not, because that's not a cheap option. It seems to me that my father is now over-ruling my decisions as the biggest shareholder, which wasn't the arrangement we had. But I only own twenty-five per cent of the company; my parents own the rest between them. As far as I'm aware, they can veto anything I put forward as he made it clear it's two votes to one.'

Ross is literally fighting for what he feels is right for the company, but his father is well aware that any disagreement between them would go in his favour, not Ross's. You would think that Ross's mother would get involved, or at least hear what Ross has to say as he's been running the business success-fully ever since they left.

'Do you have a plan of action?'

He lets out a deep breath and it's gutting to hear how dejected he is. 'It sounds lame, which is why I wanted to run it past you and hear your thoughts on it. Basically, I'm going to sit back and watch it all unfold.'

I gasp. 'You don't intend to challenge him at all?'

'I can pay a small fortune to get legal advice and start the long, slow process of paperwork going back and forth, or I can wait and watch. For all I know he might be setting up this new office under a different company name. If that's the case, and it means jumping through a few hoops while he's here tinkering with the way I run things at Treloar's before he flies back to Spain, it's not the end of the world. He'll feel like he's won, and I'll be left in peace again to get on with it.'

'Have you thought about calling your mother to get her on your side?'

Ross's jaded laugh tells me that's a no.

'She does what he tells her to do. My mother doesn't have a head for business, and she hasn't forgiven me for tarnishing the Treloar name with my messy divorce. Do you think I'm doing the right thing?'

I pause, wondering if Ross is burying his head in the sand in the hope that it will all turn out right in the end. But what if it doesn't? He has always worked for the family business and it isn't just a nine-to-five job for him; he lives and breathes it. To lose that would be devastating, as his world would instantly fall apart.

'There's so much at stake for you, Ross, but you must do what feels right. Be guided by your gut instincts. All I can say, if it helps, is that whichever route you decide to take there's an element of risk. Only you know how far your father is prepared to go to get his own way.'

The line goes quiet, and I say nothing, allowing my words sink in.

'I appreciate your honesty, Kerra. Until I can get a handle on things, while he's here when you and I meet up it must be well away from Penvennan. He asked who was in the car and I told him it was someone here clearing up after I'd had a few friends around for Sunday lunch.'

My heart constricts inside my chest. 'I think you're right, Ross. Let's not risk angering him in any way.'

'Listen, I don't want this to throw *us* into a downward spiral. Let's both act as if things are normal, as once word gets out that he's back everyone will be watching. If you appear down, then there's a chance people might twig what's been going on. I'm going to square my shoulders, continue on as normal and if anyone asks, I'll give the impression that nothing he's doing comes as a surprise.'

Every hour of every day is going to be a strain on Ross until this is over.

'I'll try really hard to keep up a happy front, I promise.

And you're right, continue on as normal and plaster on a smile. When will I see you next?'

'It's a busy week for me as I'll be out and about looking at jobs and then back in the office preparing the quotes for Evan to send out. In between I'll be checking in with my site foremen, to warn them my father may well decide to turn up on site unannounced. It might be best if we catch up on Thursday night at the village hall and then plan to grab a little alone time at the weekend. I can book a hotel room somewhere for Saturday night, what do you think? By then I might have a better idea where this is all leading and what the fallout is likely to be.'

Thursday feels like such a long time away, but I know it's the right thing to do.

'Let's aim for that, then. Maybe it won't be quite as bad as we both imagine.'

'I'll let him flex his muscles, but there is a limit to what I'm prepared to put up with, Kerra. He's going to stretch my patience as far as he can, I know that, because it's how he works. But if he unwittingly pushes the wrong button at the wrong time, he might end up wishing he hadn't started this battle.'

It's the first time I've ever heard Ross this angry and that took less than a couple of minutes on the topic to get him to that point. He's repressing his real feelings for now, but this is an explosive situation and he's trying to protect me by keeping me at arm's length.

'We'll make time for us, as and when we can. I'm a phone call, or a text, away and I'll come running if you need me. Speak soon. Love you.'

As we disconnect the sadness is overwhelming. It takes the shine off everything. Jago Treloar thinks he can bully his way through life to get what he wants. But Ross is a different man now and he has self-belief that comes from the respect he has earnt from his customers and everyone who knows him. On reflection, I think Ross's plan is clever, but Jago doesn't always play by the rules and that's what concerns me the most.

* * *

After a dire start to the day, standing in front of Gwel Teg and turning the key in the lock my spirits do lift a little, but the joy has been tarnished.

'Kerra?' The sound of Dad's voice makes me turn my head in surprise, as he draws to a halt.

'Hi, Dad.'

'What are you doing here?'

He's been so caught up with things at Green Acre that I haven't had time to catch him up on my plans.

'After you mentioned it was up for sale, I took a look around it and we completed this morning.'

His jaw drops. 'You bought it? Why?'

Oh dear. This is another reason I've held off telling him, as Dad thinks cash in the bank is safer than any investment.

'Why don't you come inside and have a quick look around?' I really don't want to be seen idling on the doorstep and I hurry inside, assuming Dad will follow me.

'I was on me way to get a paper. This is the last thing I was expecting,' he replies, shutting the door behind him.

'The thing is that I'm selling the apartment in London. The wise thing these days is to spread your investments out and I intend to rent this once it's had a fresh coat of paint.'

Dad raises his eyebrows to the ceiling. 'All these things

you're getting into, Kerra, I certainly hope you know what you're doing...' He tails off, looking uncertain.

'I wish you wouldn't worry so much, Dad,' I reply, trying hard not to sound as exasperated as I feel. But my problems are nothing compared to what Ross is facing. 'I've survived in business this long and my brain is way too active to sit back and take it easy.'

He shakes his head warily, as I lead him around the ground floor.

'Well, it's not in bad shape. You do know who used to live here, although she's been gone a long time now,' he reflects.

'I've been trying to cast my mind back. I always liked this little cottage, but I can't recall who owned it when I was a kid.'

'Mrs Enys, yer grandma Rose's friend. I bet you both popped in a few times on the way to the bakery, or when you were out for a walk at the beach.'

Is that why I was instantly drawn to look around Gwel Teg? No specific memories spring to mind, although it's rather nice to think of Grandma Rosenwyn bringing me here to see her friend.

'I don't remember, so I must have been quite small.'

Dad scratches his chin. 'You was walking, so around three I expect. Mrs Enys died before you started school I reckon.'

'Ah, I wish there were some photos of those days,' I reply, nostalgically.

'Maybe there's some in the box up in Green Acre's loft, but I haven't pulled them out for years now. One day we'll do that when you're not so caught up building your little empire.'

Goodness, that sounds like a bit of a reprimand.

'Dad, I'm thirty years old and I don't intend to take it easy. I'd go crazy.'

'Well, perhaps it's time you considered settling down. The

last thing I want is you heading off again. It's easier now you're on me doorstep, although as it turns out I'm still the last to know what's going on. I'd best get off and get that paper, as I've left Ian in charge.'

Oh, here's my chance.

'I know what went on in Ian's past, but people grow up and move on. He never got himself into any real trouble, it was just larking about. I know his brother is different, but that's the whole point. They had a tough upbringing and Ian has chosen his own path, but no one will give him a chance because of his family's reputation.'

Dad frowns at me, narrowing his eyes. 'I am giving him a chance, lovely, but I'm not gonna make it easy for him. I know you're looking out for the lad, and that cuts some sway with me. But I'm no pushover and I'm watching him closely.'

I swallow hard. I know that Ian was straight with Dad, telling him he was taking on some part-time painting and decorating work, but I hope Ian didn't mention Polly by name. I'm sure she would have told Ian to be discreet, as the last thing she wants is for Sam to find out before she knows what the future might bring. I think I should be a little careful now not to push Ian's case, as Dad will make up his own mind as the days go by.

'If this is going to keep you occupied for a bit, then that's something. Now I'm off. I'm glad I bumped into you, though. I'm sure Gryff will be full of talk about the new owner of Gwel Teg as I grab a paper, and how would it look if I didn't even know it was me own daughter?'

I walk up to him and plant a kiss on his cheek. 'Expect the unexpected, Dad. You should know me by now.'

'Pity you're not into these online dating things, rather than websites. I'd like a grandkid, or two, before too long. Unless there's someone you already have your eye on, of course.'

My heart leaps in my chest. If he's hinting about Ross, then this is a huge step forward. Then Jago pops into my head and I decide this is a subject best avoided.

'Dad! If the right man comes along then maybe, but I don't know how my life is going to pan out yet,' I reply, cautiously.

I wait, thinking that if he does mention Ross by name, I might open up to him.

'This isn't the little job Ian was talking about, is it?'

Relief washes over me. Polly's cover isn't blown. 'I think I can handle painting a few walls. And you can let Gryff know that someone will be moving in, but it won't be me.'

'Well, give me a heads-up when you know who it will be. It's not easy keeping up with you and your goings-on.'

Goings-on? If only he knew, but I'm also a little relieved he doesn't know everything right now, even though it feels like I'm back-pedalling. The last thing Ross and I need is another complication to throw into the mix.

NINETEEN

ACTING NORMALLY

'Felicity has handed in her notice. Her father went ballistic, apparently, but her brother is pleased, obviously.' Well, that's not quite the news I was expecting to hear from Drew, but he seems delighted.

'That's wonderful news,' I enthuse.

'It's almost unbelievable... how can I put this?' I pass him a glass of wine and wait patiently for him to continue. 'After all these months, and the guilt Felicity feels because you know that her parents hate the thought of her moving away, she didn't discuss it with me beforehand. She told me on Friday night and this all happened more than a week ago.'

Hmm. It seems Felicity hasn't told Drew everything.

'But you have talked about it a lot in the past,' I point out.

'Yes, in theory. But to hand in her notice before she knows what she's going to do next is worrying.'

I need to be careful here. 'Did you explain that to her?'

'I did and she told me that she's looking at her options and thinking of setting up her own business. She said that accountants are always in demand.'

I smile at him, good-naturedly. 'That's good, isn't it? Something she can do from here with relative ease.'

'Yes, but two of us with no fixed income is a concern. My work is, as you know, up and down. The gaps between a lucrative project ending and a new one beginning sometimes lengthen when dates get pushed back and back. What if it takes longer than Felicity thinks to get a client base up and running? I'd feel that I'd enticed her away from a cast-iron job and what if she ends up resenting me for that?'

'What, for being here with you and guaranteeing your future happiness together?'

'That's the fairy-tale story, isn't it? But this is real life. She'd have a much better chance if we lived in a city and she rented an office. Felicity is good at what she does and yet I'm dragging her far away from all her contacts, as well as her family and friends.'

Felicity knows him so well. He's in panic mode and that's without knowing he's going to become a dad.

'But she loves it here, Drew, and as you said, she's a clever woman. Felicity is astute enough to know when the timing is right, and she wouldn't have taken that step if she weren't confident that she could make it work. Give her the space she needs to sort herself out and simply be supportive.'

He nods his head, looking troubled. 'You're right, I'm looking for things to go wrong because I can't quite believe what's happening. She was so happy at the weekend and Sunday really made it for us. Thanks to both you and Ross for inviting us. It was fun and I finally got to see the inside of Treylya.'

The doorbell rings and Drew answers it for me. I put together a little platter of nibbles to go with the wine. Ripley, I notice, is nowhere to be seen. She was more settled this afternoon and, ironically, I don't think she's bothered Bertie at all today.

'What a breath of fresh air it is to walk into Pedrevan, Kerra,' Nettie comments. 'Sixties-style houses might have large rooms and big, panoramic windows but it's like being in a box. You can take character out, but you certainly can't put in what was never there in the first place.'

I smile at her, as we hug. 'I always felt the same way about Green Acre, and I know Dad did, too. But I did love having all that space as a kid – and the orchard.'

She smiles back at me warmly. 'Your mum didn't care about the house. She only had eyes for the garden and her vision for the kennels. She'd have loved Pedrevan now. It's bigger, brighter, modern and yet the character of the old cottage is still very evident. You are one talented architect, Drew, to have the vision.'

It's lovely to watch his reaction and Nettie has no idea what a boost that has given him when he's second-guessing everything.

'Red, or white?' I ask as Nettie slips off her coat.

'Oh, red for me please. It's been quite a day. I've had some good news. It looks like I have a publisher, a real one.'

'As opposed to?' Drew enquires, cocking an eyebrow.

'Oh, there are lots of vanity publishers out there who jump at your book, get you excited, and then send you their schedule of charges. A bona fide publisher doesn't ask for money up front from the author, although they do expect you to spread the word about your book.'

'Well done, Nettie. That deserves a toast. Here's to making dreams come true!'

We clink glasses and in a bizarre way I guess it applies to us all, in different ways.

'And I took possession of the keys for Gwel Teg, today. I knew it was special, but it wasn't until Dad told me that my grandma's best friend had lived there that I realise why. Apparently, as a small child it's likely I was a frequent visitor when she took me out for walks.'

'Ah, he did mention that you'd bought Gwel Teg and he was a little shocked to hear it,' Nettie replies, her expression uneasy.

'There's been so much going on lately and as there wasn't a chain it was all executed within a couple of weeks. But the truth is that he worries about the impact of every decision I make, as if he's terrified that I'll lose everything if one little thing goes wrong. The world is a much bigger place than Dad imagines and after ten years in London I know a thing, or two. If there's anything you can say to help my cause, Nettie, I'd be grateful.'

'I'll try, Kerra, but some of us don't really understand the world of finance. We work all our lives to pay off the mortgage on our homes and then put whatever money we have left by to see us through our old age. The hope is that we can leave something behind for the generations to follow. In my case, that's a niece I dote on every bit as much as your dad dotes on you and Alice. Just keep him updated every now and again, preferably after the fact, or he'll feel he should be warning you about something, although he doesn't know what!' She laughs, but it's sad if he worries about it. 'Eddie simply can't get his head around why you bought Gwel Teg when you have Pedrevan.'

'Just reassure him that this is my forever home. I am trying to keep a low profile still, believe me.'

'I might be about to take the spotlight off you, Kerra,' Drew throws in for good measure and we exchange a look of acceptance. 'When Felicity moves in curtains will twitch and I'll be the talk of the pub again, no doubt.'

'Ah, it's lovely to hear that the two of you are getting your lives sorted at last,' Nettie remarks.

'Big changes are to come; watch this space.' Drew grins, happily.

'Right, let's talk about Ripley and Bertie,' Nettie says, sounding upbeat. 'I can't pretend to have a vast knowledge of experience in this area, but I did attend a couple of very interesting seminars entitled *How Dogs and Cats Can Coexist*.'

'Let's take a seat,' I offer, pulling out a chair for her.

'Thank you, Kerra. I'll just grab the notes from my bag. I've only had occasion to refer to these once before, and ironically that was in connection with a Bengal, too, but the situation was totally different.'

Drew settles himself down opposite us so we can look at the sheets Nettie begins laying out on the table.

'Miniature Schnauzers were originally bred to hunt. They are known for their high energy levels and intelligence, but I know Bertie's history. His owner took him to dog training sessions to quieten him down. I think the problem from Bertie's viewpoint is that he can't understand Ripley's reaction to him. He barks because he's intimated and it's a form of self-defence.'

Drew nods his head in agreement. 'I think you're right, Nettie. Aside from his reaction to Ripley, he usually only barks when we're playing if he gets overexcited.'

'I've noticed that, too,' I add.

'Bengals, and I've known a lot in my time,' Nettie continues, 'tend to be incredibly loyal to their owners, are highly energetic, vocal and they love to climb. But their personalities are quite complex. They like to supervise and stay nearby the people they get close to – the equivalent of a guard dog. Sleeping on the bed with you is quite typical for this breed, and they don't do well when left alone for long periods of time. They can get into all kinds of trouble when they're bored and left to their own devices, such as clawing at furniture and carpets. Can we just pop our coats on and take a look outside?'

Nettie has an empathy with animals, and it shows. Ripley's absence is notable, and I wonder if she sensed the apprehension in me tonight? She still hasn't appeared and that's unlike her because, more than anything, she's curious about everything and everyone.

We step outside and I pull the doors shut. It's chilly, but not so cold that it's unpleasant and with the garden lights on I love the ambience.

'Right. You need to remember that for several months at least the top part of the gardens had no divide at all between them. Ripley regarded both as one, and it was her territory. Suddenly, the gap is replaced by a six-foot-high fence and she can no longer see part of her domain. And then, without warning, Bertie moves in. She can't see him, but she can hear and smell him.'

Oh. I see what Nettie is getting at.

'One other observation I'd like to make is that Bengals enjoy playing, chasing, and investigating. They have a frisky spirit and love to climb. What's the first thing she does when she comes out into the garden, Kerra?'

'Usually, she jumps up onto the fence if Bertie is around. If not, then often she'll sniff her way along the boundary and then head off to the other side of the garden to disappear beneath the laurel bushes. There aren't any mice left in the garden.'

Drew laughs. 'They know better than to hang around here. I don't have mice, either.'

'As I said, I'm no expert, but there are two things I'd try before seeking a professional's advice. One is to build her a platform in the trees down in the bottom corner. A place she can sit and look over the fence. Bengals are curious by nature and while she can hear Bertie, she has no idea what he's doing. If she had a perch to sit and watch him, it might reassure her that he has his own confined area and he has no intention of encroaching on her territory.'

'That makes a lot of sense. Ripley is definitely more confrontational when she exits the cottage if Bertie is in the garden.'

'The other suggestion will probably sound a little strange. The standard practice for introducing a new pet into another animal's territory is short periods of supervised time together. The key is that both animals must be at eye level. Gradually these periods are extended until the two animals are comfortable around each other. If one is higher up than the other, on a fence for instance, I should imagine that it can appear one has an advantage over the other.'

'It's a little late for that in this case. Ripley has already asserted her authority over Bertie.'

Drew is right. I wouldn't relish the idea of getting them together, as I can envisage having to restrain a hissing Ripley, as Bertie stands his ground, howling.

'If you think about it from Ripley's point of view, she comes out of the cottage and her first thought is probably whether Bertie is in the garden. If a hole was cut at floor level and a piece of clear polycarbonate was fixed over it, she'd instantly be able to see what was happening. It might stop her jumping up onto the fence and scaring Bertie. Once they catch on to the fact that it's a solid barrier, they'd both be on the same level and yet within their own boundaries.'

'I'm up for that,' Drew replies. 'What about you, Kerra?'

'It sounds like it might be worth a shot. A window in a fence to stop a cat terrorising a dog. It almost sounds revolutionary.' I chuckle.

'For the sake of a fence panel we can replace quite easily if it doesn't work, it's a no-brainer. I could get that sorted tomorrow.'

'It's just a suggestion and if it doesn't solve the problem then it will mean getting someone in to work with Bertie and Ripley. Patience is usually the key to overcoming negative behaviour. Encourage them by giving treats as a reward when they're calm in the presence of another animal. It can be a slow process, it's true, but it's not like Bertie and Ripley have to live together, they simply need to learn how to be neighbours.'

'Well, let's give it a go, then,' I reply, looking at Drew with determination. 'Anything is better than a constant round of hissing and barking.'

Right on cue, madam appears.

'Here she is,' Nettie calls out, as Ripley heads straight for her. 'See, she can probably smell the dogs on me but she knows they're not a threat to her. And I assume Bertie is inside snuggled up, Drew?'

'He is; I'll be taking him out for his evening walk in about an hour.'

Ripley ignores Drew and heads straight over to wind herself around my left leg. 'She wants treats,' I explain, seeing the disappointment on Drew's face. 'Let's go back inside. You can give them to her; you might get lucky and she'll deign to sit on your lap.'

'I doubt it,' Drew replies, sounding miffed. 'She's transferred her affections to Ross these days.'

'Ross? Why Ross?' Nettie asks, looking at me blankly.

'Oh, he used to bring her treats when he was on site. Cats remember things like that, don't they?' I reply, quickly.

Nettie nods in agreement. 'They do. It's funny, they say the way to a man's heart is via his stomach and the same can be said for animals.'

Both Drew and I find that funny, but I think Nettie is serious. And she has a point.

'Are you ready for some nibbles, Drew?' I enquire and Nettie flashes me a smile as Drew is the first one through the door.

TWENTY
THE END OF THE WORLD AS I KNOW IT

Driving into the church hall car park, I see Dad's car isn't here, but I notice that Ross has brought one of the work vans. When I walk into the building, there's a hand-written sign on the swing doors into the hall itself saying: *Rehearsals in Progress – silence, please!*

Ross is walking up the corridor towards me and my heart leaps to see him in the flesh.

'Hey, how are you doing?' I whisper. He points his finger to the external doors and we walk back outside.

'It's been the week from hell. I still don't really know what's going on, which is worse than having my father on my back all the time. He's hired a car now and I haven't seen much of him. I spend every evening in my room and as far as I can tell he watches films downstairs.' His face looks grave. 'I need to bring in a large piece of chipboard, if you don't mind giving me a hand. Is Eddie coming tonight?'

'I assumed he'd already be here. I saw him briefly this morning on my way to the shop and he was dog-walking with

Ian. I'm sure he would have said something if he wasn't coming. He's probably just running late.'

Ross opens the back of the van and jumps up to slide out a huge piece of wood. It's probably three metres long by a metre wide.

'Are you sure you can manage this?' Ross checks, as he slides it towards me. 'Just steady the end for a moment and I'll stand it upright, then I'll lock the doors back up.'

As I stand here with the piece of wood towering above my head, Dad's car appears and he drives into the space next to Ross's van. When he flings open the door, he's on his feet in seconds and he looks angry.

'It's about time people started telling the truth around here,' he bellows, looking from me to Ross.

'Dad, what are you on about?'

'Leading my daughter up the garden path. You didn't think I had an inkling about what was going on between the two of you? And now I find out everyone has been talking about it behind my back, because they all knew this wasn't going to end well. And now your father has made that very plain, Ross.'

We're both stunned by his rant. But Dad isn't finished. He turns to me, his eyes blazing.

'And you, Kerra, saying how you know what you're doing and then I find out you've been letting Ross take advantage of you as if you're totally naïve.' He runs out of steam, but he's red in the face and sweating. I feel like the blood has just drained to my feet and Ross doesn't know what to say or do.

'What have you heard, Dad?' I ask, gingerly.

'For a start, no one told me Jago was back and I'm guessing you knew that, Kerra. And secondly, he says you've been up at the house because he recognised you. I laughed it off, of course, but when I thought about it, things started to add up. What builder turns up on a Saturday to do a favour and ends up staying all day?'

Ross goes to speak, but Dad puts up his hand to stop him.

'Oh, Jago had a good laugh, alright. He says you're selling Treylya and then you'll be moving away when you open a second office in Launceston. Your father tells me that you have big ambitions, and they're bigger than Kerra here, or Penvennan.'

'Now look, Eddie, I don't know—'

'You think you can explain your way out of this? Don't even try, because your track record speaks for itself. Jago got a few backs up tonight and that won't bode well for your business. Folk don't like to be talked down to or laughed at. Or used.' Dad turns to look at me. 'Kerra, you and I need to talk. Now. Jump in your car and follow me back to Green Acre. I want you to hear what Jago said from me and not on the grapevine.'

Feeling horrified, I glance at Ross. He nods his head, indicating for me to go and reaches out to take the wood from me. As his fingers graze mine, my eyes fill with tears. I want to stay and yet Dad is so angry I'm afraid his blood pressure will go through the roof.

'Now, Kerra,' Dad shouts, as he gets back in his car, slamming the door shut.

I can hardly see as I stumble forward, digging my hand into my pocket for my keys. Why did this have to happen now? It's the hardest thing I've ever done walking away from Ross when I know none of this is his fault, but it's obvious that Dad won't believe that.

* * *

'There's no point in losing your temper, Eddie,' Nettie says, keeping her voice even. 'Now, both of you sit down at the table and sip your tea. It's time to take a deep breath before you say something you'll live to regret.'

'Thank you, Nettie,' I say, my voice hoarse with the tears I'm desperately trying to hold back. I can't even look at Dad anymore. He has even accused Ross of talking me into having work done that wasn't necessary.

Several minutes pass in awkward silence, broken only by the ticking of the kitchen clock.

'Right.' Poor Nettie looks traumatised. 'I think both Kerra and I would benefit from knowing what exactly happened earlier on this evening to explain your behaviour, Eddie.'

Goodness, Nettie sounds like she means business and even Dad does a double take.

'I'm not apologising for anything,' Dad states, angrily. 'I was talking to Ian and wanted to check out something he said, so I walked down to the pub.'

I groan inwardly. Ian is walking on eggshells around Dad and if he was pressed about this other job of his, then giving Dad Polly's name wouldn't have helped his case. Dad has no idea what Polly is doing and it wouldn't have made any sense to him, at all. I bet he called in to see her, suspicious of what Ian might be up to. But what has that got to do with Jago?

'It seems there's things going on around here that people are hiding and that's shifty in my book!' Dad continues, his nostrils flaring. I quietly sip my tea, dreading where this is going. 'Well, I didn't have time to get to the bottom of that, because when I walked in it was me own daughter's name I heard as I stepped into the bar. And it came out of the mouth of Jago Treloar.'

I put the mug down on the table because my hand is now shaking.

'Yep, I got all this from that jumped-up, pompous fool of a man. I marched over and he was standing there, chatting with Gryff and Zacky, as if he was a regular there in my local, which he ain't. I told him straight that if he had anything to say about me, or me family, then he'd best say it straight to my face.'

I swallow hard as a lump seems to have worked its way up into my throat. Poor Dad – what an awful thing to walk into and Jago rarely visited The Lark and Lantern when he lived here. No, he went there tonight to ask questions and cause trouble. Zacky would tell him whatever he wanted to know in his harmless way, but Gryff just happened to be in the wrong place, at the wrong time. It's one thing nattering away with friends, but Jago is no one's friend around here.

Nettie and Dad look across the table at each other. 'I can appreciate this isn't easy for you, Eddie, but getting all het up and angry isn't going to help and it's not good for you. Take your time and just tell us what exactly he had to say.'

Dad picks up his mug, taking a slurp of his tea, and the sigh he lets out tears at my heart. It wavers, as if he's struggling to control his temper.

'I walked right up to Jago and he was within arm's reach, but Gryff stepped in between us.' Dad pauses, expelling another calming breath. 'Gryff said they were just talking about the work on the two cottages and what a good job Treloar's had done. He tried to pull me away and said he'd walk back up the hill with me.'

It's obvious that it didn't end there.

'I knew what he was trying to do, and I appreciated it, but

Jago wasn't going to miss his chance. He said he was surprised to hear that you were back, but he was glad that Ross had sorted you out. Jago said Ross could be a little too accommodating at times, but that it was good for business and he laughed. "It's all money in the bank," he said. But then he went on to add that it was time the lonely, single women around here stopped taking advantage of his son. His sights are set a lot higher, he informed everyone, and Treloar's is about to double its operations. Ross will be heading up a new office as they expand up country.'

Dad looks directly at me.

'Ross isn't going anywhere,' I state, adamantly.

'Ha! Not that he's told you, Kerra. Don't you see? He's been stringing you along. I wish I'd known what was really going on. He's made a fool of us all. I was starting to trust him, too. I saw how you looked at each other, but I would have had something to say if I'd known you'd been staying up at his place. What hurts is that you hid it from me, so you knew all along that something wasn't right.'

How can I explain my actions without accusing Dad of being prejudiced?

'You're wrong, Dad. I'm not a child anymore and I make my own decisions. You don't like change and I was trying to ease myself back into village life to avoid causing an upset. I don't care what everyone else thinks, and neither does Ross, but we've been keeping our relationship behind closed doors out of respect for you.'

Dad bangs his mug down on the table, making us all jump. 'For me? Creeping around behind me back with a Treloar when you know that Jago is little more than a crook. Giving back-handers is how he got to where he is and you know it, my girl.'

Nettie reaches out to touch Dad's hand. 'That's as may be, Eddie, but you can't lay that on Ross, too.'

'Thank you, Nettie.' I speak up before Dad can respond. 'It's the same way that you're making Ian prove himself when he hasn't done anything wrong in the first place. Yes, his father and his brother are known for their dodgy dealings, but aside from youthful pranks name one serious accusation that his name has been linked to?'

The minute I stop speaking, Nettie flashes me a look of warning.

'So, I'm not allowed to protect my niece either, am I? Old values don't seem to count for much anymore, but I'm not having it.'

Anger is bubbling up inside of me and I need to quell it, or I will end up walking out.

'All I'm saying is that you should judge people by what they've done. Ross didn't worm his way into my life. I invited him in. If it wasn't for the extension, our paths might not have crossed for a long time. We can't help how we feel about each other and that's a fact. Being discreet isn't wrong, it's a choice we made together.'

Dad rolls his eyes. 'I'm disappointed in you, Kerra. Linking yourself to that family is shaming. You know how Jago tried to destroy your mum's dream of building the kennels out of spite. She was the innocent caught in the middle of a long-standing argument between Jago and me. He went too far, and I dug up enough proof to make him back down and let the planning committee come to an unbiased conclusion. Don't you think he'd do anything to get his own back, even after all this time? He knows what's dear to me and he'll use his son to break your heart and think nothing of it.'

Nettie looks appalled. 'Eddie, think about what you're

saying.' She's sitting on the edge of her seat, dithering over whether to stop us, but it's too late.

'Mum knew that in all the time I was away I never forgot Ross and every man I met I compared to him. What I didn't know is that Ross felt the same way about me.'

'He's got a funny way of showing it, then. When he married that Bailey woman it seemed to me like he didn't have anything else on his mind, other than marrying into a family his parents approved of.'

'That's unfair, Dad. No one, including me, thought that I'd come back here to live. But Mum knew this was where I was supposed to be and that's why she wanted me to come home.'

Dad gets to his feet, pushing his chair back so forcefully it falls to the floor with a crash.

'She wanted you home so you and I could keep an eye on each other, that's all,' he shouts, pounding the table with his fist. 'Family meant something to her, God bless her soul. I didn't think you'd stoop so low as to bring your mum into this conversation as if she'd approve of what you're doing. Ross will ditch you soon enough and when he does my door will be open, because family support each other in times of trouble. But until then, there's no more to be said between us. Because of him you've kept things back from me and I don't feel I know me own daughter anymore.'

TWENTY-ONE
PREPARING TO FIGHT THE GOOD FIGHT

I lean back against the front door of Pedrevan, my body quivering. Dad has it all wrong, but his parting words give me no choice other than to leave. My legs feel like jelly and the sound of the doorbell makes me jump, my nerves jangling.

Easing the door open just enough to peer out, I see Alice standing in front of me. I swing it open a little wider to allow her inside.

'Sorry, Kerra. I was upstairs and I heard everything Uncle Eddie said. Nettie asked me to pop over and check on you. He doesn't know I'm here.'

I slip off my coat as I walk, and Alice follows me inside and stands watching, uncomfortably. There's nothing I can say... nothing I want to say at this moment.

'That wasn't fair of him, Kerra. He makes it sound like everyone knew, but that's not true. It might be what Jago implied, I can't say for sure as I wasn't there, but it's not common knowledge. Believe me.'

It's hard not to blurt out 'well you'd be one to know,' but that would be lashing out unfairly. Alice learnt her lesson back in the summer. I like to believe that there was never any malice in the gossip she spreads, but chatting away in the salon there are topics that are off limits. It would be unfair of me to rake that up now because she's not the enemy – no, that's Jago Treloar.

'For that matter, even I didn't know. Ross is very discreet, isn't he?'

'Why don't you take off your coat? It might be a good idea to give Nettie and Dad a little time alone together. If anyone can calm him down, it's her.'

She looks relieved. 'Thanks, Kerra. Ian is out working and won't be back until 10 p.m. and I feel awkward as Uncle Eddie is being so kind to us.'

'I guess we're both in the doghouse with our dads, then,' I declare, shaking my head sadly.

'I've been meaning to pop over to thank you for listening to me that night I arrived on your doorstep, and for supporting Ian. It means a lot to us both. We wouldn't still be with Uncle Eddie if it weren't for your help and it's going to take a while to get on our feet.'

We sit down onto the sofa, as the horror of what just occurred begins to sink in. I'd offer to help them financially, but – with the way things are going – Dad would probably read something into that, as well.

'I kick myself, Alice, as I really thought I had everything under control. No big moves, no huge upsets and it would all be fine. Maybe Dad is right, and I am naïve, but only when it comes to other people's perceptions.'

Alice frowns and it doesn't suit her sunny disposition, which I've always envied. When you're the serious one, you tend to overthink everything and, often, that's what trips you up.

'The thing is, Kerra, Jago knows exactly how to wind up Uncle Eddie. I don't know who else witnessed what went on, but enough that everyone will know by morning. I doubt any of them will be on Jago's side or believe the story he's spinning.'

'It's kind of you to try to reassure me, Alice, and it's appreciated. But it's Dad's pride that's been shot down and he feels I've made him look foolish. That never was my intention, of course, but the way it looks to Dad now, whatever I say will sound like I'm making excuses.'

'What are you going to do?'

'Nothing. People will have to make of it what they will. I hope that in time Dad will come around, but in the meantime I'm sick and fed up watching what I do and say.'

Alice's face freezes. 'Won't that make it worse?'

'How much worse can it get?' I throw back at her and she nods her head, sadly.

* * *

When I'm able to pull myself together, I call Ross.

'Bloody hell, Kerra. What a mess!' Ross's voice makes me cringe as I hold the phone to my ear. That's precisely what it is. 'My father didn't say a word to me when I arrived back quite late. It was obvious that something was up, but we literally passed in the hallway as he was on his way upstairs and he didn't even say goodnight, so I ignored him.'

'Where do we go from here?' I ask, feeling everything is beginning to spiral out of control.

'Clearly my father's plan is coming together. He avoided me because he knows he went too far tonight. There is no way my father recognised you and he doesn't know what car you drive. No, he got this information from someone else, and he's been asking around, digging up whatever he can to see what's useful to know.'

'Zacky wouldn't have known anything. The only people who did were with us for lunch on Sunday and it wouldn't have come from any one of them.'

'But it could have been someone at Pennington Hall Hotel. My father is no doubt busy touching base with all of his old contacts. That's where he'd take them for lunch. He knows the chef, Louis. I bet that was it. I can't believe my father went that far, though, to make up that story. Selling Treylya has nothing to do with him and to imply that I'm going to be moving away is a malicious lie, especially given the way he framed it. I feel so bad about this and no wonder Eddie was angry.'

Ross's distress mirrors my own, but there's no way to undo what's been done, and it's best to let things settle and then decide what to do next.

'Look it's Friday tomorrow, so let's bide our time and see what the weekend brings. We'll stick to our plan for Saturday night. I'll make sure I've finished my rounds by 3 p.m. I'll come straight from work. I can shower and change at the hotel.'

I take a deep breath. 'I think you're right. But why don't you just come to the house. No more hiding ourselves away from anyone.'

'Are you sure about that, Kerra?' Ross asks, clearly having doubts about whether that's the right thing to do.

'I'm positive. I'll be calling in for a quick visit with Mrs Moyle and Arthur in the morning, and I'll see what type of reception I get from them.'

'I never meant to come between you and Eddie, Kerra. If I

thought for one moment this would happen, I couldn't have inflicted that on you – or on Eddie. I'd rather walk out and cut all ties with my father than subject either of you to this sorry state of affairs.' The sadness in his voice is poignant.

'You're my future, Ross, and it pains me to say that because it sounds like I'm choosing you over Dad, but I'm not. I love my dad and always will, but I can't change his mind for him. He simply must stand back and begin to see things for what they are. If he can't, or won't, it's totally outside of my control and there is nothing at all I can do about it.'

The silence between us is a sobering acknowledgement that there are no guarantees a rift like this can be fixed.

'Does Dad love me enough to let go of his determination to be at war with your father? That's the real question here. This isn't our fault, Ross, not really.'

Love and *war*... two words that should never be in the same sentence together. And yet this is where we find ourselves.

'Jago only has power over Dad if he believes Jago is telling the truth. Dad feels I've disrespected him, but where is his respect for me?'

Ross sighs, and it has a hollow ring to it. 'Your dad is angry, Kerra, and that's understandable given the circumstances. Just let him have some space for the time being. Try to get some sleep and see what tomorrow brings.'

A chill runs down my spine. What if other people begin to take sides? Will the ripples created as word goes round bring out the naysayers? I wonder. No one relishes the thought of people thinking badly of them, well, no one with good intentions at their core. People will back Dad, not Jago, but by being with Ross will they then think I've changed sides and see that as a betrayal?

* * *

'Morning, Polly.'

'Kerra! I didn't know whether to give you a call, or not. Give me a minute and I'll ring you back. I'll just grab my coat and head outside, first.'

It is as bad as I feared, then. It's agonising as the seconds tick by. Poor Ripley can sense how demoralised I'm feeling this morning and she hasn't left my side. She's curled up on my lap as I drink my third cup of coffee, because I have no appetite at all.

Buzz, buzz. 'I'm back. How are uh... *things* this morning?' Polly asks, cagily.

'Not good. Dad told me what Jago said to him in the bar.'

'Is it true about you and Ross?' Polly sounds taken aback. That doesn't bode well for other people's reactions, does it? 'I mean, your dad and Jago have never seen eye to eye.'

'Yes, that part is true. Just don't believe everything you hear, Polly.'

'Of course I won't, Kerra. I've always respected Ross. Jago, well, to my knowledge I think that's only the second time he's ever been in the pub. Dad was telling me afterwards that the first time was years ago. That visit didn't go down well either, and Dad said he ended up asking him to leave.'

This isn't why I rang Polly, as there's no point in distressing myself any further. I can't help wondering if that occasion was when he was trying to rile people up about objecting to the change of use at Green Acre.

'It is what it is, Polly and the rumour-mongers will have their day. Ross and I will try to let it all go over our heads. Anyway, it's not common knowledge, but I've bought one of the little fisherman's cottages in the cove.'

'Oh, Gwel Teg! How lovely! I'd heard it was up for sale but when I didn't see a board appear, I assumed that the owners had changed their minds. The Bartletts haven't been down in a long while. It's nice to know it's in the hands of a resident.'

'I'm going to rent it out, but it needs a little cosmetic lift inside. Just a general paint through, and I'll be ordering some new furniture. There are a few pieces that would look lovely painted, including a wonderful old wardrobe. I wondered if you could collect the key from me sometime and pop in to give me a quote? I'm not in a rush and I'd rather keep this between us for now.'

'You don't fancy having a go yourself? You did a great job on those pieces you made over for Pedrevan. You're a dab hand at shabby chic!' Given what's happened, Gwel Teg is the last place I want to be seen. Every little thing is now fuel for the fire, but it's already stoked up and there's no point adding a new element into the equation.

'Ah, thank you, Polly, and I did enjoy getting hands-on, but I have way too much on my plate right now. I won't be advertising it, as there's someone I know who would make a perfect tenant.'

'You can trust me one hundred per cent, Kerra, like I trust you, my dear friend. When word gets out, it certainly won't be from my lips. I'll make time to pop into Gwel Teg sometime next week and I'll text you beforehand about the key.'

'That's appreciated, Polly, thank you.' How telling is it that something that gave me a little thrill, now represents another potentially hot topic of conversation?

'Try to keep heart. Who the heck is going to listen to someone like Jago anyway?' Polly retorts, sounding cross. 'It's pretty obvious he has his own agenda and that's to upset

Eddie. People trust Ross and that's why Treloar's is so well respected. It wasn't like that before Ross took over. I'm not saying the work wasn't good, but Jago isn't well-liked for a reason. Try not to worry; most things that cause a bit of a stir are short-lived. And about Gwel Teg, it might be quicker if we pop in together, but I'll be in touch as soon as possible.'

As I press end call, Ripley shifts on my lap. 'I have to go and see Arthur now, Rippers. Why don't you head upstairs for a bit?' Smoothing her back along to the tip of her tail, her purring ribcage rumbles against my legs.

'It will be alright, I know it,' I say, adamantly, as she jumps down and pads away from me. It's unlike Ripley not to reply when I talk to her and I think we're both in the doldrums today.

Right, it's time to get my things together and head to the shop to face the next test. Ready and armed, I push open the door of the convenience store and walk up to the counter. Mrs Moyle's face freezes the moment she spots me. She has a small queue of people waiting to be served and she appears flustered.

'Oh, Kerra. Are you here to see Arthur?' she asks, eyeing my computer bag. I nod and she tilts her head in the direction of the doorway behind her. 'Go on up. He'll be delighted to see you.'

As I squeeze past the line of people waiting, heads nod and I plaster on a relaxed smile.

'Morning, Kerra,' Zacky says, as he stands back to allow me through to walk behind the counter. I can feel his eyes on me, watching for my reaction.

'Morning, and what a lovely one it is! Can't beat a blue sky to kick off the day,' I reply, cheerily and keep walking.

When I get to the bottom of the stairs, I call out, 'Arthur, it's Kerra.'

'Come on up,' he calls out. 'I saw you crossin' the road and hoped you were comin' to visit me.'

I act normally as I greet him with a warm smile. 'Are you ready for the handover?'

He beams back at me. 'Ready and waitin' – it's excitin' and I have a list of people keen to be invited.'

'Wonderful, we can work through that together. If someone wants a friend of theirs added, they will need to contact you. I'm assuming that's going to be manageable, as how many people are on your list?'

As I slip off my coat and pull out the shiny new laptop, Arthur studies the notepad in front of him. 'Twenty-eight, all in. Over half of 'em are housebound and on their own.'

'Well, just remember that you're in control and you set the criteria for joining. I think you will all enjoy being able to chat online, share things and support each other. We'll run through it in detail and then this little beauty is all yours!'

Arthur looks at me, his jaw dropping. 'Yer givin' me yer' computer?'

'Your old one is slow, Arthur, and I wanted to thank you for looking out for me. That night when you alerted Mrs Moyle and she rang to warn me about the guys loitering in the shadows at the side of the cottage, it prevented what could have been a traumatising event. Being on my own, and with Drew away, the thought of facing a break-in is horrifying to contemplate even now. And poor Ripley was staying with me – anything could have happened that night.'

He nods his head slowly, his expression grave. 'It was a bit of a to-do, wasn't it? But Ross came to your aid.'

The look we exchange is one of understanding and I can see he appreciates the gesture.

My phone pings. 'I'd better check that first, Arthur. It won't take a second.' I dig in to pull out my phone and am relieved to see it's a text from Drew.

I'll pick up some thick polycarbonate this afternoon, and cut the hole in the fence over the weekend, if that's okay with you. My new project has just had the green light, so it's all go today!

I'm thrilled for Drew and the timing couldn't be better.

Thanks, just whenever you're ready. And that's great news that you're off and running at last. I won't be around much this weekend. Would you mind popping in to feed Ripley tomorrow morning? I'll catch up with you early next week. You're a star!

My pleasure and please mention that little fact the next time Felicity is here. She values your opinion. 😊

'Right, Arthur, let's make a start. I've also loaded up a document for you that explains in simple steps how to access the Penvennan Community Link-Up and what's on offer. You can email it as an attachment and I've also printed off a pile of them in case anyone would rather have a hard copy. But remember that I'm happy to pop in to help anyone who has problems setting themselves up.'

'You think of everything, Kerra, and I'm much obliged, as will be a few other folk, too. This is a lifeline, a bit of fun and a nice distraction for me.'

We could all do with that right now and if I can keep myself busy then it will stop me dwelling on things that I can't do anything about at present.

* * *

'I bet you put a smile on my Arthur's face.' Mrs Moyle looks up as I step into the shop. She's putting packs of butter into the chiller cabinet. We're alone and I'm a little dismayed, as I was hoping to say a quick 'goodbye' and get back to Pedrevan.

'It will be a bit of a learning curve at first, but he seems confident he'll soon get the hang of it,' I tell her. 'Well, I must get—'

'I'm sorry to interrupt you, Kerra, but there's no point beating around the bush. I just wanted to say that I won't put up with any gossip in here, no matter who it's from. If I end up turning customers away, then so be it. Now, I won't say another word, just thank you for supporting Arthur. That man has a heart of gold and he's never happier than when he's helping someone out.'

To my shame, my eyes start to fill with tears. 'Thank you, Mrs Moyle,' I say, huskily. 'If he has any problems, please give me a call. I'm only too happy to help.' I don't wait for her to respond but turn quickly and hurry out through the door before anyone else enters. Battle lines are being drawn and that means Mrs Moyle has already had a preview of what's to come and she didn't like what she heard.

Just get through the rest of the day as best you can, Kerra, I tell myself sternly. No one has died and the earth is still turning. If this is fate, then there's a reason all this is happening. I'm feeling helpless because I don't have a plan, but tomorrow afternoon Ross will be by my side again. He'll know more about what's happening, but until then it's time for some TLC. I'm going to run a hot bath with oodles of bubbles, slap on a mud face pack, grab my Kindle and pamper myself. I want to look positive and glowing when I see Ross tomorrow. Everything he's worked for is on the line and he'll be reeling.

I intend for us to return on Sunday ready to face the week ahead, whatever it brings, without self-recrimination. We've done nothing wrong and my days of trying to stay in the shadows are over.

TWENTY-TWO
FINDING A WAY FORWARD

The Crosslands Hotel, situated on the outskirts of Trehoweth, is a manor house set within its own grounds. I tap lightly on the hotel room door and wait for a minute or two before tapping a little louder. The seconds continue to pass before I finally hear the clunk of a lock turning. Ross pokes his head around the side, a beaming smile on his face when he sees it's me.

'Come in. As you can see, I was in the shower.' The sheepish look he gives me is endearing. Seeing him standing there with the white bath sheet wrapped around his waist and water dripping from his hair puts a huge smile on my face.

The moment the door is shut, and I drop my bag onto the floor, I rush into his arms and we just stand here hugging, loath to let go even to grab a kiss.

'Sorry about the change of plan,' Ross whispers into my ear. 'In hindsight I figured it was best not to risk inflaming the situation with Eddie by brazenly picking you up at the cottage.'

'When I read the text message I kinda guessed that was the reasoning behind it.'

'Is that your phone I can hear pinging away?' Ross pulls back, expecting me to dive into my bag for it, but I just let out a huge sigh.

'There's a whole raft of texts from various people checking to see that I'm *okay*. I wanted to speak to you before I answered. And we've had a dinner invite for tonight – a special one.'

Ross looks at me, screwing up his face. 'Tonight? I'd rather hoped we could get room service and just chill.'

'Me too,' I reply, as he helps me off with my coat. He immediately drops it onto the floor so he can scoop me up into his arms, carrying me over to the bed, squealing. Every time he moves his head little splashes of water flick down onto me. After dropping me gently down on the bed, he heads back into the bathroom and then returns, rubbing his hair with a hand towel before joining me. I could spend all day just watching him. All those years we were apart and yet the first time I saw him again it was as if the time that had elapsed counted for nothing.

We lie back on the bed, and it's only when you completely relax that reality begins to sink in. There are things that need saying, which aren't going to be easy to hear, but the sooner it's over and done with, the better. But neither of us wants to move and we stare up at the ceiling. How did it come to this? I find myself wondering and I bet Ross is feeling the exact same way.

'It's been a horrible couple of days, hasn't it?' I declare, irritably.

'If we're going to have a serious conversation, I'd better throw on some clothes,' Ross says, grimly.

Scooting up the bed, I plump up the pillows to support my back and watch his every move. Ross is a strong man, but not thick set. He's lean and muscular, given how hands-on he is when he's on site, but not bulky. I know he goes for a run several times a week and that's his thinking time, too. He would never ask someone to do something he wouldn't be prepared to tackle himself, except for roofing, he once told me. Heights are not his thing and his respect for the guys who clamber over the tiles shows that he's a man who isn't afraid to admit he has weaknesses, as well as strengths.

'What's going on inside that head of yours, Kerra Shaw?' Ross demands to know, naked to the waist and looking like a model in a jeans ad. With his damp curls falling down over his forehead, his muscled torso, and the way he's unaware of the effect he's having on me, it sums him up perfectly. Ross thinks he's a man like every other, but he isn't. He's special. Like your favourite movie actor who dazzles in every part he plays, he has that unknown quality – some people call it charisma, but it's more than that. In Ross's case it's enhanced by his honesty and sense of fair play. And yet he's spent his entire life battling prejudice and, from his father, arrogant antipathy. I firmly believe that Ross is the man Jago always wanted to be, but Jago lacks moral fibre. Instead, he took the easy route, using bribery and manipulation to get the desired results.

'As I've always said, women want to be with you and men want to be you.' I smirk at Ross as he shakes his head at me.

'Hardly. I'm the poster guy for relationship disasters and our current situation proves that. If I were a better man I'd walk away and leave you to pick up the pieces of your life, but I'm not.' He makes a sad face, and his tone is apologetic. 'I can't exist without you and that's a fact. Not quite the hero of the piece now, am I?'

'You'll always be a hero to me and none of this is your doing. We do need to decide how to move forward, though.' I pick up my phone and scroll through the messages. 'Sy and Tegan have invited us for dinner at The Forge tonight. I'm sure they've heard some of the rumours, but there's something special they want to ask us, and I don't want to spoil it for them. Do you mind if we go?'

Ross pulls on a T-shirt and comes over to sit next to me on the bed, stooping first to kiss me on the lips. There's a kiss and there's a *kiss*; this one is comforting, and it tells me I need to be strong.

'If it's important, then that's fine. Who are the other messages from?'

'Sissy, Yvonne, Logan, Uncle Alistair, Georgia – James's mum – and even Kate. She used to drive one of Tegan's two minibuses, but now she has her own little van, given that they are all self employed under the new set-up.'

Ross shakes his head, sadly.

'What a mess that we've unwittingly pulled everyone into.'

'The problem is that I don't know what they've overheard, and I think the less I say the better, for fear of sounding like I'm making excuses or trying to get people on our side. I was going to do a simple reply, saying I'm fine and not to believe everything they hear. But does that sound like I'm dodging the issue when everyone will know that Dad isn't supporting us?'

'You are, but so are they. If your gut instincts are telling you to do that, go ahead. At least you can copy and paste the message.'

I give him one of my fixed stares. 'I'm being serious here.'

Ross reaches out to grab my free hand. 'I wasn't being flippant, Kerra, because it's going to get worse before it gets any better. We have a big decision to make and everything could hinge upon it.'

'Before you go any further, Ross, I need to tell you something. I've spent my entire life either trying to please people or melt into the background and not put myself out there for fear of... rejection. I'm not even sure that's the right word. I am who I am, but I don't fit the mould and that's a fact. And now I've had enough. I'm like a firework and the fuse paper has been lit. I'm about to explode and that thought scares me, but it also makes me feel free.'

Ross gazes at me, his eyes full of concern, and I can see my words resonate with him.

'My father intends to leave me with no option other than to move to Launceston to set up the second office. He thought that by upsetting Eddie it would make you walk away from me and the humiliation of that would make me only too glad to get away. I found out this morning that he has already approached my foreman, Will, about stepping into my shoes as a manager. Effectively, taking my place here.'

My jaw drops. Ross stares down at his hands before rubbing them together, nervously.

'You see, my father didn't know you were back. He thought I was burying myself in work and he'd waltz in, hand me a huge budget and I'd bite his hand off for the opportunity.'

It takes a moment, or two, for me to take in what Ross is saying. Was Jago's reaction, when he found out what was going on, fuelled by anger? I wonder.

'Considering he had to think on his feet, I can now see that he panicked,' Ross continues. 'His trip to The Lark and Lantern was a clever move, if devious.'

'Your father deigned to lowered himself to go there because he knew it would pay off. He could ask questions, and no one would bat an eyelid, because he'd been away. Whatever information he could glean was key, because he had to suddenly change his strategy.'

'You're right. When he found out that it wasn't general knowledge that we are seeing each other, he knew that was our weak spot.'

I let out a groan. 'Some people are sheep, aren't they? I mean people like poor Zacky, blindly allowing themselves to unwittingly give Jago the ammunition he needs. But your father can't have expected my dad to walk in like that. I wonder if Jago was made aware of the fact that the three of us would be at the village hall?'

Ross shrugs his shoulders. 'It's likely. Sam told me he bought several rounds of drinks because he was celebrating.'

'You've spoken to Sam?'

Ross looks back at me uneasily.

'Sam rang me, but it was about you really. He mentioned it afterwards, saying how it all got a little out of hand.'

Ross is trying to skate over something here.

'What did he say about me?'

Ross squeezes my hand, and I can see this isn't easy for him.

'Sam thinks you're helping Polly to set up her own business and that he's going to lose her. If it's true, he told me that his days are numbered if she walks away. He can't afford to replace her, as she's his right arm and the pub is barely making a profit. Sam is at the end of his tether, Kerra, and he wanted to know if it was true. I said that Polly is her own woman, and it was her he should be speaking to, not me and not you.'

My stomach begins churning. 'I put Polly in touch with Oliver Sinclair. Polly would never leave Sam to cope on his own, but she needs something to keep her sane, Ross. I can only assume she gets her creative spark from her mother, but it's a part of who she is and not being able to express herself is eating away at her. If Sam doesn't let Polly spread her wings in her own free time, he will end up losing her. Of that I have no doubt.'

'From his viewpoint you're an unsettling influence, Kerra. It's true that she's setting up her own business, then?'

I feel utterly crestfallen. 'Yes. But she'll be doing small jobs on the side. Ian is going to help her, as he's a painter/decorator. As *Designed to Sell*, she'll be renovating furniture and buying bits and pieces to get previously rented houses ready for sale. I can't imagine her getting a flood of work, but she has her first job and I've asked her to make over Gwel Teg afterwards.'

'I thought you saw that as your fun, hands-on project? You were excited to get stuck in.'

'That's true, but with all that's happened it's taken the shine off everything. If Dad can't understand why I snapped up Gwel Teg, then others will no doubt feel the same. When it's *little Kerra Shaw* it raises eyebrows.'

'Most of them don't know you at all, do they? Or what you're capable of achieving.' Ross's voice softens. 'Eddie's life is relatively simple and much of what you do is unfathomable to him. The unknown is scary. Sam is in the same boat because he knows Polly has aspirations.'

'If Sam knew what was going on, I'm sure it would be easier all round. But Polly is scared it will come between them before she has a chance to prove that she can make it work and continue at the pub.'

'But it's obvious that if she does well, at some point it will command her attention full-time.'

I look at Ross, my expression one of resolve. 'Polly can't

hide her natural-born talent. In the same way that I'm an entrepreneur. She studied hard to get a qualification in interior design and yet Sam doesn't even acknowledge it. If his business is failing, then it's because he won't open his mind to the opportunities out there. Anyone in business these days has to move with the times, and those who don't will go under. Her success is nothing to do with the struggles at the pub. Polly has no control over the decisions her dad makes. If he turns it around, then he'll be able to pay for the staff he needs.'

Ross looks stunned. 'That's fighting talk, Kerra.'

'You know exactly what I mean, Ross, and I'm not wrong. Polly will end up leaving anyway if Sam doesn't wake up to the reality of his situation. It's a case of either one life being ruined, or two, when they could both be happy. At some point she'll hopefully meet the love of her life. What will Sam do then?'

'I think you'd better warn Polly before it all blows up. Something tells me that you're not convinced the days are numbered for The Lark and Lantern, though.'

We smile at each other and I find it exhilarating that we're so in tune.

'I should imagine he could attract a buyer with ease because of the location. But the place means a lot to him. If Sam approaches me of his own accord, then with a willing investor on board he could turn things around. I guess it's time for everyone to stand up and take responsibility for their own actions, because there's no point in reaching out to someone who doesn't want to be helped. And if he's had enough, I wouldn't blame him taking the money and running. But what would he do, then? I suspect Polly would go her own way and I'm not sure he's ready to be on his own.'

'You could be right. It's daunting for anyone having to start all over again, at any time of life. Now, what are we going to do about this Launceston thing?'

That's a bit trickier. 'If you do as your father bids, then everyone will believe that he was simply telling the truth.'

'If I refuse, a simple vote would be sufficient to oust me. As I'm also an employee my parents would have to sack me if they wanted to totally get rid of me. I might have some legal redress there for unfair dismissal, but as I'm opposing plans for expansion, it could be a costly battle and one I might not win.'

'Does Jago have anyone on the sidelines, whom he trusts enough to take over from you?'

Ross sucks in a deep breath. 'Only Will. My father doesn't really trust anyone unless he's known them for a long time. Despite our frequent disagreements, I've given him no real cause for complaint until now. What I don't know is why it's suddenly come to a head. Reading between the lines, I think he's come into some money and I know that over in Spain he dabbles in the property market. If he's made a quick profit on a deal, then he'll be keen to sink that into something solid. And what better than the family business, over which he has control?'

'You still have the upper hand, surely? Will might be able to step up, but not to your level. Managing one site isn't quite the same as running an entire business with multiple jobs on the go at the same time.'

I like Will, he's a good man and he was in charge of the extensions to Tigry and Pedrevan cottages, but he relies heavily on Ross's input and that was very evident.

'I'm guessing that my father is counting on the fact that I'll be on call to troubleshoot Will's teething problems, at the same time as getting the new office up and running. He says it'll be less work for me, as we won't have employees as we do now, but contractors in and around the Launceston area. I've seen other building companies make that mistake and I know of two outfits using contractors who went bust. It works for a business like Clean and Shine, but the building trade is different. Reliability and good skills don't always go hand in hand, so good workers look for good wages. Give a man a proper job, and pay him the rate he deserves, and he'll be loyal. That's where Treloar's, as a family business, scores. In a day and age when large companies don't really give a damn about their customers, we've prospered. Keeping local men in employment is as important as seeing a rise in profits each year. When greed and cutting corners are thrown into the mix, they put everything in jeopardy.'

I turn sideway, hooking up my leg to sit looking at Ross face to face.

'It sounds to me like you've already made up your mind. What's the plan?'

I can tell from his general demeanour that he's well aware it's a gamble that might not go in his favour.

'I'll stay, but I'm going nowhere. If Will is prepared to take on the job at Launceston, then I'll do what I can to support him from a distance. Treloar's means everything to me and if the way to show my father that he's wrong is by comparing results, then so be it. The bottom line will speak for itself. Either the new idea will fly, or it won't. He won't be happy, but I can't see what other options he has. He won't want to hang around here for too long and this is the solution I'm going to put on the table.'

In a way it's relief to know that Ross can stand back and see the situation for what it is, but tough to accept that after all the hard work he's put in it counts for very little.

'And how do *we* proceed?' I ask, tentatively.

'That's a decision only you can make, Kerra. Losing my job would be gut-wrenching but Eddie cutting you out of his life forever would break your heart. We both know that.'

I let out a huge sigh because he's right. 'If we were living in London few would know, or even care, what was going on. Unless it's political, or a scandal that hits the headlines and the news, lives get turned upside down every day and it goes unnoticed. This is so damned annoying and unnecessary!' I exclaim, feeling helpless.

Unfortunately, in a small community like ours it's rather like the situation between Ripley and Bertie. Neither of them likes change. Ripley can't understand why Bertie can run unfettered in the garden that was once hers, even though Ripley was the one who decided to move in with me. And Bertie can't understand why Ripley resents him, when he'd love to be friends. The root of discontent is uncertainty, fear of change and sometimes even jealousy, but you'd think human beings would know better.

'As much as it pains me to toe the line,' I admit, 'I think it would be best at least for the next week to keep our heads down. After that, we act like any other couple and you can come and go as you please. You'll no doubt appreciate being able to get away from Treylya, and your father, for a break. If Dad can't accept that, then so be it.'

Ross gives me a nervous look and I can tell that he still has doubts. 'There's no real rush, Kerra. If all it takes is a little more time, then maybe we simply need to be patient.'

I put my hand up to his cheek, running a finger down to his chin. 'It's bizarre,' I reflect. 'I've always thought of Dad as someone who is essentially a fair man when it comes to judging people and situations. Look at how he's taken in Alice and Ian because Uncle Alistair disapproves of their relationship. Dad feels strongly that it's not for my uncle to dictate what Alice can and can't do. And yet he's doing the exact same thing to me, simply because of his feud with your father. I'm not sure I can forgive him for that, Ross, as awful as that sounds, because it makes no sense.'

We lie for a while in each other's arms, each engrossed in our own thoughts. I might be a very private person, but I'm also determined and strong-willed. When the other kids laughed at me for being the techie, the geek, I realise now that I never wanted to change myself to be more like them. I thought of it as me not fitting in, but if that were the case, then I would have made the effort and hidden my true self. I didn't. What I did was to avoid being, as Ross said, the centre of attention. I was happy on the edge of things looking in and thinking what they were doing looked like fun, but I knew it wasn't right for me. Messing about was all well and good, but I was happy sitting at my desk and writing code.

On the other hand, Ross *was* the one for me and my heart knew that all along. I can't let anyone, or anything, come between us now – it's time to be true to myself whether people can accept that, or not.

'I'd better respond to these texts and then I'll have a quick word with Polly before I get myself ready. I think it'll do us both good to have some company this evening and then we have all night and most of tomorrow to—'

'Forget about what's going on around us and have some fun.' Nothing keeps Ross down for long and that's what I love about him. Knowing that we have each other is enough to cling on to no matter how rough a ride it's going to be.

TWENTY-THREE

A COSY EVENING AT THE FORGE

'This looks different and inviting,' Ross remarks the moment we walk into the sitting room at The Forge.

With the log fire roaring, a line of candles lit on the mantelpiece and the lovely little finishing touches Tegan has added, Ross is a convert. I start laughing and he looks at me, questioningly.

'What?'

'I told you that it needed a few touches to soften that bachelor-style life of yours.'

Sy shuts the door behind us as Tegan walks over to give me a hug. 'I'm so glad you guys could come tonight. We figured you could do with a meal out somewhere quiet.'

Sy steps forward to kiss my cheek, as I watch Tegan hug Ross, giving him a sympathetic pat on the back.

'What have you heard?' I ask, wondering where to start.

'Let's go through to the kitchen to get a drink, first. You might as well sit at the table and I can cook as we talk. I'm doing spiced, crispy squid for starters.'

Tegan flashes Sy a look and he gives her a discreet nod, as we follow him through to the kitchen/diner.

'I love that dresser, and doesn't the old Cornish pottery look wonderful, Ross?'

'Hmm, it does. I like the blue in here; it makes it look fresh.'

We settle ourselves down as Sy lights the two large, church candles in the middle of the table. With the soft light from the side lamps on the dresser, it's both cosy and romantic.

'We love it here, Ross,' Tegan says over her shoulder as she dips the squid in a dish of batter.

Sy cracks open a bottle of red wine, while Ross pulls the cork on a bottle of white.

'We didn't know what to do for the best when we heard about what happened at The Lark and Lantern. We'd intended asking you both over this evening anyway.' He looks across at Tegan, who does a half-turn to smile back at him. 'But we also wanted you to know that we're here if you need any support.'

Ross is watching the interaction between Sy and Tegan, with interest.

'What's going on with you two?' he enquires, a hint of amusement making his eyes sparkle.

'Go on, Sy,' Tegan encourages, as she lifts the basket of squid out of the fryer to give it a shake. The smell that emanates reminds me that I've hardly eaten anything at all today.

'We wondered if you two would do us the honour of being the witnesses at our civil wedding ceremony. It's on Friday the twenty-seventh of November, which also happens to be Tegan's thirty-first birthday.'

'Congratulations!' Ross immediately responds, looking

genuinely delighted. He glances at me accusingly. 'You knew all along!'

'Not the exact date. We'd be honoured, guys.'

'We've doing it on the quiet,' Sy explains. 'We can't really afford to have a big do just yet and we'd rather have a party in the spring when the weather is better, anyway.'

'And the other reason,' Tegan interrupts him, 'is that my brother and I still aren't speaking.'

Sy takes a seat and I give him a quick glance, but he looks back at me warily. Draining the squid on some kitchen towel, Tegan continues. 'Trev made no contact at all when we invited him to the little engagement party at your place, Kerra. Mum and Dad are afraid to even mention my name whenever he's around. It's time I did something about it. I don't want to celebrate our wedding until Trev and I have settled our differences once and for all.'

Ross doesn't have a clue what it's all about, but it's yet another example of a rumour, based on a lie, that caused an awful lot of trouble and heartache. And unfortunately, Alice was the instigator even though she didn't know at the time she was repeating something that wasn't true.

'I can understand that.' But it's still an unfortunate situation to be in because Sy and Tegan are so happy. Sy is like a new man since he came to Penvennan. Catching glimpses of him playing Santa in a couple of the rehearsal sessions, I've noticed that his angst has been replaced with a quiet confidence. He no longer takes himself so seriously and he's enjoying life. And Tegan fusses around him like a mother hen because she needs to be needed.

'We'll head off rather discreetly to Polreweek on the day, then afterwards find a nice little pub to sit and have a leisurely meal together.' Tegan carries the platter across to the table.

'Sy, if you can grab the small plates, I'll fetch the garlic and herb aioli. Help yourself. Oh, I forgot the lemon. Here you go. Enjoy!'

When Tegan takes her seat, we all raise our glasses.

'And I'm going to invite my family to the party – whether any of them will come, is up to them, but it's the thought that counts,' Sy reveals, surprising me. He was always the odd one out growing up and moving to London was the perfect solution for him at the time.

'Here's to a forthcoming birthday for Tegan that you guys will never forget!' Ross says, warmly. We chink glasses, as Sy leans in to kiss Tegan swiftly on the mouth.

'And here's to great friends. You've both been instrumental in making our happiness complete. Kerra for introducing us and tempting me down to the depths of Cornwall.' Sy fakes a suppressed shudder, which instantly makes me laugh.

'The man who said life doesn't exist outside of London!' I declare, before allowing Sy to continue.

'And Ross for being generous in allowing us to rent The Forge at a price we can afford. Tegan and I realise that it has made all the difference to us. It's not that the past is forgotten...' Sy pauses, knowing that Pete will always be Tegan's first love. 'Life simply goes on, and it's up to us to make the best of it. Which is what we're doing.'

As we begin eating, it makes me feel downcast that here is another couple having to downplay their excitement because of family woes. It's gone very quiet and it's time to address the proverbial elephant in the room.

'This squid is amazing, Tegan,' Ross interjects, licking his fingers and then wiping them on the paper napkin. He's signalling for me to take the lead.

'Can I just ask what exactly it is that you've heard about me and Ross?'

Sy's face pales and he looks directly at Tegan.

'Only whispers, mostly things we've overhead as we're keeping well out of it. Not least because we don't really know what happened. Only that Ross's dad is back and something about Ross leaving Penvennan.'

I suspect there's a little more to it than that, but Tegan is trying not to make a big deal of it.

'Dad and I have fallen out. He says I'm not welcome at Green Acre while I'm with Ross.'

Tegan puts down her fork, pushing her plate away. 'That's ridiculous. What has Ross done wrong?'

Sy stands, clearing the plates and Ross sips his wine. Both men are feeling uncomfortable about this conversation and it shows.

'Jago and Dad had a bit of a shouting match in The Lark and Lantern. Given that the name Treloar is a red rag to Dad, it's obvious why Ross and I wanted our relationship to come to light gradually. However, Dad has decided to take everything Jago said as the truth. Just don't believe everything you hear, because this isn't about Ross and me, it's about Jago and my dad.'

'Ross isn't going anywhere, then?' Tegan queries, and it's obvious even she found that part credible.

'No, not if I have any choice in the matter,' Ross replies, emphatically. 'But it is complicated. My father won't leave until the setting up of a new office near Launceston is under-way. I can't endorse his plans for expansion, although if he brings someone else in to handle it, then I'll obviously do whatever I can to help. After all, it is a family business, but this

260

is where I belong. Kerra has only just returned, and things will inevitably change because we're together now.'

The implication is that whatever we do from here on in, it's as a couple, and Tegan looks relieved.

Ross turns to look at Sy. 'What else have you heard? It helps to know what's being said as the next week is going to be tricky.'

Sy clears his throat, taking a sip of wine first. 'There's a rumour going around that Kerra is actively seeking to invest in Penvennan.'

It's nicely put, but something tells me that Sy is being diplomatic, and I look at him, narrowing my eyes.

'Okay. The word is you're going to snap up any house that comes on the market. You were seen in the bakery having a meeting with an estate agent and some of the locals fear you're working on behalf of a client in London.'

'Seriously?' I look at Ross, my eyes widening, and he snorts in disgust.

'I recently purchased Gwel Teg but I'm going to rent it out. It's not a secret and a few people know about it already. It's no big deal.'

Tegan jumps up to sort out the main course, leaving us to it.

'You warned me about village life, Kerra, when we were back in London. First you do an expensive renovation on Pedrevan, then you make a sizeable investment in The Design Cave, and now you've bought one of the fishermen's cottages. I bet you've been the subject of more conversations in the few months you've been back, than even Ross here. That might not be what you want to hear, but it's true I'm afraid.'

'I believe Sy is right, Kerra,' Ross endorses. 'Hearing it laid out like that, add in the fact that we've been hiding ourselves away out of respect for Eddie, it's no wonder wires are getting crossed.'

I knew it was going to be bad, but there's a twist here I hadn't foreseen. Why would anyone think I was working on behalf of a third party?

'What's to be done?' I ask, throwing the question out for discussion.

'No one knows about The Happy Hive, do they? Well, apart from us, of course, and Eddie. People don't understand that you're simply investing what you've earnt, Kerra. Consequently, it raises suspicions about what's going on and the more low-key you are, the worse it looks.'

Now I'm getting riled up. 'Drew is also aware, but that's it, because it's no one else's business!' I fume, trying to keep my voice level and struggling because I'm so frustrated.

Ross leans into me, placing his hand over mind and giving it a squeeze.

'I agree with Sy, Kerra. Not only have you and I been ultra-cautious not to be seen together, after my father's outburst people don't know what to make of the whole thing.'

As Sy jumps up to help Tegan carry the dinner plates across to the table, without warning I dissolve into fits of laughter. They all stop what they're doing to look at me intently, no doubt wondering whether I'm losing the plot. 'The options are endless, aren't they?' I say, as I struggle to regain control of myself. 'Wait until they put a spin on my little community project with Arthur. No doubt the next rumour to circulate will be that I'm spying on them all.'

Ross looks at me, horrified. 'What have you gotten yourself into now? I thought I knew everything that was going on.'

I wait until we're all seated again.

'Poor Arthur is the hub of Penvennan village, the cove and

the little pockets of properties within easy striking distance. Did you know that a lot of people have no one other than Arthur to contact if they have a problem? They either ring him, or a message is left with Mrs Moyle for Arthur to sort out.' There's an element of mischief in my voice.

Tegan passes the salt and pepper around the table as we begin to eat. After struggling to find an appetite since the row with Dad, it's suddenly back.

'The poor man is a virtual support network of one, but now he has the Penvennan Community Link-Up. No more phoning around to check on people who are housebound, like himself. And no need to hand in notes to Mrs Moyle. They can chat, swap recipes, talk about the weather and if someone needs a hand then he'll know about it.'

Sy still hasn't eaten a bite. 'And Arthur is running it?'

'Yes. I'm here if he needs any technical help, but he seems confident enough. It's by personal invite only, so there won't be any spamming, or trolling. I don't expect to have anything much to do with it, other than to keep the plug-ins updated so everything runs smoothly.'

Ross puts down his knife and fork, his elbows on the table and his chin leaning on his clasped hands. 'I can't see how that can be misinterpreted. This pork casserole is delicious, Tegan.'

'I get my meat from Treeve Perran. It makes a world of difference to the taste, doesn't it?'

'It certainly does,' I agree. 'I wish I could cook something as good as this. Ross is the chef when we're together.'

Sy stops eating to smile across at me. 'I'm thinking about the spotless kitchen in your London apartment. It was spotless because you never used it.'

'And that's going, too. My tenant is buying it.'

Sy looks shocked. 'You really don't intend going back to

London. I'm pleased for you both, Kerra. And as for the website, I think it was only a matter of time before you did something like that. Small communities that are a little spread out and have a good percentage of elderly or vulnerable inhabitants need to keep in touch. What's the story with Arthur Moyle? I've never see him in the shop.'

My mouth is full of food and Tegan joins in before I have a chance to answer him.

'Mrs Moyle once told me that shortly after they met, Arthur hurt his back. It was something to do with two discs getting crushed or crumbling, I think. He had an operation that was supposed to make it easier for him to walk, but it wasn't successful. Since then, he refuses to let them try again. He'd rather hobble around with his sticks, than risk losing the little mobility he does have.'

'All credit to them both that they lead busy lives and manage to keep everything running smoothly between them,' Sy remarks.

'I thought the exact same thing, Sy. It was a chance remark from Mrs Moyle about how busy Arthur was that kick-started my idea. Who knew that Arthur was keeping everything going very quietly in the background? When anyone who has pets is hospitalised, he arranges for someone to go in daily, or if he can't find anyone, he told me that Dad will take an animal in at short notice to help out.'

'The hidden side of the caring community,' Sy observes.

'It is and perhaps we should think about recognising Arthur's contribution in some way,' Ross adds. 'Are there any other little projects you have on the go, Kerra, aside from aiding and abetting Polly?'

Sy and Tegan both look at me as if to say: 'There's more?' and I at least have the good grace to look a little sheepish as I begin to explain myself. Having ideas and sharing them with people who then act upon them, isn't wrong, surely? It's common sense and I won't be apologetic.

Ross is now looking amused as he tucks into the delicious meal in front of him. Having dug myself into a hole, it's time to find my way out. I'm not ashamed of the way my brain works, it's just the way I'm wired.

PART TWO
NOVEMBER

TWENTY-FOUR
REVELATIONS

Arriving back at the cottage after having had a traditional Sunday lunch with Ross in a small country pub, I call out to Ripley. She doesn't appear and I walk through to the glass doors to look out. Drew has fitted the see-through panel into the fence. It looks a little weird, like a window at floor level. Weirder still, is that Ripley is sitting in front of it looking at Bertie. And neither of them is making a sound. I hurry back to grab a tube of treats and quietly slide the doors back.

Kneeling down next to Ripley, I smooth her back as she turns her head to look at me. 'Good girl,' I whisper. 'Such a good girl.'

Popping the lid off the tube, I place four chunks of dried salmon in front of her. Bertie's nose comes close to the window and he snuffles around.

'Are you there, Drew?' I call out, but there's no response.

Ripley hasn't moved a muscle. Her back is straight, and her head held high, but she's not upset because her tail is curled around her paws. I slowly back away and go inside to grab my phone.

'Drew, I'm back. Are you in?'

'Yes. Why?'

'Ripley and Bertie are eying each other but they're quiet. I'm giving Ripley some treats but Bertie is wondering why he doesn't have any.'

'I'm on it now! They've both been avoiding it all morning, so this is a first.'

It doesn't take long until I'm lying flat out on the deck next to Ripley, and Drew is waving at me from the other side. It isn't until Bertie lowers his head and begins eating his dog biscuit, that Ripley daintily picks at her treats before walking off and disappearing into the laurel hedges on the other side of the garden.

'Well, that was pretty amazing. And you did a great job of making our pet window,' I call out, as Drew jumps to his feet, landing heavily.

'We just reward them every time they spot each other and are quiet?' he checks.

'I think so.'

'I'm glad you're back. Can I pop round?'

'Please do.'

I'm in such a happy mood. Last night's dinner with Sy and Tegan was cathartic, and I felt that a weight had been lifted from my shoulders. It's time to stop worrying about being me. Echoing the sentiments of poet John Lydgate, made famous by Abraham Lincoln no less, you can't please all of the people, all of the time. It's a fact, so why am I kidding myself that I can do the impossible?

And we talked Tegan into coming to stay with me the night before the wedding and Sy is going to stay at Treylya.

The sound of the doorbell announces Drew's arrival and when I swing the door open, he's buzzing.

'What's happened?' I ask, letting him in and he's bursting to share his news.

'I'm going to be a dad. Me. I mean, heck, I don't even know what to say, except that I'm pleased.'

He's also in shock.

'That's wonderful news. When did you find out?'

'About half an hour ago. Felicity said she's been trying to tell me but wasn't sure what my reaction would be. She went on about the fact that I didn't have to worry about money and she already has her first client and several others in the pipe line. But I was blown away. It's still sinking in.'

'I can tell. Go through and sit down.'

'It changes everything, Kerra. We're going to need a nursery. When Felicity first told me that she'd handed in her notice, I will admit for her to just go ahead and do it without any forewarning felt odd to me. And then after that weekend, when we spoke she didn't say much and I wondered if she was having second thoughts about moving to Penvennan. It's an enormous relief to know why she was acting a little odd, because this is the last thing either of us expected. She just blurted it out and I... I'm so happy!'

And there was Felicity, worried sick that Drew's first concern would be how they would manage financially. It just goes to show how wrong we can be at times when we try to predict other people's reactions. I can see that Drew is alternating between moments of disbelief, utter joy and trepidation. But I have never seen him as animated as he is right now.

'A dad, eh?' he repeats, as if to himself. 'I can't believe it!'

* * *

'Kerra, it's Arthur. I hope you don't mind me interruptin' your Sunday afternoon, but is there a limit to the number of people I can invite?'

'Hi, Arthur. No. It's entirely up to you. Is everything working okay?'

'Perfect. It's buzzin', actually. A group of the gardeners are goin' to get together and plant up some indoor containers for Christmas – for those who can't get out, to cheer 'em up. One of them has talked a couple of nurseries and garden centres into donating some plants and compost.'

'Oh, Arthur, that's wonderful. I'll tell you what, I'll buy the containers. If you send me a link and let me know how many you need, I can drop them over to you once they're delivered.'

'That's good of you, Kerra. Thanks. There will be an apple pie with your name on it, next time you pop in. I'll let Mrs Moyle know.' It's hard not to laugh out loud. He rarely refers to her by her Christian name. They are two wonderful characters, and the village wouldn't be the same without them.

As I put the phone down it pings and it's a message from Ross.

There's a viewing on at Treylya at 3 p.m. tomorrow. They left a message on the house answerphone. I'm just about to ring Tegan to get one of her ladies in first thing tomorrow. Two men living alone in the house means it's not up to spec. Miss you already. The week hasn't even started, and it already feels like it's going to be a long one...

Aww. Ross should be here with me. But I want to give Dad a chance to rethink what he said and I'm hoping, really hoping, that Nettie can knock some sense into him.

Keeping everything crossed for you. And I feel the same way but after this coming week is over, the gloves are going on! xx

Ding dong.

Goodness, I haven't stopped since I arrived back home.

'Sissy, how lovely to see you.'

'I got your text, Kerra, but I was worried.'

'Come on in. I'm fine, really I am.'

'I knew you would be, but I don't like some of the stuff I'm hearing, and I can't hold back. There are folk around here who should know better, and it's time they got their comeuppance. They need to engage their brains and think about who is saying what, and about whom.'

It's obvious something in particular has upset her, and I hope it's not affecting business. I can't have my personal problems affecting Sissy.

'You're getting flak at work?'

'No. This was in the queue at Pascoe's bakery yesterday. Someone was bad-mouthing you and Polly put them in their place. I joined in and they didn't hang around for long, that's for sure.'

Oh dear, Sissy and Polly wading in to protect me. I don't even want to know who the person concerned was, but I'm rather dismayed that either of them is getting pulled into it.

'I don't expect you to fight my corner, Sissy, even though it's extremely kind of you. If things are going to turn nasty, then please distance yourself from it. Ross and I are prepared for what's to come and it's easier if the people we care about don't get involved.'

I indicate for Sissy to take a seat on the sofa and Ripley appears, jumping up next to her.

'You're honoured. Ripley rarely comes to greet a visitor if it isn't Ross.'

'Oh, that part of the tittle-tattle is true, then.'

That's the trouble with keeping things close to your chest – either you'll slip up or forget who knows and who doesn't as time goes on.

'Yes, it's true. It's unfortunate that our two families have never got on and we were hoping everyone would be accepting once they could see how happy we are together. That's not the case and my dad is no longer speaking to me. I've never even registered on Jago's radar until his return, and he's managed to use the information he gleaned to upset Dad. It's an old griev-ance between them and most of what Jago said wasn't true, anyway.'

'I am sorry to hear that, Kerra. For what it's worth, you and Ross make a perfect couple. You both work hard, are fair, and don't take yourselves too seriously. Ross did pop in and I'll have that quote early this coming week. Logan is coming on Tuesday and Ross has already marked up the wall where the face plate for the modem needs to go. You're still sure it's necessary to make this outlay, are you?'

'Has hard-wiring the internet solved the problem?' I check.

'It's been fine ever since.'

'Then it's a go. Ask Logan if we should get the modem replaced anyway. There is a chance it might have been knocked over at some point and if that's the case, we can order one from our internet provider.'

'Leave that with me, Kerra. You have enough to sort out for the time being. If there's anything I can do you will let me know, won't you?'

'That's so kind, Sissy. Just be prepared for some weird and

totally incorrect rumours to surface. My intentions are always for the best and no one is going to come between me and Ross.'

She bursts into a beaming smile. 'I like a woman with gumption,' she declares.

'If you don't mind me saying, you're looking very... upbeat at the moment.'

Her smile increases. 'You might not be the only one around here who is seeing someone in secret. Sorry, *has been* seeing someone in secret, in your case. I think everyone within a fifty-mile range knows by now and most of them will wish you both well.'

Well, well, well – what a surprise and one I didn't see coming!

* * *

I want to text Nettie and see how things are going at Green Acre, but it's too soon. The last thing I want is to cause trouble between her and Dad, so it's best we don't have any contact. If she has something to say, I'm pretty sure she'd call me, or pop in.

Ripley has been going in and out for the last two hours and I think she's a little disappointed that Bertie hasn't been out in the garden once. It's amazing what a difference that little pet window has made. I don't know why I didn't consider the fact that for weeks on end she was mistress of one large garden when the builders were here. When the new fence was erected to replace the section of hedging that was ripped out to allow the mini-digger access, it no doubt confused her. Not only did she lose some of her hunting ground, Bertie arrived shortly afterwards, eager to mark his territory.

She's outside now, miaowing to come back in because she

can't be bothered to go around to the front to use her cat flap. *Ding dong, ding dong.*

Argh, I should have known her cat sense was kicking in. I wonder if it's Dad and I steel myself but when I swing open the door, Sam stares back at me, sheepishly.

'I owe you an apology, Kerra. I might have said some hasty things to Ross.'

'You'd better come in, Sam.'

I leave him to shut the door and follow me into the sitting room, indicating for him to take a seat but he remains standing.

'I can't stay long, but my conscience is bothering me. Polly and I had it out and fair play to the girl, she was right. I can't fault the way she's supported me since she left college. And she never complains. It was wrong of me to flare up like I did.'

He's a proud man and considering he brought Polly up single-handedly while running a business, he deserves a huge pat on the back. That was no mean feat, although Polly had her hand in everything from washing up in the kitchen, to serving at an age when other kids were sitting in front of the TV. But it didn't do her any harm and her loyalty is unwavering.

'It's a bit special in here, now, Kerra. I bet Polly loves it. Right up her street this modern stuff mixed in with the painted furniture. Your mum would have approved, but I bet Eddie took a bit of convincing.'

He's making a real effort to be friendly and, given the circumstances, it means a lot to me.

'Sam, please take a seat, if only for a few minutes.' It's nice to know that there is no ill feeling between us. He settles himself down, and I sit in the armchair alongside. 'I'd like to explain what happened. I had no intention of causing trouble between the two of you. An opportunity came up and it was perfect for Polly. Not least because it's something she can fit in around working at The Lark and Lantern.'

He puts up a hand to halt me. 'I know. She told me straight, and that it was none of my business anyway as she didn't intend to let me down. You see, I don't want to stand in her way, but I'm stuck in a rut trying to make ends meet. I'm so tired at times that I can't even talk about it when she tries to get me to sit down and sort through the figures. It's never good news and that's depressing. I'm sorry if my words with Ross came across as trying to blame you – that was wrong of me. It's high time I faced facts: that our days in the pub are numbered, for Polly's sake, as well as for my sanity.'

'It can't be easy, Sam,' I reply, gently.

'I've had more than one approach over the last year or so. The vultures are circling.'

I look at him, soberly. 'That would be the end of an era, Sam, and a real shame. I'm assuming the interest you've received is from incomers?'

He nods his head. 'It's a sizeable plot being underutilised. I've never been able to afford to staff the business properly as it was in its heyday. It's too much for me and Polly, the chef, and our small rota of part-timers to keep it all going. That's why we let the bed and breakfast side of the business slide. Polly, bless her, does a bit of everything. She keeps the paperwork up to date, she helps in the kitchen, waitresses, cleans, gets behind the bar. I can't ask for more, but she does it for me and she's more than paid her dues.'

The poor man, he sounds totally defeated.

'Running a business when you live on site is probably one of the biggest tests of anyone's endurance. But Penvennan thrives because of the three main businesses that are the heart and soul of the community. The pub, the shop and the bakery.

They are all owned by local people and that makes an enormous difference.'

'We've tried to improve things and trade is good, even off-season. But we're still only keeping the bills paid and there's never any real money left in the pot to reinvest. If I sell, then it will go to a big brewery or one of the food chains. They're the only people with the money. They'll probably sell off half the site. Or maybe level all the outbuildings, and the guest accommodation, and build one of those new budget hotels. They usually manage to get it through planning, don't they? The car park is a good size, and that's half the battle these days. It would create more jobs, I suppose.'

'And more traffic through the village, which won't go down well.'

'You're right. But big investors look for high-volume turnover, don't they? That's probably why I've failed.'

'I don't think that's true to say, Sam. I think the only problem you have is that you never had the capital that you needed in the first place.'

Sam scratches his head, tilting it to one side, and it reminds me of my granddad. He used to do that whenever he was thinking.

'Well, I can't dispute that. After Polly's mother ran off, I had to find a way to look after Polly and keep a roof over our heads at the same time. We sold up and what was left had to do to get Polly and me started. I had no choice but to take on a sizeable mortgage. But aside from that I don't believe in debt. If I sell up, I'll be able to buy a little place somewhere, no doubt. Not in the village, of course, but close enough for Polly if she wants to stay with me until she's ready to find her own way in the world. Anyway, I'd best get back. They'll be wondering where I am.'

As I see Sam to the door I'm conflicted. I'm in enough trouble as it is and it's easier to say and do nothing, given my current situation.

'It would be a real shame for The Lark and Lantern to lose you as its landlord, Sam. It wouldn't be the same without you. Most people know I'm a silent partner in The Design Cave and now Sissy is installed in her new premises, I've taken a step back. Admittedly my skills are mainly in IT, but having built a profitable business from nothing, which I sold before I returned home, I know a good opportunity when I see one. Have you ever considered looking for an investor?'

Sam's surprise is very evident. 'I didn't think anyone would be fool enough.' He laughs. 'I haven't exactly turned it into a little goldmine, have I now?'

'I'm serious, Sam. Think about it. What harm would it do to sit down and have a more in-depth discussion? If the buildings for the accommodation are still sound and it's just a case of bringing the interiors up to date and employing some extra staff, it wouldn't take long to pull some figures together to see if it makes sense on paper.'

'It's a risk, Kerra. Not one Eddie would thank me for letting you get yourself into.'

I look Sam straight in the eye. 'I wouldn't waste your time if it turns out that it's not really viable, Sam. There's a point at which quitting and walking away with a cheque in your hand is the sensible thing to do. I did just that myself. But it would be a shame if you want to stay and you're considering selling up for the wrong reason. Give it some thought and if you're curious, give me a call.'

He doesn't know quite what to say and I give him a pleasant smile. 'I appreciate your visit, Sam. It took a lot of courage for you to knock on my door. And I hope Jago and my dad don't cause you any more problems.'

He chuckles. 'It was the most excitement we've had in The Lark and Lantern in a long time. We ended up packed by the end of the evening as word got around.'

'Now an incomer wouldn't understand that, would they?'

Sam puts his head back and belly laughs. 'They wouldn't for sure. A bit of gossip keeps the world turning and it makes them hungry, too. The kitchen was working flat out.' Sam gives me a wink as he steps out onto the path. 'We will have that chat, Kerra. I'll get my thinking cap on, I promise. See you soon.'

TWENTY-FIVE

CLOUDS AND SILVER LININGS

Nothing motivates me more than when I encounter negativity. Well, apart from apathy, which makes my blood boil. If everyone stopped caring, what sort of world would we find ourselves living in? This morning I'm up early. I've just fed Ripley and she pads off to climb the stairs, too tired to run up them. She was out from just after 3 a.m. and I'd say she found something worth chasing but she hasn't brought a mouse back for ages, thank goodness.

Considering it's the second of November and the dark, dingy mornings don't exactly make me want to spring out of bed, I have a whole list of things to get through today. I'm going to give serious thought to Sam's situation. I meant what I said to him and the locals would be horrified if they realised that he's thinking of giving up. Out of sheer desperation, people tend to grab the first solution that presents itself when their backs are up against a wall. But rebuilding your life from the ground up is a daunting task for anyone. I know all about that and yet I had no regrets leaving. Sam sounds like he's about to give up simply because he doesn't know what else to do and that's a red flag.

When I sit down in front of my desk, the first thing I do is to order the planters for Arthur. It restores one's faith in human nature to think that although the link-up has only been live for three days, one of the first things to come out of it is such a heart-warming gesture.

All the while, my brain is thinking about The Lark and Lantern. While I can guess at the potential that isn't being fully utilised, Sam is right: any investment is a risk for all parties concerned. All I can do is look at the various options open to him and selling up is a major one.

If Sam does ask me to call in to continue our little chat, I want to have a general idea roughed out. Once I can walk around and see it for myself, then I can run some figures and see how things shape up.

When the phone lights up my heart leaps as I wonder if it's Ross, but it's Mrs Moyle.

'Hi, Kerra. I have an apple pie here waiting for you. Arthur asked me to give you a call. Would you mind popping over to collect it *now*?'

The way Mrs Moyle put the emphasis on the word *now* is strange. Something is up and I'd better go and see what's happening.

'Of course. I'm on my way.'

As I lock up the office door and turn, I can hear Bertie running around in the garden next door. When I draw level with the little window I kneel, putting my head down low to the decking and Bertie comes up to say hello. 'Morning, Bertie. Good dog.'

I put my hand up against the see-through panel and he puts out his paw! Aww... I really hope this does the trick, but we'll soon find out. It was a novelty yesterday, so I'm waiting to see what develops when Ripley wakes up. But at least Bertie has a couple of hours with no distractions. 'See you later.'

Heading inside to grab my coat, I pop my wallet into one pocket and my phone in the other. When I step outside, I gingerly look up and down the road, but there's no sign of Dad. It's well past the time when he pops down to the cove to pick up his paper and that thought reminds me how much I miss him. More so because I know I'm not welcome at Green Acre at the moment.

'Morning, Kerra,' Mrs Moyle calls out as soon as I step inside the shop. She beckons me around the counter, barely pausing as she scans the items in front of her.

'It's in the downstairs kitchen,' she half-whispers as I pass by.

'Thank you. Appreciated.'

Walking through the passageway, I notice there's no sound overhead so I assume Arthur is in his chair and no doubt working online.

When I push back the door to the kitchen, Nettie is standing there, looking agitated.

'Don't worry, your dad is fine. I just didn't want him to look out and see me at your front door.'

I've never seen Nettie looking so overwrought, or emotional.

'We've had a falling-out.' She sniffs as she draws in a deep breath and I can see that she's fighting tears. 'You know that I would do anything for Eddie. That man is dear to my heart for many reasons.'

She's referring to Mum, of course, but it's easy to see how deep Nettie's feelings go, because whatever has happened is clearly devastating to her.

'I refuse to stand by and watch his blind stubbornness ruin his relationship with you. You're the centre of his world, Kerra. But he's as bad as your uncle – he just can't see that. Eddie is beginning to warm to Ian, and he rants on about how Alistair should be supporting Alice, because Ian is the man she wants to be with. That's wonderful, touching even, but look at how he's treating you and Ross. Anything connected with Jago and he loses his sense of perspective, and I can't stand by and watch this situation go from bad to worse.'

My jaw drops. 'You're walking away from the kennels?'

'I don't have a choice, I'm afraid.'

I was expecting people to take sides, but I never thought Dad and Nettie would be pushed apart like this.

'In hindsight, I wish I'd confided in Dad at the start, but I didn't want to upset him, Nettie. Having Jago throw it all in his face in such a public way is horrifying and I understand how hurt and let down he feels. I'm hoping he'll get over it, but I feel crushed that it's come between the two of you.' I berate myself for the way I've mishandled things.

'Even if you'd done things differently, I suspect the reaction would have been much the same. I'm more like your mum than Eddie figures. She wouldn't have put up with this nonsense. I'm only his employee but I spoke my mind and he gave me my marching orders. I won't stay where I'm not wanted.'

For goodness' sake! No wonder Dad is clinging to Alice and Ian, if he's pushing away the few people with whom he's really close.

'Is there anything at all I can do to help?'

She shakes her head, sadly. 'Some stories don't have that fairy-tale ending, do they, Kerra? I guess mine is one of those.'

Oh, my! My instincts were right. And this is all my fault.

Nettie is a strong woman and she decided to come back into Dad's life to see what might develop between them. And now she's done.

'I am so sorry, Nettie. I really am.'

I lean in to give her a hug and she pats my back, fondly.

'Grab your chance of happiness with Ross, Kerra. Don't let anyone get in the way of that. It's time I was gone. I know it will inflame the situation if he thinks we've spoken. Call me if you want to offload at any time. And give my regards to Ross. Oh, and that's your apple pie.'

She points to a box on the worktop, and we exchange weak smiles before she turns to leave. I decide it's best if I hang around for a couple of minutes to avoid people spotting us together. What would they make of Nettie and me talking in private? I wonder.

When I walk out into the passageway, Arthur calls down from the landing.

'You got your pie, then.'

I glance up at him, raising the brightest smile I can, given the circumstances. 'I have and it's kind of you.'

'We've had a surge,' he says.

'A surge?'

'We're up to eighty-three members now.' Arthur's excitement lights up his face.

'Go you! Where are they all coming from?'

'Each of me contacts probably knows a dozen different people and word is getting round.'

'And they're all managing to work out how to get in and what to do?' I'm a little puzzled, as I'd assumed at least a few of the elderly members might not be au fait with the internet, even if they have a phone.

'We've got a few in the know who are retired and are

poppin' out to get people sorted if they're strugglin'. I'm getting a few questions, like how do you post an emoji.' He grins down at me.

'Oh, Arthur, I do hope this doesn't turn into a bit of a monster for you.' I thought he was going to keep it to a small, core group.

'I can't remember the last time I had so much fun, Kerra. It certainly keeps me occupied and I'm grateful. Enjoy your pie!'

'I will, thank you.'

* * *

Shortly after lunch, Ripley slowly makes her way downstairs, stopping several times to have a quick lick of her fur. She saunters up next to me as I wash a couple of mugs and my lunch plate.

'Are you ready to go out and say hello to Bertie, Ripley? He's in the garden with Drew – I can hear them out there.'

Ripley walks over to have a drink from her water fountain, bypassing her food bowls. I quickly wipe up the few dishes on the draining board as the morning has run away from me, and feeling dispirited after my talk with Nettie, I'm eager to get back to work. I pop a tube of cat treats into my jacket and grab my phone.

When I pull back the glass doors to step outside, Ripley comes running out after me.

'Good afternoon, neighbour,' I call out. 'The sun is putting in an appearance again, but it's freezing still.'

'It's not that bad; at least it's dry. How's Ripley?'

When I glance down at our little portal, Drew's face appears. He's wearing a beanie hat pulled down over his ears. I hunker down, lying flat on my stomach, my padded coat acting as a bit of a cushion.

'She's here, but she's being cautious. I'll put a couple of treats down. I was talking to Bertie earlier, bless him. He put a paw up to acknowledge me.'

Drew grins. 'That's my Bertie. Hang on, I'll pop inside and get him a dog biscuit.'

Ripley is sniffing all around me, slowly making her way towards the fence as I lay out three cubes in a line.

Bertie suddenly appears and Ripley steps back, sitting down and eyeing him suspiciously. I wonder if Ripley thinks Bertie will steal her treats? Bertie lies down, laying his head to one side, watching us as Drew reappears.

'Oh, this is interesting,' he comments, placing the bone-shaped biscuit in front of the window.

'Who is going to be the first one to take the bait?'

The seconds pass and nothing happens.

'Have you had a good start to the week?' Drew enquires, as the boredom begins to set in.

'Awful. Nettie and Dad have had a row and he's dispensed with her services.'

Drew's look is one of disbelief. 'That's crazy, Kerra. It makes no sense at all. Well, let's be honest, none of it does in the grand scheme of life.'

I sigh. 'I know but—'

Ripley approaches and stoops down to begin eating her treats. Today we've both placed them right up against the window. Bertie has been lying there not taking his eye off his biscuit and now he, too, jumps up and grabs it in his mouth, his tail wagging.

'Well, that looked to me like Bertie was waiting for Ripley, as if he needed her permission. Is that a good, or a bad thing do you think?' Drew asks, puzzled.

'They're still quiet and that's odd given how noisy they usually are around each other.'

Ripley finishes eating and then turns tail, to run across the garden. 'I'm going to ask Ross to build a little platform in the tree like Nettie suggested. This pet window is working but I wish you'd made it bigger. Seriously, there's a limit to how long I can lie on the decking like this.'

We both start laughing and I ease myself upright.

'So how was your morning?' I ask the fence.

'I'm head down getting stuck into the new project. But every now and again I find myself sitting back and thinking about Felicity and the baby. It's scary, I will be honest.'

'You'll be fine. You might want to consider buying a garden office though,' I suggest.

He chuckles. 'I've been mulling that over, actually. Right, it's time to get back to work. See you later.'

Thinking back to the day I returned, I thought Drew was a bit strange at the time. I can't believe I even tried to talk him into selling me Tigry Cottage. But now I wouldn't be without my trusty neighbour. Isn't it ironic how when different elements of one's life are slotting nicely into place, there's always some big, thorny issue or other to cast a shadow over it? As if my thoughts are steering the weather, a series of little clouds float in front of the sun and when I look to my left there are a lot more of them gathering on the horizon.

I glance at my watch before unlocking the door to the office. Another hour and the estate agent will be escorting a potential buyer around Treylya. Wouldn't it be nice if the buyer falls in love with the view and before long, Ross can move in with me for good? I can't even begin to imagine what it would be like waking up next to each other every morning, knowing that Ross's face would also be the last thing I see at night before I fall asleep.

Ripley comes trotting over, no doubt her cat senses warning her that rain is on the way and it's cosy inside with me. It's time to stop daydreaming and get on with it, I suppose. What I need in here is a little fridge, and a coffee machine. And Ripley would no doubt appreciate having a water bowl and some dried food. This isn't just my office, it's also my den and a little oasis away from Penvennan.

'Only positive thoughts in here, eh, Rippers? And Bertie was very respectful to you just now, I hope you give him credit for that.'

Ripley raises her head from her little nest and miaows, then gives a big yawn. Life is simply exhausting sometimes, isn't it?

TWENTY-SIX

ONE FRUSTRATION AFTER ANOTHER

Swinging open the door, Ross steps straight into my arms.

'What kept you?' I demand as his lips meet mine. He kicks the door shut with his foot, walking me backwards into the sitting room.

'After I called you, the estate agent rang. It's not the news I was hoping for and it wasn't the first upset of the day, but to my shame, I let it get to me.'

Even though he's feeling forlorn, it warms my heart to see him here.

'Is it awful that I can't keep away? I know we agreed we would tread carefully, this week, but I can't bear to be living under the same roof as my father.'

Ross sounded at the end of his tether when he rang earlier on to ask if he could sleep here tonight, and I wasn't going to refuse him. It's unlikely Dad will come knocking on my door after banishing Nettie.

'It's been the same for me. Plans are all well and good, but sometimes it all goes pear-shaped. I'm glad you're here.'

Ross releases me with reluctance, so he can ease off his

coat. His fingers are freezing cold as I take it from him, and he looks windswept.

'There's a storm coming,' he mutters, flopping down onto the sofa. 'It sort of sums up my life right now.'

I hang up his coat then kneel down next to him, unlacing his work boots and easing them off.

'Right, tell me exactly what happened.'

He rubs his hands across his eyes, and it's not tiredness, it's frustration.

'In no particular order then, the people who viewed Treylya earlier this afternoon put in an offer way below asking price, which I rejected. They immediately came back with a small increase, which was equally insulting. I'm afraid I was on site at the time inspecting a water-logged pit, so I wasn't my usual courteous self. The estate agent knows my bottom line and it wasn't anywhere near it, so I reminded him of that fact and told him not to bother me again unless the offer is at, or above, that number.'

I can see that Ross is angry with himself for losing his temper. I say nothing as I help him swing his legs up onto the sofa and settle myself at the opposite end, lying alongside him.

'Legally, I think they are required to put forward every offer they receive. But you're right, it's their job to inform interested parties of your instructions to save you being both- ered unnecessarily.'

'I know that, but it was the final straw at the time. It's this new site – it's just one problem after another.'

'The one where you had to shut it down as the ground- workers thought they'd uncovered something of archaeological interest?'

'The very same. Now it's an old, bricked-up tunnel entrance and we don't know how far it goes, or even why it's there. I met with the owner and agreed I'd pull everyone off site until he can get someone in to investigate it further. For one thing it could be dangerous if it goes deep underground. I suppose there is some good news for Sissy, in that I have seven men standing around doing nothing. I'll rejig the schedules and hope to be able to send two guys over to The Design Cave tomorrow.'

'Sissy will be pleased. I'll text her to let her know. Is that it?'

'No. The problems on site were just the tail end of a stressful day. My father and I had a head-to-head this morning at the office.' Ross grimaces and I reach out to touch his foot. His toes are like ice and I wrap my hands around them, trying to rub a little life back into them.

'But you reached an agreement?'

Ross looks so dispirited, but as he watches me rubbing his toes he chuckles.

'Now that's a sign of true love, Kerra. The water seeped into my boots and although those socks are now dry, they really need to go straight into the washing machine.' His spirits are definitely lifting as he warms up. 'Anyway, we had a meeting with Will. He's agreed to set up the new office and my father has leased a small industrial unit with office space above in Launceston. I'll spend a couple of days there helping Will get the basics in place. My father is bringing in two office-based staff on short-term contracts, one to put together a big publicity campaign to get the jobs rolling in and the other to help Will recruit a small team of contractors to carry out the work.'

'Jago isn't expecting you to be responsible for both offices, then? That's good news, isn't it?'

'Yes, and no. I'm losing a site foreman and I'm not allowed

to replace him, so my workload will increase. Something's off, though, and I can't quite put my finger on it, Kerra. My father gave in too easily. Will is going to report directly to him now and I'm not the back-up plan anymore. Which is great, given the travel involved and the potential problems that might arise, but... I don't know. I just have this feeling of unease.'

There's another question floating around inside my head, even though I might not like the answer.

'Does Jago have plans to fly back to Spain?'

Ross's jaw tightens. 'He hasn't said how long he's staying but he asked if he could use Treylya as his base. There are a few meetings he wants to conduct in private. He's been treating my house like it's his own property, so that alone was out of character for him. As he'd just conceded to the terms I laid down, I could hardly refuse. But he knows we can't both stay under the same roof. Another thing that struck me as odd, when I dropped in briefly to pack my bag after talking to you, he didn't ask how the viewing went. Admittedly, it was the agent who escorted the people around, but my father is aware that I would have had a phone call by then just as a courtesy, even if there wasn't an offer on the table.'

Ross's unease is growing as he sifts through the events of the day. He needs to stop his brain from churning and unwind.

'I'm going to run you a hot bath and then cook you something nice for dinner.'

He flashes me a cheeky grin.

'Oh no, is this an experiment?'

'Do you like curry?'

He looks surprised. 'I love curry.'

'And mango chutney?' His eyes light up. 'Right, I have a box of magnesium flakes somewhere that are good for relaxing sore muscles. I'll dig those out and turn the taps on, then I'll pop over to the convenience store as I don't have any chutney.'

He laughs. 'But you do have time to make a curry and pappadums?'

'Wait and see, I might just surprise you. And there's apple pie for dessert!'

It goes without saying that I won't be making my own curry sauce. Ross knows me well enough by now not to expect that and, besides, my talents lie elsewhere. But as long as the curry is on the hob, bubbling away in the saucepan, and the jar is in the recycling bin before he comes back down, it will keep him guessing. After all, it's the thought that counts.

* * *

'What on earth is that leaning against the fence?' Ross places his hands around his eyes to peer out into the gloom, the lights around the edge of the decking reflecting on the shiny surface.

'It's a pet-friendly portal.'

'A what?'

'It's a little pet window so that Ripley and Bertie can see each other. It was Nettie's idea, and it seems to be working.'

Ross walks over to me, barefoot, looking relaxed and at home, slopping around in track suit bottoms and a long-sleeve, white T-shirt. His hair is still damp on top and his curls tumble down over his forehead. He closes in to wrap his arms around me as I stir the contents of the saucepan.

'That looks good. Sorry for offloading on you like that. Do I gather that your day was equally trying?'

'It was better than yours in some respects. The good news is that Arthur is having a ball running the Penvennan Community

Link-Up. It has really cheered him up.' I pause, remembering the day when I saw Arthur walking across the landing with a hot mug in his hand and he wasn't using his sticks. It would truly be a miracle if his back does begin to improve and he started to have more good days than bad ones. But this might be something Arthur has been through before, only to find it doesn't last.

'And?' Ross leans his head around the side of mine to catch my eye. I stop stirring and turn to face him. 'Nothing really. Well, nothing that you or I can do anything about. The real upset today was with Nettie.'

'Really? That's a surprise.'

'Nettie spoke her mind about how unfair Dad's being about us and it didn't go down well. She said that he made it clear that she's only an employee and I could tell she was in shock when he asked her to leave. As far as she's concerned, that's it between them.'

'Oh, Kerra. Nettie is usually such a calming influence so I can't even imagine what was said between them for him to act in that way. Who would have thought they'd have ended up on opposite sides of this argument? Eddie is entitled to think what he wants, but to push Nettie away when she's simply expressing her opinion takes stubbornness to a whole new level. He respects her, he always has, and if she can't get him to stand back and see it from both sides, no one can.'

'It seems none of us are indispensable. Thankfully, he still has Alice and Ian to keep him company, until he alienates them, too.'

Ross's frown wrinkles his brow and I pull away from him, not wishing to prolong this conversation. 'I'll dish up; you open a bottle of wine.'

As we busy ourselves, Ripley suddenly rushes downstairs.

She was probably asleep, and when she awoke and heard Ross's voice it was like her tail was on fire.

Miaow, miaow, miaoooooow, she begins, almost tripping him up, as she weaves herself between his feet.

'Hi, Rippers. I hear you and Bertie are making friends, then?' Ross gives her a quick stroke along her back, gingerly holding the open wine bottle in his other hand. 'You might be seeing a bit more of me for a little while.'

That thought is like a hug and a surge of warmth runs through my entire body. Ross is so at ease here and he is the missing piece to my happiness. He pours out the wine and then heads over to the cupboard where I keep Ripley's food. After washing out her bowl he empties a sachet and as he bends to place it on the floor she begins purring, rubbing up against his leg before even attempting to eat.

'That's a welcome, if ever I saw one,' I declare, and Ross smiles up at me.

'I can't be all bad if Ripley is on my side.' He laughs.

'Hey, I'm on your side. Something else came up today that was... erm... interesting, let's say.'

As I carry the plates across to the table, Ross takes a seat. 'Interesting? Well, that makes a change from shocking, or worrying.'

He looks down hungrily at his chicken and mushroom curry. When I return to get the pappadums and chutney, he has a little smile tugging at his lips, but he's appreciative. 'Just what I fancied – thank you for looking after me, Kerra.' As I take the seat opposite him, he raises his glass. 'Here's to an easier future once it has all played out. I often feel that life is like a game of chess, and just when you have your next few moves all figured out, something blindsides you and suddenly it's checkmate. The big question is, how many countermoves will it take to win, because losing is not an option.'

'To winning, then,' I affirm as our glasses touch and our eyes meet. 'It's good to have you here, Ross, and I have a favour to ask. Nettie suggested building a little platform in the tree down in the bottom corner so that Ripley can sit and watch what Bertie is doing.'

Ross has already put a huge forkful of food into his mouth and it's hotter than he realised. I shake my head at him, rushing over to the sink to get him a glass of water.

'That was a daft thing to do. Here you go.'

'I'm hungry but you're right. You were saying?'

'Oh, yes. And Sam called around.'

I watch as Ross downs half of the glass of water, then looks across at me with interest.

'Is this about the explosive incident the other night at the pub, or when he tackled me about Polly?'

He scoops up another forkful of curry, blowing on it, but he's waiting for me to continue.

'Sam said he owed me an apology and he was sorry he sounded off at you. We got to talking and I didn't realise quite how close he is to jacking it in. He has a couple of interested parties by the sound of it who have been circling for a while. Sam acknowledged that as things stand it's not the best future for Polly. This has simply made him stop and think.'

Ross puts down his fork with a clatter. 'From what he said to me it was clear he's struggling, but that's a real shocker, Kerra. The Lark and Lantern is the heart of the cove. There will be an uproar if one of the corporate chains snap it up and stamp their identity all over it. The reality doesn't bear thinking about.' He shakes his head, sadly.

'And this thing with Polly is making him seriously consider the future,' I reply, guiltily.

'Is he very deep in debt?'

'No, it appears not. But he doesn't have any capital, so all he's doing is making ends meet. We only had a brief chat, but I pointed out that he could look for his own investor and take a partner. Even if I just take a look around and do a rough assessment of what it would take to bring the accommodation up to date and run some figures for him, it might make his options clearer.'

'You're thinking of offering to invest?'

'I did mention it briefly, but it's too soon to say. His decision could have a real impact on life here. Selling up might not be what any of us locals want to hear, but it might be Sam's best option financially when he looks at the figures. Sam isn't used to taking risks and even with investment, it will take a while to get it up to speed. I'm not sure he has the motivation to see through the changes that would be required.'

Ross breaths out heavily through his nose. 'Something like this can devastate a village this small. Overdevelopment of a site is as bad as underdevelopment. Even with the planning laws as they are, we all know what happens – it's often a trade-off. There's a thin line between being swamped with tourists and causing traffic misery at peak times, and the other end of the spectrum, not having the facilities tourists look for to keep them coming back.'

We eat in silence for a while and Ross is clearly enjoying his not-so-homemade curry.

'If I can sell Treylya, I might be interested in putting up some money if it helps.'

I can't hide my amusement. 'I should imagine everyone who uses the pub would put their hands in their pockets to keep it running as it is. When Sam left, I got the distinct impression he was grateful to talk to someone who could at least understand his dilemma. If he decides to look for a partner, two investors could be better than one.'

Ross's eyes narrow and a frown creases his brow. 'The key word being *if*, of course.'

'You'll find someone. But it might not be through your current estate agents,' I reply, soberly and he shrugs his shoulders, as if to say only time will tell. 'You're still thinking about your father, aren't you?'

'Confrontations with my father rarely leave anyone feeling that they have the upper hand. I've never known him to back down on anything before, especially when the outcome is in my favour. It's a big step for Will and a lot of additional pressure. I was expecting more of a battle, that's all. Unless my father is mellowing in his old age and is prepared to give Will the ongoing support he's going to need.'

That makes me laugh and Ross joins in. Jago isn't the mellowing sort and, as surprising as it is to me, neither is my dad.

TWENTY-SEVEN

THE EDGE OF REASON

The last two and a bit weeks have been frenetic to say the very least, but tonight the focus is firmly on the pantomime. *Christmas in Wonderland* begins tomorrow and runs for five consecutive days. I didn't realise how nervous some members of the cast would be after all the rehearsals they attended, but Sy seems to be in his element.

Ross and Zacky are at the back of the stage, ready to move the scenery around on cue. After Dad pulled out, I helped Ross as best I could. He battled on single-handedly at a time when he's been under immense pressure at work. If everything goes smoothly tonight, he won't just be happy, he'll be ecstatic. Having spent three days in Launceston helping Will set up at the new depot, it set him back. In the past, Will acted as Ross's deputy when he wasn't in work, mainly checking in with the other site managers to ensure that materials were arriving on time. Communication between the office and the site is crucial. Now Ross no longer has a front runner with enough experience to handle stepping into that role. Ross was troubleshooting the problems by phone while he was away, and we only spoke briefly as he was working long days.

There's a creak and Tegan's head pops around the side of one of the double doors. She smiles and beckons to me. I tiptoe out, but Nettie is still giving her pep talk and running through the timing of the scenery changes.

'Hey, Tegan. On countdown now,' I say, lowering my voice and giving her a hug. 'Eight days and you will be Mrs Tegan Anderson.'

She beams at me. 'I know, and I'm so excited. But until the panto is over all Sy can think about is remembering his lines. He loves it, though, and I'm sure he'll be doing it again next year.'

It's hard not to laugh. 'I can't believe how they've turned him into a credible Santa. I mean he's tall and lean, has no facial hair and is on the young side, but he looks the business.'

'He does, doesn't he? And his voice, it's spot on. But it's hot in that suit with the wig, beard and make-up.'

'I always called him a drama king, as that's his nature. He runs hot, or cold, never lukewarm. Anyway, are you all ready for the big day?'

We walk down the corridor and I tentatively push open the door to the meeting room. 'Good, there's no one in here,' I confirm as we head inside.

'There's not a lot to plan, really – dress, tick, rings, tick and turn up on the day. Afterwards we'll find the jolliest pub we can with a table to seat the four of us. Weddings are usually a stressful occasion and we're both so relaxed about it, which is wonderful. Sy understands that Pete will always be in my heart, but this is my way of reassuring Sy that he is, too.'

'Ah... Tegan, it's so lovely to hear you put it like that. Sy has waited a long time to find true love and the way the two of you have focused on what's really important, while getting the business stable, is refreshing.'

'I don't know about that, but it suits us and that's all that matters. By the time we arrange a party in the spring, hopefully I will have convinced my brother that it's time to put the past behind us. It'll be a fun event to arrange. None of the waiting around at the church and endless photographs, just a real celebration of the fact that Sy and I are a couple. But it does mean so much to us both that you and Ross will be there on our special day. My parents were surprised, but they can see how happy we are. I also spoke to Pete's Mum and Dad. We shed tears together as we talked about the past, but they said that Pete would want to know that I wasn't alone. Their words meant a lot to me.' I can see how moved she is and I realise that Sy and Tegan aren't settling for a simple wedding solely because of the cost – it goes way deeper than that and I applaud them.

'We're looking forward to it, Tegan. It's a bright spot after what has been a trying couple of months.'

She gives me a troubled look. 'The rumours are getting worse, aren't they? Some people just seem to feed off negativity. I feel sorry for them, but a lot of it is also triggered by jealousy, Kerra. I'm sorry that you and Ross are two prime targets. But compared to so many folk who live around here, your lives are never dull. Locals are beginning to wake up to the fact that Kerra Shaw returned home an equal match for Ross Treloar. It's like watching the storyline of their favourite TV programme unfolding on their doorstep.'

That kicks us off giggling, like we used to do way back.

'Like reality TV, you mean. What's the latest news, then?'

'Word is that you're buying The Lark and Lantern and you and Ross will be replacing Sam and Polly behind the bar.'

She grins at me. 'Me and Sy belly-laughed at that one. They don't know you at all, do they?'

I shake my head in disbelief. 'Seriously? Is this a new rumour, or an old one?'

'I think it's new. One of my clients mentioned it and I dismissed it out of hand, of course.'

'And this came from someone in Trehoweth?' I'm aghast.

'It's to do with this group thing some of them are in. They have a chat room, apparently.'

I can feel the blood draining from my face.

'Oh, right. Well, thanks for the warning. I am talking to Sam about business in general, but how that translates into buying the pub and becoming a landlady just goes to show how easily two and two can make five in some people's imaginations. Everyone knows Sam struggles and that's been obvious for a while, but it's old news.'

Tegan shrugs her shoulders, wearily. 'What we need is a good scandal. Someone going off with someone else's husband is always a good one,' she muses, and I chuckle.

'Are you staying for the whole rehearsal?'

'No. I've only popped in to give Sy a bit of support. He'll be anxious for my feedback, but I can't stay long as one of the ladies who helps make the costumes for the panto is popping in to alter the hem of my new, woollen coat ready for the wedding. It's not fancy, but the colour matches my dress and it's warm. The forecast is dry, but with a bitingly cold wind. I wasn't going for a hat initially, but I decided it was that, or end up looking like I'd been dragged through a bush backwards.' She laughs. 'It's easy for the men, isn't it?'

We head back to the hall, but my stomach is in knots. I need to speak to Arthur and find out if this stems back to the Penvennan Community Link-Up.

'I think I've done all I can here. On my way back I have something to drop in to Arthur. Can you let Ross know that I'll see him back at Pedrevan?'

'Will do, Kerra. It's a bit wet out there, now. Keep your spirits up; the rumour mill is bound to run out of steam before too long.'

I can only hope that Tegan is right because this latest turn of events will put pressure on Sam, and that's the last thing he needs right now.

* * *

'Mrs Moyle, it's Kerra. Sorry to spring this on you but I thought I'd just drop off the planters. I'm parked outside, but if it's inconvenient I could leave it until tomorrow morning.'

'Oh, and it's raining; you poor dear! I'll be down directly.'

Mrs Moyle appears in record time, bustling me inside the darkened shop as I carry in the first stack. It's weird seeing it like this, spooky even. I make three trips and end up a little soggy, but not soaked.

'They've been in my car since yesterday and as I've just driven back from the village hall, I thought I might as well drop them off.'

'Come on up for a minute,' she says, warmly.

'I'll just lock the car.'

When I return, she lowers her voice. 'I'm glad you're here, actually. Arthur has been in two minds whether or not to ring you.' She sounds almost apologetic, and my heart starts to beat a little faster. 'He'll explain. Come on up.'

I'm guessing there might be some truth as to the source of this latest speculation.

'Good evening, Arthur. I've left Ross at the village hall as it's the dress rehearsal ready for the kick-off tomorrow night. I hope you don't mind me popping in with the planters, but my car was packed out.' I keep my voice upbeat as Mrs Moyle indicates for me to slip off my damp coat and take a seat.

Arthur is sitting in his usual chair, but he now has a free-standing, adjustable table on wheels and the laptop is open in front of him. Beside it is a notebook and a pen. Mrs Moyle, I notice, was knitting and plonked everything down on her chair when she came to let me in.

'That's champion, Kerra, and thanks. I'll make a call in a bit to get them collected first thing tomorrow mornin'. While yer here, I 'ave a bit of a problem I'm not quite sure how to handle. I know yer eager to get home, but I'd be grateful if you could take a quick look.'

'Of course. Fire away.'

Please let it be a technical issue, please, my inner voice calls out, unheard.

'Well, it's this... person. I'm not sure who it is, but they're out of order in my book. You'd best take a look for yourself.'

There's a long thread of messages and I start skimming through them. The subject at the top says *Penvennan in Bloom*. The first fifty, or so, are general back and forth between various users. Some of them are saying they have greenhouses and will have spare plants they are happy to donate. There's talk about using them in and around the village and then there's a whole string related to the idea of the Christmas planters. As I scroll down, I can feel Arthur watching me intently. Then a new comment throws the topic slightly off course.

SallyM: I have loads of bulbs ready for planting in the spring and I'm always taking cuttings of everything. More than happy to donate what I can to pretty up the village. Count me in!

BoatMan: *If Penvennan is facing a takeover, what's the point? T'aint fair for incomers to benefit off the backs of our hard work for free.*

SallyM: *Takeover?*

LionMan: *I heard the same rumour. Someone buying everything up. Won't be the same, for sure.*

SallyM: *Like what?*

LionMan: *The pub for one. Another cottage gone, too. Crying shame, it is. Shouldn't be allowed. Enough is enough!*

Fiddle832: *Rubbish! I don't believe a word of it. I'm in the pub every night and haven't heard a peep. It's the same old, same old.*

Moderator: *Polite reminder that the topic is Penvennan in Bloom.*

LionMan: *Well, I think we deserve to know what's going on before we go any further.*

BoatMan: *I hear that Polly's leaving The Lark and Lantern, says it all.*

SallyM: *No! Polly would never leave Sam on his own!*

BoatMan: Doing up houses, apparently. It's the beginning of the end, you mark my words. You can count me out. As I said, ain't no point prettying it all up for some incomer to benefit.

Razzle101: I'll ask Sam when I pop in for a pint later. No point hiding the truth but, gawd knows what we'll do if it turns into one of these upmarket wine bars. They won't welcome the likes of me.

BoatMan: Me neither. Couldn't afford one drink, let alone something to eat!

LionMan: An incomer? I heard it's one of us, working for one of them.

BoatMan: Some firm from London are trying to buy up all the independent estate agents for miles around. It's the thin end of the wedge.

Moderator: This topic is now closed.

BoatMan: But we haven't finished discussing it. I'll report back later.

LionMan: The truth is the truth, no point pretending when it's staring us in the face!

'Is this the only thread that's gone off track, Arthur?' He nods his head, looking uncomfortable.

'As far as I can tell. I'm not sure what to do next.'

'It's not supposed to be a place for gossip and speculation;

that doesn't help anyone. Do you know who BoatMan and LionMan are? It seems to me that it's bouncing back and forth between them.'

'Can't say I do. We're at two hundred and sixty one members now and growin'. A few of them are obvious. *SallyM*, she lives over by Polreweek. Lovely lady, lives with her son but he works away all week.'

I'm staggered by the number.

'I thought this was going to be a bespoke group of people, Arthur. Are you happy with the way it's expanding?'

'I was until yesterday and this started. Take a look through the other topics, Kerra, I think you'll be amazed how it's taken off.'

Everything else looks fine and there's a great diversity of subject matter. People offering things free to collect, other swapping books and CDs. SallyM has posted some recipes she says come from a book her great-grandma passed down to her.

'It's wonderful, Arthur, but I can see why you're worried. There are only two ways to deal with this unfortunate situation. One is that you close the topic down and restart it with another name. The other is that you contact the individuals you feel are breaking the rules and give them a final warning. If I remember correctly one of which mentioned *incorrect, or misleading information*. You can also delete any comments you feel are in breach.'

'Am I allowed to contact people direct?'

'As the moderator, of course you are. Especially if someone breaks the rules. You've already given them two warnings. BoatMan and LionMan seem to be ignoring your polite request. I'll just bring up the list of subscribers. If you click on *dashboard*, then *users* and *all users*, this will give you a list of usernames and the associated email addresses. There you go. If we scroll down to BoatMan—'

'Zacky Carter, I should've guessed. Bit of a giveaway that one?' Arthur laughs. 'That's well handy. Can you find the other one?'

Zacky's email address is simply his full name, but LionMan isn't easily identifiable.

'Hmm. *Sunnygate701* could be anyone.'

I type it into the search engine but there's no exact match.

'Do you keep the emails when people ask you to send invites out, Arthur?'

'They're in a folder on the desktop. Let's do a search.'

Within minutes one entry comes up. 'Well, whoever LionMan is he didn't respond to your email, but he obviously joined up. Oh, and look who put him forward. None other than Zacky.'

Arthur looks worried. 'What should I do?'

'Just close down the thread as I showed you, so that no one else can post a comment. Start again with a slightly different heading, say Christmas planter arrangements or something, and a clear outline of the topic. You could email both Zacky and sunnygate701 to explain what you've done and just copy and paste the rules into the email.'

'Why do people want to spoil it? And Zacky should know better. I'll be more careful in future.' He looks crestfallen.

'It happens. But you did the right thing, Arthur, and you don't have to stand for it. Nipping it in the bud will put an end to it. If the two of them start up again, then simply go into the user list and delete them. And if you have the time you can go to the comments section on the dashboard and simply delete whichever ones breach the rules. Remember, you're in control.'

'You are a star, Kerra.'

Mrs Moyle reappears. 'I made this for you, Kerra,' she says, holding out a bulky parcel wrapped in silver paper and tied with dark blue ribbon. 'You can open it now. It might come in handy.'

I pass the laptop back to Arthur and open my present. It's a woollen scarf.

'Ah, thank you so much, Mrs Moyle. This is so kind of you.'

'It's merino wool, the fleeces are the softest and it will also keep you warm,' she informs me.

After carefully refolding it, I loosely wrap the paper around the parcel, securing it with the ribbon. 'I'm touched. This is such a lovely gesture. Well, I'll leave you to it then.'

As Mrs Moyle follows me downstairs, I chatter away.

'Ripley probably isn't too happy about the rain. Ross isn't due back for at least an hour, so I'll have a play with her. Her favourite toy is a fluorescent green fish that I can wiggle as if it's real. It keeps her occupied when she's stuck inside.'

'Bless her. She gets through those treats pretty quickly, doesn't she? I'll keep my eye out if I see anything a bit different and a bit cheaper. You never know, she might like a change.'

'That would be great. She's starting to make friends with Bertie, at last, and it would be nice to have something different to give her as a reward.'

'I'll see what I can find and add a box to my next order so you can try them out.'

'How is Arthur these days?' I enquire when we're out of earshot of him. 'He's remembering to move around a little, I hope. I know what it's like when you're in front of a computer – the hours fly by.'

'Nothing he does seems to make it any better, or any

worse, to be honest. At least he isn't bored anymore and that's a marvellous thing. And thanks for sorting him out; he was a bit worried.'

'I could see that. The thing with gossip is that it unsettles people. Often for no good reason.'

She raises her eyebrows. 'No point in worrying about what might happen until something's been decided, is there?'

Mrs Moyle can read between the lines and she's aware of Sam's struggles. We exchange a look of acceptance as I bid her goodnight.

TWENTY-EIGHT
PEOPLE MATTER MORE THAN MONEY

I'm lying next to Ross in the darkened room and the bedroom curtains are open as usual. Ripley likes to jump up on the windowsill during the night if she hears a noise outside. It's a habit which is fine in winter, but annoying in summer as it means wearing eyeshades. Tonight, a waxing moon is a sharp crescent set against a dark blue background and as Ross intertwines his fingers with mine, our heads are touching.

'It's relaxing looking out at that, isn't it?' he remarks, sounding content.

The rear of Pedrevan Cottage abuts a swathe of land that runs down to a stream and it's a mass of trees. The fact that there are no lights visible beyond the end of the garden does make the view from here pleasant, when lying in bed. It's just the tops of bare trees and the sky, not breath-taking like the views from Treylya, but it's a nice outlook.

'Everything went well tonight, then?' I ask, knowing full well that he arrived home in a buoyant mood.

'Apart from having to oil a couple of squeaky wheels on the Winter Palace, it went a lot smoother than I expected. It does need two people and Zacky has offered to make himself available for the entire run of shows.'

'Just be a little wary what you say to him, Ross. We both know that Zacky has an unfortunate way of repeating things out of context.'

Ross lets go of my hand, rolling over onto his side to look at me.

'My lips are sealed.' He laughs. 'Why did you suddenly head off to see Arthur tonight? I thought you intended to stay until the end.'

'I, um, had to drop off those plastic pots. And I wanted to check everything was working well with the link-up.'

'And Arthur's coping with it alright?'

'Arthur is au fait with the internet in general and it's amazing how quickly he's familiarised himself with the dashboard. I was a little surprised how many members he has already but overall, the interaction looks lively and interesting.'

'Overall?'

'Zacky and another person, who isn't identifiable, are going off topic. The usual doom and gloom you'd expect from those who see any change at all as a threat. Arthur has put out a couple of reminders and if it doesn't stop, then he'll delete Zacky.'

The bed starts shaking a little and I realise Ross is laughing.

'What's funny?'

'Your new scarf. It must have taken Mrs Moyle hours and hours to knit it.'

Now I'm chuckling, too. When I showed it to Ross, he insisted on wrapping it around my neck and it took an awful lot of turns, so many that it ended up like a collar, stretching from shoulder to shoulder. After unravelling me, he folded it up and placed it on the sofa. When we turned around, Ripley had jumped up and was using it as a nest, looking cosy as the wool is so soft. I think it's a present we're going to be fighting over.

'Has Sam made any decisions?' Ross asks, his voice beginning to show signs of tiredness.

'He asked me to pop in to see him in the morning. Sam also said to thank you for getting those quotes over to him to so promptly, as he knows you're rushed off your feet.'

'It's not going to be easy for him, is it?'

'No. And Polly is buzzing, having completed her first job as *Designed to Sell*. The feedback she received via Oliver from his client has gone down well. He's arranging for new photos of the property to be taken to update the marketing literature and he suggested increasing the price. Fingers crossed a buyer steps in soon, as that will really reinforce the fact that the way a house is presented can affect the price.'

'Hmm, I'm glad to hear it's gone well for her. But if it continues then it will add to the pressure on Sam. Is Polly going to start work on Gwel Teg next?'

'She is and I'm going to approach James to see whether he's interested in renting it. Sissy speaks so highly of him. Together with Sienna, she reckons that when she's ready to take some time off they'll be able to cope without her, no problem at all. Did I tell you she has another part-timer now to help out on Saturdays and one of them is happy to do extra hours during the week?'

'Oh, that's good news all round, then. How's she finding her new office?'

'I haven't had a chance to pop in and see for myself, but Sissy sounded delighted with it. She takes her dog, Willow, to work with her now. It saves having to get someone to pop in every day to take her for a walk. Sissy is finally beginning to relax and stop worrying that something will jinx her good luck.'

'She certainly deserves every bit of it, because she's earnt it.'

'It was the last day that Quentin guy was shadowing you today at work, wasn't it?'

'Yes, thank goodness. After three days of answering his constant questions as he followed me around everywhere, I'm glad he's going back to the Launceston depot. Mr Quentin Armstrong-Jones isn't giving anything away, but there's no doubt he's one of my father's old contacts. I'm not saying he doesn't know the building trade, because he does, and seeing how Treloar's has worked in the past will hopefully help with targeting the right platforms to get those new orders rolling. I've given him some contacts within striking distance that are really on the edge of my patch, but that should be it from me now.' Ross stops to yawn. 'I can just get on with my own job again.' His voice tails off sleepily, as his eyelids begin to droop.

Throwing his arm over the top of the bedcovers, Ross snuggles into me as I continue to stare out at the sky. The longer I look, the more stars I notice as my eyes adjust and it's calming. It isn't long before he's breathing deeply. I'm still wide awake though, and troubled. Zacky's comments weren't exactly untrue. Big changes are coming to the cove whether anyone likes it, or not, but nothing stops the march of time, or progress.

* * *

'Are you ready for this?' I ask as I turn the key in the lock of Gwel Teg. Polly nods her head enthusiastically.

'Mornin', Kerra, Polly. It was you who bought it then, Kerra. I said to Logan that I'd seen you here a couple of times.'

'Hi, Mrs Williams, how are you keeping?' Betty is Logan's grandma and she's a lovely woman. The sort whose door you can knock on and always receive a genuinely warm welcome.

'Not too bad, considerin'. My great-grandsons keep me smiling – they're lovely boys. Will I be gettin' a permanent neighbour?'

I can understand her concern. She bought this place when Logan's granddad died because it was more manageable for her.

'I'll be renting it out, so no more holidaymakers – just someone local, hopefully.'

She smiles. 'That's good to know, lovely. I have been keepin' an eye out as you never know these days. Word gets around when a house is empty.'

'It won't be for much longer, I promise.'

Polly and I quickly step inside and her eyes light up.

'Ooh, this is nice. What have you in mind?'

As we walk through the rooms Polly stops to write in her A4 notebook. Mostly it involves looking at the paint colour charts she brought with her and deciding what furniture can be sanded and painted, and what needs to go.

'I'm assuming you'll sort the curtains and blinds? Did you know that Sissy is giving me a discount?'

'Yes, I'll pick something up. And Sissy did mention it. A good salesperson knows which clients to look after,' I declare firmly and Polly grins.

'What about the floors?'

'The laminate running throughout the ground floor is sound, but the carpet upstairs needs replacing.'

'I have an account now in The Carpet Store, in Polrewcck, if you want me to sort that for you. They did a good job on my first project and I'm confident I can get a good price for you.'

It's good to see Polly beginning to build her contacts and the fact that she's working with local retailers will go down well.

'Perfect. Anything that saves me having to phone around. What about the white goods?'

We head into the kitchen and Polly has a quick look inside the fridge and the freezer.

'They're both fine, in my opinion. There's no point in replacing the oven, or the hob either, but it would be worth getting someone in to do a professional clean to make them sparkle.'

'Could you maybe speak to Tegan and when you've finished get her to do that and a clean-through including the windows?'

'The final clean-through comes as a part of my service as I have an arrangement with Tegan all set up, but I'll remember to ask for the oven and hob deep-clean.'

Polly isn't going into this half-hearted.

'The patio at the back needs weeding, I notice. Ian is happy to tackle little jobs like that if you're interested?'

'Go ahead. When do you think it will be ready for a tenant to take possession?'

'Four weeks from the date you accept the quotation,' she replies, confidently. 'The carpet people will want to come in and measure up. At the same time, I'll ask them to drop in the samples and I'll pop them round to you. As soon as you decide what exactly you want, I'll be able to send you an itemised breakdown of the costs including my fee.'

'Sounds good, Polly. I'm impressed. I might as well give you the spare keys now.' I unhook the small silver ring on the main bunch and hand them to her. 'I'm popping in to see your dad next. We can walk back together.'

'I'm not heading to the pub, I'm afraid, as I'm off to look at another potential job for Oliver.'

'Oh, I thought you'd dressed up just to impress me,' I joke, and she smiles.

'We might be friends, but I wouldn't have turned up in my jeans. I've learnt a lot from you, Kerra, and you always look smart. It makes people take you more seriously and I'm serious about Designed to Sell.'

As we make our way back outside, I know Gwel Teg is in good hands. And I have a sneaking suspicion that Polly's business venture is going to fly.

* * *

'It's bewildering, Kerra, that's for sure.'

I feel for Sam because he doesn't know what to do for the best.

'What you need now, Sam, is some professional advice. Someone who can approach the two parties who are interested in making you an offer and get them to put their terms in writing. What you have here—' I place my hands on the document Ross emailed across '—is the cost of updating the holiday lets. You have three, family-sized units that haven't been used for what, ten years now? Ninety thousand pounds for rewiring, new windows, bathrooms and kitchens, plus installing new central heating systems may seem like a lot of money to you, but an investor would look at the potential for future profit. If you could reclaim the wild orchard, with views like that those holiday lets could be booked all year round and that's a substantial income.'

Sam looks at me, anxiously. 'Let's see if I've got this straight. The investor puts in all of the money in exchange for a share of the business, is that right?'

'Yes. It's a big site you have here. It wasn't until you showed me and Ross around, that I realised quite how much land you have, as some of it is so overgrown. If you want to stay, then the first thing to do would be to get in an independent valuer. You can then work out what sort of percentage you'd be prepared to offer a partner by comparing the level of investment to the value of what you have here – not just the business, but the entire site.'

'What you're saying then, is that the decision is do I want to sell up and walk away, or stay and get things back on their feet?'

I nod. 'Yes, although another option would be to see if you can get a buyer for the three holiday lets and the parcel of land in front of them.'

'Carve it up, like? If I sell up lock, stock and barrel, the money is all well and good, but I can't help wondering what I would do with myself afterwards, Kerra. Starting again somewhere else, even close by, is hard to get my head around and that might be a better solution.'

'Can I ask why you gave up on the holiday lets? The bed and breakfast in the pub, I can understand. That was an additional pressure and not ideal when you had a young child under your roof.'

Sam fiddles with the pad of paper in front of him.

'Polly was about eight, or nine, at the time when I called a halt to the bed and breakfast. 'Course, I had more staff in those days, but costs were creeping up and I was being pulled in too many directions. I had an assistant manager back then. He upped and left to work at a big hotel in Truro. His job was more defined there. Here, he was like me – doing a bit of everything, as Polly does now. It was a tipping point at the time. Polly was spending hours on her own upstairs and something had to give. She needed help with her homework and to know her dad was there for her. I stopped advertising, pared down the staff numbers and organised it so that I could slip upstairs every night and have a few hours with her before bed. It was a big weight off my shoulders, but I wasn't thinking long-term.'

It was perfectly understandable given his situation, but tough to think that he didn't have anyone to turn to who could help him through that period.

'You might not remember, but Polly spent some half-terms and a part of the summer holidays up with my parents over in Norfolk, back then. But when my dad developed dementia, it was tough on my mum. And Polly got to an age where she wanted to stay here and be around her friends. Her mother walked out on us when Polly was a toddler. The last I heard she was living in the States, but that was a long time ago.'

I don't interrupt him as it's cathartic to talk and he knows it will go no further.

'Then when Polly went to college, she was only able to help out evenings and weekends. The holiday lets were a big drain on my time and staff turnover was causing problems. I should have realised then that things were going one way, and that was downhill. I appreciate it's time to give this some real thought and what you're saying about getting professional advice, Kerra. But you're saying you'd be interested investing that sort of money if I consider taking on a partner? The reason I ask is that the pub is rife with talk and it won't be long before someone asks me outright if I'm selling up. Polly's new venture hasn't gone unnoticed for all she's trying to be discreet and it's sounding warning bells.'

Poor Sam. No doubt Zacky isn't exactly his favourite customer right now.

'I would, Sam, but remember that talk is cheap, and you don't have to explain yourself to anyone. Just don't be pushed into making a quick decision for the wrong reason.'

He hangs his head, expelling a deep breath.

'A pub is supposed to be a relaxing place to visit, but everyone is watching every little thing that happens behind the bar. Polly is on such a high – even if no one knows the full ins and outs of what's going on, it's obvious something is up. And I'm... well, frowning more than I'm smiling these days, fearing I'll do the wrong thing for her and for me, and end up being miserable.'

'Then put an end to the speculation. Say that you're considering your options and thinking of refurbishing the holiday lets.'

Sam looks up at me, laughing. 'Spin a tale, like, but that's only half the story.'

'No, it's not. You are looking at all your options and that's one of them. At least it would put a stop to the fear-mongering. There's no point in people getting het up when you don't even know what you're going to do yet. And information like that is commercial in confidence, anyway.'

'You're right!' he replies, robustly. 'It would give me some breathing space.'

'Long enough to get the advice you need to understand what you have here and get those outside offers on the table. If you decide it's not the way you want to go, that's when I'd be happy to sit down and talk figures. It wouldn't be right to do that now, Sam, as I don't want to influence you either way. When it comes to business you have to think with your head and not your heart, and that's not easy when you have such a connection to this place. Share your thoughts with Polly, as she knows you better than anyone.'

'I'm proud of my girl and you're right: she's got a business head on her. I hope we'll be sharing the same roof for a few more years to come. Thanks, Kerra. There is one other thing... and this is just between you and me for now. I don't want to unsettle Polly while she has a lot on her plate, but I'm, um, seeing someone.'

Keeping my expression under control while I flounder for a suitable response isn't easy. 'Well, that's... wonderful, Sam. Naturally I won't say a word to anyone.'

'We met online and we talk most days, as it's not easy for me to get away. Occasionally I can slope off for a couple of hours and I'm being discreet because it's not something I planned. I know you can sympathise with that. It just happened and no one is more surprised than me. But now it might be another thing to consider going forward if it works out well.'

'Ah, I see. Ironically, the timing couldn't be better, then. It's important that you end up with no regrets... about anything, Sam.'

TWENTY-NINE

UNITED WE STAND

Sy, dressed in full Santa regalia, is sitting in the sleigh, waving at the audience.

'Off we go, Rudolph! We're heading to Alaska as we have a special request this year from a queen who lives in an ice palace!'

The curtains close to a rapturous round of applause and it's time to change the scenery. Zacky pulled out last-minute as he has a cold and I'm the fallback option for tonight. I suspect that the real reason is that Arthur read him the riot act and Zacky is sulking.

Santa is about to arrive at the Winter Palace and meet the Dark Queen, who is going to freeze him into a man-sized ice cube so he can't deliver the presents on Christmas Eve.

'That was amazing, Sy,' I comment, as he steps out of the sleigh.

It's gone from an enthralling silence to a loud rumbling of chatter as the audience make their way out to queue for refreshments.

'Did you notice the not-so-deliberate mistake?' Sy looks at us, anxiously.

Ross and I shrug our shoulders, a blank expression on our faces.

'Thank goodness for that. I got in a bit of a muddle and ended up saying a bad word by mistake. If Nettie were here, she'd have picked it up immediately, so I'd better make sure I don't repeat it tomorrow night,' he confesses.

'Does anyone know why she isn't around?' I enquire, tentatively.

'A problem cropped up as she was about to set off. She sent her apologies and said she'd get here as soon as possible. Sod's law, eh?'

'It's a real a shame. But you're all doing a grand job, Sy. I've been peeking from behind the curtains and judging by the expressions on the faces of the kids in the front row, they were spell-bound. I always said you'd be a natural at amateur dramatics and I was right.'

'Cheek,' he throws back at me. 'I miss the old days.'

'How did you put up with her, Sy? That's what I'd like to know. I can't keep up with her!'

I shoo Sy off to get a drink, so that Ross and I can start moving things around. It's not difficult, but you need to know what you're doing and keep a close eye on the floor markers.

The Winter Palace is the most complex bit of scenery because it's comprised of two rooms. At one point the action is going on in both rooms at the same time, which is hilarious – it's a real, old-fashioned farce. The Dark Queen goes from one to the other, so that she can reveal her evil plan to the audience, while Santa is unaware. When the Dark Queen turns Santa into a block of ice, the lights are dimmed for a few seconds.

The two rooms are on a simple turntable, which Ross operates from the back. When the lights go up all the audience can see is the room with a full-sized, stuffed version of Santa inside a see-through box. With one arm extended in the air as if he's pointing, it really does look like the Dark Queen has frozen him solid. Ross and I spent ages scratching large areas of the shiny surface to make it look more like an actual block of ice.

'How did your talk with Sam go this morning?' Ross asks as we begin doing up the fastenings anchoring the walls to the floor.

'It's not easy for him, he has a lot of history at The Lark and Lantern. It's already obvious that Polly's interior design business is going to fly, and he knows that. But he's a little overwhelmed and he needs to appoint a professional adviser to talk to the parties interested in buying him out.'

Ross nods his head in agreement.

'He's sitting on a valuable plot of land and I don't think he realises that, Kerra. I vaguely remember the orchard from my childhood, but it's been left untended for so many years, it's an impenetrable forest of brambles. That stunning sea view is non-existent now from the holiday lets. Aside from the renovation work, it would take a small gang of men with the right equipment maybe two weeks to cut it back, thin out the trees and turf it. If it were me, I'd gravel an area for sitting out. It's all doable and the potential to grow his business is there alright.'

'I thought the same thing. He has a lot to think about.'

'Do you fancy grabbing me a drink and bringing it back here?' Ross asks as he fiddles with the turntable beneath the palace.

I lean in to give him a quick kiss and hurry away, as the

interval is only twenty minutes long. On the way I bump into Tom and Georgia in the corridor.

'How are you both? It's been a while. Is James here?'

'Hey, Kerra. No. We did buy him a ticket, on the off chance he wanted to come but he's doing a late delivery for Sissy. Somewhere the other side of St Columb, as the customer doesn't get home from work until 6 p.m.'

'Ah, shame.'

Georgia grins at me. 'We didn't think he'd want to come with us – not really. He would have made some excuse, or other. I bet he pops along over the weekend, though, on his own. Still, he loves his job and he's happy. We can't ask for any more than that.'

'And how are things with you, Tom?'

'I'm doing a lot of fishing these days,' he replies, grimly. 'There's a bit of work on the fabrication side, but it's not enough to keep me fully occupied. I might start clearing out some of the junk that's rusting away for something to do.'

Georgia puts her hand on his arm, giving it a squeeze. 'It's for the best, m'dear. Perhaps make a bit of space and put up a few garages to rent out. And people are always looking for places to store stuff. You just bought Gwel Teg, we hear, Kerra. Now that doesn't have any parking. A secure place to park the car is a bonus for holidaymakers, isn't it?'

'Yes, it is, Georgia. I'm going to rent it out, though.'

'Even better,' she replies, cheerfully. 'There you go, Tom, and you could put an ad in Gryff's shop window.'

Tom looks totally uninterested and I give them both a polite smile. 'Well, I hope you enjoy the second half. I'm just off to get Ross a drink. Say hello to James for me, when you see him later.'

Moving on quickly, I join the queue for the refreshments.

The doorway into the kitchen is blocked by a fold-up table with a cloth over it and there is a selection of snacks and three people behind it serving drinks. Turning to peer through the open doors to the meeting room, I see it's jam-packed with people.

There's a tap on my shoulder and I'm delighted when I turn around to see Gawen and Yvonne.

'What a surprise. How lovely to see you!' I hug Gawen first.

When Yvonne leans in, she whispers in my ear. 'We're so excited about next Friday. Sy and Tegan still don't know, do they? We've booked the table.'

'They don't suspect a thing. I bought the vouchers. We'll hopefully arrive at The Lobster Pot around midday. Ross and I are so looking forward to it.'

Gawen comes closer. 'Is everything okay with Ross?'

I raise my eyebrows heavenwards. 'It's been a stressful time but he's hoping things will begin to settle down now. The Launceston depot is up and running and they're on their own. It should be business as usual, although he's one foreman down.'

'That's sounds like par for the course. But if Jago is off his back, that's all that matters, Kerra.'

'Next please!'

I turn to Ross's two best friends before stepping up to order some soft drinks. 'If we don't catch up before, see you next week!' It's wonderful to be involved in keeping a happy secret for a change and I think Sy and Tegan are going to be touched.

* * *

In the car on the way home our spirits are high. A gathering like tonight really pulls everyone together and Penvennan needs more events like this one. The wonderful cast received a standing ovation, and it was well deserved. But Nettie wasn't there to see it as she failed to appear. As Ross drives us back home it's troubling me.

'I must phone Nettie, Ross. It's such a wonderful storyline and everyone left on a high. Now we're all buzzing about Christmas and that's down to her. No matter what prevented her from coming, I have no doubt that she'll be wondering how it went.'

'I agree. Why don't you call her now?'

I dial her number and just as I fear it will kick into voice-mail, she picks up.

'Hello?'

'It's Kerra, Nettie. How are you?'

'Oh, Kerra. Thank you for calling – how did it go?' She sounds anxious.

'Like a dream and the buzz was amazing. They'll all be trimming up for Christmas this weekend if they haven't already. Everything went perfectly and there was a standing ovation for the cast, and for you. You'll see for yourself tomorrow night,' I enthuse, hoping she'll confirm that's the case.

There's a pause. 'You are going tomorrow night, aren't you?' I continue.

'Oh, I am. I'm just, uh, a little overcome right now.'

'I'm in the car with Ross and you're on speakerphone, is that okay?' I query.

'It's fine. I was going to ring you, anyway. As I was leaving early this evening, Alice rang and asked if I could call in to

Green Acre on my way to the village hall. My initial reaction was a firm no, but she talked me into it.'

Nettie sounds shaken and my stomach turns over while we wait for her to continue. Ross pulls into a lay-by, leaving the engine idling.

'When I called in, Eddie was upstairs. Alice and I sat in the kitchen and had a little chat. She told me that she's never seen him as down in the dumps as he's been recently. It was obvious that it was her idea, not his, to invite me around but when he came downstairs to join us for a cup of tea, he was on his best behaviour. And then she left us alone to talk. And that's why I didn't make it, as I've only just arrived home.'

I glance at Ross, making a face. Poor Nettie – this isn't easy for her.

'He's confused about so many things, Kerra. And Alice is right: he's down because he doesn't know what to think, or what to do anymore. It's not a case of forgive and forget, it's never that simple, is it? His pride is hurt but what was heart-breaking for me was that... oh, I don't want to upset you, my dear. We all loved your mum, we still do, but I didn't realise that Eddie could return the feelings I have for him. And now I'm conflicted, because you know that your dad and I are on different sides of an argument that is still very raw.' She stops talking to blow her nose.

'Oh, Nettie. But it's good news that he's reaching out to you, isn't it?'

A quiet sob fills the car and Ross and I look at each other, apprehensively.

'I feared you might not understand, Kerra.'

'If Dad needs you, Nettie, then nothing would make me happier than to know you're there for him. Please don't feel this is a case of divided loyalty. The argument isn't yours, it's between Dad and me. Your situation is no different to Ross's, is it? You're both caught up in it but only Dad and I can resolve it. If, and when, he's ready.'

Nettie sniffs, determined to pull herself together and I don't rush her. We sit in silence until she's ready.

'Bless Alice, she was concerned for him, and it showed. I think it worried Eddie a little, too. He said he regretted losing his temper but at the time he couldn't even think straight. Eddie also said that he's angry with himself, first and foremost, and that if I'm not around the likelihood is that he'll end up alienating everyone, before too long.' I can hear the depth of emotion in her voice and my heart goes out to her.

'If you're by Dad's side, Nettie, then at least I'll be able to sleep at night. The only chance I have of him realising how wrong he is, is for him to sit back and watch everything play out. Ross isn't going anywhere, in fact he's living with me for the time being at Pedrevan, as Jago is still up at Treylya. I appreciate the timing is unfortunate, but it's how it has to be for now. Please don't feel Ross, or I, will judge you for supporting my dad, simply because you care about him so very much. It's a huge relief and I think I'm speaking for both of us here.'

'Kerra is right, Nettie. Eddie is a lucky man if you give him a second chance and I imagine he's well aware of that. I bitterly regret I wasn't around when it all kicked off in the pub, because if I'd been there it would have been a totally different story. I'm ashamed of my father at times, and that's the truth.'

Hearing Ross speaking from the heart, makes me feel tearful and I'm sure Nettie, too, is welling up.

'That's extremely gracious of you to say that, Ross. And I can't thank you both enough. My heart is telling me that Eddie needs me more now than ever, and tomorrow morning I'll let him know that I'm prepared to start afresh. We'll continue to have our differences, of course, but we have a lot of genuine respect for each other. And I know he's been pushed to the edge, but it seems he's gradually stepping back, and I see that as a start, don't you?'

'I do, Nettie, I really do. And thank you for your honesty. It's comforting to know you are going to be a part of his life going forward. I'm just sorry it's been so traumatic.'

'Right.' Nettie takes a deep breath. 'I'm thrilled the first night went well and so wish I'd been there to congratulate everyone, but I'll make up for it tomorrow night, I promise.'

'Sleep well, Nettie,' I reply.

'I hope you both do, too.'

As the line disconnects, Ross leans in to place his arm around my shoulder and I have a little cry out of sheer relief, not sadness.

THIRTY

GETTING READY FOR THE BIG DAY

Tomorrow is Tegan's birthday, and it's one she will never forget. I'm lounging on the sofa, waiting for her to arrive. My phone rings, but it's not Tegan, it's Ross.

'Hey, you. How are you doing?' I lie back, slipping off my shoes, and put up my feet.

'I'm just finishing off some paperwork and then I'll be heading off to The Forge,' Ross informs me, sounding in high spirits. 'When's Tegan arriving?'

'She didn't mention a time, but I'm chilling. I'm so glad that you're going to The Forge and not Treylya. It would have been too awkward with Jago there and a hotel isn't quite as relaxing, is it? Are you sure you have everything you need?'

'Yes. I checked and double-checked before I left Pedrevan this morning.'

'You sound very bright and breezy. You and Sy aren't planning some sort of stag do for two, are you?'

'Of course not. If we were, we'd have invited Drew along.'

'It's a pity he's heading off tomorrow to stay with Felicity for the weekend, but he's helping her to go through the loft in preparation for the big move in a few weeks' time.'

'Rather him than me. Anyway, I have some good news to share,' Ross announces. I can tell from his voice that it's something significant.

'Well, don't keep me in suspense!'

'After a lot of back and forth, I've just phoned Kenneth Truscott to accept an offer from my father for Treylya.'

'Through your agent?'

'Yes. And I'm glad. It was worth the commission to keep my father at arm's length during the negotiations. He only expressed an interest after I'd signed the agency contract and that's the way it works. Anyway, I managed to play him at his own game, and he isn't even aware of that fact.'

I'm confused. 'What game?'

'That insulting offer and the counter offer I received, were no coincidence. As soon as I heard the surname, I connected the dots back to my father. I had an inkling that it was a tactic. Naturally, afterwards Kenneth came back to me saying maybe the price was too high and I'd get more viewings if I dropped it. Like it or not, a house is only worth what a buyer is prepared to pay for it.'

'But you achieved your bottom line?'

'I did, and some. My response to Kenneth was to leave the price as it was but to increase my bottom line. He advised against it, but then he had no idea what was going on, or how dirty my father plays.'

'Even with his own son?'

Ross laughs at the level of shock in my voice. 'To him business is business, no matter whom he's dealing with.'

It is good news, but the mere thought of Jago living so close to Penvennan sends me reeling.

'He's staying, then?'

'No. But he'll be flying over on a regular basis to keep an eye on the Launceston depot. And me, as well, but he was in a good mood and left that bit out. He thinks he's made a killing on Treylya and the reality is that I've made an additional one hundred thousand pounds. I figure he owes me that for all the extra hours I put in that go unnoticed and unrewarded.'

'Why buy something so expensive, though?'

'Because he can. Because it's iconic and an investment. And because he knows I didn't cut corners. Besides, my mother loves it, so he might entice her back for a visit. I think he's missing the UK, but I hope I'm wrong and I doubt she'd come back for good, anyway. Even for a house she admires.'

I can't stop thinking about how Dad and Nettie will react when they find out. But I doubt Jago will be in a hurry to show his face in The Lark and Lantern again or be likely to pop into the convenience store. Ross is clearly ecstatic.

'You're really going to be free of that place, then,' I reply, my mind beginning to whirl. This is huge for us as a couple, life-changing in fact. 'Goodness, I can't really take it in.'

'It means freedom, Kerra. No huge loan repayment to make each month and a small uplift in my original nest egg once the money is back in the bank. It wasn't the best investment, but it wasn't a loss as I feared,' he confirms.

'Well, I hope you and Sy can enjoy a nice meal, a couple of drinks and a relaxing evening to celebrate. We're having takeaway and a film.'

'And hours of chat, no doubt. I know what you two are like when you get together. Right, I'd better get off. Can't leave the groom to fend for himself on his last night of freedom, can I. Especially as I'm the chef tonight.'

I snort, which isn't very ladylike. 'Just check that Sy turns up with the rings in his pocket and he doesn't leave them in a drawer,' I instruct him.

'Will do! I love you, Kerra. I'm not all about the money, you know that, but there was a principle at stake here.' He's being serious now and I can tell that a part of him wishes his father was different.

'Yes, well, just don't go thinking your nerves of steel when negotiating mean you should try your hand at poker next.'

Ross starts laughing. 'I'll stick to trudging around muddy building sites and constructing cat platforms in trees. I knocked something together for Ripley today and I'll put it up at the weekend.'

Ah, that's my man. Even though he's busy he makes time for the little things that matter, even when it's for Ripley. It's funny, they say lead by example, but the irony is that Ross has turned out to be the very opposite of Jago. When the gloves come off, Ross still plays by the rules because that's the sort of man he is, and I love him even more because of it.

* * *

When Tegan finally arrives, she's flustered, and I help her in with her things.

'What a day!' She groans. 'I thought it was never going to end. I'm all jittery – is that normal?'

'How would I know? I haven't even been a bridesmaid before, so I'm the last person to ask. But after tomorrow I will have been an official witness!' I declare, returning her expansive grin. 'You need a drink by the look of you. Who's manning the phone tomorrow?'

'Kate, bless her. She loves the new set-up, but I reckon she misses driving the old minibus around and our time together in the office. We had a few good laughs over the years, for sure.'

'Let's start carrying this lot upstairs and hang up the garment carriers, then I'll pop to the Chinese while you have a relaxing bath. There's a basket full of goodies in the guest bathroom, which includes a mud face pack, a bath bomb with rose petals in it and a coconut body moisturiser.'

'Ah, Kerra, that's so kind of you!'

'I'll bring up a glass of wine before I go.'

As we start to gather everything up off the sofa, Ripley comes running down the stairs.

'Hi, Ripley! It's just us girls tonight, then,' Tegan jokes, and Ripley gives her the longest miaow I think I've ever heard her utter.

I indicate for Tegan to follow me upstairs as I talk over my shoulder. 'Alice will be here at 9 a.m. to do our hair, nails and make-up, and the taxi is all booked. So, it's all looking good.'

'Isn't it silly – this tradition of not seeing the groom the night before the ceremony?' Tegan ponders, as I push open the door to the guest bedroom.

'I know what you mean, but I think it's sort of romantic. It's like Christmas Eve when you're a kid and you know Santa will be here very soon. That sense of anticipation is a part of the magic, and I think that applies to a wedding, too.'

'You old romantic you. I do hope that Ross has sussed out that deep down you're the sort of woman who wants to be swept off her feet, Kerra. Me, I like to keep mine planted firmly on the ground.'

It's good to be bantering away like we used to do when we were teenagers. We'd sit and talk for hours about all sorts of things. And now here we are on the eve of Tegan's thirty-first birthday and she's about to make Sy the happiest man alive.

'You do know that Sy doesn't really like dogs, don't you?' I throw out there, thinking about the comment he made.

'I know. But he didn't like Cornwall either, so I'm hopeful.'

* * *

Hurrying to bundle ourselves into the taxi, I hope that no one noticed the two unusually glam-looking women who sprinted across the road. Alice has, once again, worked her magic.

'Are you ladies good to go?' the driver asks, half-turning in his seat to look at us.

Tegan's wearing full make-up and her new bob is so perfect that she decided not to wear the hat she bought – and with my hair straightened and without a single kink in it, we've obvious made an impression.

'I'm guessing someone is getting married, given the destination. Right, off we go.' He smiles as he turns back around, and we set off.

'Just look at my nails,' Tegan exclaims. 'Alice makes it all look so effortless. At least I was able to grow them a little now I'm no longer Mrs Mop.'

We grin at each other.

'She certainly knows what she's doing but I wish Uncle Alistair appreciated her skills.'

'Why is he so hard on her?' Tegan asks and we both know that's the truth; it always has been.

'Uncle Alistair's problem is that he's a man's man and Auntie Marge is a practical woman. They make a good team. And then they had Alice. Alice was the little girl who shunned her schoolbooks, had no interest in the skills Auntie Marge wanted to teach her – finding office work boring. She was a princess, and he was baffled by it.'

Tegan nods. 'She was always dressing up in sparkly things.' She starts laughing and I look at her, questioningly.

'What?'

'Well, think about it. You were Little Miss Serious, your nose always in a book and, later, nothing could prise you away from your beloved computer. Alice, on the other hand, wanted to be a ballerina, even though she never attended an actual class. She was a dreamer.'

I shake my head, laughing at the memory. 'That was only from the age of three up until she started school. The other girls didn't think it was cool. In fact, poor Alice spent a lot of her school years being bullied and I had no idea at the time.'

'But she's doing well now and look at us – I mean, this is little short of a miracle!'

The driver keeps glancing in the mirror, and I wonder if he thinks we've already cracked a bottle of wine, but we haven't. We're just on a natural high after having Alice join us for a big, celebratory birthday breakfast. She was too young to hang around with us at any point while we were growing up, but it's funny that you get to a point where age no longer matters.

'Given the latest development,' Tegan asks, careful not to mention any names, 'what's the plan going forward for you?'

I glance out the window as we pass one of our former haunts, known as The Rocks. It's a steep path down to a tiny beach.

'It's funny, but we've never really talked about the future. Our future together. It's been all we can do to get through each day. I mean, Ross is living with me right now but even that wasn't planned – he simply had to get away from Treylya for a while.' I glance at her making a face and Tegan knows that if Ross had stayed under the same roof as Jago for a moment longer, all hell would have broken loose.

'I bet you're glad all the work on Pedrevan is out of the way and you can both simply relax and enjoy some quality time until he's in a position to move in for good.'

'That's the dream. It's just taking a little time to sink in that it really is going to happen,' I reply, truthfully.

'None of us know what the future holds, Kerra. Even when the major stumbling blocks begin to tumble, it's still a case of living life one day at a time, believe me.'

Of all the people I know, Tegan is the one who understands that as we speed towards the registry office in Polreweek. She thought her life would revolve around Pete and it did for the few wonderful years they had together, and now we're both embarking on what feels like a fresh, new start. It's exhilarating as we look at each other, eyes gleaming.

'Girl power!' she says, as we butt our fists together and then throw our hands in the air like an explosion. 'We're coming, guys, you'd better watch out, because it all starts here!'

THIRTY-ONE

A TANTALISINGLY HAPPY ENDING TO A PERFECT DAY

As we climb the stairs to The Lobster Pot restaurant in Drake-town, Sy and Tegan are beyond delighted.

'Honestly, Ross and Kerra, you didn't need to do this but thank you so much!'

'It's a real pleasure,' Ross replies and we're both trying to keep our faces straight as there are a couple more surprises to come.

It's a huge restaurant and a wall of windows look out across the harbour. It's the place to come and it's often difficult to get an evening reservation as they tend to be booked up at least a couple of weeks in advance, even during the off-peak season. But lunchtimes are much more relaxed, although at least half the tables are in use today. Ironically, it's the first time that Ross and I have been here together.

A waiter approaches to give us a warm welcome, instantly recognising Ross, and asks us to follow him. It's obvious from the way we're dressed that it's a special occasion and after one glance at Sy and Tegan, most people will suss out they're looking at a new bride and groom.

'Oh, my goodness!' Tegan calls out as we approach our table. Gawen and Yvonne jump up to give Tegan and Sy hugs and congratulations. 'We were not expecting this.'

'So much for a discreet little celebration,' Ross whispers, as we stand back watching. All eyes are on us and the waiting staff have turned their heads to watch. Happiness is infectious and glancing around I can't see a single face without a smile on it. Ross catches my hand, giving it a squeeze.

'Honestly, you guys, this is simply perfect. I wish I'd thought of it!' Sy exclaims, giving Gawen a high five.

'Right, shall we take our seats?' Ross interjects as we take off our coats.

'I'm Michael and I'm your waiter for today. And may I pass on hearty congratulations to the happy couple!' Aww, bless him. A waitress hurries over to help take our coats and as we sit down, they go to hang them up.

'Does it feel different now that you're man and wife?' Yvonne leans in as she looks at Sy and Tegan.

Tegan turns to her husband. 'Does it? I don't even know how I feel, I'm just so excited and I've been like this since last night,' she confesses.

'I can vouch for that,' I add. 'We ended up at two this morning, sitting on a pile of blankets in front of the glass doors with the garden lights on, having a picnic. Ripley loved it.'

'We've already ordered the wine and a bottle of champagne,' Gawen confirms, winking at Ross, as the waiter returns to hand out the menus.

'I love it in here,' Tegan says softly, turning to Sy. 'It couldn't be more perfect, could it?'

'Happy birthday, wife,' Sy replies softly, as he leans in to kiss his bride.

We all say 'Ah...' in tandem, as Michael heads back

carrying a wine bucket containing a bottle of champagne. He places it on the table, and we watch as he expertly pops the cork without losing a dribble.

When we finally raise our glasses to toast, there's a pause as we look around the table, not quite sure who is going to do the honours. Then Gawen and Ross begin to speak at the same time and stop short, laughing.

Instead, Sy takes over. 'To my lovely wife, the woman who made me feel that I'm enough just as I am, and I know Kerra will understand how much that means to me. I feel truly blessed. And I'm so grateful to have been welcomed into such a tight-knit group of friends. Here's to us all, and the best is yet to come!'

I don't think any of us could beat that as we chink glasses and try our best to keep our voices down, but it's hard to contain ourselves.

'Right, I'm hungry and we need to order some food.' Ross encourages us all to settle down.

Perusing the menu, I find it hard to choose.

'What are you going for?' Ross asks, having a similar problem.

'Hmm... I think the blackened sweet potato wedges with avocado aioli, then roasted hake loin with bacon, mushroom puree, pickled mushrooms and beef jus. It sounds amazing. And for dessert the blue cheese, with honey and walnut bread thins and port-glazed fig. I probably won't need to eat for a week after this, but who cares? It's not every day we celebrate a wedding and a birthday.'

* * *

By the time we get to the dessert stage, although the portions are a perfect size, we're content to linger and take our time.

'What's the latest news in Penvennan, then?' Gawen enquires. 'Or shouldn't I ask?'

Everyone looks in my direction. 'Nettie is back with Dad, which is great news,' I reply, sounding a little more optimistic than I'm feeling. But that's probably down to the champagne and the wine. 'Oh, and in a week's time I'll no longer own an apartment in London. I guess I'm back for good.'

Sy nods, approvingly. 'Thank goodness for that. I bet Ross is relieved.'

Ross turns to look at me, his eyes sparkling. 'There's no way I would let her go now, believe me, Sy.' The way his eyes crinkle up when his smile comes from deep down inside of him, touches my heart. As the others exchange a little banter, Ross leans into me. 'You look beautiful, and I feel so proud sitting next to you, Kerra.'

'Come on, you two, get a room or rejoin the conversation,' Gawen calls us out and I feel myself blushing.

'Tell them your news, Sy,' Tegan encourages.

'Yesterday morning I had my exorbitant fee through from The Happy Hive and the best bit is that Clean and Shine is now doing so well that we can earmark it for our big celebration in the spring.'

'What a result all round!' I reply, thinking how pleased Sy looks with himself.

'Well, that is exciting news. I do love a big party, but they are few and far between these days, aren't they?' Yvonne reflects, sadly.

'It's so expensive. When you think that a full-blown wedding can cost upwards of fifteen-thousand pounds, that's a hefty chunk of money for one day,' Gawen adds. 'Hey, if you two are looking for a free venue, we have a barn and a large flagstone patio you're very welcome to use for your big do. You can never bank on the weather, can you?'

'That would be incredible,' Sy replies, turning to look at Tegan, whose smile couldn't get any bigger.

'Oh my,' she says, 'that's a really generous offer. The setting is everything, isn't it?'

'It does solve what looked likely to be a big problem for us. We'd love to take you up on your offer, Gawen and Yvonne.'

Ross sits, nervously turning the stem of his wine glass in his hand, as everyone's attention is on him. 'My news is that I've sold Treylya, at last.'

'Thank goodness for that! What a turning point,' Yvonne remarks, delighted for him.

'To Jago,' Ross adds and the reaction to that isn't quite so exhilarating.

'Oh.' Yvonne, like everyone else, doesn't quite know what to say.

'He's not staying for good, but he will be flying back and forth to keep an eye on the new depot. It suits me and we seem to have reached an agreement with which we can both live, for the time being.'

'Hopefully, that means you'll soon be able to move on with your life,' Tegan remarks, turning to smile at me, as Ross goes on to explain.

'I think my father might have learnt a lesson, or two, after the uproar he caused that night in The Lark and Lantern. I don't think he'll be seen around the village or down in the cove for a long time to come. At least up at Treylya, he can keep himself to himself. Which suits me and everyone else, I think.'

It's hard for anyone around the table not to agree with that sentiment and Sy changes the subject.

'I see that it's out in the open about you and The Happy Hive now, Kerra. It's about time and will put an end to a lot of the speculation.'

'It is?' I'm aghast. What on earth does he mean?

'I thought... assumed, that you knew? Kate was talking about it yesterday. One of her elderly clients asked if she could help her to sign up to the Penvennan Community Link-Up after she received an email. It's on the home page now, apparently.'

'What is?'

'I don't know because I can't access it, but some reference to it being set up by you, the creator and former owner of The Happy Hive, or words to that effect.'

Ross grimaces and it all goes rather quiet.

'Oh Arthur... he probably meant well, but this isn't good news.' I don't know how he found out, probably searching around on the internet, but I wish he'd mentioned it to me first.

Ross reaches down in my lap for my hand. 'It's out there now and do you know what? It's one thing less to worry about, Kerra. Sy is right, it might even help matters. No more guessing games about how you can afford to do what you're doing. Let me top up your glass,' he says, encouraging me to let it go and enjoy myself.

'So much for coming back and trying my best not to make waves,' I mutter, half to myself and they all begin laughing. I notice that Gawen and Yvonne aren't quite sure what exactly we're talking about and at some point, I need to enlighten them – but not today.

Excusing myself to go and sort out some wayward strands of hair that conveniently work loose, I head to the bathroom. Instead, I walk straight past the door to a quiet corner beneath a turn in the stairs, which lead down to the ground floor, and I pull out my phone.

'Hi, Arthur, it's Kerra. How are you feeling today?'

'Not the best, I'm afraid. The relief never lasts long, but I've felt worse. Is somethin' up?'

Darn it – my slightly hesitant tone of voice has given away my concern. 'It's just a small thing, but a friend mentioned that you've put a credit up on the website mentioning me?'

'I know you professional folk have bios and I was searchin' around online for yours. After all the work you put in it seems wrong for you not to get the glory. Mrs Moyle and me were blown away, Kerra. We had no idea you made it big in London!'

Oh dear, how can I put this so he won't be offended.

'Ah, that's most kind of you, Arthur. The problem is that having sold one website, I wouldn't want anyone to think the Penvennan Community Link-Up could end up being commercialised. It fear it might put some of your members off.'

The line goes silent, and I let Arthur mull over my words.

'Oh, I see what you mean, Kerra. I'd best take it off. I was going to show it to you next time you called in as a surprise.'

'I think it's for the best. It would be a shame to undermine all your hard work, Arthur. But it's the thought that counts and I'm grateful to you.'

'Well, I'll do that right away. And I'm glad you rang because I have a bit of information you might be surprised to hear. Just between us, I had a stern chat with Zacky and you'll never guess who LionMan is... none other than Jago Treloar. He's now deleted and I told Zacky straight that if he causes trouble again he'll be next.'

My initial reaction is to suck in a sharp breath at the mention of Jago's name.

'Thanks for letting me know, Arthur, and well done for sorting out the problem. I think you're right and this should go no further. Anyway, I'm always available if you need me. Bye for now.'

I'm in shock as I walk back into the restaurant. The last thing Ross needs now is another upset linked to his father and, thankfully, Arthur has it under control.

* * *

'It was a great day, wasn't it? I'm so glad that none of the surprises we planned turned out to be an unwelcome shock.' Ross's voice is soft as we sit cross-legged on the floor in the darkness, looking out over the garden. It's such a lovely setting at this time of night with the uplighters outside casting their gentle glow. Ripley is curled up next to me, exhausted because Ross has spent the last half an hour playing with her.

'The best and we were lucky with the weather, too. Sy and Tegan were a little overwhelmed when you handed them the vouchers we all chipped in for, but they'll appreciate a long weekend away to recharge their batteries. Hopefully, they will choose a location they haven't visited before. It will be a nice memory for them to share a *first* to mark their wedding,' I point out.

'I'm glad things are coming good for those two, at long last. It gives the rest of us hope.'

'It's been an awful couple of years for Tegan and Sy, well, he was a walking disaster at times. I can't believe what a perfect fit they are, because being together has changed them both, albeit in different ways.'

'And what about us?' Ross asks, tentatively.

'What do you mean?'

'Are you convinced that we're a perfect fit?'

I look at him, unable to make out his expression because a part of his face is in shadow.

'I'm surprised you need to ask me that question,' I retort, laughing. 'I've never shared my home with any man before.'

'Okay... this is a theoretical question, as I'm not actually proposing to you now – I'm a bit more romantic than I've probably given you cause to think... but if I were going to ask you to marry me, what would your answer be?'

I stare at him, pretending to give it some serious thought.

'A theoretical *yes*, but there are no guarantees – it pays to keep a man on his toes.'

He grins at me. 'That's all I wanted to know. I was just checking.'

Ross crawls over on all fours to cuddle up next to me. With him on one side and Ripley on the other, as Ross's arm snakes around my waist, I feel as if everything is finally beginning to fall into place.

As for Dad, he will come around, I'm sure of it – especially now he's back with Nettie. She is a voice of reason and understands, as I do, that the bond between father and daughter can never be broken – just a little bent out of shape when they fail to agree. And I'll prove to Dad that being with Ross makes me feel complete and then he'll see what I see – not Jago's son, but the man I'm destined to be with.

And my knight in shining armour is already getting ready to sweep me off my feet. Ross doesn't intend doing it in a low-key manner. It looks like we'll be making even more waves in our little community, in the not-too-distant future. I see that as a positive thing. The best way to take the wind out of the sails of the naysayers, is to stand firm in your own beliefs. It's time for Ross and me to grab the happiness coming our way, because I firmly believe that love is the greatest force in the universe. It arms you with the power to overcome whatever life throws at you.

'You make me a happy man, Kerra Shaw, even if you are a bit of a handful at times.'

I guess I am, at that, but I know that Ross wouldn't change a single thing because that's what falling in love is all about. You simply can't help yourself and he's caught – hook, line, and sinker, as my granddad would have said.

Watch out Penvennan Cove – the best is yet to come!

ACKNOWLEDGMENTS

Cornwall has always been an enchanting destination for me and whenever I've visited, I return home feeling renewed and uplifted. It was the perfect setting for this three-book series in which Kerra Shaw rediscovers her first love, Ross Treloar.

I'd like to give a virtual hug to my new editor, the wonderful Hannah Todd – it's a pleasure working with you and your input has been invaluable!

Ripley, too, gets a special mention as she is a cat with attitude and a well-loved family member.

Grateful thanks also go to my agent, Sara Keane, for her sterling advice and motivation. And to the wonderful Vicky Joss – who is a dream of a marketing manager. Her hard work is much appreciated!

And to the wider Aria team – a truly awesome group of people I can't thank enough for their amazing support and encouragement.

Also, a special mention to the fabulous Tregolls Lodge book club in Truro. It's run by Howard and Jeannie, and the whole group gave me such a wonderfully warm welcome when I popped in to do a talk on one of my research trips.

There are so many friends who are there for me and who understand that my passion to write is all-consuming. They forgive me for the long silences and when we next catch up, it's as if I haven't been absent at all.

As usual, no book is ever launched without there being an even longer list of people to thank for publicising it. The amazing kindness of my lovely author friends, readers and reviewers is truly humbling. You continue to delight, amaze and astound me with your generosity and support.

Without your kindness in spreading the word about my latest release and your wonderful reviews to entice people to click and download, I wouldn't be able to indulge myself in my guilty pleasure – writing.

Feeling blessed and sending much love to you all for your treasured support and friendship.

Linn x

ABOUT THE AUTHOR

Linn B. Halton is a #1 bestselling author of contemporary romantic fiction. In 2013 she won the UK Festival of Romance: Innovation in Romantic Fiction Award.

For Linn, life is all about family, friends, and writing. She is a self-confessed hopeless romantic and an eternal optimist. When Linn is not writing, she spends time in the garden weeding or practising Tai Chi. And she is often found with a paintbrush in her hand indulging her passion for upcycling furniture.

Her novels have been translated into Italian, Czech and Croatian. She also writes as Lucy Coleman.

Hello from Aria

We hope you enjoyed this book! If you did, let us know, we'd love to hear from you.

We are Aria, a dynamic fiction imprint from award-winning publishers Head of Zeus. At heart, we're committed to publishing fantastic commercial fiction – from romance to sagas to historical fiction.

Visit us online and discover a community of like-minded fiction fans.

You can find us at:

www.ariafiction.com
🐦 @Aria_fiction
📘 @Ariafiction